#1

BECOMING ALPHA

AILEEN ERIN

First published in 2013 by Ink Monster LLC
Ink Monster, LLC
34 Chandler Place
Newton, MA 02464
www.inkmonster.net

ISBN 9780989405034

This book is dedicated to my best friend, partner, husband.

Thank you for encouraging me to follow my dreams, for your unwavering support in all things, and for believing in me when I didn't even believe in myself.

You have my heart always.

Chapter One

The noise from the party raging downstairs seeped into my quiet space. I palmed my blue and red bouncy ball as I lay on my bed facing the wall. I threw it in the air a few times to watch the colors blur together before bouncing it off the wall above my headboard.

It was ten o'clock at night on a Thursday, and the party was just getting started. My parents said that having people over tonight was unavoidable. We were leaving for Cedar Ridge, Texas—a town too small to register on most maps—in a few days, and people wanted to say good-bye. Any other seventeen year old would probably be excited about sneaking a drink or having an excuse to buy a new dress, but not me. I wasn't much of a party person. Or a people person.

With my stuff already packed up and the TVs unhooked, I was beyond bored. Still, there was no way I was going downstairs.

I'd disappeared to my room as soon as the caterers

arrived. Since then, I'd found the end of the internet. Apparently there were only so many .gifs a girl could enjoy. Unless I wanted to pay for crappy re-runs, I was out of things to watch and left with only a bouncy ball to aid in my entertainment.

It'd been a bad idea to pack everything but my essentials so early. Twenty-three small boxes were stacked against the side of my room. Most of them were filled with books. The only stuff that I'd left unpacked would fit into a small duffel bag and my backpack.

But a bouncy ball was better than nothing, and much better than braving the crowd downstairs. I threw it to the beat of the music and counted down the seconds. Those would turn into minutes, and then into hours, and then eventually back into quiet so I could go to sleep. I was really looking forward to a fresh start. The sooner I could go to sleep, the sooner it'd be tomorrow.

Only three more nights until Texas. Until everything would change. I smiled at the thought. This girl could use some change.

A knock came from my door. "Bathroom's downstairs," I yelled. I held my breath as I listened, hoping they heard me.

The knob turned. Shit. I should've locked it.

I hopped off my bed. "Hey—"

"Whatcha doin', Tessa?" My older brother, Axel, swung open the door.

I sat back down on the bed. He knew exactly what I was doing. "What do you want?"

He leaned against the doorframe. He was well over half a foot taller than me, but that didn't mean much to my five feet and almost nothing inches. We had the same wavy dark brown hair—when he let his grow—and the same dark brown eyes, thanks to our Latina mom. "Dad wants you to come downstairs, even if it's just for a minute. People are asking about you."

I made a face. "I'd rather not. Cover for me?"

"What if I said a certain celeb was down there?" He waggled his eyebrows. "The one who I saw you drooling over last week?"

I threw the ball at him and he caught it, laughing. The jerk. Dad's combo of PR work and law degree made him a hot commodity in Hollywood. He now had an enviable number of high profile clients. If I were more into the LA scene, then maybe the guest list would've been appealing.

I chewed on my lip, unable to deny the draw of my latest actor crush—James MacAvoy. Nothing hotter than a guy with a sexy Scottish accent. "He's really downstairs?"

Axel nodded.

I thought for a second and then sighed. "Still can't do it. I don't want to destroy the illusion that my favorite Scotsman is absolute perfection. What if he has a zit? Or spills something on himself? Or worse—what if I accidentally touch him and get a vision? The dream will shatter. And that, big brother, is not worth it. Even if I was willing to risk having a million other random visions, which I'm not."

He rolled his eyes at me and stepped into my room.

"Hey!" I jumped off the bed. "Don't come in here. This is a clean zone." He knew I wasn't referring to

3

the fact that I was a neat-freak, but that everything in the room was new. Touched by a minimal amount of people. It was my only defense. A quick brush of skin-against-skin, or even skin-against-other-person's-property, was sometimes enough to give me an in-depth view into their mind. As much as that might sound like fun, it was usually more icky than cool.

He held up his hands. "Please, Tess. I know the drill." He moseyed his way to my bed and collapsed. "Come here." He patted his side.

I looked at him suspiciously. "The shirt's new?"

"Yes."

I lay down on my side next to him, resting my head on his chest.

A quick vision of a factory in some Asian country filled my mind. The humid heat had me sweating as the clacking of hundreds of sewing machines echoed in my head.

"Are you sweating?" Axel's voice brought me back to my room. "Christ. It's like lying next to a furnace."

I elbowed him as I rolled away. "Your fault. That's a sweatshop shirt you're wearing."

"Shit. I actually liked this shirt." He pulled it away from his chest, making a face as if it'd suddenly grown mold. "I should let you touch my stuff before I buy anything."

I wiped the sweat from my brow. "If you like it, then wear it. You already did whatever damage you were going to do by buying it in the first place. You never would've known if you didn't have a freak for a sister."

He was quiet for a second. "You're going to have to come out of this room at some point. You can't hide forever."

He did this at least once a month, but he hadn't gotten the family "gift." I had.

"You're not Rogue, you know," he said.

Oh God. He was on variation five-B of the speech also known as The Comic Book Rip-off. "You're not going to kill someone if you touch them," I finished for him, mimicking his deeper voice.

"Right. Well. I still think that if you learned to block it out instead of trying to avoid it, then you'd be able to have some kind of normal life."

Maybe he was right, but you couldn't wash your mind or un-see things. "Yeah, well, believe it or not, too much information is an actual thing. Like getting the glimpse of when you and Bambi—"

"Blair."

"Whatever." I gagged.

"I don't know why you're so stubborn. Not letting anyone touch you isn't the answer."

I elbowed him again. "Gross! You want people to touch me. That's so messed up."

"Shut it. You know what I meant." He messed up my hair. "I'm gone in a few weeks, and I'm worried about you."

I glanced up at him. We looked like twins, except he was all angles, whereas my face was round. Axel was only two years older than me, and was, without a doubt, my best friend. "I'll be fine without your butt stinking up the house."

He smiled like I wanted, but I wasn't so sure that I'd actually be fine. Even if he wouldn't admit it, I knew he'd picked a Texas college because we'd still be within driving distance. I hated that he'd turned down other schools, and hated myself a little for being glad that he'd done it.

He nudged me. "I dare you to find out what the deal is with Dad's new job."

"What do you mean?"

"He's leaving his celeb-filled job in LA to work for some random boarding school in Texas. That doesn't strike you as odd at all?"

I shrugged. "I guess I hadn't thought about it. I'm just looking forward to not going back to school here. I don't think I could take another year of those monsters." I paused. I shouldn't have brought that up. "Look. The gloves will work fine in a school that's clueless as to what they mean. I'm old enough not to talk about what I see anymore. Plus, I'm getting better at minimizing the number of visions I get. It'll be a fresh start, and I'm not about to poke holes in something that might actually be a good thing."

"Aren't you curious? Even a little?"

I thought about it. "Well, I wasn't…"

Axel sat up so quickly that I almost fell off the bed. "You have to go downstairs, to Dad's office, and touch some of those papers from St. Ailbe's."

"That's a terrible idea." Going downstairs during a party where people might actually want to hug me good-bye was a disaster waiting to happen. Add messing around in Dad's office, and I'd be begging for a grounding. Only a moron would agree to this.

"Come on." He gave me the look-that cocky, half-grin that told me I was about to get into trouble. "We'll go downstairs, sneak a glass of champagne, you can get an eye-full of Sir Hunkalot, and then we can find out the real story on this move. We'll be sneaky, and no one will see us." He paused. "I didn't want to have to say this, but I double-dog dare you."

I couldn't stop the grin. "What are you? Twelve?"

"What are you? Forty?" He poked me. "Live a little. You've gotta start having some fun, Tess."

I wouldn't mind seeing Sir Hunkalot. I snickered at the name. Plus, whatever we did had to be more entertaining than bouncing a ball against the wall. "Fine. But if I do this, then you've got to do something for me."

Axel crossed his arms. "Name it."

I could never think of anything good enough on the spot and he knew it. Then it came to me, and an evil grin spread across my face. "No chicharones on the road trip." I almost patted myself on the back. Fried pork skins were something that I couldn't stomach. Even if both he and my mom swore they were positively delectable.

His mouth dropped open. "What! You're talking about messing with a road trip tradition. That's sacred stuff."

I crossed my arms. "They're disgusting."

"You've never even tried them." He narrowed his gaze. "They're delicious."

"I don't need to try them to know I won't like them. Eating pig skin in any form is revolting." I stared him down. "And they stink." It might not seem like a big deal, but on a road trip halfway across the country, it was huge. Multiple bags could be avoided. Two days of a chicharone-free car ride was more than adequate reparation for one vision. "Do we have a deal?"

He left my room.

Great. Now I actually wanted the deal, and he was bailing. I wouldn't give in. If I knew my brother at all, he'd be back in ten, nine, eight, seven—

"Just kidding." He appeared back in the doorway. "Let's do this."

I started out the door and then ran back. I'd only left a few pairs of gloves unpacked. I grabbed the heather gray cotton pair and slid them on, doing up the apple buttons along the forearm as I walked into the hallway. I would've changed, but there was nothing nicer for me to put on. My jeans, white peasant blouse, and leather flip-flops would have to do. "Ready?"

He nodded.

I only had a second to think about how much fun using my visions for something useful would be before I hit the bottom stair and stopped.

This had to be a fire code violation.

A few people clogged the bottom of the stairwell that emptied into the living room. The party planner must've taken out some of the furniture to make room, but there was still not enough. There were people in every square foot available, and—except for the few actors who everyone would recognize—I didn't actually know anyone.

Waiters dressed in black pants and white button downs made their way slowly through the room, offering up hors d'oeuvres or drinks, depending on what their silver platters held. Speakers stood in the corners of the room, playing non-intrusive electronic music with a steady beat but I didn't spot the DJ. He had to be set up outside by the pool.

I swallowed the lump in my throat and entered

the madness. It wasn't long before I heard Dad's voice above the din. "There she is!"

So much for no one seeing us. I wanted to hit Axel. So I did.

Dad shook his head at me. "Come here, Tessa," Dad mouthed. His blonde hair hid most of the gray that had started appearing a few years ago. I always wished I had his blue eyes, but got my mom's brown ones instead. He was wearing a tailored navy suit, and I suddenly felt way underdressed.

I brushed against someone and their jealousy burned through my mind. I shook it off and focused in on Dad. He was watching my careful navigation through the crowd with worry. Dad knew about my "gift," but chose to ignore it for the most part. Luckily Mom understood it more, most likely because my *abuela* had the same one. She always said it made it really hard to be a rebellious teenager when her mother could read her mind. I'd say actually having the abilities made it hard to be a teenager. Period.

Dad pulled me to his side, and I tucked close to him to avoid any touchy people. I got a few flashes from him, but thankfully nothing that drew me in.

"We're so sad your dad's leaving us," said some lady in a super-tight dress. "What are you going to do in Texas?"

I shrugged. "Eat a lot of bar-b-que and go to school?"

She laughed and her fake boobs nearly popped out. I looked for my brother. He was flirting with some young girl who looked way too skinny. Must be an actress. "Help," I mouthed as soon as I got his attention.

He made his way through the sea of people. I tuned the lady out as Axel grabbed my gloved hand. "Tess-aaah," he practically shouted, drawing my short name into two long syllables. "There's someone over here I want you to meet."

Dad's hand brushed my arm as Axel pulled me away.

Dad was talking to his boss, a silver-haired man in a slick suit. His tie was a little undone.

"Jesus, John. Are you serious?"

"I wish I was joking." Dad sat heavily on the couch across the room from his boss. "I know I'm leaving soon, but this is a lawsuit waiting to happen. She's liability. You need to get rid of her."

Whoa drama.

I nearly cracked up at the look on Dad's face as he held onto my hand. He definitely didn't want to be talking this lady. I almost felt bad leaving him with her. Almost. "Oh, fantastic," I said to Axel, my voice so thick with sarcasm that Dad laughed. "I can't wait to meet this person."

Before I could get away, tight dress lady smothered me with a hug. Her hand brushed the top of my arm.

I hadn't been to Dad's office in a while, but I recognized it—the wall of glass behind his desk with an amazing view of the city. She was in his chair. In black lace lingerie.

Dad walked into the room and she stood up.

"What the fuck are you doing?" Dad yelled as he spun around. "I'm giving you five minutes to get dressed and get out of my office. When I get back, you better be fucking gone."

Axel tugged me away from her and the onslaught stopped. He brilliantly played it off as tripping, glancing at nothing on the hardwood floor and cursing. "I'm sooo sorry. Lost my balance there for a second. Must be something spilled here." He didn't give her a chance to say anything before he started walking away, towing me with him.

Holy shit. Did I just see what I thought I saw?

I spotted mom and pulled on Axel's hand. When he turned, I motioned to her. She was already heading our way.

Mom was super cute with her short, wavy dark-brown hair, and looked ten years younger than she actually was thanks to her daily power yoga routine. A boldly printed Diane Von Furstenberg wrap dress showed off her curves, and got her quite a few stares from the male contingent as she walked through the crowd.

"You decided to come down on your own?" she said to me.

I raised an eyebrow. "Not likely."

She smiled, and it wasn't a totally happy one. "That's what I thought. Thank you anyway. I know that your father will appreciate you making the effort."

Before she could leave, I stopped her and leaned close. "That lady talking to Dad—the one that's about to have a wardrobe malfunction—totally tried to come on to him. She's thinking yucky things. Fifty shades of things…"

Mom laughed her big, booming laugh.

Not the reaction I was expecting from her. "Don't worry though," I whispered into her ear. "She hasn't

11

gotten anywhere with him."

Mom sobered and stepped back to look at me. She seemed to realize something and then shook her head. "Of course she hasn't. That's one thing you don't have to worry about. Your father and I are one of the few who have a forever marriage. Your *abuela* made sure of it." Growing up with my *abuela* made Mom able to block everything but what she wanted me to see. No one else I knew could do it. So when she reached out to cup my cheek, I relaxed my head into her hand and closed my eyes.

I was flooded with the twenty or so times that they'd said they loved each other today. She kissed my forehead, and I heard the echo from her mind that she loved me.

I opened my eyes and smiled. "Thanks. Love you too, Mom."

She gave my cheek a couple of light pats before looking at my brother. "Be good, you two."

Axel scoffed. "Are we ever not good?"

"Yes. Frequently." With that, Mom slid back into her role as hostess.

"Let's go before anyone else stops us," Axel said.

We made our way to Dad's office and locked the door. Thick law texts were haphazardly stacked in his now mostly empty shelves. Bankers boxes piled high to the right of his large oaken desk. Two long file cabinets sat along the wall behind the desk. I had no idea where to even start to look for the St. Ailbe's stuff.

"You find the file, and I'll touch it." I took off my right glove and stuffed it in the back pocket of my jeans. "I'm not touching anything I don't need to."

He dug through some drawers, and then started in on the Bankers boxes. My palms were sweating. The longer Axel took, the better chance there was that Dad would look for us, even if that was ridiculous when we had half of Hollywood in our house.

"Got it!" Axel stepped around the mess he'd made and handed me a folder.

I grabbed it and my father's office disappeared.

Chapter Two

An image flashed through my mind. Five red brick buildings in a circle, surrounded by forest. Teenagers. Students carrying books walking through the center of them. Wolves running through the forest around the buildings.

Why weren't the students scared of the wolves? Were they tame? Or maybe they were just large dogs. Or maybe it was a farm school. A giant-sized, wolfish-dog farm school.

Wind blew against my face. The scent of the trees and dirt filled my every breath. I'd never had a vision so vivid before. Usually it was just one or two senses, but this was all of them.

Someone brushed past me, and before I could react, my vision shifted to a one-room cabin. It was nighttime now. The two men—one about my dad's age, one maybe a few years older than me—were sitting at a table discussing something. No, they were arguing.

"Trusting some unknown outsider with—" The younger one stopped, and looked straight at me.

I froze. He couldn't actually be looking at me, could he?

"We're being watched."

No way. This was impossible. When I touched something, I only saw echoes of the past that had imprinted in the object. There was no way I could actually interact with a vision.

I had to test it. I had to know if he could see me. "Hello?" My voice cracked.

The younger guy stood up. "There's someone here. In this room."

"Can you see them?" the other one said.

The younger guy shook his head.

Then how could he hear me? Or could he hear me? Maybe he could just sense me? But how? I was looking into the past, wasn't I? There was no way I could've linked with whoever signed the papers. Because that would be way messed up.

The younger one continued to stare in my direction. The look he gave me made my pulse race; it was like he was seeing through my soul. His muscles strained against his black T-shirt as he stepped toward me. His inky black hair made his amber eyes seem brighter. Holy shit. He was way sexier than my favorite Scotsman.

"They're not going away. They're still here," he said.

"Do you know who it is?"

"No. But it feels familiar. I don't know, but whoever it is, it's like I know them." He ran his fingers through his short black hair. "That doesn't make sense."

No. It didn't. I'd never seen that guy before. I would've remembered meeting someone that hot.

The older man turned to me and said something in a language that I couldn't understand. And then it was like something shoved me out of the vision.

The next thing I knew, I was on the ground in my father's office.

Holy shit. What the hell was that? My vision actually interacted with me. The people in it knew I was there. That could mean only one thing.

Axel leaned over me. "Are you okay?"

"I'm not sure."

"What did you see?" he asked. "What's the story?"

I swallowed. There was only one logical conclusion, but it seemed impossible. But Occam's razor hadn't failed me yet. The simplest explanation was usually the correct one. And if that were true, then holy shit. I connected with whoever signed the papers.

Out of all the visions I'd had in my nearly eighteen years, nothing like that had ever happened before.

Not only that, but the older guy pushed me out of my own vision.

Could there actually be more people out there like me? And if so, then how did I not realize this sooner?

There had to be something to draw Dad to his new job. If St. Ailbe's a school for the gifted, I wanted in. Maybe. Probably.

This was insane. I had to talk to Dad before I got my hopes up, but there was no chance of that happening tonight.

Axel was asking question after question, but I ignored him. I needed air. And fast. That sensory overload had blown my mind. Possibly literally. Well, not technically literally. But still, all rational thoughts had fled.

I hopped up and swung the door open.

"Wait. Let me pick up—"

I left Axel to clean up the mess he'd made in Dad's office. I probably looked as crazed as I felt, since I somehow managed to get to the backyard without touching anyone.

Even with our decent-sized backyard, there wasn't a spot to disappear into. The pool took up most of the space. The path around it was sprinkled with cocktail tables, and people were packed around them, mingling. A bar was set up in the back and drawing a sizable crowd. The bartender was making a rowdy group a bunch of chilled shots, and a DJ played off to the right of the pool while people danced in front of his table.

This was a disaster waiting to happen. I didn't think I could make it to the stairs without bumping into someone, but there was no other option. It was worth the risk. Being alone right now was a must.

Before I could go back inside, a hand closed around my upper arm. Full-contact skin against skin.

Shit.

I slammed into a mind I was familiar with. The fact that he went out of his way to touch me when he knew what I was only made him that much creepier. Images of his fantasies flooded my mind. Sweaty bodies. Naked bodies. Ones he wanted to be with. Those he had been with. And to top it off—a few fantasies starring me.

Was it necessary for Axel to invite every asshole in his class to the party?

I wrenched my arm away and spun to face Caleb. If his visions didn't already make me want to kick his ass, his skinny jeans and hipster smile did. Usually I'd just shake it off, but not tonight.

"What the hell is your problem!" I shoved him hard, and he stumbled back a few steps. "Do you really want me to see what goes on in your disgusting little mind? Do you think I want to see when you and Jessica were banging in your backseat? Do you think it turns me on? Because it doesn't." I poked him in the chest with my gloved-finger. "And if you think that I'd ever consider—"

"Tessa!" Axel said as he stepped between us. I don't know how long he'd been yelling my name, but from the silence in the backyard, I could tell it'd been at least a few times.

Shit. Why did DJs always lower the music for a fight? Didn't they know that drawing attention to it made it worse?

I swallowed and looked around. And there was Mr. MacAvoy in the flesh, staring at me like I was a complete nut-job. Just perfect.

"Freaky Tessa is at it again. Bitch doesn't—"

My brother spun. I didn't have time to stop him before he punched Caleb in the face.

Caleb groaned as he fell to the ground.

"No one calls my sister a bitch, you—"

Dad appeared behind Axel and grabbed him before Axel could do any more damage to Caleb. "What the hell is going on out here?" He looked from my brother to me and then to Caleb, who was holding his hand against his face. It wasn't the first time this had happened, but it was the first time it'd happened during one of my father's parties.

I stared at the ground hard. "It was my fault." I didn't choke on the words, but they didn't come out easily.

"Tessa?" Mom said. "Why don't you go upstairs, honey?"

I nodded, doing my best to not look disappointed and failing. It hadn't been my idea to leave my room in the first place. Mom reached out to touch me, but I dodged her.

The crowd parted as I made my way inside. I tried not to listen to any of the whispers that followed in my wake. When I was halfway up the stairs, the DJ started playing again. By now, Mom would have taken care of Caleb, and Axel would go for a drive to wherever it was he went. And I would be here. Alone.

I couldn't wait to leave LA. The less population density this new town had the better.

Still, I wondered if Texas would be any better. I hoped so, but Axel was right. If I didn't learn to control these visions, my life would never be any kind of normal.

***

I was in bed trying to figure out how I'd let the night get so out of control when someone knocked on my door. Instead of waiting for an answer, Mom came in. She made her way around the boxes in my room and sat on the foot of my bed.

"On a scale of one to ten, how mad is Dad?"

Mom sighed. "He's not mad, honey."

I finally met her gaze. "I'm not buying that. I embarrassed him in front of all those people."

"What's a Hollywood party without a little drama?" She patted my leg. "We're more worried about you."

I stared at the ceiling. "It's fine. I'm fine."

"No. You're not. But we're hoping Texas will be better. That's the whole reason we're moving."

I gathered my courage and hoped for the answer I wanted. "Is St. Ailbe's a school for kids like me?"

She stuck her tongue out in a look of disgust. "No!" Then she laughed at herself. "No way. You would not fit in there. Trust me."

Interesting. So who would fit in there? "Then why Texas? Why make Dad leave his job instead of making me switch schools again?"

I'd been through most of the private ones in Los Angeles while in lower school. By third grade, I'd exhausted all options. They finally sent me back to my original one. It was a good school, but that's not why I went back there. The thinking was that my brother could keep an eye out for me. Their plan sort of worked. But my brother graduated, so that was that. Why my parents refused for me to do home schooling was beyond me. It would've made life so much easier.

"There's really no one left who will take you besides Westlake, and I know you don't want to stay there."

Well that was embarrassing. "What about the public schools?"

Mom shook her head. "Not in this county. I want

you to have an excellent education in a safe setting. And with your brother going off to college, it's time for a new place. I always wanted an excuse to move back to Texas anyhow."

"I could always do home schooling."

"No way, kiddo. You're already in your own head enough. I won't let you become a hermit."

"But Dad—"

"Why don't you let me worry about your father? Okay? This job is a good one. He'll be making the same as he was here with a fraction of the workload. After you leave for college, we'll talk about coming back to LA, but I doubt we will. I have a feeling we're all going to be happier there. Plus, we'll be by your cousins. I think you'll find that you have more in common with them than you think."

That had me sitting up. "Seriously?" The crazy *brujos*? She thought I'd have more in common with a bunch of crazy people that thought they were witches. I knew my *abuela* had gifts like mine, but some of the stuff the rest of the family believed was really out there. I doubted they'd see eye to eye with me.

"It's my fault really. I didn't keep up with them after your *abuela* died." Her voice was soft, and tinged with regret. "But I tracked down my cousin Ana, and her twins Veronica and Carlos both have gifts. They're a few years younger than you, but it's better than nothing."

She had a point. They couldn't be any worse than the kids at school. Plus, who was I to judge someone for being weird.

Mom stood up, and smoothed down her dress. "I know it's been hard for you here, but it'll get easier."

"Thanks. As you can tell," I motioned to the boxes, "I think I might be ready to move."

She laughed. "Good. You can help me pack the kitchen tomorrow."

"Sure thing."

Dad popped in the doorway. "You okay, princess?"

I nodded. "Sorry, Dad."

"Don't apologize for things that aren't your fault." He turned to Mom. "People are clearing out."

"I'll be right down."

"Great." Dad winked at me. "Get some sleep, princess."

Mom stopped at the door. "Light on or off?"

"Off." She was almost out the door when I stopped her again. "Mom."

"Yes?"

"Thanks."

"You're very welcome." It was too dark to see her face, but I could tell from the sound of her voice that she was smiling.

I lay in the dark listening to the sounds of the dying party. I had been excited about the move, but now I was seriously pumped. Cousins with gifts? This could change everything. But why hadn't Mom contacted them before? What was different now?

The more I thought about it the more questions I had. And not only about my cousins, but about St. Ailbe's. And those wolf-dog things. And that guy.

Mostly about that guy.

Chapter Three

I rested my head against the window as my father drove. We were almost to our new home. After all the build up, the next chapter in my life was just around the bend, and the anxiety of meeting it head-on had my knees bouncing.

At least Axel wasn't in the car with us. He and Mom were following us in his Jetta. We'd switched on the last stop so that Axel could eat his grotesque snack of choice. He was more than annoying when he didn't get his way. Dad and I had much more acceptable munchies in the form of M&M's and Cheetos in his Lexus SUV.

Neither car was fully packed with stuff. The moving van would come later today, and Mom's car was getting shipped here from LA. She didn't want anyone riding alone, just in case we got separated. I was still hoping now that Axel was taking off, a car for me would show up. It'd be nice not to have my parents drop me off on the first day of my senior year.

I grabbed for some snacks, more for a distraction than because I was hungry. I was trying to think positively about the chances of pulling off the whole "normal" thing at my new school, but the closer it got, the more my confidence waned. "Want any?" I held the open bag of Cheetos to Dad.

"I better not. Those things are like crack. Once you start, you'll never stop."

I fake gasped. "Dad! You've done crack?"

He laughed.

"But seriously. You dare turn down day-glow cheese?"

"Hey, I'm trying to undo the damage I did to myself when I was your age." He patted his stomach, which was mostly flat. He turned a corner into a gated complex. Although the word "complex" was a stretch. The gate opened onto a dirt road. Vegetation on either side threatened to swallow it.

"What's the code again?" Dad asked.

"Eighteen thirty-six." I scratched my head. "That sounds like a date."

He leaned out of the window to punch in the code. "Yup. Year of the battle of the Alamo. Welcome to Texas, princess." Leave it to Dad, the history buff, to know the answer.

Dad clicked his seatbelt back into place, and we drove down the bumpy road. I checked the directions from Dad's new boss again. "Says here that we're the ninth driveway. If we get to the fork, then we've gone too far."

Dad grunted. "Well, we're definitely in for a change here."

"You could say that." It seemed like these tiny

driveways were more like trails in a national park. I couldn't see any houses, and the "driveways" were really spread out.

When we reached the fifth, Dad cleared his throat. "So the head of St. Ailbe's is meeting us at the house with the keys. I, uh, just…" Dad trailed off.

"What?"

He sighed. "Try not to touch anything or have any visions in front of him. I didn't exactly say anything about—"

"Dad. Seriously. It's not a big deal. I would rather not have one either, but in the event that I do, I'll try to hide it. Cool?"

He patted my jean-clad leg. "Thanks, princess."

"That's nine." I pointed to the driveway. It curved down a hill and finally opened up to a beautifully manicured lawn. A circular drive with a giant oak tree in the middle led up to the pale yellow stucco house. Butterflies filled my stomach as we stopped in front. It wasn't as big as our house in LA, but almost. The white wrap-around porch drew my attention, especially the bench swing to the left of the front door. Off to the right was a white two-car garage.

Dad parked in front of the garage to leave the drive open, and Axel pulled up beside us. I slipped down from the SUV and pulled a pair of thin tie-dyed gloves from my pocket.

Mom hopped out of Axel's car and put her arm around me. "How was the last of the drive?"

"Fine. But you still smell like chicharones." I made a face. She tried to smother my face with kisses, but I pushed her away. "Nasty!"

The screen door squeaked open, which shocked

me. Besides our two cars, there were no others here. A man stepped onto the porch, and we stopped goofing off. Mom straightened her shirt, and Dad knocked on Axel's window. "Quit texting."

I didn't fully turn to Dad's new boss until Axel was out of the car. I don't know why I was surprised to see the older man from my vision walking out of the house. He was the one who hired my dad, so he'd most likely held the papers that gave me the vision. But I was still caught with my mouth hanging open. The whole thing was weird, and that was saying something for a girl who was used to weird.

Now that I was seeing him in the flesh, Dad's boss looked a bit younger than my parents. Light brown hair curled around his neck. He hadn't shaved, giving him a rugged look that went along with his scarred hiking boots. He didn't make a sound as he walked down the steps, which was eerie enough without adding the fact that he'd co-starred in one of my oddest visions ever.

I didn't know I'd made a noise until Axel elbowed me. "Dude. You okay?"

I cleared my throat. "Totally. Why wouldn't I be?" Axel had been pestering me ever since I had the vision in Dad's office, but I hadn't spilled much. Maybe I should've told him, but I couldn't bring myself to. For some reason, my connection with the younger guy felt personal.

"Thank you for getting here so quickly, John," he said to Dad. "I'm Michael Dawson." His grey T-shirt was a smidge too tight around his arms, making it strain against his biceps as he reached out a hand.

Dad stepped forward to shake it. "Wasn't a

problem. This is my wife, Gabriela, my son, Axel, and my daughter, Tessa."

Axel and I stayed by the car while our parents greeted him. It was better to keep my distance, less chance of a vision that way. But when Mr. Dawson reached to shake Axel's hand, he abandoned me. I sighed. This was going to be awkward.

Mr. Dawson held out his hand to me, but I didn't take it. "Welcome to Texas," he said. It sounded a little like a question.

Mom gave a nervous laugh instead of her normal booming one. "It's been a long drive, and we're a little cranky. But we can't wait to get settled in."

Nice save.

A breeze picked up, blowing my hair in my face. It'd finally grown past the bottom of my shoulder blades. I pulled a rubber band out of my pocket and yanked the wavy mess into a sloppy bun.

I followed them to the house. As soon as my flip-flop hit the bottom step I had a feeling that this house was going to be full of stuff for me to "see." I shoved my gloved hands in my pockets. Better safe than sorry while Mr. Dawson was around. Mom and Dad were touring the house with him. Axel hung back with me. "What's your deal?"

I shrugged. "Didn't you see how he walked?"

"No."

"Remember when we went to the San Diego Safari Park and spent the night and we went into the tiger enclosure?"

He nodded. "Yeah. Those cats were crazy. They were inches from us the whole time, and we didn't even notice it until the guide shined her flashlight on them."

"Exactly."

"And what does that have to do with Mr. Dawson?"

"He didn't make a sound coming down those stairs."

Axel shoved me. "You're messing with me."

I shoved him back. "No. I'm actually not. Pay better attention next time."

We walked through the door and went the opposite way my parents had gone, ending up in a living room.

"Look at this yard," Axel said as he looked out a back window.

"What yard? All I see is forest."

"That's what I'm saying."

I shook my head. He was so weird sometimes. "I'm going to go claim my room." I found it upstairs, first door on the left, complete with en suite bathroom. It was even better than the pictures Dad had shown us. A bay window with a bench faced the front yard. The unpaved driveway disappeared around the corner, hidden by the forest.

Axel stomped into my new room. "Oh, this is for sure my room."

"No. Yours is next to Mom and Dad's. This is mine."

"No way. I'm older. I get this one. With the tree, it'd give me maximum sneaking-out capabilities."

"Dude." I smacked him on the back of his head. "You're not really going to be living here."

"Right. Forgot about that part."

I snorted.

"This can be your room I guess."

I rolled my eyes. "Perfect. Thanks so much."

Mom called from downstairs.

"Coming." We walked down to find her.

"How are you guys doing?" she asked as soon as we entered the kitchen. Dad and Mr. Dawson were standing around the kitchen island with her. It was a nice, bright white kitchen with granite counters and stainless steel appliances.

"My room is much better than Axel's and that's what counts, right?"

"That's right," Dad said.

"Hey!" Axel said.

Mr. Dawson chuckled and the sound gave me goosebumps. There was something off about him, and I wanted to figure out what it was.

"I opened all the windows down here to air it out a bit with that nice breeze," Mom said. "But it's so hot out, we'll need to close them in a minute. Help me with that?"

"Sure," I said.

"This is going to be great for us," Dad said.

"It's a good house. I hope you'll be comfortable here," Mr. Dawson said. "But it's important to remember that it's more secluded than you'd think."

I stifled a snort. My teeth were still rattling from the last mile of "road."

Mr. Dawson smirked. Guess I hadn't stifled it quick enough.

"Behave," Mom whispered to me.

"There's lots of wildlife in this forest, especially wolves," Mr. Dawson said.

"Wolves?" Dad laughed. "You're kidding," he said

with a slightly high pitch to his voice. Dad always did that when he was lying to us. He knew exactly what Mr. Dawson was talking about.

I glanced at Mom. She shrugged, not giving me anything to go on.

Now I knew my vision was real. Something was definitely up with St. Ailbe's and the people who went there. Mr. Dawson had my full attention. I wanted to see how he was going to explain away these "wolves" of his.

"Unfortunately, I'm not kidding." His voice was firm, leaving no room for misunderstanding. His gaze met mine with such a force that I wanted to look away but couldn't. "If you leave them alone, they'll leave you alone. You're safe here. Just stay close to the house after dark."

"Thanks for the warning. We'll keep an eye out," Mom said.

"I'd advise staying away from my St. Ailbe's kids. They're not like most other teenagers and can be a bit unstable. Even violent. Which is why we need the help of people like your Dad." He paused. "They might look normal, but they're not. Under no uncertain terms should you make friends with them. You'd be risking your life. Your future. Understand, Tessa?"

His intensity made me nervous. "Sure," I said, although I wasn't sure I understood at all. In fact, the only good his little speech did was make me want to find a St. Ailbe's kid to befriend.

His gaze was suddenly too much, and I looked down at my feet.

"I doubt you'll run into my students too often,"

Mr. Dawson said. "They stick pretty close to campus, and John, you'll be doing everything from the offices downtown. The school isn't too far from here though—just on the other side of the creek."

That sounded far. "Where's your car?" I said. Axel elbowed me. Jeeze. Was it elbow Tessa day or what? My question was perfectly valid. It wasn't out front when we pulled in.

"I hiked." I must've made a face because Mr. Dawson explained. "The creek backs up to the house. You've got maybe fifty feet of trees before you'll hit a steep drop. The bottom is the bed of the creek. It's been dry for years though. It's only a couple mile hike from here to the school." A honk sounded from the driveway. "That's one of my former students now. He graduated a couple years ago, and teaches occasionally. John, you'll get to know him well. He's my second here. I know you've got movers coming in a bit, but I thought you might want help unloading your cars after such a long drive."

"Perfect. Thanks, Michael." Dad grabbed the keys from his pocket. "Axel, get to it."

Dad tossed the keys to Axel, but I caught them. "I'll help."

Dad shared a look with Mr. Dawson. "Axel, go with your sister."

That wasn't awkward at all. Why didn't Dad want me to go outside? Axel and I walked out the front door, but I stopped just outside.

He was here. The younger guy from the vision. The one who could tell that I was having the vision. The one I linked to.

My breathing was shallow as I watched him move.

I didn't want to make a noise, not even from breathing. I wanted to watch him in real life for a second. He was at least as fit as Mr. Dawson, and had the same soundless stride. I could feel his restlessness as if it were my own. He pulled off his sunglasses and stuck them in the collar of his blue t-shirt. I smiled when I noticed the band artwork on the front—The Helio Sequence. That album was in heavy rotation on my playlist.

Axel called out to him and my moment of watching unnoticed was shattered. I stumbled back a step.

"Tessa?" Mr. Dawson said, suddenly close. "Are you okay?"

I tried to move away, but he was already reaching out to steady me.

"Don't touch her!" Dad said.

Too late. He gripped my bicep, skin-to-skin.

Running. Panting. Wind ruffled his fur. His paws slammed the ground at a fast pace.

Faster. Must go faster.

Mr. Dawson was there with me. I could feel him in my head, an unwelcome visitor, seeing what I saw. It felt like an invasion, and I wanted him gone. I pushed him out as the vision faded. And just as quickly as it started, I was back on the porch, staring into Mr. Dawson's hazel eyes.

I knew I should pull away from him, but the look he was giving me warned me not to even try. I was paralyzed as I waited for one of us to break the silence.

That was the second time my visions had gone wonky. This time was way more unsettling than the last.

And shit. Dad was going to be pissed.

His lips turned up as that thought ran through my mind. "I see we've both got our secrets," he whispered so that only I could hear it.

Crap. Was he reading my mind? If he were telepathic, that could explain why my visions were weird with him. I'd never met anyone with gifts before, not since my *abuela* passed, and I was too young to really remember her anyway.

He smiled.

Crap. I've got to stop thinking stuff.

Mom stepped between us and pulled me away from him. "You okay, Tess?"

"I think so." *Sorry*, I mouthed. So much for making a good impression.

"My daughter doesn't like to be touched." Dad tried to explain. "She's got this condition—"

"It was my fault." Mr. Dawson stared at me as if he could see right through me. Then he nodded, and took the keys from my gloved hand. "Head's up, Dastien!" He threw the keys.

Dastien caught them without looking from fifteen feet away. He didn't take too much notice of me. Not like I wanted him to. He walked to the cars as a breeze whipped through the house, slamming the screen door shut behind me. He spun. His eyes, dark before, flashed to glowing amber.

That had to be a trick with the light.

We stood there staring at each other. I couldn't look away, and I was sure he couldn't either.

He was too far away for me to hear, but his lips moved and I knew what he said. It was the same thing

I'd been thinking. "It's you."

Mr. Dawson cleared his throat. "Maybe it's best if we leave you to it."

"Yes, but thank you for your offer," Mom said. "Tessa's not great with strangers."

Perfect, Mom. Way to make me sound like a freak. I shot her a look that said as much.

"Let's talk on Wednesday, John." Mr. Dawson walked to the car. His movements were not only silent, but also graceful and efficient. Almost like a dancer's, but somehow more dangerous. The two men argued, but then Dastien's shoulders drooped. He placed the keys on the hood of our car and headed to his. He stared at me before getting into the passenger side.

I didn't realize I was holding my breath until they were gone and I was left gasping for air.

"You okay?" Axel said.

I swallowed. "Yeah. Of course. I'm fine."

"You sure, *mija*?" Mom said. "You look pale."

"I'm fine," I said it with a little more force than was necessary, but didn't apologize for it. I headed to Dad's SUV and stared at the keys. I thought about taking off the gloves and holding them for a second just to see what would happen, but I had a feeling my mind had taken in all the information it could for today. The gloves had to stay on, at least for now.

I unlocked the doors and started unloading our bags.

Chapter Four

For days I kept staring out the windows, hoping Dastien would come back, but he never did. I guessed he didn't really have any reason to come back. That didn't stop me from wanting it. I was curious about him and needed to figure out why I was so drawn to him. Hours filled with unpacking endless boxes went by, and I started to wonder if what I'd seen, what I'd felt, had been a figment of my imagination. For a girl who was used to seeing things that weren't there, it wasn't completely out of the realm of the possible. But it'd be a damn shame. Just the thought of seeing Dastien again had my palms sweating and I kind of liked it.

But Dastien wasn't the only thing on my mind. The house was a minefield of visions. Sometimes they were normal, everyday stuff—people laughing, fighting, getting ready for work. Then I'd touch something and rage would fill my body. My blood would boil and an animalistic urge to destroy things would consume me, but I wouldn't exactly see anything. It was all emotions, which I was adding to the weird and new category. So far, Texas was turning out to be pretty interesting.

By the end of the weekend, the house was mostly in order—all the essentials in the right spots even if they weren't totally organized—so I started attacking the boxes in my room. I dusted my books off, placing each one—sorted alphabetically and by genre—on the shelves Dad installed. What some people might call "anal," I'd call efficient. What good was it to have a book if you couldn't find it when you wanted it?

When I was done, I sat on the bed and stared at my collection. Axel and Dad were arguing over what station to stream music from. Dad wanted classic rock and Axel wanted hip-hop. Dad informed Axel that there were no "thugs" in the house.

I was laughing at their verbal sparring when Mom came into my room holding a stack of clean towels. She pointed at my gloveless hands. "How's it going in here?"

"Fine." I waved toward my books. "Got them unpacked."

She set the pile down on my bed. "What about the rest? The house giving you any trouble?"

I shrugged. "Define trouble."

"Anything you need to talk about?"

"Nah. I think I've got it covered. But thanks for the offer."

She settled down next to me. "You okay? Your brother's leaving in a week and half, we're living in a different state, and your new school starts tomorrow. It'd be totally cool to admit you're nervous."

"Have you met me? This whole no-brother, new school combo is going to rock."

Mom gave me her patented I'm-not-buying-the-line-of-crap-you're-selling look.

"Axel leaving is gonna suck."

She kept silent as she stared at me.

"Okay, so I'm nervous about next week. I'm a freak, but I'm also human. Who wouldn't be?"

"That's what I thought."

"I don't know why admitting it was helpful. It didn't do me any good."

"Well, it made me feel better."

I laughed.

"Kidding. But admitting your nerves is the first step to getting over them." She smiled. "And you're not a freak. You're gifted."

"There's a difference?"

Her smile turned into a full-on grin. "I'll admit. It's slight, but there *is* a difference." She put her arm around my shoulders, and I leaned into her. "You're going to do great. People here are nice, more down to earth."

"So you've said." But I wasn't holding my breath. I was a freak to the core, and even if the people were "down to earth," chances were they wouldn't be down with me.

"And now your cousins are only an hour away. Once we get more settled, we'll have them over for dinner. They'll understand you, even if the other kids don't."

She had me there. If they were "gifted" too, then maybe I could finally figure out how to have a normal life. "Sounds like a solid plan."

"Have you eaten anything?"

I thought for a second. "Zone Bar?" I might have forgotten to eat again. When an organizational task was put in front of me, I was a girl on a mission. Puny matters like eating faded away.

"A woman cannot live on Zone Bars alone." She gave me another squeeze before getting up. "Don't worry so much. It's all going to work out. Your dad and I are leaving for dinner. Date night, remember?"

I nodded. Every Sunday, rain or shine, Mom and Dad had a date. It was cute. I kind of envied them, but I had time to figure the whole boyfriend thing out. One day I'd find a way to be a regular girl with a totally awesome guy by my side.

Okay, so I'd take an average one. I'd even settle for a mediocre one at this point. The blame wasn't on them; it was totally me. No one needed to be inside the head of a teenage boy when you're the object of their thoughts. Because seriously, eew. Which defeated the purpose entirely.

"There are frozen pizzas in the freezer, and we'll leave money in case you and your brother want to go somewhere. Eat. It's an order."

"Got it. Starvation-chic is not my look." I grabbed an old Nora Roberts book and settled down in my window bench to escape for a bit. The predictability of her books drew me in quickly. There was nothing more certain in life than the ending of a good romance novel.

A few chapters in, Mom yelled that they were leaving. I watched them get into the car and disappear around the curve in the road.

Alone at last. I'd been feeling antsy since we got

here, and it'd only gotten worse. For me there were only two things that would quiet my mind, dancing and running. I'd already gone for my morning jog, and had been waiting for a chance to blast some music.

I clicked on last week's BBC One Essential Mix, turned the volume up as loud as I could stand it, and started dancing around my room.

Axel walked in without knocking and turned off the music. "Are you trying to make everyone in the state deaf?"

Or not. "Who said you could come in here?"

"I did. We're parentless!" He hammed it up with some cheering, and then collapsed on my bed.

"That's hardly cause for celebration." I rolled my eyes. "Come on. I've been listening to what everyone else wants to for days now. Can I just—"

"No."

I kicked his shin.

"Ow. Don't be so violent." He rubbed his shin. "It's your last night before starting a brand new school year."

I groaned. "Not you too. Can we please drop the whole 'school starts tomorrow' talk? I'd like to live in denial for a little while longer."

"One thing, try not to bite the head off of the first friendly person you meet. Promise me."

I crossed my arms and gave him my best tough-girl look. "Dude. I'm not a bitch. I'll be as friendly as people are to me."

"Riiiiight." I went to kick his shin again, but he hopped out of the way. "Let's go for a drive. We can scout out a pizza place."

"Fine, but I get to pick the toppings."

"No way. You picked last time."

I grabbed a pair of gloves and my flip-flops. "Yeah, but you like to experiment with nasty combinations. The fact that you actually picked pineapple and anchovy means that you should be banned for life in the topping-picking department."

"I still think the combo of sweet and salty could've been a good thing. It was nearly genius."

"Near genius doesn't count." I shoved him. "Moron."

He clutched his chest. "I'm hurt by your name calling."

"Good." I grinned. "Your ego could stand to lose a few pounds."

"What's wrong with knowing that I'm awesome?" He messed up my hair.

***

When we were on the way back with the pizza, a strange sensation tingled through my body. It was like a weight had settled over me. This intense sense of foreboding mixed in my blood making me cold.

By the time we got home, it was dark. Axel went into the house, but I lingered outside for a minute, sitting on the porch swing as I tried to figure out what was making me feel that way. I knew that staying outside after dark was a bad idea, but I couldn't help myself.

Goosebumps ran up and down my arms. The full moon hung low and yellow. The crazies would be out tonight, or so Mom always said when it looked like that. I smiled. I was outside, so she had a point.

I hadn't even realized that there had been noise outside until it was suddenly gone. The cicadas song cut off. The owls stopped hooting. There was no rustling of the leaves. Everything was still. A healthy dose of fear pumped through my veins.

A wolf crashed out from the woods. Then three more. They were playing, not really noticing I was there as they rolled around on the ground and pawed at each other. I probably should've been scared, but in that moment, I wasn't. They were on the other side of the driveway, and I felt safe on the porch. I relaxed in the swing as I watched them. One of them bit another one's tail, making the bitee yelp. I laughed.

One of them suddenly stopped playing and looked straight at me.

Dumb. I was so unbelievably dumb. These weren't wolves in a cage. These wolves could actually come over here and eat me.

I thought about darting inside. It probably would've been the smarter choice, but I didn't want to spook them by moving.

One of them came closer to the porch.

I stood up, torn between going down the stairs to pet it and rushing inside. I wasn't stupid, but the way it was moving—with its head down and tongue out— it looked more curious than dangerous.

Before I could do anything, another wolf jumped out of the woods. It was beautiful, mostly white with patches of gray sprinkled along its face and back. The coloring seemed much more regal than the shades of brown the others were. It slid to a stop in between me and the approaching brown wolf, snarling.

Shit. That one was pissed and was more likely to eat me. I should've gone inside.

The new wolf stared down each of the others, and they started to whine and rolled over, exposing their stomachs. It had to be the alpha of the bunch. It howled and the others scrambled up, fleeing back into the woods.

The alpha turned to me.

My heart pounded. I stepped back into the front door until the doorknob of the screen door dug into my back. The wolf sat down on the ground to watch me.

Something about it seemed familiar. I couldn't quite place it, but the face and its eyes just had this quality like I knew I'd seen it somewhere before. But I knew I hadn't.

"Tess!" Axel swung the front door open. "You're eating or what? The pizza's getting cold."

I turned away from the wolf for a second, and when I looked back, it was gone.

My breath came in short gasps as I looked back to Axel and then to the drive again.

"You okay?"

I shook my head. "I don't know." I moved out of the way so Axel could open the screen door. He grabbed my gloved hand and pulled me inside.

"Come on," he said softly. "You need to eat."

I let him pull me inside. The whole exchange with the wolves went by so quickly that I wondered if it had actually happened. For the second time since I'd arrived in Texas, I was questioning my sanity.

Yet another thing to add to the weird and new category.

***

The next morning I must've changed a million times. I finally settled on casual. My favorite band T-shirt—a vintage Orb from their album *Adventures Beyond the Ultraworld*—plus jeans, chucks, and black loose-knit gloves with deep purple accents. It didn't look like I was trying too hard. Even if no one else my age knew who The Orb was, the design was cool.

Mom and Dad were in the kitchen when I got downstairs. I did a spin. "What do you think?"

"Beautiful," Mom said. She was still in her pink fluffy robe, with the belt knotted at her waist.

"That's not helpful. You have to say that. You're my mother." I looked down at my T-shirt. "Too weird? I might not need any extra help in that area."

Mom laughed. "You have to be who you are."

Dad was already in his full suit. His hair was still a little damp from the shower. "Except let's not take off the gloves today. Okay, princess?"

"John!" Mom was about to dig into Dad again.

"It's too early in the morning for contradicting parents. Be yourself. Don't be yourself. My head hurts already. Someone get me my AM medicine quickstyle."

Dad opened the fridge and handed me an icy cold Diet Coke.

I popped the top and took a long chug. "Okay. Brain function returning. So which one of you lucky parental units is going to drive me to school?"

They shared a look. "Neither," Mom said.

I set down my Diet Coke. "Well, if you think I'm

going to go wake up Axel, then you're going to be disappointed. I don't feel like getting slugged."

"He's not driving you either," Dad said.

"Are you guys high? I can't walk to school from here. It'd take me all day." No way. "Please don't tell me I have to catch the bus for my first day of senior year. Even you two wouldn't be that cruel." It wasn't that I had anything against taking the bus, per se, but for me it presented all kinds of problems. The goal was to minimize the number of visions I got per day, not add to them.

They just stood there smiling. Waiting for me to realize something.

Holy shit.

My only defense for being so dense was that it was before eight AM. Anything before ten AM and I'm lucky if I can speak my native language coherently.

I ran out the front door. A new black VW Tiguan sat in the driveway with the other cars. "Nice." Any car would've been amazing, but they'd picked the exact one I'd been lusting after.

Dad stepped out onto the porch and handed me the keys. "Have a good day, princess."

I shocked him by giving him a big hug. Then ran inside and did the same to Mom.

"Thanks, guys. Way to start my year off in style." Dad wrapped an arm around Mom as she stepped outside to wave good-bye. "We try," he said. "Now go, or you'll be late."

Once inside, I took a deep breath and inhaled the lovely new leather scent. The car was a classic black on black. And it was perfect. I set up my iPhone to link to it, and once I had the navi going and my music playing, I headed for school.

Chapter Five

The school was made up of two four-story buildings in an L-shape. The parking lot faced a football field with full-on stadium style seating and lights. Another smaller field backed up to it, but didn't have as nice of a scoreboard or the seating. This place wasn't messing around when it came to football.

I slid down from the car and grabbed my backpack. If my life were a movie, everyone would've noticed me walking through the parking lot and stared. Good thing I lived in real life, and was blissfully ignored. I even moved through my first few periods managing not to speak to anyone. But as I doodled over the fourth syllabus of the day, something tapped against my back.

I glanced behind me.

The girl with long fire-red hair had been in my last class, too. She passed me a note, and I slid it under my textbook as the teacher looked my way. As soon as she turned, I opened the carefully folded note.

Hot pink ink gleamed off the paper. Not my favorite choice in pen color, but who was I to judge. "Are you really from LA?"

I wrote a quick reply asking her how she knew, and twisted my arm to place the note on her desk without looking back.

A second later, the tap came again. "Small town. Word gets around. Plus, Mrs. Kelly—the front office lady—has a big mouth. That's so cool!" The exclamation point was dotted with a heart. "Let's talk at lunch."

This was probably a bad idea. Psychometrics—people who got visions from touch—didn't make good friends. I didn't need to take my gloves off to know that we probably weren't going to hit it off. Still, if I wanted friends, I had to keep an open mind.

The redhead appeared by my side before the shrilling bell had time to end. "I'm Rosalyn." She was wearing a short frilly skirt and tank top. Her bright smile faltered as she took in my T-shirt. Maybe I should've gone with something less obscure, more Beiber-esque. I snorted before I could stop it.

She didn't look amused. I cleared my throat and her gaze met mine. Her smile returned, but this time didn't reach her eyes.

"Hi. I'm Tessa." I loaded my arms with books just in case she had the urge to shake hands.

Her smile dimmed again. Shit. I should be smiling, too. I smiled, and she looked at me funny. I almost laughed at the awkwardness of the situation.

"Okay, well, I need to grab my lunch. Meet me here." She strode off without waiting for a response.

Christ. This was going well. I made my way to my

locker. It took me a couple of tries to get the combination right, but finally, the lock clicked. I shoved my books inside and grabbed the brown sack lunch Mom had packed for me.

Rosalyn was waiting for me when I got back to the door of our last class. She was holding a similar brown bag, and I said a silent thank you to Mom for being awesome.

"It's a good thing you brought yours, too," she said as we walked toward the cafeteria. "The food here is gross. No one eats it unless they're desperate."

I didn't know how to respond to that, but she didn't notice.

She eyed my bag as if she could see through the paper. "What did you bring? Tofu? Sushi?"

Guess she had some ideas about what a proper Angelino should eat. "A turkey sandwich and some chips."

"Oh." Her mouth pressed into a firm line as she studied me from head to toe.

I nearly walked away right then. Mom and Dad were kind of right this morning. I couldn't change who I was, even though I needed to hide my visions. I was a walking contradiction—equal parts wanting to fly my freak flag with pride and bury it in a deep dark hole.

"What's up with the gloves? Are you a germaphobe or what?"

And there it was. This was why I didn't talk to people. I needed a lie. A good one. Just my luck I was possibly the worst liar ever. "I guess it's hard to stay current with fashion here."

I held my breath, hoping she'd buy it. My cheeks

weren't heating, my usual "tell." That was something at least.

"Ugh." She stuck out her bottom lip. "We never get any of the new trends till they're already over. I've got to get out of here."

I couldn't believe she bought it. If everyone here started to wear gloves because of this, I was going to laugh. Hard.

Rosalyn walked up to a round table that was almost full and sat down. Taking my cue, I slid into the chair next to her. Everyone stopped what they were doing, some in mid-chew, to gawk at me. One might think being a pariah at my old school would give me the ability to deal with these kinds of situations, but they never got any easier. I wanted to slouch, but didn't dare. Showing weakness only made things worse.

"This is Tessa," Rosalyn said. "She's from LA."

I counted eight other people besides Rosalyn sitting around the Formica. Two of the guys had on blue and white jerseys. Hiding my abilities from one person, hard. From nine? This could very easily be a disaster of epic proportions.

"Is that Tokidoki?" The girl to the right of me asked as she pointed to my bag. Her brown hair was done in some elaborate braid that would've taken me hours to attempt even though my hair was long enough to try it. I was jealous for a split second and then realized she must've gotten up at the butt-crack of dawn to get ready, a feat I would never dare to try myself.

"Cool hair."

She grinned. "Thanks."

I tapped my messenger bag. "Yep. I have kind of an obsession with Tokidoki."

"Jealous! My dad won't get me one. Says a teenager doesn't need such an expensive backpack. But I found my Harajuku Lovers one on eBay for a sweet deal." She rummaged around in it and pulled out a copy of Us Weekly. "Have you ever met any stars?" She flipped through pages, stopping on a picture of my favorite Scotsman.

I flashed back to the party before we left LA. The look on his face when he stared at me was something I wished I could erase from my mind. I could've probably impressed the group by saying that he'd been one of Dad's clients, but that would've required a bunch of explaining and would probably come off as bragging. Not a good option.

I took a closer look at the photo. "That's Larchmont Village, one of my favorite streets in LA." I shrugged. "You see them every once in a while. I mean they're normal people. Just like us." I quoted the magazine's tag line, but got a bunch of empty stares as I glanced around the still silent table. I quickly re-thought my no-bragging approach. "My dad had a lot of stars as his clients, including him." I tapped the picture. "Plus, there were tons in my neighborhood—Bel Air."

"No way!" Fancy Braid Girl said.

"Isn't that where the Fresh Prince lived?" the boy across the table asked. His dimples winked at me as he spoke.

"Yep." He was cute, but nowhere near Dastien's level of hotness. Perfect. I was obsessing over a boy I didn't even really know. That made me officially ridiculous.

Fancy Braid Girl grabbed the corner of my T-shirt. "Who's this? I'm Lindsay, by the way." She cocked her head, waiting for me to answer.

It took me a second to realize she was talking about my shirt. "Um...The Orb is one of my favorite groups."

"It's really soft. Has to be printed on something better than American Apparel for sure. Lemme check." She reached toward me, but I leaned away. "Don't freak. I'm just checking the label."

Her fingers brushed against the back of my neck.

"Oh, Lindsay. You're so soft," Dimple Boy said. His voice was muffled as his lips moved along her neck.

Ew, gross!

The seatbelt dug into Lindsay's back. She was giddy as his wet lips pressed against hers.

I banged my elbow on the table, jolting me back to the lunchroom.

"Yup. Printed on Splendid," Lindsay said.

I looked around as I rubbed my elbow, but no one seemed to notice anything weird. At least I hadn't said anything to give away the vision.

"Her jeans are J Brand," Rosalyn said. "I bet she has good stuff stashed in her closet. She'll be a good addition."

I slowly inhaled and exhaled to let the aftershocks of the vision fade from my body, before trying to speak. They were going to be sorely disappointed if they thought they were going to raid my clothes. I'd never be able to wear anything they borrowed again, and shopping really wasn't my thing. "I don't really pay much attention to brands, but I like to do screen

51

printing. Splendid's shirts are my favorite to work with."

Lindsay made a face at that, but then Dimple Boy asked a question. From then on it was a solid twenty-five minutes of being barraged with a million and one questions about LA. By the time the bell rang, my palms were sweating. I itched to take off my gloves and let my skin breathe, but that was so not an option.

Rosalyn and I left the cafeteria together since it turned out we had almost the exact same schedule. We'd better end up being actual friends, or else this school year would be really painful. Someone shouted my name. Dimple Boy was chasing after us.

"I wanted to let you know we're having a party on Saturday night. You know, to celebrate the start of a new year. You should come." He winked at Rosalyn. "She knows where I live."

Rosalyn took a step forward and linked her arm in mine. We were both wearing short-sleeved T-shirts. Our skin touched.

Rosalyn's face was red. "I can't believe you'd do this. You know Lindsay is coming over later, and look at this place!"

An older woman was laying half-on, half-off a couch. Beer cans littered the floor. A grease covered pizza box was on a coffee table in front of her. Cigarette butts covered the rest of the table. "I'll clean up. Don't you worry, baby." Her words were slurred.

The stench of alcohol filled the air, stinging my nostrils. Rosalyn's anger and frustration consumed me.

I stumbled, and my arm pulled free from hers.

Rosalyn stared at me. "You okay?"

"Yeah. Just a little clumsy. Sorry," I managed to

say. Rosalyn might seem normal, but from what I just saw, her home life was a hot mess. I was starting to feel bad for her.

"Carlos' parties are always crazy."

Wait. Did I get invited to a party? Nice.

"Just so you know, Carlos and I are together. He's probably only inviting you because you're new. No offense."

…and not feeling bad for her anymore.

I barely contained my eye roll. I hated when people said "no offense" or "I don't mean to be rude." If someone is going to say something rude or offensive, they should just say it or not. Trying to pawn it off as something not rude or offensive when it clearly was, was beyond insulting.

She might have thought she was doing herself a favor by warning me off her manwhore of a boyfriend, but she really should've been more concerned about what her "friends" were doing behind her back. When I thought about it, the whole thing was kind of sad. And damn it. Now I was feeling bad for her again.

"Anyway. I'm sure we can find something to make you look presentable for the party."

Every time I started to feel a little bit of sympathy for the girl, she hit me with a backhanded comment. I officially decided to cut off my feelings for her. She was clearly using me to feel more "LA," whatever that meant, and I was using her to get to the party. With any luck, I'd make some actual friends there.

Pathetic as it was, my mind drifted back to Dastien. I couldn't help but wonder if he'd be there. The chances seemed slight, but still, a girl could dream.

Chapter Six

When Saturday finally came around, I didn't even want to get out of bed. Rosalyn's friends had tentatively let me in their group, but they grew even more touchy-feely with every day that passed.

What was it with Texans and invasion of personal space?

It was exhausting keeping my visions under control. I'd thought about ditching my new friends, but there was no mistaking that my family had moved here for me. I owed it to my parents and myself to give it my all. When I hit my breaking point, I'd reassess what my goals were. But for now, I could handle it. I would try to be a normal kid. And normal meant having friends and hanging out with said friends.

Still, a little escapist therapy in the form of a new book would help cleanse my brain of all the unneeded background information I'd gotten over the past few days.

I rolled out of bed at noon, and got ready as quickly as my sleepy body would allow. I threw on a pair of well-worn yoga pants, the first T-shirt I could find, threw my hair up in a messy bun, and headed downstairs. Axel was in the kitchen digging into a bowl of cereal.

"I'm hitting the bookstore. Wanna join?" Bookstores were my kind of place. All those shiny books, lightly touched by only a couple of people. Each one held a different world, a different life to disappear into.

That said, libraries were a total nightmare scenario. Too many hands touched those books and turning pages with gloves on was a bit too cumbersome.

"You want me to go to a bookstore?" Axel narrowed his gaze at me. "Yeah. Not going to happen."

Axel hadn't read anything cover to cover ever. I wasn't sure how he was going to do the whole college thing when I wasn't there to help him with his homework. I grabbed my purse and dug through it for my keys. "It's at the mall, dork."

"In that case, yes." He put his now empty cereal bowl in the sink. "But I get to drive your car."

He made a grab for my keys, but I dodged around the center island. "What! No way. Only I get to drive my car."

"I picked it out, but Dad drove it here. I should at least get a turn before I leave. Deal?" He held out his hand, as if I'd just hand over the keys.

"No deal. I'm not having you imbue the driver's seat with whatever stuff you've got going on in your head. There's such a thing as TMI between siblings. I'll go by myself."

He sighed dramatically. "Fine. You can drive, but I pick the music."

"Fine." Now I just had to let my parents know where we were going. "Where are Mom and Dad?"

He shrugged. "Dunno. They were gone when I got up."

Weird. They were usually around on the weekends when Dad wasn't working. I headed for the door.

"Wait. You didn't eat any breakfast."

"Not hungry." I usually didn't get hungry until after I was up for a bit. Today was no exception. I had too much on my mind to be hungry.

The bookstore was attached to the only mall in town. It was a brown blob of a building, with a JCPenny's and Macy's on either end. The bookstore branched off the mall on the Macy's end, and had an entrance from the outside. I left Axel to his search for a new pair of jeans, and pushed open the glass doors to the bookstore.

Fans blasted me with cold air, refreshing after the 110-degree weather outside. The scent of flavored coffee wafted over me. The baristas were hard at work, making yummy caffeinated concoctions. I closed my eyes for a moment, letting the calm seep in. There wasn't much to this town, but at least I had this bit of zen, and that was nothing to look down upon.

I veered over to the science fiction and fantasy section, and searched for any new epic fantasy releases. I was still looking through titles when I bumped into a body.

That wasn't like me. I was usually hyper-aware of the people around me. "Excuse me," I said without looking up. "I didn't hear you."

"It's okay."

That voice made goosebumps spread over my skin. I spun.

He was taller up close. At least a foot taller than me. But it was his golden eyes that held me captive.

Dastien.

It took me a second to speak. "Hi."

"Are you okay?" He asked.

It took me a second too long to answer. "I'm sorry. My mind seems to be MIA."

Then he smiled, his eyes scrunched at the corners and his lips spread to reveal perfect teeth. His black hair was flecked with auburn highlights. And there was something sexy about the way he held himself, standing up straight with his right hip slightly cocked.

I melted on the spot. Who could withstand him?

More importantly, who would want to?

"You're Tessa McCaide, right? Staying at the yellow house?"

I stared down at my feet, unable to keep eye contact for one more second. And crap. Why did my beat-up-to-hell Nine Inch Nails t-shirt have to be the one on top? The one with the silver dollar sized hole just to the left of my belly button.

Perfect. On the day I looked like a homeless weirdo the hottest guy ever wanted to talk to me. The one guy who made me feel things I couldn't even begin to describe. It was more than attraction, though that was there in spades. I was drawn to him.

"I'm Dastien Laurent." An accent peeked through

as he spoke and held out a hand.

I couldn't turn it down.

"Do you always wear gloves?"

"Usually." My face burned. "I'm not supposed to be talking to St. Ailbe's kids."

He laughed, golden eyes glittering. "I'm not exactly a St. Ailbe's kid anymore. I graduated already." He leaned in closer to me, and his warm breath tickled my cheek. "I'm okay. Promise," he said with a low voice. He hadn't let go of my hand, and I didn't want him to.

"Nine Inch Nails, huh?"

"Yeah. Why?"

"You look too sweet to like Trent."

I dropped mouth open. No one had ever accused me of being sweet.

He narrowed his eyes. "What's your favorite song?"

Now that was a serious question. Did I go old school or new? I loved most everything. Song titles quickly ran through my mind. 'Survivalism.' No. 'God Given.' No. Maybe I should say 'Ringfinger.' Yes. That was it. "I'm going with 'Closer.'"

My face was intently hot as he laughed. Holy Freudian slip, Batman. Leave it to me to tell the hottest guy ever that one of my favorite song's chorus was a guy yelling about how he wants to fu—"do" them like an animal.

I covered my face with my hands. "I meant 'Terrible Lie.' I swear. Seriously. Forget the other song I mentioned."

He was still laughing. "Don't think that's going to happen, but I won't mention it. Both choices were

59

solid. Pretty Hate Machine is a classic album, so your second choice was pretty good." He leaned in again. "But I liked your first choice better."

Oh. My. God. Was he flirting with me over my favorite band ever?

This was it. We had the same musical taste. He was clearly meant for me. I wouldn't fight destiny when it brought something like this to me.

He stepped into my personal space, and I didn't step away. "You know—"

Another guy appeared in the aisle saying something in a language I couldn't understand. His chartreuse eyes stood out against his fair skin.

I took a step away from Dastien, but he shook his head at me. Why, I had no idea. I couldn't begin to imagine what was going through his head when I couldn't form a coherent thought.

Dastien and his friend spoke rapidly in what might have been French. They were wearing identical outfits—black jeans and black t-shirts. It was weird, but neutral enough that it could've been a coincidence.

Dastien's friend nodded at me and then walked away.

I didn't have time to wonder what their exchange was all about. Dastien kissed the back of my hand, and my brain turned to mush.

Wait. He was going to leave?

My pulse echoed in my ears.

"I'll see you soon," he said as he let my hand go.

"Sure," I said but his back was already to me as he walked away. He looked over his shoulder at me and winked.

That should be illegal. Seriously.

I leaned back hard against the bookshelf. It rattled, but thankfully didn't tip over. I fanned myself for a second. That guy made me sweat.

"I'll see you soon?" I whispered his words to myself. I glanced around the bookshelf to see if he was gone. What did that mean? When would he see me?

The bookstore suddenly lost its appeal. There was only one thing for a girl to do when she had a close encounter with a guy that hot.

Ice cream. I needed lots and lots of ice cream. Even if it was my breakfast. It had milk and maybe eggs. That totally counted.

I peeked at my watch. I still had twenty minutes before I was supposed to meet up with Axel. I meandered through the mall until I found the food court, grabbed a sugar cone with a scoop of chocolate chip, my favorite, and went outside to wait.

A lone cement bench sat outside the front of the entrance closest to where I'd parked. I settled down to eat my cone as I watched three guys try to hit on a girl. They were laughing and punching each other as they vied for her attention. The boys were hot and so ripped their T-shirts could be mere seconds away from tearing at the seams. There had to be something in the water here. I didn't recognize the guys from school, but I knew the girl was in my Pre-calc class. I searched my memory for her name and drew a blank.

I angled away from them, hoping she wouldn't see me, but I couldn't stop myself from watching. One of the guys, a blond one with a bit too much muscle for my tastes, seemed to be in the lead. She flirted with him, brushing his shoulder as she talked. He sat down on an oversized planter that held a half-dead shrub, and drew her in closer to him. The other two guys started to make fun of the blond one.

A group of guys I definitely knew from school came out of the mall entrance. Four of them. Including Carlos.

Shit. I pulled my hair out of the bun and let it block my face. I didn't have it in me to play off any visions, especially the kind that came from Carlos. Just dealing with the party was going to be enough for one day.

I shouldn't have worried. They went straight for the girl.

"Stay away from Jess!" Carlos said. His hands were balled at his sides.

Holy crapola. Where was Axel? He was going to die when he found out he missed a fight. I quickly texted him.

"Carlos. I was just—" She stepped away from the golden boy.

Carlos shoved the guy with blond hair. "What do you think you're doing talking to our kind?"

Blondie budged only enough to move off the planter, rising slowly.

I took another bite of my ice cream as the girl tried to stop the fight. Ice cream and a fight? Best mall trip ever.

Carlos' face reddened, and then he looked at the ground, backing down.

Lame. After all the visions he'd given me, seeing his ass get handed to him would've been nice.

One of the boys glanced toward the entrance. "We're busted," he said.

Dastien strode from the mall with two other guys dressed just like him—black T-shirt and black jeans.

"*Retour sur le collége. Maintenant*," Dastien said.

I wondered what that meant. It sounded sexy.

Blondie's fists clenched at his sides, but instead of saying anything, he started walking toward the parking lot.

Axel ran out the mall exit. "Did I miss it?"

My face heated as everyone turned to me. "Shut up." I tried my best to ignore them, instead focusing on my brother. "No fight."

Axel looked around at the crowd now dispersing into the parking lot. "Bummer." He took my ice cream cone before I could stop him and took a big bite.

"What the hell? That was my breakfast."

Axel snorted. "No. This was dessert." He ripped off the paper covering the cone, and licked the length of it. "And now it's mine."

Licking a food item was the ultimate in claiming. "You're a dick."

He took another big bite. "Mom and Dad are waiting to have lunch with us." He threw his arm over my shoulder. "We've got to do something about your eating habits before I go."

I rolled my eyes. I ate plenty. Sometimes got distracted and forgot about it, but I wasn't anorexic or anything. My curves were still visible as ever.

"Where's your book?" He asked as we started toward the parking lot.

My face burned once again. Dastien was a few feet away by the mall entrance. I snuck a peek at him. Yup. He was waiting for me to answer, arms crossed and a slanted grin on his face.

He totally knew what he was doing to me. What a jerk.

The easiest thing to do would be to lie, but Axel knew the face I made when I lied. It wouldn't work. I took a deep breath. "I got distracted."

He looked back at Dastien and took a big bite of my cone. He chomped for a second, and I thought he'd dropped the subject.

"By what?" He asked as he turned to look at Dastien again in a totally obvious way. He took another bite, and I wanted to hit him.

I pulled my keys out of my purse. "None of your business." I heard a chuckle and looked back again. God. This was so embarrassing.

Axel snatched my keys out of my hand while I wasn't looking. "That's what you get when you hold the good stuff back."

"Who said I was holding anything back?"

He made a show of shoving the last of my cone in his mouth.

"Gross."

He put his arm around me again and started half-dragging me towards the car. "Little sis, let's talk about crushes," he said way too loudly.

I shoved him away. Dastien's laughter echoed through the parking lot.

Why, God? Why me! Why did you have to give me this jerk of a brother who was hell bent on humiliating me any chance he got?

I ignored Axel's ramblings and looked one last time at Dastien. He was still standing by the entrance. One of his friends was saying something to him, but

Dastien was watching me. I faced forward and waved as I stepped into the rows of parked cars.

Axel was right. Maybe I had a crush on this guy. But he had been watching me, so he had to feel something for me, too.

Chapter Seven

As I got ready for the party, I wondered if I'd made a good decision. It was too late to second-guess myself, but I already knew that Rosalyn and her friends didn't have that much in common with me. I didn't like to shop or gossip. I liked to read and loved to listen to a good DJ set.

Every once in a while, I'd convince Axel to take me to a club and we'd dance all night. I wore something to cover most of my skin, and Axel kept people away from me. It was one of my favorite things. Not like they had much of that around here and Axel would be leaving next week, but still, Rosalyn and I just didn't see eye to eye on music. Which might not seem like a big thing, but it was most likely the beginning of a fatal flaw in our relationship.

I'd bitten my nails down to the quick. When Axel saw me gnawing on my fingers, he offered to tag along with me, but I couldn't—wouldn't—let him do that. He was leaving soon. I had to do this on my own. But I was keeping my cell in my pocket just in case I needed backup.

By eight, Rosalyn was waiting for me outside. Her crooked smile spelled mischief as I closed the door to her little silver Honda. Her red hair hung halfway down her back in perfect curls. "You ready?" she asked.

Nope. Not at all. "Totally."

Rosalyn's country music filled the silence as she drove through the winding streets. I tried to tune it out, but the singer whining about losing some lame boyfriend was like needles digging in my eardrums.

"This song is great," I said, my lame attempt at trying to start a conversation.

"I know, right? It's one of my faves." She turned it up.

Thankfully, only a few minutes passed before she pulled into a packed driveway and parked. "Nervous?" she said.

I wondered if the gleam in her eye meant that she was hoping I was nervous. "I'm more curious than anything."

"It'll be fun. Plus, it's Texas. We're all nice," she lifted one shoulder, "for the most part."

Yeah, I wasn't buying that one. I had a feeling that if I got on Rosalyn's bad side, she would become a huge pain in my ass.

She grabbed her purse and pulled out a glittery tube of lip-gloss. "Here. Try this one."

Oh God. That was a terrible idea, but one I couldn't refuse without being rude.

"Thanks." I took the tube from her, and with a

shaking hand, started to apply the gloss in the vanity mirror.

Short, staggering visions popped through my mind of the different places she used the gloss.

In a bathroom. In her car. In English class. In Carlos' car.

And then she was at a pharmacy. She looked around as her pulse pounded. The coast was clear. She put the gloss in her pocket as she walked down the aisle, toward the exit. Her fear and excitement filled me.

And then I was back in her car. I pulled the tube from my lips. Rosalyn was texting and hadn't noticed a thing.

I exhaled slowly and focused on my reflection. The gloss was slimy and sticky, but it made my lips look Angelina-plump. My eyes were lined in my favorite midnight shadow, making their brown look richer.

"Ready?" she said.

"Sure." I flipped the vanity mirror shut and hopped out of the car.

We walked across the lawn to the large brick house. A lilting beat floated across the yard. I took a look down at my outfit—black skater dress, thin silver belt, flip-flops, thin silver scarf, and black over-the-elbow gloves—as my nerves started to reach an all-time high. I smoothed my skirt down and centered the knot on my scarf as my nerves rose.

If I could make it through the night without freaking out from some vision, then I had a chance at finding a place where I belonged—even if it wasn't with Rosalyn's crowd.

Rosalyn went straight for the door, and opened it

without pausing to knock. I might have been a little bit naïve—it was my first party after all—but I wasn't expecting everyone to be drinking. Thirty kids or so were scattered around the entryway screaming at each other over the music. They all had red plastic cups in their hands.

How in the hell did a bunch of sixteen and seventeen year olds score enough booze for everyone?

I shook my head. Some of those cups had to be filled with soda.

One girl gestured while talking, unaware that the contents of her cup were spilling all over the floor. A guy was falling all against a girl, who pushed him away.

Nope. They were drunk. Unreal.

Guess there were no parents here.

"Good. We're perfectly late." Rosalyn grabbed my gloved hand. "Let's get a drink." She led me through the crowd to the kitchen. I spotted Jess as she rushed past me, knocking me into the wall. She ran to a powder room and slammed the door.

"Gross. She's always sick before the party even gets started," Rosalyn rolled her eyes. "She seriously needs to learn to control her alcohol."

No kidding. And from the looks of things, there were a few people who wouldn't be far behind Jess' state. I knew right then that I was in over my head. I thought about calling Axel, but was too stubborn to admit that I'd been wrong about telling him not to come.

Rosalyn towed me along with her to the kitchen. It was big with an island in the center. The counters were light speckled granite, but I couldn't really see them under all the booze. Liquor bottles and red cups, along with an assortment of sodas and juices were spread all over the place. In front of the sink was an extra-large plastic trashcan filled with ice water and a keg floating in the center. Three boys stood around it as they filled red cups and handed them down a line of kids.

I checked my watch. It wasn't even 8:30 yet. How were there so many people already drunk?

Carlos was filling shot glasses on the counter with some amber colored liquor.

Right. That was how.

He looked up at me. "Hey, Tessa. Glad you could make it," he said with a grin. His dimples made him look more charming than he actually was.

He hadn't said anything to Rosalyn, and by the look she gave him, she was pissed. I so didn't want to get in the middle of that.

"How about a proper welcome to Texas? Take a shot of tequila."

Rosalyn dropped my arm and stepped back. I glanced at her, and she shrugged. "Go ahead."

At that the other three boys who were lined up for a shot looked at me. My palms started sweating. I'd never taken one. I'd never even had a drop of alcohol before. Would it make me act stupid? Or worse— would my visions go crazy?

That was *not* appealing at all.

Finding a way to be normal was my goal here. I snatched the glass that Carlos held out for me with my gloved hand.

"We take 'em Texas style here," he said.

I gave my best fake-confident smile. "Okay. What

exactly does that mean?"

"Here, let me show you. Take off your glove."

There was no way I wanted to do that, but I'd already committed.

As soon as the glove was off, he grabbed my hand and, looking me straight in the eye, licked it.

I was instantly drowning in his hormones.

Glimpses of half-dressed girls. Moans echoed in the backseat of his car. Flashes of wet skin.

As soon as he dropped my hand, I was back in my own body. I grabbed onto the counter as the dizziness faded. That was the fifth time I'd been in the backseat of Carlos' car this week, thankfully never in my own body. I made a promise to myself to keep it that way.

The wet streak glistened on my hand. Was that supposed to be sexy?

He grabbed a saltshaker and put some onto the wet spot.

Oh no. Please don't mean what I think that means.

He reached down to a bowl of sliced limes, and handed me one. I took it with my gloved hand.

"All right. So, we motion up and say, '*Por arriba.*' That means for above. Then we motion down and say, '*Por abajo.*' For below. Then we motion out and say, '*Por alcentro.*' For the center. Then we say, '*Por aldentro.*' For inside. And then lick the salt, take the shot, and suck on the lime. In that order. Got it?"

I nearly rolled my eyes. Most people heard my last name and just assumed I was white, but my mother was Mexican. Thanks to her I could speak Spanish.

"*Lo entiendo, chavo.*"

Carlos' face went blank for a second. "You Latin?"

71

I nodded. "My mother is. So, yes."

"Cool." He paused. "What's *chavo* mean?"

Christ. With a name like Carlos Rodriguez and his explaining of how to take the shot, I totally thought he spoke Spanish. "It means dude. I said I understand it, dude."

"Sweet."

"Yup." But still I wished I didn't have to eat spit-salt.

"You know you don't have to do this. They're just stupid boys," Rosalyn said. She crossed her arms.

Fantastic. She had to say that after I said I'd do it. There was no backing down now, not without looking like an idiot.

Damn it. I was already an idiot. Her boy had been a little flirty with me and now she wanted me to make a fool of myself. I should've noticed before I agreed to the shot. "No, I've got it." I tried to keep my hand steady as I held the tiny glass.

"Whatever," she said as she started to inspect her manicure.

"All right, everyone. Shots at the ready," Carlos lifted up his shot glass in salute.

"Ready!" the boys yelled.

"*Por arriba. Por abajo. Por alcentro. Por aldentro.*" I said with the boys, and then quickly licked the salt, forcing myself not to grimace as a new flash of visions burned my brain courtesy of Carlos. I drank the shot in one swallow, and tried to ignore the burning in my throat as I shoved the sour lime in my mouth with my gloved hand.

That wasn't so bad.

The boys laughed, and one gave me a high five as I

put my discarded lime on the counter.

"Good work," Carlos said.

"Thanks." Smiling back at him, I finally felt the confidence I'd been faking. I could do this. I could be one of them. I could control my visions and come off as cool. As normal. I was totally rocking it.

Chapter Eight

"Oookay. Well, thanks for that Carlos." Rosalyn's words were clipped, bringing me crashing back down to reality.

That was nice while it lasted. I shook my head as I pulled on my glove. I'd have lost with her either way I played it. I was going to have to figure out who I wanted to be actual friends with and fast. Keeping up with Rosalyn and her mood swings was enough to drive anyone mad.

Rosalyn held up two fingers. The boy closest to the keg grabbed two red plastic cups and started filling them with beer. Being totally underage, I had no idea what my limit was in terms of alcohol, but I was going to have to watch it. I wanted to blend in, not end up like Jess.

When he handed us the beers, Rosalyn grabbed my hand again. "Bye, boys. We're going to go see who else is here."

She pulled me into the living room, where some

hip-hop was blaring. Not anything I would ever choose to listen to, but a vast improvement from the country music that Rosalyn favored. I hadn't had my dancing fix in a while, so I'd take it.

All of the furniture in the room had been pushed against the walls. A bunch of people danced in the middle of it, grinding into each other. Others sat on the couch and chairs around the room. I couldn't help but stare at the couple making out on the couch. Didn't they feel weird doing that out in the open? The guy grabbed the girl's boob, and I looked away.

There was no way I'd let any guy maul me in public. I don't care how many shots I had. It'd never happen. I respected myself too much for that.

I took a sip of the beer and gagged. It tasted like pee, not that I'd ever actually tasted pee, but what I imagined pee might taste like.

Rosalyn chugged her beer and then dropped the cup on the floor. "Let's dance," Rosalyn yelled into my ear as she pulled me into the middle of room.

Not sure what to do with my drink, I held onto it. I tried not to spill as I swayed back and forth. When I went out with Axel, I usually stayed off to the side or in dance circles where there was more room, and I always wore something that covered nearly every inch of my body. But this was out of control, especially in my dress.

I should have worn long sleeves, but I couldn't bring myself to do it in the Texas heat. Just the four inches of exposed skin between my gloves and the cap sleeves of my dress was enough to drive my second sight crazy. The press of bodies moving to the music was overwhelming. Wave after wave of visions hit me.

I hope he likes me.

I think I'm going to be sick.

That guy is totally checking me out.

I can totally see down her shirt. This drink is gross. She's totally into me.

Iamtotallygoingtogetlaidtonight.He'sabadkisserIthi nkIsmellImtotallyhotterYeahbabycometopapa

The floor rocked. All the emotions that everyone was feeling built on top of each other. The visions were crazy. Usually when I got one from physical contact with another person, I saw the last thing that affected them emotionally. But since everyone was well on their way to wasted, whatever they were thinking and what they were feeling were the same thing. So I was seeing what everyone was thinking.

That might've sounded like a cool superpower before, but now I knew mind reading wasn't something I enjoyed. At all. The only thing I was feeling that was all mine was the nausea. I needed air.

I crossed my arms in front of my chest, and hunched over them so no one else could touch my skin. To the side of the dance floor there was a sliding door. "I'm going to go get some air," I yelled in Rosalyn's ear.

"Cool," she said and went back to her swaying.

The air outside hit me in the face with a wall of wet heat, but one by one, all the other feelings and visions faded away until I was left alone with my nausea. The backyard was so dark that I couldn't see where it ended.

Mr. Dawson had said that there was a big creek behind the neighborhood. The dark part was probably where the drop started. I walked toward the edge of the darkness, where the ground started to slope. Yup. My house had to be somewhere down the edge here since both our houses backed up to the creek.

I sat down on the grass and contemplated walking home.

Listening to the sounds of the night, I took another sip of the beer and gagged again. Even though I was dying for a cold drink, I couldn't choke it down. I looked around to see if anyone else was outside, and then pitched the liquid into the creek.

"Hey!" A voice shouted from the darkness.

I jumped up. "Oh my God! I'm so sorry! I totally didn't see you." A shape of a guy stepped into the light—tall, definitely over six feet, with dark hair. He was brushing himself off. His eyes glowed yellow in the moonlight. My breath caught.

"It's fine." Dastien motioned to my now empty cup. "Not to your taste?"

"No." My face flamed. "I really am sorry. I didn't see you." He was wearing the same black jeans and black T-shirt he had on earlier. When he shoved his hands in his pockets, a line of his skin peeked from beneath the shirt.

I looked down at his feet to get away from the overload he caused, but even the sight of his bare feet on the grass made my heart stop.

Where were his shoes?

He put his finger under my chin, lifting my head until our eyes met. I squeezed mine closed, dreading the vision that would come.

Running through the forest. Smell of grass and trees. And a rabbit. Hunt.

He dropped his hand to his side, and the vision

went away. "Don't worry about it."

That was it? A feeling of running, the smells of nature, and a slight urge to chase animals. What kind of guy thought about those things? And why didn't I see the usual triple-X rated show? A guy that hot had to be a chick-magnet of extreme proportions. No way was he celibate.

I didn't realize I had been holding my breath until I gasped for air. I seemed to do that a lot around him. The burning in my cheeks slowly spread through my whole body.

"*Vamanos*, Dastien," a deep voice said from the dark.

Squinting, I tried to find where it was coming from.

"I'll catch up with you later," he said, keeping his gaze on me.

I smiled. I didn't think I could stand it if he left so soon.

"Dude," said a different voice. "Not a good idea. You know—"

Dastien had his back to me before I even saw him move. I stepped away from him as a growl echoed through the darkness.

The guys must have a dog out there. Some kind of really big and scary sounding dog.

"Fine. It's your funeral if anything happens. Come on, Cody. Let's go."

Dastien turned back to me and sat next to my feet as if that little exchange hadn't happened. "How was your day?" He smiled as he held out a hand.

I laughed at his so very ordinary question. "It was okay, I guess." I couldn't figure this guy out. There was something different about him. He didn't act like any other guy I'd ever met.

I tried to tell myself that I took his offered hand because I was curious. It had absolutely nothing to do with the fact that for the first time ever that I was attracted to someone real. Movie stars and characters in novels didn't count.

His hand was so warm that I could feel his heat through my glove. When I settled down next to him, I thought he'd let go, but instead he laced his fingers through mine.

I stared at our joined hands. Mine fit perfectly in his, and at once I felt completely relaxed, which never happened. Not around people. Especially not when someone was touching me.

I was losing my mind. I had gloves on. That was the only reason that I could hold his hand.

I searched for something to say. Something not stupid. "You said you went to St. Ailbe's, but Mr. Dawson said you were taught there sometimes."

"Yup, graduated two years ago. I'm taking a year or so more before college to help out at the school."

"You don't look like any teacher I've ever had." I nearly slapped a hand over my mouth. I could not believe I'd just said that.

He smiled. "Is that a good thing?"

Whoa. Dangerous territory alert. This called for a major subject change. "You only have an accent sometimes."

"I've lived in the area for most of my life, but I was born in France." He grinned at me. "And don't think I didn't notice the subject change."

It's like he knew what I was thinking.

I'd almost forgotten he was holding my hand until he squeezed it. The fact that he'd done that twice now—held my hand like he didn't want to give it back—made me exceedingly happy. I had no idea what I was doing with this boy. Man. There would be plenty of time to freak out later. For now, I'd enjoy it. Him.

"So you like books and Nine Inch Nails?" Dastien said.

"Yes to both."

"And how about Texas?"

"It might be growing on me." Did I just say that? Someone needed to shoot me before I embarrassed myself any more. Flirting was so not my bag.

He was quiet for a second. "Do you mind if I kiss you?"

I laughed. "That's kind of abrupt."

"I guess. Thing is I can't concentrate on the conversation right now because all I'm thinking about is kissing you—"

"What!"

"It's true. I could tell you things like you're beautiful and have the most amazing eyes, but any guy could say the same thing." He smiled. "You're amazing—I mean judging by your T-shirts alone, I'd say we were on the same wavelength, but that doesn't even come close to all of it. I feel this connection. It's more than attraction, although that's there, too. And I really, really want to get to know you, but there's this thing hovering—this need. If we just got it out of the way, maybe it'd help. It might just make things worse, but you can't blame me for trying."

My heart rate skyrocketed as he talked. He felt the

connection too? "You're a no bullshit kind of a guy, huh?"

He shrugged. "I'm just honest. I don't like to play games." He paused. "So what do you say? Can I kiss you?"

My hormones were screaming, *Hell yes! Please, for the love of God, kiss me now!* But I made myself think about it.

A kiss could be disaster. Totally nightmare worthy. And yet, even though I didn't know Dastien at all, I couldn't ignore that connection either.

All of a sudden he was closer.

Had I moved?

I licked my lips and nodded, saying a silent prayer that I would see nothing.

I closed my eyes as his lips touched mine. They were warm and soft. I opened my mouth a little, and he moved in deeper, placing his hands on my shoulders drawing me close. His tongue brushed mine and desire blossomed. I was lost in a wave of sensations. Through my visions I could feel what he was feeling as well as my own too, and it made me want more. I moved closer, and we tumbled back onto the ground.

He laughed as he hovered over me. He murmured something in French, and then kissed me again.

I wrapped my leg around his hip and pulled him closer to me.

I moaned and he growled in response.

His teeth bit down on my lip. Something ripped into my shoulder.

I pushed at his chest. "What the hell!" He was up and ten steps away from me before I could blink. His eyes were glowing yellow. He took a long slow breath.

I reached for the back of my shoulder, and touched something wet. It couldn't be blood. The black gloves showed nothing in the dark. I quickly pulled one off and touched it again. I got up and moved closer to the porch light.

A drop of blood dripped off my fingertip.

I ran my tongue along my bottom lip. It tasted faintly metallic. I was bleeding.

"You bit me?" I knew it was my first real kiss and all, but I seriously doubted bleeding was normal. Pain blossomed across my left shoulder. "What? Why?"

"I'm so sorry, Tessa," he whispered. "It was an accident. I didn't mean to do it. God! Please know that I—"

Music spilled out from the house as the screen door opened behind me. Rosalyn, Carlos, and the other guys that I'd taken the shot with came outside.

"Tessa. Where'd you disappear—" Carlos stopped mid-sentence as he looked back and forth between Dastien and me. "Is he bothering you?"

"I don't know," I said. I really had no clue what the hell was going on. My mind was stuck on one thing. It had been an amazing kiss. The best I could ever imagine a kiss being. Even now, in pain, I'd do it again. No doubt. Something in the core of me needed him, and from the looks of him right now, the feeling was mutual.

When it came to Dastien, all I had were questions. And attraction. But mostly questions.

Carlos and his friends were closing the distance. I pulled my glove back on before any of them got closer. The last thing I needed was another vision.

I glanced back to Dastien unsure of how he wanted to play this off. Tears shimmered in his eyes. The sight took my breath away. I was hurt and pissed, rightfully so, but there was nothing to cry about here.

At least I hoped there wasn't.

"I'm sorry. I honestly didn't mean…I can't…" Then he melted into the darkness.

What the hell. Why would he do that—kiss me like that—and then just run away?

"That guy is one fine piece of meat," Rosalyn said.

Her words brought me back to reality. Suddenly I was jealous, and I didn't like that one bit.

"Rosalyn," Carlos said sharply. He really didn't like the St. Ailbe's guys.

This was a nightmare. Now I was standing there, bleeding, hurting, and any hopes I had of a good reputation were destroyed. These guys were going to think I was a slut.

Rosalyn scoffed as she walked over to me. "What? I'm not allowed to look just because he's one of them?" She stopped short. "Oh my God. Are you bleeding?"

"It's no big deal. It's only a scratch."

She took a couple of steps back.

"There's blood on her shoulder too," Carlos said. He turned a sickly color of green and swallowed.

This wasn't the reaction I was expecting from them. Why were they freaking out about the blood?

"Holy shit. That was one of the guys from St. Ailbe's," one of the other boys said, clearly a bit slow on the uptake. He took a step away from me.

"Kind of," I said, trying to downplay it. "Look I know the people from there are supposed to be dangerous, but he's already graduated, so I'm sure he's all reformed or whatever."

The boy smirked. "It's not a reform school. It's a school for—"

"Shut up," Carlos said and glanced at Rosalyn. "Take her home. She's not welcome here anymore."

There was no stopping the gasp. "I don't understand. I'm hurt here and you haven't even asked if I'm okay or offered up any sort of first aid."

Carlos and Rosalyn didn't even acknowledge me. "I don't want that in my car," Rosalyn whined.

"I'm not a that. I'm a person!" They'd lost their minds. And I had apparently become invisible since no one was paying attention to anything I said.

"Tough shit. You brought her." Spit flew from Carlos' mouth as he yelled. "You're responsible for her. Take. Her. Home. Now. And don't you dare think about making her walk. If she changes tonight out in the open, it'd be on your head." He strode back into the house, the other boys close on his heels.

"Hey! I'm right here!" The sound of the door slamming shut made my stomach knot. That was the sound of my social status at Cedar Ridge High going from cool to freak in no time flat.

"Let's go." She stormed off toward the cars.

I broke the uncomfortable silence as we got into her car. "I don't understand. Why is it such a big deal?"

"You don't understand." She rolled her eyes. "Weren't you told to stay away from St. Ailbe's guys?"

Mr. Dawson did say that. "But Dastien is totally normal."

Her laugh was harsh. "No. No, he's not."

I shivered. I was missing something, something huge. "What aren't you telling me?"

"You'll find out soon enough." She pulled over at my house. "Get out," she said without even looking at me.

"Fine. Thanks for a great time. Really cool, Rosalyn." I hopped out and slammed the door.

Chapter Nine

The TV was on in my parent's room when I walked in the house. I slowly closed the door behind me.

"You're back already?"

I jumped at the sound of Axel's voice behind me.

"What the fu—"

I slapped my hand over his mouth. "I don't want Mom and Dad to know." I paused. "Seriously."

He nodded, and I moved my hand slowly away from his mouth, ready to slap it back if he started yelling again.

"Who did that to you?"

Axel was in protector mode. He reverted to it whenever I was hurt or being picked on. I prayed for patience. "Can you please find wherever Mom put the first aid stuff and meet me in my room?"

He narrowed his eyes at me. Yup. There was no way he'd let this one go, but he went in search of the kit anyway.

My shoulder was full on throbbing by the time I got upstairs. This night had been a disaster of epic proportions. If I could get into my room without Mom or Dad checking on me, I'd be happy. I couldn't face telling them that come Monday, life would go back to status quo in Tessaland.

I crept up the stairs, desperately trying to remember if there were any squeaky boards.

"I'm home," I said from my bedroom door.

The TV muted. "You're early. How was the party?" Mom's voice came from their room.

"Fine, but I'm pooped. Can we talk about it in the morning?" I held my breath as I waited for her to answer.

There was whispering back and forth as they debated. "Okay. Get some rest," Mom said finally.

I breathed a sigh of relief when the TV's sound came back on. I threw my belt and shoes in the closet. In the light I could see the blood staining my gloves. I chucked them in my trash.

What was I going to do now? I couldn't lift my arm up to take off my dress.

Oh well. It was a nice dress while it lasted. I grabbed a pair of scissors from my desk. There was a soft knock on the door. I had a moment of panic before Axel opened it.

"Get in here, and help me," I said.

He closed the door and dumped the first aid stuff on my bed. I handed him the scissors. "You're going to have to cut the dress off me."

I could feel his breath on my back. He was investigating my cut without touching it himself.

He sighed. "This looks really bad, Tess. You need

stitches."

"Don't say stitches. That involves needles and I don't do needles." The thought of them made me queasy. "It doesn't even really hurt. A few butterfly bandages will do. Just cut the strap and move the material away from it. Then pour a bunch of peroxide on it until it stops fizzing."

"Yeah. Yeah. I'll do it. But Mom's going to find out in the morning and she's going to say you need—"

"Don't you dare say the 's' word again. I really don't need them. I've had cuts worse than this."

"No. You haven't," he muttered. The scissors sliced through my strap. "Stay still. This is probably gonna burn like a motherfucker."

He poured it down my shoulder, and tears filled my eyes. "Shit. Blow on it or something."

"Seriously? I don't want to get that close to it. It's bubbling up like crazy."

"I don't care what you do. Just do something!" I dug my fingernails into my hands to take my mind off of it.

"Okay. Okay. Hang on." He grabbed a book off my shelf and started fanning it.

It totally wasn't helping. "The peroxide was a bad idea."

"You know what a good idea is? The emergency room. In fact, it's a fantastic idea."

I rolled my eyes. "That'll take hours. No way. I already said it twice, but I'll say it again. I don't need stitches. You can't make me get them."

"Fine. But you're just being a stubborn baby." He poured more peroxide on it.

"Fuck! That burns," I said when I could get air

enough to talk again.

"See. You're such a baby." Axel started digging through the clear plastic bin that had all the first aid supplies in it. He came back with a tube of antibiotic ointment.

"Don't use your finger."

He showed me the Q-tip in his hand. "Please. I want to touch that as much as you want me to." He rubbed it on and put an extra-large bandage over the cuts. "So you going to tell me whose ass I need to kick?"

Nope. Not a chance in hell. "It doesn't matter."

"It definitely matters. No one hurts my sister and gets away with it."

I wanted to cry and scream and hit something, but none of that would help me right now. "Can we talk about it tomorrow? Please. I'm hurting and tired and sad. Really, really sad."

He stood there, staring at me for a while. "Okay," he said finally. "We'll talk tomorrow." He handed me an ice pack.

"Thanks," I whispered.

"Take care of your lip. Okay?"

I nodded.

When he left, I grabbed the scissors again, and cut down the front of my dress. It was one of the only dresses I actually liked. It was a damn shame to have to destroy it completely. Once it was off, I studied the material and saw four inch-long rips where my left shoulder blade was.

How did Dastien manage to do that with his bare hands?

I snorted. It didn't matter how he'd done it, but it

sure sucked that he had.

I threw it in the trash and grabbed a giant sleep shirt, slowly easing my arm into it. As I put peroxide and ointment on my bottom lip, my mind drifted back to Dastien. Something was off about him. Okay, so maybe the biting and scratching thing was it, but I couldn't get over the fact that I didn't get any visions when we kissed. And that connection. Intense didn't even begin to cover it.

He was different from everyone else I'd ever met. And, even accidental biting aside, I was still drawn to him.

This was stupid. Why was I pining over some lame guy who I kissed and then who ran away? I couldn't lose my shit over one kiss. Hopefully the cuts would be better in the morning, and I could forget this whole thing ever happened.

A shiver rushed down my spine. Something was watching me. Someone was waiting for me outside. Dad had put curtains up on Friday night, so no one could see in, not that anyone ventured down our road, but I couldn't shake that feeling.

I slid the curtains silently along the rod and leaned close to the window and jumped back.

Oh crap.

A wolf was in my driveway. I stepped back toward the window to double check.

It was sitting there. Watching me with its golden eyes. I wanted to go out to it, but that was crazy. It was a wolf. A dangerous, wild, totally not-tame wolf. I threw the curtain closed and slid into bed.

It wasn't until that moment, as I waited for sleep to come, that I realized how much I wanted friends. I liked to think I was fine alone, but sometimes being alone was flat out lonely. Axel was great, but he had his own life to live. With him gone soon, I was going to be the outcast again.

The wolf howled outside, and I wanted to howl with it.

***

"Tessa!" Mom was yelling through my bedroom door. "I know you went out last night, but you are not missing church!" The alarm clock glowed 9:45 AM in red.

I moaned, feeling more than a little groggy and nauseous. Probably from that stupid shot of tequila. "I'm not feeling so good."

Mom opened the door and peeked through the crack. "What did you say? I couldn't hear you."

"I feel like shit on a stick."

"Language!" She came over to my bed. "Did something happen to your lip?" She ran her cool hand against my forehead.

I tried to tune out all the thoughts she was having, but failed. Worried that I'd caught something. Worried that my father would get sick and have to miss work after only just starting. Then worried that I'd pass it along to my brother who had to leave soon.

The woman worried way too much.

"You're burning up." She hurried out of the room, and came back seconds later with a glass of orange juice and a couple Tylenol in her hand. "Sit up."

I winced and grabbed at my left shoulder.

Mom's eyes narrowed. "What's wrong with your

shoulder?"

"Nothing."

"Take off your shirt."

"Mom, it's fine real—"

"Take off your shirt, Tessa. Or I *will* take it off for you."

That was her patented you-better-do-what-I'm-telling-you voice. Once that showed up, there was no arguing with her.

I sucked in air as I slid my arm from my sleeve. I left the shirt dangling in front of me. It was too much work to take it off completely. My eyes watered as she pulled off the bandage. "Gentle please."

She was going to flip out in three...two...

"Who did this to you?"

My cheeks heated.

"Was it someone at the party?"

"Please, don't tell Dad."

"God, Tessa. This looks bad. Your skin is so hot, which means it's probably infected. Why didn't you tell us last night?" She brushed her finger against the skin next to the wound, and I saw what her next move was going to be.

Yep. That's what I thought. She was thinking about how to tell Dad. He was going to be extra pissed when he found out that someone from St. Ailbe's—let alone his bosses second in command—had hurt me. And when I told him how the Cedar Ridge High kids wanted nothing to do with me now, he was going to flip. We moved all this way for nothing.

"Well, let's get it cleaned." She looked at my shoulder again and then back at me.

"I cleaned it last night." Tears welled, but I

wouldn't let them fall. "The kit's still on my desk."

Somehow Mom taking care of my shoulder made it real. I had actually kissed Dastien last night. Thinking about him made me anxious to see him again. Which was beyond stupid. The guy was obviously dangerous.

"Turn around." The second the peroxide filled cotton balls touched my shoulder I nearly threw up. Last night was nothing compared to today. Mom held my shoulder still when I tried to move away. The pain was enough to block out anything Mom was thinking. It was getting worse, not better.

"You need stitches."

God. Not the stitches talk again. "Can't we put the Band-Aids on it and see what happens in a day or two?"

"We'll see." The pain exploded, radiating across my back as she rubbed the Neosporin into the cuts and put on the band-aids. Gently, she helped me back into the shirt.

"Let's see the lip." She gave my lip the same treatment, going light on the Neosporin and leaving off the band-aid.

She sat down beside me on my bed and gave me that look, the one that said that if I even tried to lie I would be in serious trouble. "Did someone hurt you?"

"Please, Mom. Can we talk about it later?"

She pressed her lips together as she thought about it, and then finally sighed. "Fine. Go back to bed. I'll come check on you in a bit."

It was humiliating the way everything always went wrong for me. I lay back down and Mom tucked me in.

"We will talk about this after you get some rest."
She kissed my forehead and left my room.

The next time my eyes opened, the clock read 1:56
PM. Mom was back in my room, sitting on the bed
with her hand to my forehead. A million of her
unasked questions slammed into me. She wanted to
know what happened, who did this, and why. But she
was mostly worried about me and angry that someone
had hurt me. Angry was the wrong word. She was
furious.

"It's really high," she said to Dad who was
standing over us. "Definitely over 100."

He raked his fingers down his face, and then
patted Mom on the back. "We're going to take you to
the hospital, Tess."

Dad left my room, shutting the door quietly
behind him. Mom grabbed a pair of jeans from my
closet. I sat up and picked up my bra from on top of
the comforter.

"Don't worry about the bra. It'll only make your
shoulder worse." She crossed her arms. "You ready to
talk?"

I cleared my suddenly dry throat. "Not really." I
didn't know if I'd ever be ready. It was too
embarrassing. Only Tessa McCaide would have to get
stitches because of a kiss.

"It was a boy at the party?"

God. She wasn't going to let it go.

I nodded.

"He can't get away with this. Tessa." She paused,
taking a deep breath. "Did he do anything else to you?
Hurt you—"

My face burned. "Jeez, Mom. No. He kissed me

and got a little carried away. I don't know how he did that to my shoulder. He must have had something in his hand or I dunno..."

"Sweetie. They're deep. There's no way it wasn't on purpose." She sat back down on the bed, putting her face on my level, so that I was forced to look her in the eyes. "We're going to have talk to your principal about this. Get a meeting with the boy's parents. He could have really hurt you. What if he does this or something worse to another girl?"

The thought of Dastien with another girl made me monumentally pissed off. I tried to rein my anger in, but my shoulder burned, deeper into my arm and torso.

Somewhere underneath it I knew I was losing my mind over a boy who hurt me. "I don't want to make a huge deal out of this. It's fine. Really. It wasn't even one of the guys from school."

She crossed her arms. "If it wasn't someone from school, then who was it?"

Perfect. She thought I was trying to lie to her. "Dastien," I whispered. Saying his name felt equal parts relief and betrayal.

"*Madre Santa.* The teacher from St. Ailbe's?" She sucked in her breath. "Teresa Elizabeth McCaide!"

And now she'd used my full name. Only I could manage to get in trouble for being hurt.

"I hope this doesn't mean..." She paused for a second, and my heart started to pound.
"We're going to have to talk to Michael Dawson when we get back from the emergency room. This could be really bad, Tess."

That was so not cool. "Mom. Seriously. It's fine."

"No. It's really not. You're a minor."

"Only for like a few more weeks! And he's only two years older than me. That's like nothing. Let's not make a national disaster out of this. He was really nice. I'm not even sure how it happened. He seemed pretty shocked. He apologized and everything." I don't know why I was defending him.

Mom sat there quietly, waiting for me to continue.

It wasn't embarrassment anymore. I was mad. Furious even. Those people at the party had been flat out rude to me. For no reason. It wasn't even something I could blame on my weirdness. I was physically hurt, bleeding, and they kicked me out. Not even an "are you okay" or "do you need some ice for that" before they shoved me out the door.

I willed myself not to cry. "I wanted to have friends and go to parties like everyone else. Not be Freaky Tessa who sits at home on the weekends reading books and watching TV with her parents. Begging her brother to hang out with her."

Mom sat down next to me, holding my good side. "I know it's hard, but you're here for a reason. You have to have faith in God and in yourself. If there is anything I'm sure of, it's that you're meant to do something great with your gifts."

I snorted. "Right. Because these 'gifts' are so useful for oh, I don't know, nothing."

She kissed my forehead, and her guilt surged through me before she could block it.

I felt like a real jerk for not being nicer about what she said. But I couldn't get my hopes up that one day I'd find my curse was useful.

"This is my fault. I've kept you away from my side

of the family for too long. You are meant for something."

What the hell was she talking about?

"I have something to tell you later. First, let's get you to the hospital." She started for the door.

"Mom," I called after her. "I'm sorry. Thank you for taking care of me."

"Anything for my baby."

I'd make it up to her. Tomorrow. When my shoulder wasn't hurting so bad. Sliding on my sweatpants and flip-flops took all the energy I could muster.

I was so out of it that I nearly forgot my gloves. Number one place I didn't want to have a vision: the emergency room. Talk about a minefield of pain and drama. I grabbed a pair of white cotton ones that stopped halfway to my elbow.

Axel was waiting with my parents at the door by the time I got down the stairs.

"Ready?" Dad's arms were still folded in front of his chest. No hint of a smile on his face.

"Yeah, but I'm feeling a little—" Gray dots filled my vision. Then, there was nothing.

Chapter Ten

The car bounced over the gravel road, but I couldn't muster the energy to lift my head. It took a second to make my eyes open. "What happened?" I was lying across the backseat in Dad's SUV.

"You fainted, sweetheart." Mom brushed my hair out of my face. "We're almost to the hospital."

"That's good, I guess." A cold drop of sweat rolled down my forehead. My mom's face spun in my vision, and I had to close my eyes to keep from throwing up.

When the car jerked to a stop, I nearly rolled off the seat.

"Dad's going to carry you inside."

The world tilted as he lifted me into his arms. Mom walked ahead of us to the front desk. The nurse stood as Mom started rattling off information. "My daughter has a very high fever. And we think she has infected scratches on her shoulder."

The nurse gave my mom a bored look as she

snapped her gum. "How did your daughter get these scratches?"

"She was at a party last night, and a teacher from St. Ailbe's—"

The nurse's mouth fell open, and a ball of wet gum plopped onto the desk.

Gross.

She picked up the phone. "Stand by for a possible Code Black." The nurse slammed the receiver down, grabbed a clipboard, and ran around the counter. "Follow me."

Code Black? Code Blue was what they said on TV when someone was dying. Code Black better not mean death. Because if I died from one measly kiss, I was going to freak out.

My nausea was back with a vengeance. I leaned my head into my father's shoulder. He smelled like a juicy steak.

A steak? Really, Tessa?

I was already kinda crazy, but this fever was making me full-on insane-o.

"You okay, sweetheart?"

"Yeah, Dad. Just a little queasy." And by little, I meant on the verge of hurling.

"Hang on for one more minute. Almost there."

I closed my eyes and my sense of smell strengthened. Disinfectant stung my nostrils. Someone must have gone overboard with the bleach.

That was enough of overbearing smells for this girl. I tugged the top of my shirt over my nose.

Mom put the back of her hand to my forehead. "You hanging in there?"

"Yup." Barely. "Where's Axel?"

"Don't worry about him."

Oh, no. That didn't sound good. What was Axel up to? I hoped he wasn't chasing down Dastien.

Dad set me down on the bed as the nurse slid the privacy curtains along the rail, hiding us from view. She snapped on a pair of rubber gloves. That sound made me antsy. Any time plastic gloves were involved, things were not going to be fun.

The nurse grabbed an electric thermometer from the small counter, and slid a plastic protector on the tip. "Do your ears hurt?" she said.

"No." Was she dense? What did a shoulder scratch have to do with my ears?

She shoved the thermometer in my right one. A screeching beep sliced into my head, and I jerked away from her.

Maybe they did hurt? I stuck my finger in my ear and wiggled, trying to get the sound out of my head. "Can you turn the volume down on that?"

The nurse gave me an "are you nuts" look and then stuck the thermometer back in my ear. "Hold still."

I ground my teeth as a digital beeping pierced my eardrums.

"Don't let this be what I think it is," she said so softly I could barely hear her.

What was her major malfunction? Weren't nurses supposed to have seen it all and be calm in emergencies?

With a final series of screeching beeps, she glanced at the readout and cleared her throat. "108."

"That's not right. She'd be dead if it were that high," Mom said.

The nurse grunted and searched a nearby tray. "I need to see the scratches."

"Who cares about the scratches? She has a fever of 108! Get a doctor," Dad said. He was standing guard at the end of the bed. He was so pissed that he was nearly vibrating with it.

"Sir, it'd be best if you could calm down."

Oh no she didn't.

Mom put a restraining hand on Dad as he stepped toward the nurse. "She's just doing her job."

The nurse cleared her throat. She had to know she'd stepped in it with her comment. "The doctor is aware of her situation and is waiting on my assessment."

Nope. She was an idiot. "I'm fine, Dad. Feeling much better. See." I smiled. He didn't smile back. I must've looked worse than I felt.

Mom sighed. "They're on the back of her left shoulder."

The nurse reached toward a tray of pointy objects. The metallic clang as she looked through them made me shake. I bet there were needles on that tray.

"Please, stay calm. I'm only going to cut your shirt a little bit."

I tried, but with each snip of the scissors, my chest got a little bit tighter. She was going to say I needed stitches. I just knew it. My hands were so sweaty that the soft jersey gloves stuck to my skin. The stink of the nurse's fear made me even more anxious.

Wait. I could smell her fear?

I sniffed the air. It reeked like someone had poured cheap perfume over rotting fruit. Something inside of me knew that smell was fear, even if I had no rational explanation for it.

She pulled my shirt away from my shoulder, and started ripping off the band-aids. She gasped and the scissors clunked to the ground.

I looked over my shoulder. The nurse's plump, rosy cheeks had gone sheet white. "What? What is it? What's wrong with my shoulder?" I glanced at Mom, but she only shrugged.

The nurse backed out of the room and didn't turn away from us until she was halfway down the hall. Her clogs clunked on the floor as she started to run.

Forcing myself to take slower, deeper breaths, I gathered up the courage and twisted until I could see it. The cuts weren't bleeding anymore. They were an angry red and didn't have scabs yet, but puss wasn't seeping from them. "It doesn't look that bad. Why is she freaking out?"

My dad leaned down to brush a kiss over my forehead. "I don't know, honey." He peeked at the cuts. "How did you say you got those cuts again?"

A doctor in his white lab coat came into our makeshift room before I could answer.

"Hello, I'm Dr. Schel." He was tall and thin, with dark circles under his eyes. Someone was overworked. He slid the curtain closed behind him. "Nurse Tilden filled me in, but I'm sure she must be misunderstanding something. I need to see the scratches on your back, if that's alright." He frowned. "And what's that on your lip?"

"It's a bite," I answered as softly as I could manage. My cheeks burned. I could never look my father in the eyes again. Never. Again.

Dr. Schel walked around the bed. The sound of

102

his throat clearing startled me. He suddenly smelled just like the nurse.

"I've never seen scratches quite like those. How exactly did you get them?"

This was beyond mortifying. I couldn't say in front of Dad. Especially if Mom hadn't already spilled the beans.

"I'm sure you won't get in any trouble. Right?" Dr. Schel looked at Dad.

"Of course she's not in trouble. She's hurt." Dad came to stand in front of me and patted my leg. "Go ahead. He's here to help, but you have to tell the truth."

"I never lie, Dad." He stared me down until I started talking. Still, I couldn't tell him that it was a teacher, even if he was only a couple years older than me. "I was kissing a guy who used to go to St. Ailbe's—"

Dr. Schel held up his hand. "You're absolutely sure that he was connected with St. Ailbe's?"

"Yes, but—" I stopped talking as the doctor took a slow step away from me. What was wrong with this place? He jerked his gaze to the floor and cleared his throat again. The stink of fear increased, radiating from him. I wanted to plug my nose, but that would've been rude.

"Unfortunately, it seems the nurse wasn't misunderstanding anything. I'm sorry, but we're not going to be able to help you here," he said.

"What do you mean you're not going to be able to help her? This is a hospital, for Christ's sake!" Dad's face had gone red and his fists were clenched.

"There's nothing I can do for her. That anyone

can do for her," he said.

"Of course there's something you can do for her. She has a fever of 108, goddamn it. She needs some antibiotics for whatever infection is giving her the fever. And some more Tylenol and fluids. Even I know this shit and I'm not a damn doctor!"

"I'm sorry. I truly am. But no doctor can fix what's wrong with your daughter."

What did he mean no doctor could fix me?

He held up his hands to stop us from moving. "Please. Please, wait here. Stay calm. I promise you that she's fine for the moment. I'm going to get someone who can help you. A specialist." He took some hurried backward steps and slid to the other side of the curtain.

Dad suddenly walked around the bed and stared at my back.

"Dad?"

"Oh, Christ Almighty."

I twisted to look at him.

"You're sure that it was someone from St. Ailbe's that did this?"

I nodded.

"It was Dastien, the teacher that came to the house the day we got here," Mom said.

Dad cursed again. "With what, Tessa? What did he scratch you with!"

My heart was racing. I'd never seen Dad so pissed. "I don't know. His hand?"

Dad cursed up a storm, knocking the tray next to my bed to the ground. The sound had him freezing. He stood there, facing the curtain, breathing heavily.

"Dad?" I waited, but he didn't say anything.

"Dad?"

"Stay calm, John. If there's a chance this is what we think...just stay calm. It's early. We caught it. There has to be a way out of it."

It was like he couldn't even hear us. Dad paced back and forth in the tiny area next to the bed, but he wouldn't speak a word.

I tried not to freak out—Dad was freaking out enough for both of us—but everything smelled too strongly. It was almost as if I could taste my parents' growing anger and frustration. It was too much. The world started to spin again.

My whole body trembled. It felt like I was lying on hot coals. "Mom." It came out a whisper.

She held my hand. "I'm right here, baby."

"I feel like I'm on fire."

Mom dug through cupboards and found a cream colored plastic pitcher. "Get her some ice and a bottle of water."

Dad left without a word.

Chapter Eleven

Dad still wasn't speaking by the time Dr. Schel came back with another man. I didn't have to look up to know who the man was. I watched the floor as he walked toward me in that graceful, soundless way. I took a breath and glanced up at him. His eerie hazel eyes bored through me. I had to stop myself from squirming under his gaze. Mom patted my glove-covered arm.

What was he doing here?

"This is Michael Dawson. He's the head of St. Ailbe's Acad—"

"I know damn well who he is."

The doctor stepped back out of Dad's way. Probably a smart decision.

"What in the hell did that boy do to my daughter?"

"I'm so sorry, John. I warned her—"

"Bullshit you did. Don't give me that crap like it's an excuse." Dad raked his fingers through his hair.

"You will not blame this on my daughter. Her life is ruined. Ruined!"

"John!" Mom said. "Not yet. We don't know anything for sure yet."

I cleared my throat. "Why is my life ruined exactly?" They ignored me.

"I can help her," Mr. Dawson said. "It won't be the end for her."

The end? Holy shit, this sounded bad.

Dad blocked Mr. Dawson's way as he tried to look at my shoulder.

"Let me look. I have to confirm it. It'll only take a second. If it's shallow or small, it won't be enough to turn her."

Dad stepped in Mr. Dawson's space. "I don't give a shit about this job. Someone hurts my girl, they pay. Understood?"

"Perfectly. No matter what this is, we will make it right." Mr. Dawson didn't back down, but he didn't get mad either. He had some major *cojones* to stay calm while facing Dad's anger.

"You've got exactly thirty seconds," Dad said.

Mr. Dawson walked toward me. I tried to retreat, shaking. He stopped and held his hands up. "I won't hurt you. I won't even touch you. I promise. I'm only going to look."

He won't touch me? How much did he know about me?

"It's okay, honey." Mom tried to get free of my grasp. For some reason I was afraid of Mr. Dawson, and he hadn't done anything. As he walked toward me, the overhead light hit his eyes, making them glow for a split second.

Mr. Dawson hung his head and scrunched his shoulders, and the motion made me feel more comfortable. "Let's get this over with." I sat up with Mom's help, and he bent toward me. I could have sworn I heard him sniff before he straightened and took a step back.

"We should talk outside," he said to my parents. They followed him past the curtain and down the hall.

Free of his gaze, I could breathe again. But why did they leave the room? I was the one who was going to be affected by whatever he had to say. I wasn't a child.

I could hear their voices faintly moving away from my room. Squeaky wheels turned beneath beds as they rolled down the hallway. I focused on them, but everything got too loud until I was drowning in sound. Footsteps on the floor. Beeps of the machines. Frantic murmurs of the nurses. Weeping down the hall. Every little noise filled my head.

I plugged my ears and started to hum. I had to concentrate on my parents and Mr. Dawson. I could do this. I had years of experience blocking visions out. When I pulled my fingers from my ears, the noise had gone down to a reasonable level. Now I had to find their voices in the din.

I visualized the hallway. The sounds grew, building onto each other until I could pick out Mr. Dawson's calm, deep voice.

"—a danger to everyone in this hospital, including you," Mr. Dawson said. "It is essential that we—"

"Is there any cure?" Dad sounded seriously pissed off.

"We can ask my family," Mom said. "They have to

know something—"

"Please, Gabby." Dad growled. "You know how your family is."

If they were talking about Mom's family, this was going to be bad.

"I don't want to start anything with the Texas coven," Mr. Dawson said. "The wolves that attend my school aren't dangerous. If you go to your family, this could turn into a war."

There was silence. I wasn't getting it and felt incredibly dense for missing whatever the rest of them knew.

"This is the first incident we've ever had, and there's something going on here that we're missing. If your family is what I think it is, you know what I mean. And you also know that she has to come with me," Mr. Dawson said. "For both her safety and yours."

"I can't believe you did this to us, John. And I can't believe I let you talk me into going along with it. That you exposed our children to their kind. You know who I am. Who our children are, and yet you still did this."

"Gabby, please—"

"You can't take Tessa," Mom said, cutting off Dad. Her words were clipped with anger. "You don't understand who my daughter is. Once *La Alquelarre* finds out, there's no telling what they'll do."

What did *Alquelarre* mean?

"She's part of the Texas coven?"

"She's supposed to take it over."

What was she talking about? What was I supposed to be doing? It didn't matter what they were talking about. I didn't want to go with anyone. I wanted to go home.

My heartbeat pounded in my ears. They couldn't make me go with Mr. Dawson. I didn't care what they said. Pain rippled along my hands. I looked down at them, and saw my nails growing longer, poking through the tips of my gloves. The seams ripped.

What the hell?

I grabbed the thin mattress. This was so not happening. It was a vision. A druggie must have been on this table before me and had some weird hallucination. That had to be it. That was the only rational explanation.

Hands do not turn into claws. Especially not my hands.

Panic made it worse. My knuckles popped, and pain rolled up my arms.

"I know this has come as a shock. You have to understand that she is extremely dangerous—"

Dangerous? My panic turned to anger. Rage boiled my blood. It consumed me.

The pain grew. A growl escaped me as I squirmed in my bed. My growing nails shredded my gloves. My knees popped, sending shooting pain through me, and I screamed.

Mr. Dawson appeared by my side. "Shit," he said under his breath. "We need a tranq in here. Now!"
I tried to sit up, but he dodged my swinging monster-arms and pinned me in place. I growled again, struggling to get free as he brought his nose to mine. All I could see were his eyes as they turned from hazel to bright olive.

Mr. Dawson made a low rumbling noise that

rippled through me. The pain and heat lessened, clearing my head enough so that I could think about what had just happened.

This was a nightmare. My hands had transformed into beast claws.

And that anger. I'd never felt anything like it before. Not in any of my visions. Not ever.

I shivered. Was Mr. Dawson right? Please, God, don't let Mr. Dawson be right.

The nurse, stinking of fear, rushed in, and stabbed my arm with a needle.

I couldn't stop the tears as they rolled down my cheeks. Mom's soft whimpering caught my attention. They were standing outside the curtain, staring at my deformed hands. Only a piece of the shredded white glove hung around my left wrist. Dad's arms held Mom up as he stared openmouthed.

They looked how I felt.

If this is a dream, I want to wake up now.

"Oh my God. This is my fault." Dad turned to Mr. Dawson. "Please. Help my daughter," he whispered as the world faded from view.

Chapter Twelve

I threw the covers off, gasping for breath. Sweat covered my body, thanks to some half-remembered nightmare still fading from my thoughts.

Where was I?

Right, hospital, for my shoulder. Because Dastien had hurt me at the party. I moved it slowly, but it didn't even twinge. That was a good sign.

I hopped out of bed and the ties to my hospital gown got caught in the IV stand next to the bed. Thankfully it wasn't hooked up to my arm. I grabbed the tie, and managed to somehow ram my elbow into the hard wall. Tingles exploded up my arm. I rubbed my funny bone as I glanced around. The room was excessively closet-like.

I backed up to take in the room, and fell on top of a springy metal box. Sighing, I turned around to kick the obstacle, but stopped before I made contact.

What the hell. Why was there a cage in my room?

I squatted down to take a closer look. There

wasn't a bowl or food in there like a normal dog kennel, but it was big enough for a large dog. Maybe a Great Dane or a Mastiff. But the cage was spotless inside. I reached out to open it without thinking. The metal bars of the cage were cold on my bare hand, and I pulled my hand away. I hadn't gotten a vision, but something much worse.

I remembered huddling in the cage. Shaking. Pain. And I remembered needles. Lots and lots of drug-filled needles.

It was way past time for me to get the hell out of here.

I wasn't going to get far in a hospital gown. I needed something less conspicuous. I frantically searched the wall of cabinets opposite the bed. Anything would do.

I hit the jackpot in a bottom cupboard. A fit-and-flare black cotton dress was neatly folded in the cabinet, along with my favorite worn-in boots and a pair of gloves. I didn't have time to wonder how my stuff got in there or how I'd gotten to wherever the hell I was. If someone had caged me up like an animal, I wasn't sticking around long enough to ask questions.

I pulled on my clothes and ran to the door. The knob wouldn't move. I jiggled it, twisting one way then the other.

Locked. I was so screwed.

High heels click-clacked down the hallway toward the door.

I needed another way out. A tiny window let light in beside the bed, but it didn't look like it'd open. The footsteps were getting louder. I was running out of time and options.

I grabbed the IV stand and smashed it through the window, shattering the glass.

The person coming down the hall was running now.

I didn't look down as I pushed myself onto the windowsill, careful to avoid the glass edges.

The door flew open and a tall, thin woman in a lab coat ran through the doorway. "Tessa! Wait—"

Before I could think better of it, I threw myself out the window.

Three stories up.

Shit. Shit. Shit.

I screamed the most girly scream ever as I flipped through the air. My breath ripped from my lungs as I thunked down on the ground. On my feet.

What the...

I didn't have time to question my luck. I brushed myself off and scanned my surroundings. A courtyard full of kids my age stood frozen, staring at me. Some were wearing backpacks. Others carried books in their hands. One girl stopped with an apple halfway to her mouth. She looked at me like I'd lost my mind. Little did she know, I never really had it to begin with.

This had to be St. Ailbe's.

I hoped I hadn't flashed anyone.

Forest encircled the buildings. I picked a direction and prayed it was the right one.

I gave a demure wave. "No time to stop and chat. Things to do. Places to escape from." I took off running. Something howled, and I glanced behind me.

What the hell? A blond wolf was chasing me.

My day really couldn't get any better.

I pushed my legs to move faster. My lungs burned, but I kept going.

The forest teased me, only a few yards ahead and I'd hopefully disappear through the brush and trees. Out-running a wolf seemed like a long shot at best, but if I managed to get away from it and find the creek, then I probably could get to my house. Maybe. I'd figure out the rest when I got home.

I hit the tree line, and another wolf howled. I looked back. It was the white and gray one, along with the blond-ish one from earlier. They were right behind me.

Sweat dripped down my face, but I wouldn't give up. I zigzagged through the woods hoping that would buy me some ground.

"Tessa! Stop!" Mr. Dawson yelled from behind me. He yelled something to someone in a language I couldn't understand. There was more howling.

I didn't look back. Adrenaline pumped through my veins.

And then something slammed into me from the side.

I hit the ground hard, rolling a few times before crashing to a stop against a tree. I gasped for air, but somebody was weighing me down. Hot breath brushed my face, and the person lifted up enough so that I could see his face.

Oh my God. Why the hell had a naked guy tackled me? "Move, you perv."

I focused on his crystal blue eyes. They were laughing at me. "Do you believe in love at first sight? Or should I tackle you again?"

"Spare me the tired pick-up line. Where are your clothes!"

A big cloth fell over us.

"Mr. Matthews. Off Miss McCaide. Now," Mr. Dawson said.

The guy winked at me, and hopped up. "Caught her," he said as he pulled on a robe before I could see more than I needed to.

The wolf had disappeared, and some naked guy had appeared.

Goosebumps ran up my arms. There was no way what I was thinking could actually be right.

He reached down to help me, but I ignored it, getting up on my own.

The lady in the lab coat stood behind Mr. Dawson. Her high heels didn't slow her down too much. Impressive, but I still didn't trust her. I took a step back. She wasn't getting near me again. No way in hell.

The gray and white wolf stood behind them. He growled at the blue-eyed guy and then turned around and ran back to the buildings.

Weird.

Mr. Dawson inched toward me. "Why are you afraid, Tessa?"

I was trying to be more angry than scared, but somehow I was venturing into full-on terrified-mode. "I don't know. Maybe because someone put me in a cage and stuck me with an assload of needles!"

"Tessa—" Lab Coat woman said, but Mr. Dawson cut her off.

"You were in the cage because you were feral."

Blue Eyes let out a low whistle. "Impressive."

"Thank you for your help, Mr. Matthews." Mr. Dawson kept his eyes on me as he spoke to Blue Eyes. "You can go back to campus now."

"Anytime. I love catching pretty ladies." He winked. The air grew heavy and shimmered with heat. Blue Eyes' arms and legs morphed as he got down on all fours. His face changed too fast for me to follow. The robe slid off as he moved. And then, instead of looking at a guy, I stood in front of a blond-colored wolf.

Someone cursed as the world faded to gray.

Chapter Thirteen

A high-pitched noise whined in my ear. Something slimy brushed against my face as everything came back into focus. The wolf was licking me. I sat up and scooted away until my back hit a tree.

"What the hell is that?" My breath came in hollow gasps.

"Good work, Mr. Matthews. I think she's fully terrified now." The wolf lay down and rolled over, exposing the length of his stomach. "Go back to the dorms," Mr. Dawson said.

The wolf gave one more whimper before he jumped up and took off running.

Mr. Dawson squatted in front of me. "Don't be scared. I won't hurt you."

"Bullshit. Tell that to Dr. Needle-Happy over there."

The doctor took a single step closer, and held out her blessedly empty hands. "I did what I had to do to keep you safe and ease your pain. I know it's hard for you to understand, but you've been very sick for the past week. A hurt and confused wolf is a dangerous thing."

Did she just say what I think she said? "I'm a human of the female variety, not a wolf."

"No, you're not a wolf, but you're not just a girl anymore either," she said.

"If you ever were *just* a girl," Mr. Dawson said.

I didn't like where this was going.

"You're a werewolf," Mr. Dawson said.

That's what I was forgetting. He was out of his mind. Certifiable. I stepped toward him. "There are no such things as werewolves."

"Then there are no such things as *brujas*."

I laughed. "With you on that one. My cousins are a bunch of crazy hippies. Thinking they can talk to spirits and cast spells and do magic. Whatever their little religion is, it's fake."

"Fake? So you don't get visions when you touch things? Because that's so very, very normal."

He had a point, but I didn't have to like it.

"I won't lie to you. St. Ailbe's is a school for werewolves. Dastien is a werewolf. When he bit you and scratched your shoulder, he turned you." Mr. Dawson put his hand on my knee as I tried to get up. "No more running, Teresa Elizabeth McCaide." The way he said my name, like it held some sort of power, made me pause. "You have to face what's happened."

This was a nightmare. My parents had left me with some lunatic. "I'd be happy to face something, if you were speaking the language of a sane person."

"What do you think you just saw?"

I thought I saw a guy turn into a wolf. But that

was impossible.

"Christopher Matthews changed into a wolf in front of you." Mr. Dawson spelled it out for me like it was totally possible. "A man who can also be a wolf. Human, but more. A werewolf."

I flinched as the needle-loving doctor squatted down next to Mr. Dawson. "I'm Dr. Gonzales. I apologize if I scared you, but I only want to help."

They were completely batshit. What were they trying to pull? Annoyance became anger, and my skin started to crawl.

"Take a look at your hands," Mr. Dawson said.

As I watched, my fingers lengthened, ripping my gloves along the seams again. Memories from the hospital came rushing back to me. "This is *not* happening. This is so *not happening.*" I was yelling, but I didn't really care.

"I can stop it for now. But you'll need to face it soon. You don't want the wolf to gain control again."

Pain rippled down my body. My knees cracked. "Why does it hurt so much?"

"It only hurts when you fight it," Dr. Gonzales said.

I couldn't help but fight it. I would not be a wolf. Ever. "What about my parents? They let you take me?"

"They had no choice," Mr. Dawson said.

I groaned as the pain spread to my stomach. My organs moved and mushed inside of me. I didn't need this. I didn't want it. "Stop it. Help me. Please. I'll do any—"

Mr. Dawson's eyes started glowing as he leaned in close. "Shhhh," he said. Power rolled through my body, taking my pain with it.

I stayed on the ground, panting. My muscles ached but everything was back where it was supposed to be. I was too grateful to question how he'd done it. "Thank you."

"I've settled the wolf within you for now, but you must learn to walk your new path soon." Mr. Dawson stood and reached a hand down to me. "I'd take it back if I could, but I can't change what Dastien did. So we're going to have to go from here."

I blinked back tears, unwilling to let them fall in front of either of them. "How do you know it was him?"

"You smell like him." He crossed his arms. "And he told me. Now that you're better, Dastien's got some answering to do."

He gave me a distraction and I snatched it up. "What do you mean?"

"He broke our Law."

"Law?"

"We don't bite. Not ever."

I almost laughed at that. "If you don't bite, then how come I'm here?"

"I have an idea, but…" He shrugged.

Admitting they didn't have all the answers made me trust him a little more. No one was perfect. And he seemed reasonably upset that this whole thing had gone down like it had. I took the hand he offered, and let him pull me up. "So, what now?"

Dr. Gonzales stood with me. "You'll take classes here, and learn to be one of us. It's going to take time, Tessa. You have to be patient."

I snorted. "Patience isn't one of my virtues."

"You'll learn it," she said. "You'll control your emotions, and hopefully one day, you can go to college, grow up, and take a place in our world."

Our world. Not *the* world.

Fantastic. Was there any way I could get back to *my* world?

Dr. Gonzales put an arm around my shoulder and I suppressed the urge to shrug it off. It wasn't her fault she had to stick me with needles. I'd forgive her. Maybe. But how was I going to forgive Dastien?

"Come on," she said. "Let's go back to campus. I'll show you to your new room. I'm sure Michael can find your suite-mate. Meredith's been looking forward to finally meeting you."

My new room? Suite-mate? I was going to have to actually live here. That totally blew. "I'm not sure I'm good company right now. Plus, I tend to have a hard time with making friends."

"I think it'll be much easier here," Mr. Dawson said. "We're all different."

He had that right. Visions were weird. But werewolves? Total freaks of nature. I laughed at the thought. If I hadn't just seen my hands changing, felt the pain of it, I'd have thought they were nuts.

It wasn't until we were walking through the courtyard that I realized that Dr. Gonzales had touched me skin-to-skin, and I hadn't gotten a thing from her. Not even a hint of a vision. I tugged on my gloves, making sure they were still there.

It was a fluke. No need to panic.

Okay, maybe a little bit of panicking.

Chapter Fourteen

Dr. Gonzales led me through the courtyard to a three story red-brick building. The unobtrusive sign on it read "Girl's Dormitory" in plain font. The walls inside were a pale mint. It was decorated in Pottery Barn-esque stuff. A large navy sectional and love seat surrounded a flat screen hanging against the far wall. To the right was a little kitchenette with top of the line appliances, and dual Subzero fridges. A girl was poking around in one of them. It was fully stocked with food, each item in a plastic container and labeled.

Looked like whoever organized the fridge could be my new BFF.

Three other girls were chatting on the couches as some lame reality show played on the TV. It—this building, the way it was decorated, and the girls hanging out—all seemed so normal. I don't know why that surprised me, but it did.

Dr. Gonzales cleared her throat. The girls paused

the TV and swiveled on the couch to stare at me.

"Ladies, this is Tessa."

They gave a chorus of "hi's" as they gawked at me. I almost reached for my face to check for dirt when a tall, thin girl stood up. She flicked her perfectly silky straight light brown hair over one shoulder and smirked at me.

"You look familiar. Oh, right." She laughed and tapped one of her friends. "That's the girl who jumped out the window."

I raised an eyebrow at Dr. Gonzales. "It sure will be easier here, huh?"

Dr. Gonzales had the grace to look a bit embarrassed. "I know you'll do your best to welcome Tessa to her new home."

La Bitch grinned. "We'll welcome her."

I wondered what her idea of "welcoming" would involve.

Dr. Gonzales led me to a stairwell. "We're lucky we have the space to give everyone their own rooms, but you share a bath with the room to the right of you. I think you'll find you have a lot in common with your suitemate, Meredith." She stopped in front of a door, number 27, and handed me a key. "There is no need to lock it. We're completely safe here, but I wasn't sure if you'd feel more comfortable this way."

Hell yes I'd feel more comfortable that way. The looks those girls were giving me downstairs were not exactly friendly. I didn't trust anyone here.

Inside was a small room with a desk, full sized bed, end table, and chest of drawers. They were all Ikea white lacquered. A bright purple poster in a gaudy black frame brushed with hints of gold hung above my bed. It was an outline of the Cheshire Cat's big grin. Underneath the grin was big bold font that read, "Keep Calm. We're all Mad Here."

I rolled my eyes. "My brother?"

"Yes." She scrunched her nose. "I can take it down—"

"No way." I ran my hand down the edge of the frame. She didn't know my brother or me well enough to get the joke. But it was like having a piece of him here. If she wanted it gone, she'd have to pry it from my cold, dead hands. "It's perfect."

"Your father insisted on new furniture for the room. He told me to tell you so."

I nodded. To the side of the bed, metal shelves had been attached to the wall. Each of my books was in the identical spot I had placed them in my room.

I was fully set up here, which probably meant I wasn't going home anytime soon.

"My parents…" I stopped. My voice sounded pathetic even to me, and I couldn't have that.

"They don't want this anymore than you do. But after seeing what happened to you at the hospital, they didn't have any other choice."

"So when can I go home?"

"Let's not worry about that right now, but maybe they can come visit."

That didn't sound vague at all. "But my dad works for the school. Can I see him at least?"

"He works off-site."

I nodded as I clenched my jaw shut to keep from saying something awful.

"You're going to get through this. Just remember to take it one day at a time."

I tuned her out as she rambled on. Her assumptions were a bit more than I could bear at that moment.

I tuned back in as she tapped the stack of books on my desk. "Your books are all here, as well as your schedule and a map of campus. Our curriculum is a bit different from your usual high school, so don't let that throw you."

"I'm sure it won't be a problem." Because I was getting out of here as soon as possible.

She picked up a small, brown leather bound book. "*The Werewolf's Bible*. It's basically a guide to everything about being a Were. It explains most of what you'll be going through." She paused, waving it at me. "Please read it. If you have any questions or just want to talk, I hope you'll come find me. You don't have to go through this alone."

Maybe she didn't think so, but I didn't know a soul here. I sighed. That wasn't exactly true. I kind of knew Dastien. Not that I wanted to see him again.

No, I was lying to myself again. I totally wanted to see him, but I wasn't going to let my hormones win. Not this time anyhow.

As soon as Dr. Gonzales left the room, I collapsed onto the bed. I wanted to curl up in a ball and cry. Instead, I got up and searched for my cell. Axel would have a plan to get me out of here.

My suite-mate's door slammed.

"Hello," a voice called out. There was a knock from the adjoining bathroom door. "Can I come in?"

I wanted to say no. I hadn't even had time to find my cell, let alone catch my breath.

"Tessa?"

I pulled off my ripped gloves and tossed them in the trashcan next to my desk. Clearing my throat, I tried to sound confident. "You can come on in."

A girl with long black hair flowing down her back came into my room. Two thick chunks of bright blue hair framed her face. She had ice blue eyes and rosy cheeks. She was nearly six feet and thin. My first thought was that she should be in a magazine or on the runway, not sharing a bathroom with me.

She started to walk toward me, but then stopped. "Are you okay?"

I laughed, but it didn't have any humor. "I'm so not even in the realm of okay."

She sat down on my bed, resting against the footboard. "Well, I'm Meredith—if you hadn't guessed that already—and I'm here if you want to talk about it. Dr. Gonzales said you might have some questions."

The good doctor had already sent a spy? "I wouldn't know where to start. But thanks anyways."

She reached over to pat my hand. I flinched.

There it was. My skin touching her bare skin, but nothing happened. What was wrong with my visions? I always hoped that by some miracle they would go away. Now that they might be gone, I wanted them back. Pronto.

"Being a Were is amazing. Promise."

Not sure she could make that kind of a promise. "I'm sure it is."

"It's dinner time. I'll introduce you to all the good people and fill you in on the gossip." She gave me a megawatt smile. "You've got questions. I've got answers," she said with a wink.

A surprised laugh escaped as I realized she'd quoted the RadioShack slogan.

She leaned close to me and sniffed and then crinkled her nose. "They must not have washed the stuff they put in the infirmary with you. Reeks of dryer sheets. Norms." She rolled her eyes.

Norms?

She dragged me into the bathroom. "Freshen up and I'll get you some clothes."

The bathroom vanity had two sinks. White subway tiles covered the bottom half of the walls and lined the shower. The white granite counter had plenty of room for two girls to spread out. The mirror opened in panels with enough shelves to make my inner organizer happy.

I splashed some cold water on my face, and stared into the mirror. Something was different. My hair shined. The highlights and lowlights gave the brown more depth than I'd ever had before. It looked shampoo commercial good. But the thing that stuck out the most to me was my 100% zit-free face. I always had some sort of blemish lurking here or there. Not even the tiniest red splotch marked my skin now.

They must have given me a few shots of super vitamins or antibiotics or something. Maybe a super vitamin E? Dr. Needle-happy might not be so bad after all.

I rummaged through my makeup bag that sat on the counter. Half of it wasn't necessary with my complexion being so clear. A quick swipe of gloss would be enough. I wasn't trying to impress anyone. It only had a hint of chemically smell, so I put it on.

Meredith was still digging through my clothes

when I walked back into my room. "You've got some cute stuff." She pulled out a black mini. "Love this."

I laughed. "With your body, it'll probably look better on you than me."

"Yeah, 'cause you're such a cow." She rolled her eyes. "I threw some jeans and a tank on the bed. Change. I'll wait." She moved over to look through my books.

I moved to the bed and picked up the tank top. It was one of my staples, black ribbed with black lace edging. But something was different with it. Something about it made me want to spend the night rubbing my face in it. I took a wiff of it, and smelled wood and something manly.

Totally weird. "My clothes smell—"

"Like Dastien!" She jumped in place. "Doesn't he smell like soooo yummy?"

Damn it. I didn't want to like her, but I couldn't help smiling with her. "I hadn't noticed before. I guess he does. So uuh, dare I ask why they smell like him?"

She waved me off and went back to the books. "He helped move your stuff in. I think it was part of his ongoing punishment."

"Punishment?"

She looked back at me. "For biting you."

"Is that his only punishment?"

She shook her head slowly. "No. Not even close."

I sat hard on the bed. This didn't sound good. "Is he going to be okay?"

"I don't know." She sat next to me. "I wouldn't worry about him. There might be a trial or something, but he'll probably be okay."

I took a deep breath with my face in the tank. I

couldn't believe I was torn between being repulsed and happy that it smelled like him. That guy had seriously messed with my head. And I really shouldn't care what might happen to him, but the "he'll probably be okay" thing was bothering me. "What kind of punishment could he get?"

"No one really knows, although everyone is talking about it. It's a huge deal that he bit you. I mean, it's against our Law. We're not like humans. The consequences are..." She got up and started looking through the stuff on my desk. "We just don't break our Law. So, Dastien's been keeping to himself and spending a lot of time as a wolf. And I'm sure we'll have a visit from the Seven before too long."

Was she purposely trying to not give me all the info? "The Seven?" It sounded a little sharp, even to me.

"Oh, sorry. We've never had a bitten wolf here."

I made a mental note to ask about that later.

"They're like our president, but more like a governing council made up of seven really old Alpha werewolves."

"So what's the worst case scenario?"

She made a face, scrunching up her nose. "I don't want to freak you out. It probably won't even happen."

"Okay, then don't say things like 'I don't want to freak you out.' Because first thing I do is start to freak out!"

She replaced the book she was holding back where she found it, and let out a breath. "He could get sentenced to death."

What! "Death?"

"Hey, it's not like I didn't warn you. You said you wanted worst case scenario."

"Yeah, but killing him is a little extreme, don't you think! I'm still alive. I'm fine…ish." Even if I wasn't fine, I didn't want him to die.

I looked from her to the clothes. She wasn't going to give me any privacy. I grabbed them off the bed and turned my back to her.

As I pulled on my jeans, I noticed they were a little baggy. Guess being "sick" burned some calories, but I was looking a little too thin. My ribs were even protruding a little—which was nowhere near sexy.

I jerked my top down when Meredith started talking again. "We have all of our regular classes together—math, chem, English, history. And yikes, you have Were history with the freshman. And metaphysics with them too. Well, at least you have yoga and martial arts with me. That's not so bad."

Yoga? Martial arts? *Were*? What the hell kind of classes was I going to be taking?

She grabbed my hand. "Come on. We're gonna be late." My skin froze as she pulled me out the door.

No visions. Not even a twinge.

I slid my hand from hers and rubbed it on my jeans. "Wait. What about shoes?"

"Oh. Just grab some flip-flops. That's what most of us wear. Makes shifting easier if you don't have to untie your shoes all the time. And once you change, you'll get used to being without clothes too. Gotta get used to being in front of everyone in your birthday suit." She winked.

"What! No. NO! You've gotta be out of your mind."

She doubled over laughing at whatever look I had on my face. I guessed it was somewhere between completely scandalized and totally horrified.

Changing clothes while keeping on my underwear was one thing. I could pretend it was like being in a bathing suit. And she was only one girl. No one saw me completely naked. Not even Mom.

"You should see the look on your face. I'm sorry. I had to. It was just so easy." She took a breath. "We don't roam around naked or anything. And we have special robes for when we change in groups and don't want to rip up our clothes. Plus, plenty of bushes and trees to hide behind and hidden stashes of clothes in the woods."

That was at least a little better, but still completely weird.

The sun set as we walked through the courtyard to the cafeteria. The two and three story red brick buildings dotted the campus, all of them simple in their style but beautiful, even if they did feel a little jail-esque right then. The smell of the trees, cedar and oak and pine, mixed all together made me feel calm.

This was going to take some getting used to. I hoped Dastien wasn't at dinner. Would he try to talk to me? Oh shit. What if he was there but he didn't want to talk to me? That would be completely awkward.

I held my breath as we got to the cafeteria. It was my second new school in as many weeks. That was a record, even for me. Somehow, the first time at a cafeteria in a new school never got any easier.

Screw it. It was like ripping off a band-aid. Right?

Chapter Fifteen

The cafeteria was filled with students grabbing food. There was a short order grill, bars for salad, baked potatoes, and desserts, and a station with hot entrees. No one looked shy about eating as people moved from one station to the next piling their trays high. Not one girl had a water and plain lettuce on her tray. Yet everyone was in amazing shape.

I'd definitely entered the Twilight Zone.

I looked down at my jeans and tank. Yeah, my clothes blended, but I didn't fit in. Every other girl in there looked like they could be models. They were tall, all legs. And everyone moved gracefully, as if they were choreographed into some intricate dance. No one bumped into each other. Nothing spilled or slopped around on their trays.

The guys were just as impressive. They were all tall and built—muscles stretching T-shirts almost beyond their capacity. It was like I walked into a living Abercrombie ad.

What a nightmare.

It hit me suddenly, and I started roughly counting the people in the room. There were at least three times as many guys there as girls. I never considered myself much of a women's lib person, but this was ridiculous. Sex bias much?

"Come on." Meredith dragged me the rest of the way to the brown plastic trays.

I grabbed a slice of roast beef and some veggies and started to walk away. Meredith grasped my arm, pulling me back to the line. "That's not enough food." She piled on mashed potatoes with gravy and rolls and pasta and everything else within reach onto my plate until my tray was fully loaded down.

I lifted it and it was at least ten pounds heavier than it had been a minute ago.

"Oh. You need this too." She carefully balanced a slice of pecan pie on the edge of the tray.

"So what army am I supposed to be giving this to?"

"No one told you?"

"No one's told me anything. I just got here, remember?"

A smile broke across her face. "You're going to love this."

I was?

"Being a werewolf has its advantages. You don't get sick. Ever. We heal fast. And because we heal so fast, we're slow to age. But all of that, plus shifting, burns a ton of calories. Think mega calories. So, you have to eat a lot to keep up with your new metabolism." She started scooping food onto her tray again. "Mr. D might look like he's in his mid-thirties, but think like five times that."

She'd just made my brain explode and had no clue that she'd done it. This was a lot to take in. I glanced down at my overflowing tray and wondered if I would even be able to carry it. "So what, I'm going to look seventeen for the next five years."

"Kind of. We age normally for a while, but then it slows way down once you hit your first shift." I must've made a face, because she answered my question before I asked it. "Puberty."

"Awesome." Because puberty wasn't hard enough already.

"Seriously," she said. "I'm not kidding. You need to eat all of that. If you're hungry, you get pissy. A pissy werewolf is a dangerous werewolf."

When she decided we had enough, she looked for a table. Ignoring everyone had been easy while I got food, but once I turned, the entire cafeteria stopped eating to stare at me. Low whispers spread through the room.

Fantastic. Now if I could make it to the table without tripping, that would be good.

I followed Meredith as she wove through the tables. Most people stopped talking when I walked by them, except for one table.

"Don't worry, Dastien. She won't dare approach you here."

I spun—nearly toppling my soda. La Bitch was back.

Then I saw them. A pair of golden eyes. La Bitch's hand covered Dastien's as she leaned toward him.

Motherfucker. Did that asshat have a girlfriend?

The two of them together stung way more than it

should've. We had kissed once. It wasn't like it meant anything besides irrevocably destroying my life. Still, the urge to throw the contents of my tray in his face for turning me and then sitting there all chummy with that bitch of a girl was almost too great to ignore.

He got up without saying a word to me and walked out of the cafeteria.

Meredith looked from me to La Bitch. She cleared her throat, and stared at the ground. "Come on, Tessa. Table's over here."

I didn't want to look away from the girl, but Meredith pulled on my arm, nearly upending my tray. It was either make a scene or follow Meredith.

I stared at the doors Dastien had disappeared through. I didn't need any more problems. I took a deep breath and followed Meredith.

We sat down where three people were already eating. "This is Chris." Meredith pointed to a boy with wavy dirty blond hair, and sky blue eyes. "He's our resident brooding artist."

I set my tray down with a thunk. It was the guy from earlier who tackled me. "I think we've met. Kind of," I said.

"I could never forget someone who made me fall so hard." He gave me a wink. "Recovering okay?" His voice had a deep rasp that I hadn't noticed before.

"This is Adrian," she said, motioning toward the other guy.

He had brown skin and eyes so dark I couldn't tell where the iris started. He smiled, his white teeth gleaming against the dark skin. "Hola," he said with a thick Texas accent.

"And this is Shannon." Shannon had flame-red

hair and bright green eyes. Her cold glare made me shiver. This one didn't think so highly of me. Maybe she should go join La Bitch's table.

"Listen, the cliques here can be pretty rough. I mean some of them are from families with long lines of ruling alphas," Meredith said. "You don't want to piss anyone off until you know what's what. Just try not to let anyone get to you. Like Imogene—"

"The girl with Dastien?"

She nodded.

"Right." I shrugged. "Well, I'll be nice to her if and when she's nice to me."

Meredith made a face, but I wasn't backing down on this. I'm not going to go out of my way to be nice to someone who insulted me.

A change of subject was in order. "I guess everyone's not just staring at me because I'm new?"

"Sorry, love." Shannon's lilting Irish voice surprised me. "It's been a long time since anyone's been bitten. It's simply not done."

Not done. Right. Because if that were really true, then how did I end up at St. Ailbe's?

I poked around at my mountain of food, and they started talking about some chemistry test coming up. I nodded when appropriate to the conversation that flowed around me, but couldn't stop wondering about the whole biting thing. That was the second time that someone mentioned that werewolves didn't bite humans. So why had Dastien done it?

"You should really finish that," Meredith said.

I'd eaten some of it, but hadn't even made a dent in the mound. Thinking about Dastien had killed my appetite. The thought of taking another bite made me want to gag. "You know, I think I'm good. I'm going to head back to my room."

"Are you sure you—" Meredith said.

"I'm fine. Really." I'd reached my limit. I was never great at being around people, and couldn't remember the last time I'd been alone. This was all too much, and trying to pretend that it was normal and have a nice little dinner chat wasn't working for me. "It was nice to meet all of you."

As I stood up, the room went quiet again. I left my tray where it was, and strode across the room. Everyone stared, especially a group of girls from the table where Dastien had been sitting. Their gazes could have started a fire, mostly around me. I held my chin high as I walked past them. I hadn't done anything wrong.

When I got back to my room, I found my cell phone on the bed with a note tucked underneath it.

Call your parents. They want to hear from you.
—Michael Dawson.

I stared at my phone. What would I say? What did they have to tell me? Nothing and nothing.

I grabbed my laptop off the desk and started doing searches on werewolves and their bites. I found a lot of stuff that I didn't think was right. One site said werewolves were started by a gypsy's curse. Another site said you could go back to being human if you killed the werewolf that bit you. That was a pretty thought, but I was reasonably sure I wouldn't be trying it out. I wasn't that desperate. Yet.

One blogger wrote that werewolves could only shift when there was a full moon, but I already knew that wasn't true. Chris had gone back and forth between the two forms in a fraction of a second this afternoon. A quick search confirmed that we were a little more than three weeks away from the next full moon.

I was about to close my computer in frustration when I found a local news story. A girl was found dead about 100 miles north of San Antonio with her throat ripped out. All her blood was drained.

Meredith would probably tell me vampires or goblins did it. Hell, maybe a unicorn with rabies.

I rolled my eyes and closed my laptop, placing it on my desk to charge.

Mr. Dawson's note was still on my bed. I read it again and dialed home. I snapped it closed before it started to ring.

I couldn't call my parents, but there was one person I could call. I grinned as a plan formed in my mind.

Chapter Sixteen

Meredith knocked on the door connecting my room to the bathroom when she got back from dinner. "Tessa?" she whispered as she opened the door.

I hoped the lights being off would be hint enough, but I was prepared. Under the covers, I was fully dressed—black skinny jeans and a black t-shirt, but she wouldn't be able to tell. I kept my breathing even and steady. The door quietly clicked closed.

I stayed still until I heard the noises from her room quiet. I waited another two hours after that. Then one more just to make sure.

Everyone had to be asleep by then. It was after two in the morning. I threw off the covers and picked up my cell.

Axel picked up after one ring. "Are you okay?"

"No." I kept my voice as quiet as possible. "This place is totally messed up. Come get me."

The silence on the other end nearly did me in. I

closed my eyes and prayed he'd do this for me. He had to. There was no one else.

"I dunno," he said finally. "Mom and Dad would flip. They're saying that you're…that you…"

"Axel. Please. I'm asking for help. You know I wouldn't ask if I had any other option."

He sighed. "I didn't say I wasn't going to do it. I hear they have you under lockdown."

"That's not true. I'm in a dorm, not jail. Plus, campus has been quiet for hours now. Everyone is asleep." I tiptoed to the window to double check, but nothing was moving. The courtyard was empty. Not one light was on in the buildings. The night was totally still. "I'm going to sneak out and go to the front gate of the school. Pick me up in fifteen."

"I have to get dressed and it'll take me longer than that just to get there. Give me twenty-five."

"Done." I paused. I didn't know what I was doing and this was probably going to get both of us in world of hurt with our parents. "Axel?"

"Yeah?"

"Thanks."

"Sure thing. I got your back, lil sis."

I hung up and double-checked that my cell was on silent. Even having it on vibrate could get me caught if I was actually on lockdown. Whatever the hell that meant.

Since Axel was going to take a few, I grabbed my backpack and looked around my room to see if there was something here I couldn't live without, but there really wasn't much that I couldn't replace. I grabbed a few of my favorite T-shirts I'd screen-printed, my laptop, and my signed Nora Roberts book. With my cell shoved into my back pocket, I sat down, knees bouncing as the seconds ticked away.

Waiting that last ten minutes was torture. I studied the map of campus to kill time. Judging from the scale, it shouldn't take me more than a few minutes to get to the front gate. The problem would be getting out of the dorm without waking anyone. My hearing had been a bit sensitive at the hospital, so I was assuming that was a Were thing. It would suck if one of these girls was a light sleeper.

Leaving through the door was a no go. No matter how softly I tried to close it, there was too much potential risk of waking up Meredith or one of the other girls. So I did the only thing I could think of. I opened the window gingerly.

The good thing was that I'd already survived a three-story drop. After that, two-stories was no big. Or it should be no big. That said, convincing myself to let go once I was hanging from my windowsill was harder than I'd imagined.

I made the mistake of looking down past my dangling feet. Two-stories was still one too many stories. But I had to let go. I counted down silently. When I hit three, I let go.

Next thing I knew, I was on my feet looking up at my window from the ground. I watched the windows above for any lights turning on, but nothing happened. I guessed Axel was wrong about the whole me being on lockdown thing.

The path to the right should lead to a parking lot. And beyond that, the main gate. I'd never seen it, but I hoped it wouldn't be hard to open. Or climb.

I heard someone whispering, and it was getting

louder. A three-foot hedge in front of the dorm seemed decent coverage. I moved around the end of it to hide between it and the brick wall.

When the group approached, I tried to breathe as quietly as possible.

"—reports that they're organizing and heading south." I recognized Mr. Dawson's voice. "It seems pretty convenient that they pick now to search for us."

"You can't think it's because of what I did," Dastien said.

Shit. I couldn't have been in a worse hiding spot. If either of them caught me I was going to die of humiliation.

"We've spilled human blood. They could sense that or maybe a weakening alpha because of the broken law?"

"That's bullshit. You're not weakening."

Their voices were getting softer, but I could still hear them.

"I'd rather think that than the alternative," Mr. Dawson said.

"Which is what?"

"That we have a rogue in the pack."

Dastien said something else, but I couldn't make it out. Only the tone. He was pissed.

A rogue? What did that mean?

It didn't matter. It wasn't my problem. I was getting the hell out of here.

I counted to ten before coming out of my hiding spot, and then took off down the path. Dense trees threatened to swallow it, but that look was cultivated on purpose. St. Ailbe's had something to hide. The trail snaked sharply to the right, and then to the left, and then to the right again before it straightened out.

The parking lot was filled with at least a hundred cars. The three front rows looked completely full from where I was standing, and the fourth and fifth had some empty spaces. A line of black Expeditions took up the first row. What was up with that? The popular kids needed matching cars here?

Beyond the Expeditions were fancy cars galore. Even in the dim moonlight, they gleamed and curved in a way no ordinary Chevy could. I wanted to be annoyed by it, but the private schools in Los Angeles hadn't been any more down to Earth.

A tall, red brick wall bordered the back of the parking lot. The top of the black iron gate peeked over the top of the SUVs. Both the gate and the wall were pretty high. I'd be in for a climb either way I went. Maybe the gate wasn't locked.

I made my way through the cars, and slid to a stop as I reached the gate.

A group of no less than ten guys stood leaning against it. Some were chatting. A few were sitting down in a circle playing cards.

I was so dumb. I should've gone through the creek.

One of them looked straight at me and winked. "What's the time?" he said to the guy next to him.

"2:26 AM. Damn it. That means Brandt won."

A series of curses rang through the group, followed by one guy celebrating. "Hand it over, bitches."

Axel's car screeched to a stop beyond the tall iron gate. He jumped out of the car, leaving it idling. His headlights lit up the lot. "Shit, Tess. I told you this was a bad idea!" He stepped up to the closed gate.

I hadn't said a word yet. The only thing I could think of was the fact that I was stuck here. The walls were closing in on me. Even outside.

Mr. Dawson, Dastien, and three other guys strolled up behind me. They were all dressed in black. Dastien stayed back while Mr. Dawson and the others kept walking toward me.

He wouldn't even look at me, but he'd wait up all night to make sure I couldn't run away?

Axel had been right. I was on lockdown, and they'd been waiting for me. Being predictable sucked.

"Alright, show's over," Mr. Dawson said. "Tessa, it's back to the dorm for you."

"This is bullshit." I couldn't believe that they'd been watching for me.

Mr. Dawson raised a brow. "Is it? Because I've a mind to think that you being here means it's definitely not bullshit."

"That's beside the point."

Dastien chuckled.

I pointed at him. "You shut it. It's your fault that I'm—"

"I thought we went over this." Axel wrapped his hands around the bars of the gate. "You don't get to go near my sister again!"

This was so not happening.

"You're trespassing. You need to leave. Now," one of the guys said to Axel.

"I'm not leaving. Let me in."

"Listen norm—"

Oh, hell no. It was one thing for these people to

boss me around, but there was no way anyone was going to treat my brother badly.

I strode to the gate, stepping in front of Axel and him. "No one orders my brother around." I eyed each one of the guys. "No one." Each of them dropped their gaze. Except for Dastien and Mr. Dawson.

A hand squeezed my shoulder and I spun, growling. Axel took a big step back.

"Tess? What's wrong with your eyes?"

Seeing my brother afraid of me—of something he saw in me—was like getting a bucket of ice water dumped over my head. I was suddenly exhausted.

Mr. Dawson turned to Dastien. "You should go. All of you. I've got it from here."

Dastien left without even a glance in my direction. Typical. The others followed quickly behind him.

The one who won the bet paused in front of me and held up a wad of cash. "Thanks for this."

"I didn't do it on purpose."

"I'll still give you a cut." He held out his fist and I rolled my eyes, but still bumped it.

"Go, Mr. Thompson," Mr. Dawson said.

When the audience finally dispersed, Mr. Dawson opened the gate to let Axel in. "I know that you're protective of your sister, but we're going to take care of her here."

He looked at me warily. "It doesn't seem like that when I get a phone call at nearly two AM. And I thought you said you'd keep that asshole away from her."

"I'm trying, but you've got to give her time. She's going through a bit of an adjustment period."

I snorted. "Adjustment? That's what you're calling

this?"

"Adjusting is your only option. You won't like what happens if you fail."

"That sounded pretty close to a threat," Axel said. He moved to stand between Mr. Dawson and I.

After what Meredith said about Dastien's punishment, I knew what he might mean. Scared didn't even scratch the surface of what I was feeling, but that didn't mean I could put my brother in danger. I'd already asked too much of him. No way was I risking one of these wolves biting him. "Go home, Axel. I'll figure it out. I'll be fine."

"No way, Tess. I don't like it," he said.

"Me neither." I hugged him.

He gripped me tighter and whispered in my ear. "I've been with the cousins. We're working on getting you out of here. Just sit tight for a few weeks. I'm not forgetting about you."

Our cousins couldn't do anything, but if it made him feel better, then it was good he had the distraction. "I love you."

"Love you, too," he said in a normal voice. "Don't let them push you around."

I nodded as he let me go.

I didn't wait for Axel to leave or for Mr. Dawson to escort me back to my room. I was a big girl, and it was past time for me to put on my big girl panties. I'd make the best of a bad situation or die trying. Maybe for real. Which was terrifying, but life had never exactly been easy for me. This was more old hat than anything else.

If only I could actually convince myself that it was old hat, then I'd be in a much better place.

And damned Dastien. He was driving me crazy. Why wouldn't he even look at me?

Chapter Seventeen

The sun peeked through the curtains. I threw the covers over my head. If I stayed in bed, then there could be hope that yesterday had been a crazy fever-induced dream. Or maybe someone had slipped something into my drink and I'd hallucinated the whole thing.

It was easy to pretend underneath the familiar feel of my old white cotton sheets. I touched the hole on the corner that had ripped when I trusted Axel to do my laundry once. Any second, he'd come in here and annoy me.

An inhumanly loud beeping chafed my ears.

A groan and a few bangs came from Meredith's room before the alarm clicked off.

No such luck. Guess I'd better deal with the day.

I threw the sheets off. I appreciated what they'd done, trying to make me feel at home, but it didn't matter. This wasn't my home.

Running away didn't work. I was left with only

one option.

Time to face reality.

I pulled myself from the safety of my bed, and quickly showered. Meredith walked into the bathroom as I was wrapping a towel around myself. She mumbled something unintelligible and flipped the shower back on.

Someone definitely wasn't a morning person.

I went back to my room to get changed, trying to ignore the fact that I was touching a million and one things and had exactly zero visions was getting increasingly harder. But I had bigger things to worry about. I started opening drawers as I considered my outfit options.

The kids I had seen last night were made of hotness. There was no way my short, curvy, Latina frame could compete. I dug through my clothes, trying and failing miserably to ignore the scent that covered everything. I decided to keep it simple with jeans, a black KMFDM T-shirt that fell off one shoulder, and a pair of yellow neon and gray kicks. No flip-flops for me. There was no risk of me shifting. The question was—gloves or no gloves?

I fingered a pair of cobalt ones. I felt naked without them, but did I really need them?

My visions could come back, any second. They had to. I grabbed the gloves and shoved them in my back pocket.

I made my bed as I waited for Meredith. Mom always said I was a little too much of a neat freak, but I felt more at ease about the parts of my life that I couldn't control when the ones I could control were in order. Lord knew my life was out of my hands right now.

As I smoothed out the comforter, the conversation in the room next door came through the brick like it was paper. They were gossiping. About me.

"What does Dastien see in that girl?"

"I know right? She's short. And weird. What is with those T-shirts she wears?"

My shirt today was cool. I was sure of it. Maybe everyone didn't know who KMFDM was, but they were a totally awesome electro-industrial band from the 1980s. Okay. So maybe it was weird, but I wasn't changing it because some random girls didn't get it.

"He had Imogene. And if he was tired of her, he could have his pick of the Weres. Why would he throw that away to bite some stupid norm?"

This was so not helping my confidence.

I pounded on the brick a few times. "I can hear you!" I said.

They giggled, and I wanted to plow through the brick and pummel them.

The water shut off, and Meredith went into her room. I rushed into the bathroom, trying to get control of myself. I was flipping out. Since when did I ever care about what someone said about me?

If I was being honest, I usually cared, but I never let it show.

I took a deep breath and held it in until my lungs burned. When I let it out, I felt marginally better.

What now, Tessa?

I picked up my perfume, and took the cap off. The smell of rubbing alcohol filled the room. I put my nose up to the top of the bottle and sniffed. It stank.

The florals and fruits that I loved were barely there, and the alcohol was strong enough to give me a headache.

Did perfume go bad?

I put the lid on and carefully placed it in the trash so it wouldn't break. My complexion hadn't worsened, but I'd found the best thing I could do when feeling a little lacking in the confidence department was to put on some war paint. I finished off my brown smoky eyes with some liner and mascara. Happy with the results, I grabbed a chapstick and went back into my room to try to figure out what I needed for class.

My schedule sat on top of the pile of books on my desk. I stared at it for a minute before shoving everything in my backpack. Who knew what I'd need for metaphysics or Were history? Whatever they were. I folded up the schedule and put it in my pocket.

Meredith's flip-flops clacked on the tile bathroom floor. "Give me five, and we can go down to breakfast together."

"Okay." I didn't want to face the cafeteria alone anyway. People didn't give you the stink-eye like those girls gave me and then let it go. The last thing I needed was a fight on my first day of school.

I plopped back on my bed. The whole situation was awful. One stupid party. One stupid boy. One stupid kiss. And my life was virtually over.

Disgusted with my own whining, I pulled my schedule back out and tried to focus on what it said. Normal classes were before lunch, and after seemed to be the weird stuff—Were history, metaphysics, and martial arts & yoga.

The more I thought about it the worse my nerves got. A bead of sweat rolled down my face, which was odd. Even during gym class I didn't sweat that much. Maybe I was still sick.

I took deep breaths, but that made me feel dizzy. My skin crawled. Head between the knees was all I could think to do.

My stomach twisted and my bones ached.

Not this. Not again.

"Okay, Tess. Ready—" Meredith's voice dropped off as her footsteps quickened on carpet. "Breathe deep for me. Calm. It's going to be okay. You're fine. No reason to panic. Just stop fighting the change."

"I'm not feeling super fantastic."

"You're fine. Your body's just on the verge of deciding whether or not to go furry."

"That's crazy. Do you know how that sounds? Completely batshit crazy."

"I know. It's gotta be weird for you."

I snorted.

"If you don't want to shift, then don't get too worked up over anything. Deep slow breaths. Food will help. You didn't eat enough last night."

"I ate."

"Not enough." She looked around my room. "Damn it. They should've put a mini-fridge in here. Once you get used to eating more, you won't need it. Until then, I'll get Mr. Dawson to put one in here for emergencies. You'll have to rely on the one in the common area until then."

After a minute of deep breathing, I started to feel okay, and glanced up at her. "Thanks."

Meredith knelt in front of me, her mouth quirked up at one side. "Any time. I know you don't trust me yet, but I hope we'll be friends."

I shrugged. "I'll do my best. No promises."

"Cool." She grinned. "Rad shirt."

"You like KMFDM?"

She shook her head. "No idea who they are, but love the screen print—black on electric blue is kind of my thing."

"I can tell." She'd complemented her blue streaks with blue eye make-up.

"Feeling good enough to walk to breakfast?"

I stood up slowly, and took a second to make sure I was all right. "You really think food will fix this?"

"It'll help keep your wolf happy so you'll be less likely to change."

That meant absolutely nothing to me, but it didn't really matter. "Okay. Let's go eat." I swung my backpack over my shoulder. I had to start trusting someone here, and Meredith seemed as good an option as any.

Chapter Eighteen

We walked outside in silence. A light breeze ruffled the leaves. Birds called to each other. They sounded different than before. Usually I couldn't tell the difference between birdcalls, but now I could hear distinct pitches and tones. It was more musical. More melodic.

"You better?" Meredith's voice brought me back to reality.

"Maybe?"

"Rumor is that you'll be changing with the next full moon, but you should talk to Mr. Dawson or Dr. Gonzales about it. You seem like you've already changed, and—if I'm right—you're going to need to get some control. You'll need help."

I was pretty sure somewhere in the week I'd lost, I probably went full-furry, but I wasn't trying to repeat that. The whole idea of turning into a wolf freaked me out. It was the last thing I wanted to talk about right then.

We reached the cafeteria before I could come up with something to say. As soon as she opened the door, the smells of breakfast reached me. My stomach rumbled so loud that a few people at the closest table chuckled.

My face heated. "Apparently I'm hungry," I said, trying to laugh it off.

Meredith's smile was back. "Me too. Let's get some grub."

The amount of food was intense—eggs, bacon, pancakes, French toast, bagels, croissants, anything and everything. The man at the grill station had to be a Were. He moved so fast I could barely track him as he took orders for omelets and crepes and noodles.

I piled my plate up quickly. As we walked to a table, people were quieter than they had been at dinner, focused more on eating than chatting. Thank God not everyone was as peppy in the morning as Meredith. She took forever to get up, but once Meredith finally got out of bed, she was all sunshine and rainbows.

On my way to the table, an elbow jabbed my side. I turned to see what the deal was just in time to get shoulder checked by La Bitch. I barely registered the brush of her skin against mine before I got sucked in.

Look at this short slut. There's no way he's going to dump me for her. Not a chance in hell.

Was that a vision?

I shoved away the stabbing pain in my heart at the thought that Dastien would choose this girl over me. Instead, I'd focus on the fact that my visions might be coming back. The relief was tangible. Now, if only I could get this girl to back off. "Excuse me?" I didn't care how rude I sounded. Having a little bit of my own normalcy back was enough to make me confident.

"Move out of the way." La Bitch moved to shove me, but I sidestepped in time, and managed to keep my plate from slipping off the tray. Go me.

The girl's face reddened. She leaned into my space. "Listen, whore," she whispered. "I don't know what you did to my Dastien, but you better stay far away from us."

I met her stare. "I really don't give a shit about you or your cheating boyfriend. You need to back off before you start something you're going to regret." We stood there frozen. Somehow it turned into a third grade staring contest, and I wouldn't look away first.

Time stopped as I waited for her to look away. As soon as she did, I smiled, and it wasn't in the least bit nice. "Leave," I said. "Now."

She spun, stomping her feet like a child.

Who knew telling her to go would work? I couldn't stop the grin. I was badass.

It didn't take long for the grin to disappear. Everyone in the room had been watching. Fan-freaking-tastic. I hoped that was the end of showdowns, but knew I could never be that lucky.

I found my way to the table where Meredith and Chris were sitting, and slid into the chair.

"Well, that was intense," I said.

"Intense?" Meredith said. "No. That was ah-may-zing. Do you know what this means?"

"That she'll leave me alone?"

Chris laughed. "No. You've just made an enemy

for life. No chance in hell she'll ever leave you alone now."

"Aaaaand," Meredith said, cutting off Chris before he could say anything else. "More importantly, you might be an alpha."

"I have no idea what you're talking about." I looked at La Bitch, who was now talking furiously with three other girls. "What is her problem?"

"She's Imogene Hoel. She thinks she's the shit," Chris said. "And she likes to think that she's Dastien's girlfriend."

My heart double-timed it. "But is she Dastien's girlfriend?"

"No," Meredith said. "They kind of grew up together, and a bunch of people, including her, thought that they'd end up together, but they've never really dated. I mean...there was that rumor—"

"The rumor had some truth to it, but she threw herself at him and wouldn't leave him alone until he gave her a chance," Chris said.

I stopped breathing as Dastien walked into the room. Imogene ran to him and put her arms around his waist. He put his arm on her shoulder as she talked to him. He jerked back at something that she said, and then his gaze found mine.

Shit. I sank down in my chair. Being in the middle of a soap opera wasn't my idea of a good time.

"She's really pissed. I love being right. I knew I was going to like you," Chris said. He blew me a kiss.

I pretended to catch the kiss and press it to my cheek, and then I looked behind me again. Dastien stood still, ignoring Imogene. His eyes were glowing, but I wasn't sure if he was staring at Chris or me. My heart sped up. Was he going to come over here?

Dastien spun on his heel and left the cafeteria, slamming the door behind him. Imogene stood there for a second, staring at the door, before going after him.

I ground my teeth. She was out there alone with Dastien, and I despised her for it.

I was so dumb.

I thought back to the vision I'd gotten from Imogene. It seemed like I heard her current thoughts, which was odd. It'd happened before—when someone was drunk or when it was Mom—but it was rare enough to throw me a little off. If my visions were coming back, I needed to put on my gloves. I leaned in my chair enough to grab the cobalt ones from my back pocket. I slipped them on, trying to make it look casual, and felt instantly more like my old self.

A glance around the room confirmed that everyone was still staring at me, probably waiting for my reaction. I smiled at Chris. "Hopefully Dastien won't come back to bite me this time."

Chris laughed. "So I heard you had a little early morning adventure."

Meredith dropped her fork with a loud thunk. "She didn't?"

"Yup." He grinned as he leaned back in his chair. "Brant Thompson won the pool."

"Damn it. I was listening for the door."

Good thing I went out the window.

"Window," Chris said.

How did he know? Oh God. If he knew, then who else knew?

"Again?"

The jerk was enjoying making me squirm in my seat. "Yup," Chris said.

"If you were going to try to run, why not tell me so that I could win?" There was a hint of whine in Meredith's voice.

"Uh. Sorry?" I cleared my throat. "Was everyone in the entire school in on this?"

"Yes," they all answered as one.

"Wow. That's really embarrassing. Can we talk about something else?"

Meredith crossed her arms. "No."

"Okay…"

"If you're going to run away again, you have to make sure it's next Tuesday during fourth period." She punctuated her words by banging the table. "It's the only way you can make it up to me."

Holy hell. How dumb did they think I was? "I'm not going to run away again."

"Yeah, you are. Every once in a while there will be a Were who marries a norm and doesn't tell their partner about the whole going wolf thing. It's a hot mess when their kids come here. They always run away. And you were an actual norm. So, you're due a couple more runs at least." She paused. "Tuesday. Fourth period."

Meredith had somehow managed to turn something uber-humiliating into something kind of okay. I could've kissed her for that. "I'll see what I can do."

"Fair enough."

I tried to bring the conversation back to something normal. "So, what are the teachers like here? Tough? Easy?" I said as I tugged at my gloves.

"Classes are pretty tough, but the teachers are helpful," Meredith said. She eyed my gloves, but accepted the topic change. "I mean most people leave here and go Ivy League or study in London or wherever they're from." She paused. "What's up with the gloves? You can't be cold. Werewolves don't get cold."

"I'm not cold." I shoved a giant bite in my mouth as everyone stared. I swallowed. "So I take it not everyone is from here?"

"Yeah. This is *the* place to go if you're a Were. People come from all over. I'm sure you already know all about that because of being with Dastien."

I knew exactly nothing about that. "Um, I think he mentioned that he's from France."

"Oh?" She paused, waiting for me to keep going but I wasn't going to tell her what happened. There were too many ears around. Plus, she was right. I didn't trust her yet.

A soft tone dinged throughout the cafeteria, and everyone got up and moved toward the doors.

"Well ladies, it's been lovely. See you at lunch." Chris blew us another kiss before leaving.

"That's the bell?" I said.

"What did you think it was?" she said.

"I had no idea, but it doesn't sound like any bell I've ever heard. Usually they're more fire drill-like."

"No fire drills here. Talk about insta-headache. Werewolves have really good hearing. Plus, once you know what the bell sound is, you can't miss it."

"But your alarm clock—"

"Just because I have good hearing, doesn't mean I want to get up in the morning. The more obnoxious and harder to turn off, the better. And I have a tendency to smash them. I go through a couple a month." Meredith frowned at my tray. "You didn't eat nearly enough."

The girl had lost her mind. "I ate a humungo-sized omelet, hash browns, a bagel with cream cheese, and a bowl of fruit. That's more than I've ever eaten in one sitting." There physically wasn't any more room in my stomach.

Meredith rolled her eyes. "Hang on one second." She walked back to the guy making the omelets, talking to him while pointing at me. He shook his head in disapproval.

Jeez. Why didn't she call the National Guard while she was at it?

Meredith came back with some sandwiches in plastic bags and an apple. "Take these. You might not think you need them, but when your stomach growls in ten minutes, do yourself a favor and eat them. Okay?"

I saluted. "Yes, ma'am." I shoved them in my bag.

We walked outside with a group of other students.

"The classes are all in there." She pointed to a two-story red brick building next to the infirmary. "The physical stuff is on the first floor. Don't want anyone going out a window, right?"

I laughed. "They're not so bad."

"I kind of was bummed about getting a suite-mate, but that moment changed my mind. The whole breaking the window with the IV stand and then jumping thing was kind of badass."

"Thanks," I said, grinning. "In retrospect, maybe not my smartest move, but you gotta go with what you're feeling at the time, right?"

"Totally." She laughed. "Anyway, the academic stuff is on the second floor. All of the lockers are there too, so we can stash your stuff."

Off to the side of the building was some training equipment. It looked way more Navy SEAL than high school. "What's that?"

"Anyone who wants to be a Cazador has to pass a physical test and a sparring test. Most people try it after they graduate. Although some will come back and practice after graduation if they can't pass it the first go-round."

"Cazador? As in Spanish for hunter?"

"Yup. They keep the norms safe from all the things not so normal."

My mind kept bouncing back and forth between two things: either these people were seriously demented or the world was a lot scarier than I thought. Werewolves weren't bad enough? There had to be more?

Someone darted out of the woods between the buildings. Someone with strong arms, a broad chest, and long legs roped with muscle. I knew who it was, even from this distance. I stood frozen in place as I watched Dastien run toward the course with equal parts raw power and grace. He was wearing a pair of running shorts and nothing else.

"Wow." It came out half moan as I watched the play of muscle across his body.

"Yeah. He's kind of amazing to watch. One of the best Cazadores we've seen in a long time."

Dastien ran at the hurdles, jumping over them without slowing down.

"But I thought he stayed here?"

"He goes out on assignment, but likes to keep his home base here. He teaches martial arts sometimes and gets the seniors ready for the Cazador test when he's around."

He took a running leap at the rope wall, gaining half of it by that alone. Hand over hand, he lifted his body up like it was easy. He leaped off the top of the wall, shifting midair, and landed as a beautiful white and gray wolf.

Well that was not what I was expecting to see. Undeniable proof that Dastien was a werewolf. I shoved any feelings I had about that way down. I had more than my fair share of junk to deal with for today.

Steeling my shoulders, I forced myself to turn away from him and keep walking.

Chapter Nineteen

The second floor had a long hallway lined with wooden doors and tall, black lockers. Each locker had a name on it instead of the usual numbers, and none of them had actual locks on them. Meredith pointed me in the right direction before heading to hers.

The schedule said I had English first. I left one notebook and the English books in my backpack, and dumped everything else in the locker. Meredith waited by one of the open doors.

All talking stopped when I entered the classroom.

"Ignore them," Meredith said.

I focused on keeping my chin up and followed her to our seats. The teacher strode in. Everyone in the class sat up straight in their chairs as she set her papers down on her desk. I shifted in my seat, not knowing what I should be doing. I grabbed my notebook and a pen, and waited for class to begin.

I checked my schedule again for her name. Mrs. Ramirez. Thick black hair flowed down her back. Her large almond-shaped brown eyes made her look fey. She scanned the desks and stopped when she saw me.

"Hi, Tessa. Welcome to English. We're doing Macbeth. Have you studied it before?"

I nodded.

A smile spread across her face and she stepped toward my desk. "You'll be ahead of this bunch." She handed me some papers and turned, her paisley printed maxi-skirt swirling around her legs. "Let's begin."

She started asking questions, but the syllabus distracted me. My old school had always been more of a straight out of the textbook kind of thing. But this was different. I flipped through the pages and couldn't find anything about when the standardized tests were. Instead there were descriptions after each piece of literature—two essay question exams, blue books provided.

What the hell was a blue book?

I tried not to stress, unsuccessfully. I flipped open my notebook, furiously writing down everything that Mrs. Ramirez said.

Meredith hadn't been kidding about the classes being hard. At my old school, you could get by on the Cliff's Notes version. Not here, apparently. By the time the bell rang, my hands were sweating. I should've worn a thinner pair of gloves.

I scribbled the last few points in my notebook and shoved it in my backpack. By the time I got up, everyone was gone except the teacher.

Mrs. Ramirez eyed me carefully with a small smile. "You're going to do fine, Tessa," Mrs. Ramirez said.

I forced a smile. "Sure." Honestly, I wasn't at all sure that she knew what she was talking about. I rushed to my locker and grabbed the books for my next class, where Meredith stood waiting by the door.

It wasn't just werewolf stuff I was behind on—it was everything. The new workload made it easier to ignore the wave of silence that followed me into every classroom.

By the time the bell chimed for lunch, I wanted to run back to my room and suck my thumb, but Meredith wrapped her arm around my shoulders. "Come on. It's not that bad."

"Totally not bad at all." The whine in my voice was pretty thick.

She quirked an eyebrow. "You put claw marks in the lab table."

"Oh. Um. Ooops?" That wasn't good. "Should I tell someone? Do I need to pay for it to get fixed?"

Meredith shook her head. "No way. Stuff like that happens all the time here. It's part of life. But maybe next time eat the sandwiches?"

I'd completely forgotten about them, but now that she said something, I realized that my stomach was trying to eat itself.

Shannon waited in the hall. "How was chemistry?" Her smooth Irish lilt made me smile, even though I wasn't sure that she liked me.

"It was fantastic," I said. "I think I'll go shoot myself in the face now, and avoid the pain and humiliation of flunking. How am I so far behind?"

Shannon laughed. The sound of it lessened the tension in my shoulders a little bit as we walked to the cafeteria. I didn't know how I was going to face the next round of classes after lunch.

I piled my tray high when we got there. I needed a plan, fast. In a mere forty minutes, my classes were going to take a turn for the strange and I was already at my stress limit.

Chris smiled when I took the seat across from him. "How's it going?"

"As well as can be expected, I guess."

"She's got Were classes after lunch," Meredith said.

Adrian laughed. "Be prepared to hear some funky shit."

"Don't scare the girl, Adrian. She's already panicking," Shannon said. "You should try to be open to what Mr. Dawson has to say in Were history."

"I'll do my best." But I still didn't know what Were history meant.

"Hell, I wouldn't buy any of it if I were you," Chris said. "But I know what I know." Chris' easy smile comforted me. I wasn't threatened or intimidated by him like I was with other guys.

Like Dastien.

Chris relaxed, reclining in his chair a little, muscles at ease.

"We all have martial arts and yoga class together," Meredith said. "It's fun, promise. So keep that in mind while you're in the more wolfy classes."

"Wouldn't picture you as a yoga kind of a guy," I said to Chris.

"Hey. You don't know me that well. Plus, I'm an artist. It's hip and arty to do yoga."

"Whatever, dude. You like it so you can check out all the girls' butts in downward dog," Adrian said, shoving Chris.

"Hey!" Chris shoved Adrian. "You're doing the same thing!"

"I'm a dude, dude. It's what I do."

I couldn't help but laugh at the boys. The tension in my shoulders eased some more and I smiled.

"You're really pretty when you smile," Chris said as he leaned toward me.

"Thanks," I said. My cheeks heated.

"It was merely my observation," he said with a wink. He settled back into his relaxed pose.

Yeah, I wasn't buying that for a second. The guys here were way too smooth.

The chair next to me scraped against the floor. Dastien stepped into the empty space and leaned in close to my ear. "I need to talk to you."

I froze, unable to look at him. My pulse sped up at the sound of his voice, his breath hot on my neck.

I was seriously messed up where he was concerned. He ignored me ever since he bit me and here I was, drooling at the chance to get close to him. This had to stop. My body, heart, and hormones might want to do whatever he wanted, but my head was in charge of the lot.

I turned away from him. "No. You can't just come over here and—"

He gently circled my arm with his fingers.

Jealousy. Rage. It swamped me. My stomach burned with it. My heart raced and I had an urge to rip something apart.

The intensity of his feelings made it hard for me to breathe. Was he really that mad?

He squatted down next to me. "Now. Outside."

169

His words weren't a demand, but a plea.

I tried to jerk my arm away, but he slid his hand down to twine his fingers with mine. Dastien's hair stuck out all over the place and his shoulders hunched down. He mouthed the word "please."

I glanced around the table. Shannon and Meredith's mouths hung open, but Chris sat forward, every muscle tense. His eyes were bright as he stared at Dastien.

I shook my head. I didn't need Chris to protect me. Dastien had already done his worst by turning me into a werewolf.

I was probably going to regret this. "You've got five minutes."

I followed Dastien out the door. He kept walking until he hit the tree line between the dorm and the classroom building. His grey T-shirt wasn't tight, but he couldn't have hidden his muscles if he tried.

Use your head, Tessa. "Are you going to keep walking, or do you want to talk?"

He spun, eyes glowing. "Stay away from Christopher Matthews."

I had a second to be freaked out by the eye change, before I got seriously pissed off. "You've got some nerve. You're the one with the fucking girlfriend."

"What? I don't have a girlfriend. Just please. Tessa. Just stay away from the guys."

"What do you call Imogene?"

"A friend. A very old, very loyal friend."

"Well guess what. Chris is a friend. A very new, very fun friend." My blood boiled. "News flash: I haven't done anything wrong. You have no right to drag me out here and yell at me. Hello? You bit me. Now, I'm here and struggling to keep my head above water. So you need to get your shit together."

His eyes dulled back to his normal light amber. "I—"

"No. Don't say anything. There's no taking back what you did." I took a couple steps toward him and poked him in the chest. "And now you want to boss me around? Tell me who to talk to!"

"You've been flirting with Chris." His voice was more growl than anything else.

"You're jealous. You're a big ball of lime green jelly." It wasn't a question. It was a fact. Maybe my visions were coming back. But why was it just words and emotions? Why didn't I "see" anything.

He punched the closest tree. I ducked as splinters rained down. "*Merde*, Tessa. *S'il vous plaît...*"

I took a giant step back. "What's your deal?"

He closed his eyes, breathing heavily. "I don't know."

"You have no right to tell me anything. To speak to me. To be around me. What you did is unforgivable!" I forced myself to take a breath, but it didn't help calm my anger. "You can't ignore me, and then come over, drag me out of lunch to tell me who I can and cannot talk to. I don't care—" My skin started tingling and my knuckles cracked. "Shit. This isn't happening. This can't happen. Christ. I didn't eat enough." Hair sprouted down my arms. My breath came out in gasps as I watched it thicken into fur.

"It's going to be okay, Tessa. Just let the shift take over."

I looked up at him, unable to keep a tear from

escaping. I crumpled to the ground. "No. I can't. I—" I panted as pain swept through my body, my muscles moving and shifting.

"If you don't want to shift, then let me help." Dastien leaned close to me. He brushed a gentle kiss over my forehead. "Shhhh."

The sound was balm to my soul. The pain drained away as my hands shrunk back to normal.

A branch cracked beside me. "Everything okay here?" Mr. Dawson said.

"Yes, Michael," Dastien said. He brushed the hair away from my face. "I think we've got it under control."

Yeah, maybe he thought so, but I was clearly far from being under control. Dastien helped me up, and I brushed off my jeans with shaking hands.

"Sebastian and Donovan should be here soon. We'll need to set a meeting to discuss the implications of what's happened between you two."

That didn't sound good. I didn't want to be punished for something that wasn't my fault, but I didn't want Dastien to get punished for it either. Did I?

"Understood," Dastien said like a good little soldier.

"When you say implications, what do you mean exactly?" I said.

"Don't worry about that." Mr. Dawson raised an eyebrow. "I think you've got a class to get to." He walked back to the school building.

I hated that. I was going to worry now for sure now.

Dastien ran his fingertips along my jawline. "*Je*

suis desole, mon amour."

I didn't know what *desole* meant, but I was sure *amour* was love.

Before I could catch my breath, Dastien sprinted into the woods. I kicked the tree as he ran. I wanted to call him back, have him tell me what the hell was going on, but restrained myself. The guy was pure brain-poison.

I leaned my back against the tree, and slid down until I was squatting. There was no way I could face my next class. Who were Sebastian and Donovan? And the "implications" Mr. Dawson was talking about couldn't possibly be the same ones Meredith told me about. Could they?

Leaves crunched as someone walked toward me.

"I never thought Dastien would run from anything," Meredith said.

I laughed unhappily. "Except me, apparently."

"I mean—it's Dastien. He's the strongest alpha we've seen in generations. He's amazing. Why is he always running from you?"

She gave me an expectant look, hands on her hips.

"I don't have some easy answer for you. It wasn't my bad breath that sent him packing."

Meredith stared into the forest for a moment. "I know Dastien. This isn't something that he'd do. Bite someone and then run. Hide."

I sighed. I didn't want to argue with her, but she wouldn't leave it alone. "Obviously you don't know him that well if Mr. Perfection would break the Law and bite someone. He ruined my life." I wanted to hit something, but there was nothing to hit. "And now I apparently have to face the consequences for his screw up."

Meredith flinched like I'd slapped her. "I just think that you should—"

"I'm really fucking tired of people telling me how I should feel about this or about how amazing Dastien is. I'm allowed to feel the way that I feel. And it seems to me, that I'm the one that got bit. I'm the one dealing with the change. And since there isn't anyone else here was has been bit, I don't think that anyone is qualified to give me any more fucking advice."

"Well, you clearly don't want my opinion."

"No. Right now I really don't."

Meredith shifted her weight from foot to foot trying to figure out what to say, but finally gave up and stomped back to the school building. Chris was waiting for her in the courtyard. She stopped to drag him along with her, as she gestured wildly.

I thunked my head against the tree. Shit. Why did I have to lose my temper? I'd probably lost the only friend I had at St. Ailbe's.

A group of girls had gathered in the courtyard to watch the scene. The whispers and giggles annoyed me.

"Show's over, ladies," I said.

They laughed again. If I concentrated, I could hear what they were whispering, but that wouldn't do me any good. Humming to myself I trudged back to the school building.

I grabbed my backpack and the books I needed from my locker and slammed it shut. This turning into a disaster of epic proportions. There was no way it was going to work. I pulled my schedule from my pocket, and looked down at what I had left.

As I scanned the sheet, I realized another awful gem. Didn't Meredith say that Dastien taught martial arts?

The bell rang, echoing through the now-empty hallway.

Great. I was late for the class taught by Mr. Dawson. That would really make him want to go easy on the "implications."

I dropped my head back against the locker, its metal cool against my skin. I had to stay strong. I'd been through bad times before. Nothing this bad, but still, I'd get past this. I had no other choice.

Chapter Twenty

Everyone was already in their seats when I finally walked into Were history, but Mr. Dawson had yet to arrive. The people in the room looked so much younger than the seniors, but that made it that much more apparent that I didn't belong. Having another incident was not an option. Ever. I made myself take a deep breath and then searched the room for an empty seat.

Guilt weighed heavy on my shoulders. Meredith really had made facing class easier, and I paid her back by being a raging bitch. I promised myself I'd apologize as soon as I saw her.

For now, I had to sit down. I spotted a space behind a guy with scraggly brown hair.

He twisted in his chair as I walked by. "What was it like being bitten?"

I paused for the punch line. He had to be kidding with this. "Are you seriously asking me?"

He nodded. "Did it hurt a ton?"

I dropped my backpack on the desk. "If you really want to know, you could always go find a rabid dog to bite you." I sat down and grabbed a notebook.

The girl next to me tapped my shoulder. "Excuse me, but I—we were wondering if you knew he was a werewolf?"

I scanned the room. All eyes were on me. Where in the hell was Mr. Dawson?

"The thing is Dastien is really, really nice," the girl continued. "He wouldn't have done something like that without a reason. So maybe you wanted to be a werewolf?"

Talk about an invasion of privacy. These kids had cajones for sure. "No, I didn't know. And I most certainly did not want to be a werewolf."

"But it's the rule," the girl said. "Before biting someone you have to make sure they're clear on what they're getting into. Plus you need their permission and the local alpha's."

"Well, if that's the rule then maybe you should be asking Dastien why he broke it."

She scoffed. "That would be rude."

I narrowed my gaze at her. "And it's not rude for you to ask me?"

At least she had the decency to blush at that.

"Imogene has been saying that—"

I growled. What was Imogene's problem? I forced myself to take ten deep breaths before speaking. "What's she saying?"

"Well, you know, she's Dastien's girlfriend and all..." The growl got louder and she shrank in her seat. "Well, maybe ex-girlfriend, I guess? I'm sure now that you're up and about, you'll be able to set the record straight."

I clenched and unclenched my gloved hands a few times. I had to get my emotions under control. Why should I care if Dastien had a girlfriend anyway? It just showed how much of a creep he was. I grabbed one of the sandwiches Meredith had given me this morning, took a big bite and chewed. If these people weren't going to stop asking me questions, then I needed to get a better handle on the whole hungry-wolf thing.

Mr. Dawson swept into the room, taking the focus away from me. A frenzy of movement rippled through the class as everyone pulled out notebooks and pens.

I noticed a weird phenomenon with the teachers. Whenever they walked into a room, there was this feeling—almost like a compulsion—to sit up and pay attention. It was worse with Mr. Dawson, and that bugged me. I kept my gaze on him as I slouched in my chair, slowly tucking into the second sandwich.

"Good afternoon, ladies and gentlemen. I trust that you are making our newest student feel welcome." He glanced my way, smirking when he saw how low I sat in my seat.

"Continuing from last lecture—Tenet Number Five of the Were Law. Who can tell me what that is?"

A blonde in front raised her hand. "Excuse me, Mr. Dawson."

"Yes, Nikki?"

"We were discussing Tenet Number One before class. There seems to be some issue with that right now, and the punishment for it."

What was it with the girls in this school? Mr.

Dawson scowled at Nikki. I smiled. Looked like Mr. Dawson didn't care for her either.

He pulled some papers out of his satchel and stopped at my desk. He looked down at me and sighed before handing me a syllabus. "Let's review what we know about biting humans."

Son of a bitch.

I quickly scanned the syllabus. They'd covered this two weeks ago. I plopped my head down on my desk.

Could today get any worse? *Please, I double dog dare you.*

I picked my head up in time to see a hand rise in the front row—a guy with spiky black hair.

"It's dangerous, which is why you have to have permission. Only one in a hundred guys can survive the transformation. And almost no girls live through it, more like one in ten thousand. Which is why some people think that boys outnumber girls so much." He pointed at me. "That's why everyone's curious about her."

Goosebumps broke out over my skin. I could've died? Did Dastien even think about that?

I couldn't let it show that he bothered me or they'd pick on me more. "Really with the pointing?"

"I'm willing to briefly discuss this, but let's leave Miss McCaide out of it," Mr. Dawson said.

That seemed highly doubtful.

"So, class, if it's dangerous—why bite?"

The boy in front of me raised his hand. "Because we police the world's big bads," said the boy in front of me. "We try to protect the humans and all supes— a.k.a. Supernaturals—from things that would out us. Things that would make the world into an ugly

179

place." He shrugged. "In the past, we've gotten low in numbers and so—" He chomped his teeth and the class laughed.

"And what are the big bads, as you pups like to call them?" Mr. Dawson said.

"Fairies, well the bad ones, black witches, vamps, demons. You name it, we hunt it," he said.

What in the hell were they talking about? Fairies? Demons? Vampires? Seriously?

Nikki's hand shot up again.

"Yes, Nikki?" Mr. Dawson said.

"Sometimes people find out about us and ask to get bitten." She glared at me.

I met her stare, and she looked away instantly.

"That's enough, Nikki." Another hand shot up. "Yes, Gabriel?"

"Why would someone break the Law and bite a human? We have rules for a reason."

I started a mental list of people to avoid. That dude was on it for sure.

"I know you all have questions about what happened, but I'm not going to answer questions about a private matter of one my students. Miss McCaide's been through a lot, and she still has a hard time ahead of her. I expect you all to treat her with respect and compassion. This ends now."

Nikki raised her hand again. "A whore—"

"Nikki!" Mr. Dawson said. This time power sizzled behind the command. The hair on my arms stood on end as it rolled through the room. "Did you not hear me? You will go—"

"You don't even know me. None of you know me." As much as I wanted Mr. Dawson to fight this battle for me, I couldn't let him. I'd had enough of this. "I'm not a whore. I didn't know he had a girlfriend. If he even had a girlfriend. To be perfectly clear, I sure as hell didn't ask for this. This right here is a nightmare." I motioned around the room. "And you've all just made it that much more shitacular. I hope each of you is feeling really awesome about that right now. And you," I pointed to Nikki, but she couldn't meet my gaze. "If you say one more word I swear to God I won't be responsible for what I do, you stupid—" The hot, woozy feeling was back with a vengeance. I was so done with this class. I grabbed my backpack and my half eaten sandwich.

"Tessa. Wait," Mr. Dawson called after me. Power backed the command, but I shook it off and kept moving. I heard shocked murmurs from the class but I didn't look.

I strode out the door, ran to the stairwell, and slammed into Dastien.

Why had I dared the day to get worse? I was seriously dumb sometimes.

Dastien's scent filled me. I wanted to bathe in it.

I pushed him away. It wasn't easy, but I had to. For my own sanity. I tried to step around him, but he blocked my way. "Move." I shoved him, but it was like trying to push a boulder.

"Tessa. Calm down for a second."

"Calm down? Do you know what I just went through in there?"

He tucked my hair behind my ear. "Tessa, I—"

I slapped his hand away. "No. Don't. I can't. Not right now." A tear slipped free. I wiped it away with my gloved hand. There was no way I would let him see me fall apart. "Please. Let me go."

"*Cherie...*"

"Please. Just let me be."

"If that's what you really want." He frowned and stepped aside.

I raced down the stairs and out into the courtyard. A black Expedition pulled between the buildings, narrowly missing me.

I slammed my hand on the hood of the car, like any good Angelino would do. "Hey. Watch it."

Two men stepped out of the car. Their power tingled along my skin making me stumble. I kept on walking to the dorm, but couldn't stop myself from sneaking a peek at them again.

"Very sorry, lass. We didn't see ya," one shouted to me. He wasn't very tall, but he commanded attention. The two shared a word, and then glanced at me before they walked toward the faculty building.

I tried to shake off the feeling that I should know who they were, but couldn't quite manage it. I looked back one last time before picking up my pace.

Chapter Twenty-One

Once I was in my room, I went straight for my cell. The tiny screen said nineteen missed calls. Oops. I flipped it open and pushed the number one button. Home. It didn't even finish ringing before she answered.

"Finally! Teresa Elizabeth McCaide. You called your brother but not me! And you tried to run away. What is going on over there?"

"Sorry." My voice cracked.

She took a deep breath. "Oh, baby. What happened?"

"Nothing. I'm totally, one hundred percent, a-okay." The wobble in my voice told my mother what she needed to know—that I was one hundred percent lying.

"Oh, Tess—"

"Mom. This isn't the place for me. There has to be somewhere else. Axel said something about the cousins?"

She cleared her throat. "I'm sorry, baby. The cousins can help, but they can't teach you what you need to know right now. If there's a chance that you can get a handle on your wolf without your cousins' help, then you have to try."

She was clearly mistaken. My emotions were all over the place, and I didn't feel one bit like myself. "There's no controlling this. I get so angry, and then—it's just bad. I'm afraid of what I've become."

Dad said something in the background. There was a rustle before I heard his voice. "Princess. I've talked to your mother's family, and your brother is right—they could help, but I don't think it's the best place for you right now. We've kept you away from them for a reason. Right now you have some freedom, even if it doesn't feel like it. If you got to them in the state that you're in right now, I'm worried for what they'll do to you. If there were another place, a better one, then I'd tell you. But Michael is there for you. He's a good guy. You can trust him."

"I thought you were mad at him."

"I was, but I also am your father and have to put aside any anger to figure out what's best for you now." He paused. "You know I wouldn't leave you somewhere without going over every option. Right?"

I sighed. "Yeah. I know that." But what was up with the cousins? I thought we moved here to be closer to them.

"Listen, Michael wants me to give it time, but I need to see you for myself. I negotiated him down. We're coming for a visit in two days. Can you hang until then?"

"Sure," I said, and hoped it wasn't total bull. Soft

taps came from my door. "I gotta go. Someone's here."

"I love you, kiddo. We all do."

"Love you, too." I ended the call and plugged my phone in to charge. I was stalling and I knew it. I didn't want to know who was on the other side of the door.

"Tessa," Meredith's voice came from outside. Three more knocks. "Tess? It's me. Can I come in?"

"Is it just you?"

"Yes."

I was relieved it was only her and disappointed at the same time. We were going to have to stop running away from each other at some point. "It's open."

She stopped at the foot of my bed and shoved her hands in her pockets. "I heard class didn't go so well."

I half-laughed. "You could say that."

"Well, at least you got me out of Meta."

"How?"

"Mr. Dawson pulled me. He's worried about you."

I guessed now was as good a time as any for that apology that I owed her. Taking responsibility for your actions was part of growing up, but that didn't make it easy. "About earlier…I'm sorry I snapped at you."

She held up a hand. "Don't even worry about that. We all snap sometimes and I was way out of line. I don't know what happened between you and Dastien, but you can trust me. I won't tell anyone. I swear." She shrugged one shoulder. "I know it's none of my business, but you might feel better if you talked to someone about it."

We sat there for a moment in the quiet. Bottling it

up was making it worse. I looked back at the poster hanging over my bed. Meredith had dealt with crazy just as long as I had. A different breed of crazy for sure, but she'd understand better than anyone I'd met.

So I totally spilled my guts. The only problem was that once I started talking, I couldn't stop. From my past, and embarrassing lack of friends, to moving to Texas and meeting Dastien—even about my visions. She sat on my bed and listened, with a blank look on her face.

When I finished, she didn't say anything for a minute. I chewed on my nails as I waited.

Finally, she leaned back on the bed and let out a huge breath. "Wow. No wonder you snapped. What Dastien did is unforgivable. Inexcusable. And completely unlike him. I mean, it's unbelievable. After I met you I didn't believe all the stuff about you seducing him, you just seem more real than that. But I thought it was at least consensual." She got up and started pacing beside the bed. "Why would he do that? What was he thinking! To risk his life and yours...I can't believe it. It doesn't make sense."

I opened my mouth, ready to defend myself, but she held up her hand.

"No. No. I believe you. But I'm blown away. I can't imagine what you must be going through right now. I thought you were just having trouble adjusting, but your reactions make so much more sense now." She collapsed on the bed.

I don't know what I'd expected when I started telling her my story, but for some reason, I didn't think it'd be sympathy.

"And I have a working theory about your visions."

I laughed. "Let's hear it."

She held up a finger. "One, I think they're going to come back. Some of the really powerful werewolves have special abilities. There's a Were I heard about that could move things with his mind. But since you're different now, they might be different."

The sense of relief was palpable. "Really?"

"Yep." She held up a second finger. "And tied to that is my second point—werewolves have stronger minds. We're not like humans, open for anyone to take a peek. It's why we're such good hunters. I mean what if there was a bad witch around? How would we be able to sneak up on her?"

This made sense, in an insane way. "Seriously?"

"Totally. I bet once you get settled with your wolf, you'll be able to see more and you'll have more control than you did as a witch."

"I wasn't a witch."

"You might not have known it, but that doesn't make it untrue. And now you're like a werewitch or something."

Oh God. I wasn't touching that one. I had more than enough issues to deal with.

"By the way, forget what that idiot Nikki said. In case you didn't notice the resemblance, she's Imogene's little sister."

It made so much more sense now. "What a bitch."

"I know, right? I've never gotten along with those two or any of their crew. You should've heard what they said when I put the blue streaks in my hair." She patted my leg. "Get up."

"What? Where are we going?"

"Last class of the day and we've got it together."

"No way in hell am I going." I put a pillow over my face. "I've had enough for one day." It came out muffled, but I didn't care.

"You can't hide. You can't let them win." She took away the pillow and stared down at me. "This will be good for you. You'll punch and kick all that anger out, and then the yoga will center you. It's a must. Plus, I'll be there and so will Chris, Shannon, and Adrian. It'll be fun."

"Martial arts really isn't my thing."

"It might not have been, but it is now. Trust me."

"But doesn't Dastien teach—"

"Crap. I didn't think of that." She paced beside the bed. "I hope Mr. Dawson is smart enough to sub out Dastien from our class, but if not, we need a plan." She stopped mid-step. An evil grin spread across her face. "Oh. I'm brilliant. I was going to pair up with you, but if Dastien is there, you have to pair up with Chris. It'll drive Dastien crazy."

"Wouldn't that be using Chris?"

She waved a hand through the air. "He won't mind." She went through my drawers and pulled out my usual yoga attire—stretchy fold-over pants, a sports bra, and a tank. "I'm going to get changed. I'll be back here in two and you'd better be up and ready to do some damage."

I shed my jeans and T-shirt. The thought of doing martial arts in front of class was incredibly intimidating. Not that everyone would stop to watch me make an idiot of myself, but they could. My day so far had included more than my fair share of being stared at.

I was slipping on my kicks when she rushed back

into my room. "Let's go," she said as she grabbed my wrist and dragged me to the door.

"I'm coming. Jeez. This can't be that exciting."

"If Dastien's there, it's going to be more than exciting."

Oh, perfect. She just wanted to watch the drama unfold. "For you, maybe."

"No maybe about it."

"Glad my drama can entertain you."

She pulled her blue and black hair in a high ponytail. "Me too. It was way more boring here before you came."

I probably shouldn't have liked that, but I did. Making someone else happy made me feel good.

Maybe this class wasn't going to be so bad. I trusted Meredith. She was the first person, not counting family, that knew about my abilities, and she hadn't freaked out.

How hard could it really be to get through one martial arts class?

Chapter Twenty-Two

The scent of sweat, plastic, and new wax hit me when Meredith opened the door to the gym. The center of the shiny hardwood floor was covered in bright blue mats. A fight was going on in the middle of them. They were moving so fast that I almost couldn't make out their faces, but Chris and Adrian were kicking each other's ass. They were stripped down to a pair of gym shorts. A few guys had their shirts on, but that seemed to be the norm for most of the guys there.

They were managing to block all the hits, until Chris flipped Adrian on his back. The slam echoed off the walls. A few people clapped and cheered as Adrian kipped-up effortlessly and punched Chris in the stomach. The sound of flesh hitting flesh made me break out in a sweat.

Shit. They weren't kidding about fighting. They were amazing.

And there was no way I could do this. I started to

walk back out the doors. "Tomorrow would really work better for my schedule," I said when Meredith called me on it.

She grabbed the back of my yoga pants, stopping my retreat. "You're going to be fine. I'm sure Dastien will start you out with something small. Right, Daz?"

Dastien strode toward us. He wore sweatpants, no shoes, no shirt. I'd never seen anyone with a six-pack in real life before. My heart started pounding.

Holy hotness, Batman. Someone call the fire department. This guy was out of control.

"I thought we talked about you not calling me Daz." Dastien crossed his arms, which made his biceps look huge. No wonder that tree had splintered earlier.

A pitiful whiney noise escaped me before I could stifle it. I covered my mouth with my hand.

The sounds of Adrian and Chris' fight stopped. I peeked around Dastien to see my classmates watching the drama unfold. I guessed Meredith had been right about that. Funny how I never thought I'd star in my own personal soap opera.

Chris ran over to us. "Everything okay?"

I said no at the same time that Dastien said yes.

"She smells scared—"

"I know what she smells like," Dastien said too quietly.

"Gross!" I said. "That's really fucking disgusting. Can we not discuss what your super-schnozes are smelling right now? Kay. Thanks."

Dastien sighed and closed his eyes for a second. When he opened them, they had gone from amber to bright yellow. "I was going to teach her, but maybe it's easier if I don't. Meredith?"

"I suck at explaining. Chris should do it." She nudged me.

"I'm in," Chris said.

"No," Dastien said.

This was going nowhere fast.

Shannon joined us. "You ready, love?" she asked Meredith.

"*Don't leave me*," I mouthed to Meredith.

"You're going to do fine. Kick Chris' ass for me." They walked to the other side of the gym, and started stretching.

Jerks. Leaving me alone to deal with the boys.

I glanced from Chris to Dastien and back again. "So, what now?"

"Fine." Dastien crossed his arms. His biceps bulged and I wanted to squeeze them to see if they were as firm as they looked.

Dastien cleared his throat, drawing my attention to his face. I blushed at his smirk. I hoped I hadn't been too obvious with my staring, but I had a feeling I'd been utterly transparent. Traitorous hormones.

"I'll be watching you," Dastien said.

That wasn't going to help me concentrate at all.

"Chris is the best student fighter in the school, but he'll go slow with you." I made sure to keep contact with his eyes as he talked. It was much harder than it should've been. "I'm assuming you've never taken any kind of class like this?"

"Does a Tae Bo video count?" I said.

"No," they said together.

That's what I thought. "Then, no."

"Okay, Chris. Start with basic stretches, then

stances. Make sure she doesn't break anything when she tries to throw a punch," Dastien said. "If she gets hurt, I'll make you hurt."

Yikes. Poor Chris. Chances were I'd probably hurt myself, but it wouldn't be his fault.

"I'll take good care of her." Chris winked at me as soon as Dastien walked away.

I looked Chris up and down. He'd put back on his shirt, which I was glad for. Dastien could possibly classify as the jealous type. But something struck me as off. "I thought you said you were artsy."

"I am."

"Artsy people don't fight like that."

"Maybe, but I'm a werewolf." He grinned with all his teeth.

I stared at the ceiling. "Mad. That's what everyone is here."

Chris put an arm around my shoulders and pulled me toward the mats. A growl echoed through the suddenly quiet gym. Dastien was watching us, as promised.

Chris started moving his arm, but I reached up and held it in place. "Where we headed, sensei?" I asked Chris.

Chris and Dastien were in some sort of a staring contest. Chris's blue eyes flared bright. Neither of them noticed me. Chris dropped his gaze to the ground and stepped away from me. "Let's go over there. Don't want to be too close to anyone else." His hands were balled into tight fists, knuckles white.

"What was that about?"

"Nothing." The smile he gave me was a shadow of his usual one.

"He's…what was the word you used…more alpha than you. Right?"

"He's more alpha than everyone. Except maybe Mr. Dawson. But no one knows for sure."

Interesting. I tucked that piece of info away for future reference. "What does that mean?"

"Alpha rules the pack."

He didn't add anything else to that little gem. I wasn't quite sure what he meant by "rules the pack." In what way? And to what extent? I'd save those questions for Meredith. She'd give me some real answers.

Chris stopped when we were at the opposite corner from everyone else. We spent the next ten minutes stretching every muscle—hamstrings, calves, shoulders—which gave me plenty of time to work up my fair share of nerves. Trying something new with an audience was not something I ever aspired to do.

"Feeling loose?" Chris said as he stood on one foot, stretching his quad.

I dropped my foot to the ground. "I guess?"

Sounds of light sparring filled the gym. I scanned the room, and caught a few pairs of eyes watching me, but thankfully not everyone was staring. I tried to avoid glancing at Dastien, but was drawn to the jerk. He was walking through the sparring pairs, giving notes and encouragement. When he reached Imogene, I turned away. That was one train wreck I wouldn't watch. The whole jealousy feeling was new to me, and I didn't care for it at all.

"This is a basic fighting stance." Chris' voice dragged my attention to the problem at hand.

I copied him, placing my feet shoulder width

apart and raising my hands. Chris circled around me, moving my feet into the "correct" stance. He twisted my shoulders a bit. "When you punch with your right hand, you want your right shoulder to be pulled back a bit. Then, as you punch, follow through with it."

I nodded like that made sense, but I had no idea what he was talking about. The weird part was that he wasn't joking or winking or smiling. That thing with Dastien had really gotten to him. He circled around me one more time then pointed to my gloves. "You might have some strange fashion thing going on, but the gloves have to go. You can't fight in them."

"Sure I can. What harm are they really doing?"

"I can't quite tell how you're holding your fingers. We're going to start punching and I don't want you to break anything."

Against my better judgment, I pulled them off and tucked them into my waistband.

Chris grabbed two hand targets from the other side of the gym. His shoulders were still hunched over.

It wasn't any of my business what went on between Dastien and Chris, but I felt responsible. I had to try to fix it. "I can't stand the way you're acting," I said.

He put the pads over his hands. "Look. I like you, but I can't fight Dastien and win." He stared at the pads as he talked.

What? Who said anything about Chris and Dastien fighting? "Why would you have to fight?"

"Dastien seems to have claimed you and—"

"Claimed me? What the hell does that mean?" I tapped my foot. No one was claiming me except me.

"I forgot for a second how new you are to this." I groaned, but he continued on before I could bitch about the lack of explaining going on. "We mate for life. Once you've been claimed, that's it. We all know that there's more guys than girls and—"

He was missing the point entirely. "Excuse me but I do believe I'm living in the age of equal rights for women. This claiming stuff isn't going to fly with me."

"It's not like that. I'm explaining this wrong." He started messing with the pads. "We just have a different way of viewing relationships than norms."

"Well, you boys are just going to have to deal where I'm concerned because I'm not getting claimed. I'll do the claiming when and if the time ever comes." I pulled my hair free from the band, shook it out, and sloppily put it back up.

Why were werewolves so confusing? And Christ, my life was majorly messed up if I was pondering the degree of confusion werewolves were causing in my life.

Still, I wanted to put a stop to whatever pain Chris was feeling. "Look. I'm not trying to be a bitch about it, so I'm sorry if I am being one. I like you and—"

He finally looked up. A lazy smile spread across his face. "You do?"

Oh, no. Now I'd really done it. I didn't mean I *liked* him liked him. "I mean I don't—" Dastien growled and I could physically fell his anger pulsing through me. The pain took my breath away. I cried out, silencing the room.

I hit the ground on my knees and rubbed my chest. My heart actually ached. Dastien watched us with golden eyes. The expression on his face matched the pain I felt. But how was I feeling his pain? I wasn't even touching him.

He stomped out of the gym, slamming the door behind him.

"I'm going to go make sure he's okay," Imogene said over the now silent gym. She said it sweetly, but the look she gave me was nothing nice.

Shit. Somehow I'd made a complete ass out of myself. This was not what I'd intended at all.

Chris knelt beside me. "Are you okay? What just happened?"

I took a deep breath and let it out slowly. Dastien's feelings faded when he left. He thought I was hitting on Chris, and that had hurt him. I was pond scum, total bottom feeding cockroach, for making him feel that much pain. I'd really stepped in it this time. There was no way out of it without hurting Chris' feelings. I couldn't set him straight right then. Not while everyone was watching.

I straightened and let go of the last lingering of anger and hurt. "Can we just, you know, have some fun doing this? I'm seriously nervous and everyone is staring now that Dastien…" I motioned to the doors.

"Don't worry about them. You're going to do fine. No one's expecting you to be Jet Li on your first day."

Shannon and Meredith went back to sparring in the middle of the gym. Shannon did a back flip to avoid Meredith's sweeping leg. She landed on her feet, and then kicked. Meredith grabbed Shannon's foot and twisted, sending Shannon spiraling to the ground.

They were amazing. "I don't think I'm ever going

to be able to do that."

"We train from the time we can walk. We might not be able to shift till we're teenagers, but our reflexes and strength are never as bad as a human's. You'll catch up."

"You don't know me well enough to say that. With my luck, I'll miss those pad things and hit you in the face."

"Wouldn't be the first time."

I tried to stand how Chris showed me. I needed to get out of class with the minimum amount of embarrassment. "This is so lame." I lightly tapped the pad with my fist.

"Oh, come on," Chris said. "Just do it."

"Okay, okay. Fine. But if I look like an idiot, it's your fault. I'm not taking any of the blame."

"Deal. You don't know what you're capable of yet, so don't limit yourself. Pretend that my hand is your worst enemy. The person who was the meanest to you. The one you dream about destroying." He slapped the pads together and then held them out again. "Hit it!"

For a second, I pictured the face of my ex-best friend from second grade—the one who started the nickname Freaky Tessa and spilled to everyone what I could do—but I wasn't that angry with her anymore.

The face morphed into Imogene's. Anger raged through me.

I got back in the stance and glared at the hand target. I put my whole body behind the punch, following through with my shoulder and twisting at the waist like Chris had shown me. As soon as my knuckles hit, I knew something was wrong but it was too late to pull back.

Chris flew three feet and slammed into the wall. The boom reverberated through the gym over the other sparring noises as he crumpled to the floor.

Dread swamped me. What had I done?

"Oh my God. Oh my God. Oh my God. I'm so sorry." I kneeled next to him. Chris' eyes were closed. "Wake up. Please. Please…"

He started laughing.

"Jerk." I shoved his shoulder into the ground. "This is so not funny. I thought I killed you."

He grinned. "Come on. It's kind of funny." He jumped up and grabbed me around the waist like I weighed no more than a teddy bear. "My little wolfie," he said as he spun us around in a circle.

I growled and smacked his shoulder.

He gave me a squeeze. "Don't think that this is going to get you out of doing more reps."

Maybe he really had hit his head. "No way. I'll kill you next time for sure. I don't know if you know this, but I am kind of super strong."

"I hate to break it to you, babe, but you took me by surprise and I went with the hit. Just a little drama to up the fun level." He winked.

The gym doors swung open and Mr. Dawson strode in wearing sweatpants and a T-shirt. "Dastien is sitting the rest of this class out." A series of groans echoed through the gym. More than a few people glanced my way.

Go ahead people. Blame the new kid. Not like Dastien had any responsibility in this whole situation.

"Settle down," Mr. Dawson said. "You'll be stuck with me for the next few days. I hear you haven't done your running yet. One hundred laps people. Now."

"One hundred. Is he serious?" I slapped a hand over my mouth. Oops. I didn't mean to say that out loud.

"Totally. You never know what to expect when Mr. D teaches the class. He's really good at kicking our butts," Chris said.

"How far is that? This gym is massive."

"It's about the size of four basketball courts put together and then some. Nine-ish laps is about a mile."

So eleven miles. That's nearly a half marathon. Axel and I ran nearly every morning before school, but only three miles. On a good day we hit five. This was a whole different ballpark. "This is nuts."

"Too much talking. Not enough running," Mr. Dawson said.

At least we weren't doing it outside. It was way too hot and humid to be running out there. I settled into a comfortable pace next to Chris. Something about the sound of everyone's feet slapping the wood was pleasant. It took me a minute to realize that we were all running in sync, every footfall matching. I stumbled, breaking the rhythm.

Chris grabbed me before I fell.

My feet matched the rest of the class again. "This is very *Village of the Damned*."

"What?"

"You know that horror movie where those kids all look the same and do the same thing. We're running in perfect sync. Exactly matching Mr. Dawson."

"That's part of being a pack. If we were racing, then we wouldn't match, but when you're a pack it's comfortable to move as one."

I made a face. "I never agreed to join any pack."

"Well...kinda, through Dastien, who is part of our pack."

Mr. Dawson sped up, and we met his faster pace.

"Does everyone. Join the pack?" It was getting harder to talk.

"Pretty much."

"What if. I don't want to?"

"You're a girl. You kind of have to."

I growled. Werewolves were kind of sexist. "You're pissing me off."

"Relax." He bumped me on the shoulder. "That's not what I meant. It's just, well, haven't you noticed the ratio?"

I let my silence speak for me.

"Not a lot of girls are born. That's why Imogene thinks she's so special. Her mom had two girls, which is unheard of. Those two think they're the shit because of it. Anyway, it's about a ten to one ratio. We take care of our women, and they're never without a pack."

I gave him a sideways glance, hoping he got the point. He was bringing out the feminist in me again and there wasn't that much ra-ra feminism in me to begin with.

"Look. There are tons of packs to choose from. All over the world."

Mr. Dawson sped up the pace again.

"You. Don't have. To choose. Now."

I was too winded to respond, but I didn't like where he was going with this.

The call of the pack slid over my skin, urging me

to stay in step with everyone else. It took me a couple of tries to get my footfalls to break their beat. It wasn't that I had anything against the pack stuff, but I didn't like the idea of having someone dictate my moves, even if it was just the way I was running.

"What. Are. You doing?" Chris said.

I couldn't answer him. Staying on the offbeat took all my concentration. I forced my legs to move faster until I was next to Mr. Dawson. Whispers followed in my wake. I was gasping as I reached him.

"You're just full of surprises," Mr. Dawson said with a smirk.

I matched his pace, but made sure my feet hit the ground just before his did.

Chapter Twenty-Three

Ninety-seven.

A drop of sweat rolled off my nose as I straightened my arms, completing a push-up.

Ninety-eight.

My arms felt like jell-o. I was losing form, and my lower back was starting to ache.

Ninety-nine.

I collapsed down on the ground. The grass felt cool on my hot cheek.

It hadn't taken that long to finish the laps around the gym with the pace Mr. Dawson set. He wasn't done with our torture by any means. As soon as we were done running, he took us outside next to the Cazadores track. I'd already done more sit-ups than I'd done in my entire life, a cool 124 and a half before I gave up. I was counting that half. I'd earned it. But the rest had done over 500. They were beasts. No wonder they all had amazing bodies.

Everyone was still trucking along, like there was

nothing to 200 push-ups. Their bodies moved to the ground and up together.

I rolled onto my side facing Chris and massaged my biceps. "I can't do it. I can't do one more freaking push-up." Triple digits wasn't something humanly possible. Or Tessa-possible.

Chris looked over at me, pausing an inch from the ground. "What are you? A girl?" Chris pushed himself off the ground, clapped once, before landing, and did it again.

"Oh, come on! Are you for real?" I shoved him.

"Hey! Watch it!" Shannon said as Chris tumbled into her.

A throat cleared above me. "Trouble, pups?"

I rolled myself up and sat on my heels. "Not anymore. I'm almost breathing normally again."

He crossed his arms.

"I can't do one more, Mr. Dawson. My arms have turned into cooked spaghetti noodles. And they're shaking." I held them out.

His mouth set in a firm line.

"I'm not used to this. It's a miracle I lasted this long." My stomach growled. "And I'm starving. There's no telling what could happen, and I don't want to be responsible for any more disruptions today."

He laughed. "Okay. Okay. You're done for now, but you need to be at my cabin in thirty."

If I was in trouble for not finishing the work-out, I was going to freak out. "Because I'm not as strong as Captain America over here?"

Chris picked up his pace at the attention.

Mr. Dawson shook his head. "No. You've surprised

me with how well you've done today. I expected you to drop out while we were running."

I patted myself on the back. "Give me a few days. I'll kick all their butts."

"Care to put money on it?" Chris said.

"What do you have in mind?"

"Alright. Enough," Mr. Dawson said. "You've got 30 minutes, Tessa. I don't want to have to come find you." The threat behind his words gave me the energy to get up. He started to walk away but stopped. "It's straight back behind the medical wing, okay?"

Shannon stopped mid-push-up. "Does that mean we're done here?"

"Nope. Listen, pups. We're hitting the course in five, everyone runs it once and then we'll do some asanas to finish. I want to see you working! Up and down! Now."

"You okay?" Meredith said from the ground.

"Fine." I stood on shaky legs. I was going to be in a world of hurt tomorrow. "Guess I'll see you later?" I brushed myself off and went back to the dorms to shower.

Even though I was physically exhausted, my mind raced as I showered. What did Mr. Dawson want to talk to me about? I wondered if it was because I ran out of his class. But he couldn't really expect me to stay there while that jerk, Nikki, said all those things about me. I hoped it wasn't the whole "implications" thing. Wasn't being a werewolf punishment enough?

That workout destroyed some major calories, and left my stomach feeling hollow. I threw on some clothes without really looking at what I was wearing and grabbed a thin pair of lace gloves. I took a sandwich and soda from the common room as I left, eating as I walked.

I bumped into Dastien on the way to Mr. Dawson's cabin.

"Hi?" I said.

He stopped to let me walk in front of him. I looked over my shoulder and he was right behind me. "Are you following me?"

"No." He grinned. "We're going to the same place."

He didn't say anything as we walked. I moved to walk next to him and gave him a very overt once-over. He was wearing a pair of khaki pants and an Underworld T-shirt for their "best of" album.

Why did he have to be so awesome? Next to Nine Inch Nails, Underworld was pretty much my favorite band. "Nice shirt," I said.

He rolled his eyes. "Sure."

"I'm being serious. I love Underworld."

"Fine." He raised an eyebrow. "Then what's your favorite song?"

I walked backward, facing him. "Back to testing me?"

He shrugged. "I have unusual taste in music. Most people don't know anything about the groups on my shirts, but they always have a comment."

By "people" he totally meant girls. He thought I was hitting on him. I was, but that was beside the point. I went back to walking normally before I tripped over something. "'Born Slippy.'"

He glanced at me out of the corner of his eyes, and I stuck out my tongue at him. He stopped walking. "That one's too popular."

"Fine. How about 'Cowgirl.'"

"Another."

He thought he could break my Underworld knowledge. How cute. "Pearl's Girl."

He laughed.

"King of Snake."

"Okay, I believe you."

"'Moaner.' I can keep going."

He laughed harder.

"'Push Upstairs.' 'Rez.' 'Jumbo.'"

He put his hand over my mouth. "Enough."

When he lowered his hand, I crossed my arms. "Never question my love of obscure electronic music."

"As it happens, I like your shirt too."

Crap. What shirt was it? I glanced down, and met his gaze. I waited patiently, tapping my foot.

"'Flaming June.' 'Knowledge of Self.' 'Somnambulist.'" He started singing. "*Simply being loved, loved, loved. Is more than enough.*"

He had to have an amazing voice. I shoved him. "Okay. I got it. When it comes to music, we're totally weirdo twinkies."

Dastien's smile disappeared. "I think you might find it's more than that."

I didn't know what to say to that.

He cleared his throat. "Do you really like Chris?"

I gave him my best sly grin. "Sure. He's a nice guy."

"Don't be dense."

I squared my shoulders. "You really think calling me a fancy word for dumb is going to get you anywhere?"

"That's not what I meant and you know it," he said softly.

This guy was more than frustrating. "Honestly, I have enough to deal with right not without worrying about hurting a couple of boys' feelings. I need time to figure this out." I motioned to myself.

"You're not answering my question."

"And you'll notice that I never accused you of being dense."

"Then I'll ask a different question. What do you feel for me?"

God. Like that wasn't a loaded question. "I feel so many things for you that I don't know my ass from a hole in the ground." I sighed. "Let that be enough for now."

He started to close the distance between us but dropped his hand before it could touch my face. "It's enough."

"Good. Because now we're late."

We walked around the medical building to a small cabin. I climbed up the three steps onto the porch. A well-worn, wicker rocking chair sat next to the door. Before I could knock, the thick wooden door swung open.

"Come inside," Mr. Dawson said. He'd changed from his workout clothes into a pair of faded jeans and a green T-shirt. The piney soap from his shower blocked all other scents.

The cabin was one large room. The bed stood against the wall to the right. A door next to the kitchen opened just enough so that I could see the bathroom. To the left, was a small sitting area. A kitchen with a small breakfast nook that looked out to the trees took up the rest of the room. The two men I'd seen parking the Expedition earlier stood up from their chairs in the sitting area when we entered.

"Tessa McCaide, meet Sebastian Braun and Donovan Murry. Two of the Seven," Mr. Dawson said.

Oh crap.

Chapter Twenty-Four

Dastien stepped in front of me. "I take full responsibility. She had no choice or option."

What the hell was he thinking? He couldn't say that. He'd be killed.

"We'd like a word with you. It isn't an easy thing to bite someone. Especially if you've not gone mad, which I can see for myself that Michael wasn't lying." Donovan's Irish sing-song voice was really pleasant to listen to. His hair was black, but his eyes were a crystal, clear blue. "Have a seat, lass, while Dastien tells us what he's about."

I started to step around Dastien but he rumbled a low growl.

"Quiet down," Sebastian said. "No harm will come to her."

Dastien stepped aside. I sat across from Donovan. His power whispered along my skin.

"Tone it down, Dono," Sebastian said.

Donovan capped his powers so much that I had to

check to see if he was still sitting there. Dastien sat next to me.

Sebastian's white-blond hair and fair skin made his moss colored eyes stand out. "Why'd you do it?" Sebastian said as he settled into the last spot, across from Dastien.

They cut straight to it. I shifted in my seat, waiting for Dastien to answer.

He cleared his throat. "I didn't set out to turn her. My wolf momentarily took control. It seems he has chosen her as his mate."

What the hell was he talking about?

Donovan leaned across the table. "Did he really?"

Yeah. Did he? I stared at Dastien, and he shifted in his seat before saying anything. "Yes, Sir. Once she got near, there was nothing I could do to stop it."

Sebastian studied me. "Interesting that your wolf would choose a human." His German accent showed through on the word "wolf" turning the "w" to a "v."

Great. So his wolf wanted me but I wondered if he—the guy—actually wanted me. Was that possible?

Mr. Dawson stepped to the table. "I think you might find her interesting on a couple of different levels."

"Really?" Sebastian reached his hands across the table toward mine.

I put them on my lap, out of his reach. The look he gave me, like I was a new treat to try out, didn't ease my mind.

"Don't hide them," Sebastian said. "Take off your gloves."

His power rippled along my skin. Goosebumps followed in its wake. "I'd really rather not," I said,

211

ignoring his command.

Sebastian turned to Mr. Dawson. "I see what you mean."

"Do as he says." Mr. Dawson gave me a nod of encouragement. "It'll be alright."

He didn't know that. In fact, I was nearly certain he was wrong. Meredith told me that certain werewolves had developed special powers, and I'd bet my ass Sebastian was one of those wolves.

I met Mr. Dawson's gaze. "If something happens that I don't appreciate, I will never trust you again. And I will do my best to get out of here as quickly as possible."

Donovan laughed. "She's got you by the balls, Michael."

"Just don't make a liar out of me, Sebastian," Mr. Dawson said. "You cost me the two strongest wolves from my pack and there'll be hell to pay."

I don't know what all that meant, but I figured it was something significant. And I guessed I had to do as they asked. "For the record, this is a terrible idea." I pulled off my gloves, folding them in my lap, and reached across the table.

I closed my eyes and waited for the onslaught as Sebastian grabbed my hands.

Nothing. I got nothing from him.

And then I felt it. A tingling in the back of my mind. He was reading my thoughts, my feelings, my memories.

"Hey!" I tried to pull my hands from his, but he tightened his grip. "Stop." The invasion continued. He picked at my most private memories. Poked into the worst times at school in LA. Uncomfortable didn't even begin cover it. "I said stop!" I visualized him in my mind and shoved him as hard as I could.

He dropped my hands. "I've never been so cleanly pushed out before." He clapped once. "*Ach, mein Gott!* I can't wait to see what she can do in a few years." He nodded to Donovan.

"Teresa Elizabeth McCaide, you've been pardoned," Donovan said.

"Good. Because I didn't do anything in the first place." I muttered the last bit under my breath, but from the smirk on Sebastian's face, he heard me.

"Dastien Brys Laurent," Donovan said.

He stood straight. "Yes, sir."

"You're not to leave Cedar Ridge until you have this matter well settled. She'll make you work for it." Donovan winked.

Dastien's eyes flashed to gold. "She'll be mine." The words sent a shiver down my spine.

I opened my mouth, hopefully with a snarky comment, but nothing came out. I was paralyzed under Dastien's gaze.

"We'll have a word with you in private now, Dastien." Donovan's words drew my attention. "It's been lovely meeting you, Teresa. You'll want to go eat now. Your wolf is perilously close to slipping free and from what I've heard, you're not wanting to let her out yet."

I couldn't feel it, but I wasn't going to argue with him. I barely stopped myself from running out the door.

When I got to the cafeteria, it was mostly cleared out—except for the guys. I spotted Meredith at the usual table with the gang, and waved before grabbing a tray. The boys surrounded me.

"Can I help you?" I said, a little more harshly than I meant to, but they were really invading my space. That wasn't something I ever enjoyed.

Gabriel from Were history class stepped forward. "It's you we want help. Can I carry your tray for you?"

He'd been a jerk to me in class and now he wanted to help me. Why? Because he thought I'd turned down Dastien? Yeah. That was so not going to work for me. "Thanks, but I'm fine."

The guys formed a wall when I tried to go to the table. Why were they being so weird? "Excuse me," I said, trying to get them to move out of my way.

"You didn't get enough red meat. You'll need more." Gabriel chimed in again.

A redhead that I didn't recognize from any of my classes stepped forward. "Allow me." He started to pile more food on my plate.

"Okay, I think that's good. I'm going to go sit down now."

They cleared a path for me. By the time I got to the usual table, Meredith was laughing so hard tears rolled down her cheeks.

"Laugh it up, roomie." I dropped my tray onto the table, rattling the silverware. "What the hell is going on? Where are all the girls?"

She kept on laughing. I shot her what I hoped was a mean look. She put her hand on her chest and took a deep breath. "I'm sorry. I had to wait and see your face. Word got around about how you refused Dastien in class, and well, you're fresh meat now." She started cracking up again.

Refused Dastien? "What?" I gave Chris a pleading

look.

"When you got between me and Dastien, you turned him down and opened yourself up to new claims." He took a bite of his roast beef. "The girls are pissed." He said the last word in a high pitch squeal. He was enjoying this. The bastard.

"Let me get this straight. All the girls hate me now and the guys want to see if they have a shot?"

"Yep," he said.

"Great. Just great." How did I always manage to get myself into the worst situations? "But you're not mad?" I said to Meredith.

"It's too funny to get mad over. Plus, I happen to think you'll end up with Dastien."

Chris frowned. "You don't know that."

I pushed my tray away and put my head down on the table.

Someone tapped my shoulder. "You should really eat, Tessa."

I swirled in my chair to see Gabriel standing behind me. I gave him my best scowl and he took a step back. "How come they're not like this with you?" I said to Meredith.

"Long story."

I waited for her to say something else, but she stayed quiet.

The guys backed off after I started eating. I found that eating slowly was key. If I ate too fast, then I'd feel full, but it wouldn't last for more than a few minutes. It took me forever to actually fill up, but hopefully that would be enough to keep myself from Hulking out for now.

Meredith and I walked to the dorms together after

dinner. The air had cooled. The cicadas' song soothed me as we strolled. By the time we got to the dorm, the girls were already huddled around the TV watching the news.

"What's going on?" Meredith asked.

Imogene glared at us. "Shut up."

I truly despised that girl.

The reporter on screen had hair teased into a big lump on the back of her head, making her look a little alien-like. The banner said her name was Rebecca Nunez. "...have been tracked by the FBI since they crossed the Oklahoma–Texas border. If they continue at the same speed, the killer or killers could be in the Greater San Antonio area in days. Victims have been brutally murdered, throats ripped out and their bodies drained of all blood..."

Nikki leaned into her sister. "So they were right? They're coming here."

Wait a second. Drained of blood? They couldn't be talking about what I thought they were about. Could they? "A vampire?"

Imogene glared again. "Vampire*sss*." She went back to watching the TV. "They're being messy. They want us to know they're coming."

"Why would they do that? What would they gain by finding us?"

Imogene swiveled around and shoved my arm.

I just have to hold on a couple more days and then they'll finally be here. They'll take care of her.

How did she know for sure that the vampires were coming here? And who exactly were they going to take care of? I had a feeling it was me, but maybe that was narcissistic.

Something she said stuck with me though. My first night here when I'd tried to run away, I overheard Mr. Dawson and Dastien talking about some threat coming south. Maybe it was my fault that they were coming here? Or mine and Dastien's fault.

That didn't sit well with me. Especially if Imogene was referring to me in the vision I had.

"Come on. I have a TV in my room," Meredith said.

Shannon followed us and shut the door. I sat on the fuzzy magenta rug and tried to think rationally, but that proved hard.

Meredith plopped on her bed and grabbed the remote.

"—recommend that you stay indoors after dark. Authorities asked that if you see anything suspicious, call 9-1-1 immediately. The governor's office released a statement—"

Meredith muted the TV. "The governor's office doesn't know squat." She looked to Shannon. "You think the vamps are planning something?"

"Maybe. Probably. I hope we don't have to move the school."

"Move the school?" I asked.

"Every once in a while, bloodsuckers try to find the school," Shannon said. "But they've never gotten this close to any of them. If they actually found us, we'd have to move or else face God knows how many attacks."

That made sense, but it still seemed like overkill. Not to mention bad timing. I didn't want to move any farther away from my family than I already had. "How can you be sure it's vampires?" I asked.

"Throats ripped out. Drained of blood," Shannon said. "I'm sure even you've seen a vampire movie."

I didn't like the way she talked to me, but tried to ignore it.

Meredith patted my shoulder. "Don't worry. I'm sure some Cazadores will fix this whole problem before the vamps get anywhere near us."

"Do vampires and werewolves talk at all?"

Shannon snorted. "Don't be ridiculous. The only time we talk is when we're killing them."

Maybe my visions were still off. They definitely weren't like they were before. Maybe the "they" Imogene had been talking about were werewolves since they were connected with her father. But why would she be thinking about that while the reporter talked about a brutal murder?

If I was right and Imogene had something to do with the vampires, what could I do about it? And who would believe me?

Chapter Twenty-Five

By Thursday morning, I entered full-on-annoyed mode. Everywhere I went, boys followed. And while the boys were busy fawning, the girls were driving me completely mental. If they didn't stop with their whispering and staring and rude remarks, someone was going to get hurt. I was pretty sure that person would be me, because I'd seen them in martial arts class. But still, it was enough to make me forget that.

Dastien was conveniently MIA. I hadn't seen him since the meeting with Donovan and Sebastian. I told him to give me time, so it was on me if he was trying to do that. But still. The dude needed to grow a pair.

I tried to distract myself by figuring out what Donovan meant with "getting it settled." The word "mate" reverberated in my mind constantly. For some reason, it seemed too personal to share with Meredith, so I was on my own with figuring it out. I tried to do more research on the web, but who knew how accurate that was.

The Werewolf's Bible might have the info I needed in it, but the only time I picked it up, I got one of the most messed up visions I'd ever had. I'd tried to read it with my gloves on but the pages were worn and delicate. I took off my gloves.

Anger made me sweat. Then fear made me shiver. Despair. Confusion. Anger. Rage. Fury.

I'd thrown the book across the room, and pages ripped from the old binding. It took me a full hour to calm down. To separate my own feelings from those in the vision.

Suffice it to say I wouldn't be attempting to read it anytime soon.

I was mulling it over again at lunch as I ate my thrice-daily mountain of food, but the whole thing was so alien to me.

"Look at that," Chris said.

I turned to see one of Imogene's friends—a blonde whose name I didn't know—sitting at a table alone with one of the guys—Stephen? Stefan? Something starting with an "s."

"Hope found her guy?" Meredith said.

Adrian laughed. "Yeah, right. That girl is a tease. She's got a couple more months until she turns eighteen. No way is she settling on one until then. Guaranteed. I'm still in the running."

Chris and Adrian fist bumped.

Meredith shoved Adrian. "I'm going to get more food. Anyone need anything?"

"Nah. I'll come with," Chris said.

Adrian got up too, leaving Shannon and me alone in uncomfortable silence. She and I weren't exactly clicking. We'd gotten into a habit of ignoring each other's existence, and I was totally fine with that.

I chewed on my lip, thinking to myself. "I wish everyone would shut it with the whole 'mate' thing," I muttered, not intending it to really be heard.

"Listen, love," she said in a condescending tone. "Every girl here will be mated by the time she's eighteen. It's the way that it works. Girls are precious, and the males protect them."

I tried to keep the disgust off my face. "Eighteen is barely legal. No one should decide who they're with at that age. You don't even know who you are yet."

"Some choose earlier."

"It's not the Stone Age anymore." I ran my fingers through my hair. I didn't have long until my birthday, and couldn't imagine choosing anyone…okay, I could totally picture choosing Dastien, if he were anywhere to be found. "Whatever might seem normal to you, isn't to me. It's not right."

"Tough luck. You're going to have to choose a mate soon." She pointed at the next table over. "See there, three boys have been courting Samantha. She's favoring Paul at the moment, but she could change her mind." She spun in her seat. "And there. Nikki is already promised to Jacob." She stared at me. "Look around. Loads have already made their choices."

I looked from table to table. There were only a few girls who hadn't chosen, and they had a bunch of guys with them. And there were still a few tables of just boys—who were all watching me. I did a finger wave to them. They stood—ready to jump at my request. It was beyond creepy. And more than a little sad. They didn't really want me. They just wanted a girl, and I'd do just fine.

"Don't tease them," Shannon said.

I crossed my arms. "If it's all so important to choose, how come you haven't?"

She grinned, and I didn't like the look of it. "I've got my eye on one. And since you've ditched him for the half-breed, I'm sure I'll get him."

I should've known. Every girl, their moms, aunts, and female cousins wanted a piece of Dastien. I'd seen him with his shirt off, so it was understandable, but that didn't mean it didn't bug the crap out of me. But who did I ditch him for? "What half-breed?"

"You like to call him Chris."

What a bitch.

Some people in LA liked to call me that since I was half-Caucasian and half-Mexican. It was safe to assume that "half-breed" was an insult in any culture, even supernatural ones. That she called a friend one was inexcusable. "You seem to think real highly of your friends."

"I like him fine, but he isn't a suitable mate. His great-grandfather was bitten. So it's fitting that you two would pick up."

And now she was calling me a "half-breed." Why was Meredith friends with her? "And you think you'll get Dastien?"

"Rightly so."

It took everything in me not to punch her in the face.

"If you weren't here, all of those boys around you would be vying for the attention of the undecideds. They're used to more attention, and they hate you right now." Her laugh wasn't even a little sweet. "You're a new element in the equation and have messed up the whole bloody lot. I'm quite enjoying the drama."

The one thing that made me happy was imagining her and Imogene fighting over Dastien. That would be something to watch. I'd bring popcorn. "Well, I have too much self-respect to beg some guy to be with me. Dastien's going to like who he wants, and unfortunately, none of you shewolves have a say in it. And if you think fighting over a boy is going to gain their attention, then you're sadder than I thought."

"Damn skippy," said a voice right behind me.

I jumped out of my seat. "Axel?" I turned to find my whole family standing behind me.

Well, this was awkward.

Time for a swift subject change. "Mom! Dad! What are you doing here?" My voice was way high-pitched. A clear give-away. I was nothing if not smooth.

Mom pulled me in for a quick hug and then pulled away to look at me. "You look amazing. I don't know what I was picturing, but you look beautiful...And a little thin. Are you eating?"

I rolled my eyes. "Yes. It's just that this whole change burns through a ton of calories. I'm still figuring out how much to eat."

"Tessa," Dad said.

I gave him a hug. "Thanks for coming and bringing Mom."

"I told you I would. And Axel wanted to say goodbye. He's headed to Austin in the morning."

Axel elbowed. "I'll only be a little over an hour drive away. Less if I speed. Call me if you need me."

I nodded. "Thanks."

"Who's that hottie?" Axel said.

I spun to see Meredith walking up with Chris and Adrian. "That's my roommate. She's not legal."

Axel laughed.

"Be nice," I whispered to him. "I'd like you all to meet my Mom, Gabby. My Dad, John. And my brother, Axel. This is Adrian, Chris, Meredith and Shannon."

My Dad looked less than friendly toward Shannon. Crap. He'd heard more than I wanted him to hear.

"The feeling's mutual," Meredith said to my brother.

Axel looked confused, so I filled him in. "You called her a hottie. Everyone here has excellent hearing."

He winked at her. "Thanks."

I elbowed Axel again. "Down boy."

The bell rang and everyone started filing out. "We're going to head to class," Meredith said. "See you last period?"

"Sure."

They said their good-byes.

When everyone was gone, Mom smiled. "Meredith and the boys seem nice."

"Totally."

"What was that Shannon girl saying about teenage marriage?" Dad crossed his arms.

Oh sweet baby Jesus. This couldn't be more embarrassing. "Don't worry. I didn't drink the Kool-Aid." As I said that, Mr. Dawson and Dastien walked into the cafeteria. The room felt ten degrees hotter as I watched Dastien.

Boy did he make the Kool-Aid appealing.

Axel stepped in front of me, blocking my awesome view. "You're supposed to be staying away from her. That was the deal. This is the second time I've seen my sister since you attacked her and both times you were there."

I slapped Axel on his arm. "What the hell, dude."

"Why don't you go take over my class?" Mr. Dawson said to Dastien.

"I think that'd be best," Dad said.

Dastien nodded and left without a word.

I wondered how much of him staying away from me had to do with his guilt and giving me time, and how much was everyone trying to keep us apart. "I know everyone thinks I'm fragile right now, but I'm okay. I think with everything that I've had to deal with, you should trust me to figure out the whole guy thing on my own."

Axel got in my face. "You can't actually want to date that guy. He attacked you—"

My cheeks burned. "Attacked is a bit of a harsh word for what happened." I couldn't stand by and let them think that about Dastien. "It was an accident."

"And the next time he hits you?" Mom asked.

My mouth dropped open. Holy crapola. They thought I was in an abusive relationship? "Not you too. Everyone can calm down. No after school special needed here. I'm not really in any kind of relationship, so it's fine." I sat down in the chair, and everyone moved to take a seat around the table.

"It'd be best if everyone moved to the opposite side of the table from me and Tessa," Mr. Dawson said.

I scowled at him. "I'm not going to hurt my family."

He laughed.

My scowl must not have been as intimidating as I thought.

"It's a necessary precaution if you want to continue this conversation," Mr. Dawson said.

My family got up and moved across the table. The cafeteria was completely deserted. Even the staff had left, probably just in the kitchen cleaning, but it was enough to give me the feeling of privacy.

Which was essential because my blood was boiling. Keeping my cool was a struggle. Mr. Dawson had a point, but that didn't mean I had to like it. "Look. I'm not saying I'm going to marry the guy—"

Mr. Dawson cleared his throat.

My heart skipped a beat before it raced. "What? You know something that I don't?"

"I wouldn't confirm or deny anything at this point. Let's wait and see what happens."

Dad did not like that. He slapped his hand down on the table. "No one is forcing a man on my daughter."

"I would never..." Mr. Dawson took a breath. It was the only hint that he was pissed. "We're keeping this quiet, but I guess you should know that Dastien Laurent is her mate. His wolf took control to claim her. It was an accident and one Dastien wishes he could undo. Or re-do in an entirely different manner. But what's done is done. Now's the time to support Tessa as she figures out what this means and what it is she wants."

Axel sat back in his chair and crossed his arms.

"You can call it whatever you want, but that asshole turned my sister without permission. That's not okay. Not in my book."

My parents nodded. My family was on my side, but it sure felt like they weren't.

A man with chin length straight blond hair streaked with gray came to stand next to the table. He wore a charcoal three-piece suit—which was overkill for Cedar Ridge, Texas. "I see you're still having trouble controlling your student body, Michael."

Mr. Dawson stood in one fluid movement, forcing the man to take a step back. Their gazes clashed, and the man's fists clenched as he looked away.

"And what have we here? Three humans on campus?" His gaze fell to me. "Ah. This must be the bitten girl."

"Careful, Rupert," Mr. Dawson said. "You'll not insult any member of this family."

I didn't like Rupert standing over me, so I stood. Everything in the room fell away as I waited for him to look away. When he finally did, fur rippled along his face and was gone so quickly I thought I'd imagined it.

Mr. Dawson put his hand on my shoulder. His grin made me feel like I'd just done something awesome, and I couldn't help but return it.

"This is Rupert Hoel. Nikki and Imogene's father."

That didn't surprise me in the least. I liked this guy just as much as I liked his daughters.

"This is the McCaide family." Mr. Dawson turned to fully face Rupert, crossing his arms. "Is there a reason why you're on my campus unannounced?"

"I wasn't aware I needed to announce myself." Mr. Hoel smoothed down his vest.

"It's always necessary. This is a closed campus and you know that. Wait in my office."

Go, Mr. Dawson. I snickered as Mr. Hoel stormed off, slamming the cafeteria door behind him.

Mr. Dawson winked at me. "He's not going to like my office much. Donovan and Sebastian are there and the three of them don't get along."

"I won't pretend to know all the ins and outs of what's going on here, but I'm learning fast." Dad had his no-bullshit face on. "I want to be perfectly clear—what might be normal for you is not normal for my daughter. She is—was—human and I won't have anything forced on her that she's uncomfortable with. Or that her mother and I are uncomfortable with."

Thank God the cafeteria was empty. I shifted in my seat. "I don't think anyone is going to forget that I was bitten, Dad."

"I think the thing to remember is that this is a transition for all of you." Mr. Dawson's voice was calm and even. He was taking Dad's intimidating stare better than I could. "You've lost the old Tessa, but she's not really gone. She might have had a rough time before, and maybe at the moment it's harder—but I think it's all set her up to become a very strong person. I think you'd all be surprised by what she's already accomplished here."

My cheeks burned. I wasn't sure I'd accomplished anything.

"I would never intentionally make a member of my pack uncomfortable. I swear that I will watch her as if she's my own. I've given you full access to St.

Ailbe's. Feel free to visit her whenever you feel the need. She's not my prisoner. I'm only here to help as she learns her new abilities."

The rest of the conversation went normally enough. They asked about classes and my friends, and ignored all things Dastien-related.

After a bit, I walked them to the parking lot with Mr. Dawson supervising so I wouldn't accidentally wolf-out on them. They'd brought me my car, just in case I needed it for some reason. My parents said their good-byes, promising to come back and visit whenever I wanted them to.

It was harder to say good-bye to Axel. He was going to college, and I wouldn't see him for months. I knew that he was always going to go, but the reality proved to be a bit harder than I expected.

Axel held out the keys to my car. "I picked out an awesome car for you."

I snatched them from his hand. "You better have been good to her."

He pulled me in for a hug. "I might be farther away, but I'll always be here for you."

"Thanks. Love you."

"Me too."

My heart was heavy as I watched their car disappear from sight.

Mr. Dawson put his arm around me, and turned me back toward school. "Come on. Let's get you some ice cream. I hear it can help at a time like this."

"That'd be good. Thanks."

When we got back to the cafeteria, he disappeared into the kitchen. He came back carrying two light brown pints with gold lids. "Here you go." He slid one to me.

"Blue Bell?"

He set his spoon down. "Please tell me you've had Blue Bell."

I shook my head. "But I like Cookies 'n' Cream, so I'm sure this is fine."

"Blue Bell is more than just fine. It's *the* Cookies 'n' Cream. Trust me. I'm a connoisseur of all things ice cream."

I pulled off the top. It looked like ordinary Cookies 'n' Cream to me. "If it's so amazeballs, why haven't I heard of it before?"

"Because you're from California. They make it in Brenham, Texas and they only deliver it themselves to locations that they can easily get to in their refrigerated trucks. Although when I've lived other places, I've had it shipped to me from the factory. Costly but necessary."

I shook my head. Dude was out of his mind. I took a bite and moaned. "Holy shit. This is good."

"Told you."

"So you and ice cream, huh?" It made him more of a real person, instead of this odd authority figure.

"Food. All kinds. When you've got to eat so much of it, you get to know the difference between good, bad, and excellent." He pointed to the ice cream with his spoon. "This is excellent."

"So do you cook too?"

He nodded. "Most wolves do. Especially those my age."

That made sense. I wanted to ask him how old he was, but he beat me to the next question.

"Can you cook?" he asked me.

I shrugged. "Mexican food, for sure. With a recipe—anything else."

We got into a conversation about Mexican food, most importantly the differences between Mexican food among the border states.

A pint of Blue Bell Cookies 'n' Cream later and I was feeling better.

I stared down at the empty carton. "I can't believe I ate the whole thing."

Mr. Dawson laughed. "I can. You've got to eat more. And you're about to burn all that off, so it's not even going to do you any good. Let's go."

I patted my stomach. "Just when I thought I had a nice food baby going on, you gotta ruin it."

As we walked to class, I was more relaxed. Everything felt a little more okay.

But then again, it could've just been an ice cream high.

Chapter Twenty-Six

That evening we were watching the news on Meredith's TV. It'd become a nightly habit. Every time we huddled around and waited to see how close the vampires were, but this time there was no mention of the "killers."

"Maybe the Cazadores finally found them?" Meredith said as she muted the sound.

"We would've heard," Shannon said. "Yesterday they were only fifty miles away from here."

"But they won't come here, right?" I said.

"I hope not, but they must be close." Shannon sighed. "If the Cazadores are having this much trouble the school will have to relocate again."

"Again?"

"It moved in the fifties," Meredith said when Shannon didn't answer. "It was in the Northeast, but the town got too big. It's never had to move because of vamps finding us. You'd almost think they had help."

I chewed on my lip as I thought. Maybe from the rogue Mr. Dawson had mentioned when I overheard him talking? But what if Mr. Hoel had something to do with this?

My imagination was taking my dislike for the Hoel's and turning it into some crazy plot against St. Ailbe's. I clearly needed more sleep. "I'm going to bed."

Shannon ignored me and Meredith said good night. They whispered theories as I got ready for bed, but I tried not to listen too much. Just because I had great hearing didn't mean I should use it all the time. People still needed privacy.

I was on the verge of sleep when St. Ailbe's version of a siren—a modulating low-pitched hum— cut thorough campus.

Howls echoed through the night. Answering ones came from the dorm.

What the hell was going on?

The smell of rotten eggs filled my room.

"Oh my God." I heard Meredith say from her room. "They're here!"

Everything was still for a moment, before doors in the dorms slammed open. Girls were shouting in their rooms.

I ran to my window. At least thirty people were running though the courtyard.

No. Not running. Gliding.

"Vampires." I whispered to myself as I pressed my nose against the glass. The cold bit into my skin but I couldn't look away. Both werewolves and vampires moved silently, but this kind of silence turned my stomach. It wasn't natural.

How were they moving like that?

I gasped as one of the dark figures stepped into the light. It swirled around, and then stopped. It was searching for something in the windows. Meredith yelled something, but I couldn't make it out.

Its gaze pierced me—red eyes called to me.

Everything slowed. I could hear my heart beat and count the time between each thump-thump.

A voice in my head ordered me to open the window, and I did.

All I could see was red. It filled my vision as it got closer, larger.

Cold wrapped around me and I floated to the ground.

"Tessa!" Meredith shouted from far away.

The sound stirred something in me, but it was quickly shoved aside.

Red eyes stared out from the darkness of his hood.

Cold fingers dug into my arms. He sniffed me. "Witch blood," it hissed. The vampire shoved my head to the side and something hot dropped on my neck. It burned like acid.

"Teresa Elizabeth McCaide!" Meredith yelled as another drop fell onto my skin.

Suddenly I was too aware of the pain. Of the stench. Of the cold hands grasping me.

I snapped out of the trance and screamed.

The howls answered my scream, but they were too far away.

I was alone in the courtyard. Vampires surrounded me, hovering in the air. Their long black coats swirled around their feet. Their faces were half-decayed.

His teeth grazed my neck as I struggled to break free.

"Awake now? I love the taste of scared witch."

I choked on his putrid breath.

The vampire threw me and was on me—pinning my arms and legs—before I could even register hitting the ground. I screamed again as I twisted, trying to break his hold, but couldn't get free. The fighting I'd been learning all week didn't help me one bit. Even with my new strength, I was helpless.

A tear rolled down my face as I started to flip out.

I wasn't proud of it, but I used the only weapon I had. "Dastien!" I yelled louder than I ever had before, hoping my voice would somehow reach him. I knew I'd die right then if he didn't come. If he was too far away.

A pained howl echoed through the courtyard.

The vampire's teeth scraped my neck, not yet breaking the skin, like he was teasing me. I whimpered.

Dastien was going to be too late. My skin was ice cold with fear. If I got out of this okay, I was going to start paying attention in martial arts class.

And then I heard him. "Tessa!" He grabbed the vampire and tossed him into the nearest tree. Bark splintered down, and the vampire slid to the ground.

Three more vampires jumped onto Dastien.

I tried to get up to help, but another vampire jumped on me.

I punched him, but it didn't faze him. He pressing me into the ground, and I shoved my fingers in his eye sockets. Black ooze streamed from the holes where its eyes used to be, and it screamed, rearing back.

A gray wolf leapt—grasping the vampire's neck in his jaws, and slammed it into the ground beside me.

Holy shit.

I rolled away from them as chaos broke out around me. It was a flurry of movement as wolves and vampires moved almost faster than I could track. I tried to spot a way to get through them and back to the dorm, but every time I tried to get up, a vampire would step toward me. There were too many of them, and I was attracting them when I moved. I crouched down on the ground, trying to make myself the smallest target possible.

Dastien was fighting his way back to me in his human form. He wore only a pair of gray sweatpants.

Only one vampire stood between us. Dastien charged at it, but an auburn wolf jumped in between them, taking the vampire to the ground.

This was my chance. I got up and ran as fast as I could, meeting Dastien halfway. A warm arm wrapped around my waist and lifted me from the ground as he ran back toward the building. He threw open the door to the girl's dorm. "Stay inside. No matter what." He gave me a tight smile. "I'll be back." He stepped back into the courtyard. "Seniors, outside now. The rest of you, stay in the dorms."

The sound of cloth ripping filled the night as people raced out of the buildings, shifting mid-sprint.

Now I felt like a total wuss. The rest of my class was outside fighting, and here I was hiding. This was all kinds of lame.

"What is it with you and windows?" Meredith met me at the stairs. "Are you okay?"

"I don't know." I didn't have time to wonder why she wasn't out there with the rest of the seniors. I raced up the stairs, taking two at a time. I had to get back to my window so I could see what was going on outside. The thought that Dastien or one of the others could get hurt—possibly because of me—made me sick.

One of the vampires separated from the group and circled around, trying to surprise-attack Dastien.

"Behind you!" I yelled, leaning out my window.

Dastien shifted instantly into a white and gray wolf. He lunged and tore into its neck. Black sludge spewed from the vampire. Its head rolled off and it crumpled to the ground. Meredith cheered from behind me.

A blond colored wolf jumped into the fight.

"That's Chris," Meredith said.

A large brown wolf ran into the courtyard, followed by two more–a black and a white wolf. My hands shook as I watched them fight.

The vampires moved with quick, slashing movements.

A yelp rang in my ears. One of the vampires had torn Chris' leg. His blond fur stained with red.

The brown wolf ripped into a vampire, ripping off its leg.

"That's Mr. Dawson," Meredith said.

I had no idea how she could tell them apart, but I took her word for it.

Before it could rise, wolf-Dawson slashed a paw at the vampire's neck, severing the head.

My throat was dry as I watched the gore.

The other vampires fled, taking off through the

woods. The wolves howled and all but two followed them into the tree line.

Mr. Miller, the chemistry teacher, ran out from the medical building with a bag in his hand. "I'll finish. Go!" he said.

Mr. Dawson and Dastien disappeared after the escaping vampires.

Mr. Miller opened the bag and took out a bottle. Then he punched through the chest of a vampire, and ripped out a ball of black goo. He dumped the bottle on the vamp and lit a match.

I turned away from the window as my dinner started to come back up. "That's disgusting."

Shaking, I sat down hard on the ground.

"Totally," Meredith said.

My breaths started to come easier after a few minutes. But then the worry for Dastien seeped in. I hugged my knees into my chest.

Holy shit, that was close.

I owed Dastien my life.

There was a knock on the open door. Dr. Gonazales didn't wait for me to answer. "Are you okay?"

I started to say yes, but hesitated. "I don't know." My neck still ached. I ran my fingers over it. "Something burned me."

The doctor set her bag next to me. "Vampire venom. Toxic stuff. But he didn't bite you, so that's good. If it gets into your blood stream, then you've got a bigger problem." She cleaned my neck with an alcohol swipe and spread sticky goo over the spot. "Keep this covered and dry for tonight," she said as she taped on a bandage. "It should be fine by tomorrow."

"I thought werewolves healed quickly."

"This is a supernatural injury. It'll heal slower."

Just when I thought I'd get some use out of the whole werewolf thing, it failed me. Typical. "Is Chris going to be okay?"

"He ran off with the others, most likely making his injury worse. But he'll be fine once I fix him up."

Mrs. Ramirez took a step into the room. "Girls, stay in the dorm. We're under lockdown. Windows bolted. Curtains closed. No matter what you hear going on outside. Understood?"

"Absolutely, Ms. Ramirez," Meredith said.

"Good." She left. A second later we heard her knocking next door, spreading the word.

Dr. Gonzales shut the window, clicked the lock and pulled the curtains tight. "You didn't read the book?"

"What book?"

She stepped over to my desk and picked up the thin volume—*The Werewolf's Bible*.

I shrugged. "It's been a bit of a rough week." I probably should've put on gloves and read the damned thing, but no one expects a vampire invasion. "How come it hypnotized me so easily?"

"You met his gaze?"

I nodded.

Meredith slapped my shoulder. "Next time, don't do that."

"We're not as weak as humans," Dr. Gonzales said. "It's like when someone punches you when you're not ready. It takes you by surprise. But if you are braced for it, it'll graze on by. Just stay away from the window and never ever meet their gaze unprepared." She placed the book back on my desk. "Please try to read this. It explains a lot."

"Yeah, sure."

"I guess maybe we should get ready for bed?" Meredith said when Dr. Gonzales left.

Bed? Was she kidding? Vampires attacked the school. One nearly killed me. Dastien and Mr. Dawson and the rest were out there. Fighting. Not to mention the adrenaline still working its way through me. "I don't think I can sleep."

"It must be weird for you to see that. But really, it's going to be fine. They can't come out during the day, and the Cazadores will come soon and watch over us at night." She squatted in front of me. "Are you sure you're okay?"

I pulled my hair back and saw my hands shaking. "I don't know." I thought for a second. "What else can vampires do?"

"You mean besides controlling your body if you meet their gaze and drain all the blood from you?"

Holy shit. "Yeah, besides that."

"Some of them are said to have magical powers, not that I've seen it. Their saliva is poisonous to us, but usually if you're close enough to find that out you're going to be dead soon. You got lucky." She paused. "And they glide over the ground, so they don't make sound. And they can glamour humans into thinking they don't look nasty. Also, they can leap really high. And—"

I waved my hand through the air. "Enough. I don't think my puny ex-human brain can take any more tonight."

Meredith laughed. "Listen. How about you get ready for bed, and then we'll watch a movie in my room? Something fun and silly."

I grabbed some pajamas, but kept looking toward my window. I didn't dare go near it. That feeling when I looked at the vampire, like that thing had control over me, chilled me. It invaded my brain. I never wanted to feel that again.

I pulled on some shorts and a tank, and snatched a pillow off my bed.

"*Sixteen Candles* or *Mean Girls*?" Meredith said as I walked into her room.

"*Mean Girls*."

"Done."

I snuggled down on her fluffy rug and hugged my pillow.

I swore I could hear Dastien howling in the distance.

Mr. Dawson had been right. Too much of this was a coincidence. I come here and then the vampires. As much as I didn't want it to be about me, what if it was? Or what if I was the excuse?

What if Mr. Hoel was the rogue? And Imogene was helping him?

I hoped I was wrong. That this blew over, but if it didn't—then I'd made some pretty powerful enemies already. I was going to have to start watching my back.

***

The sound of scratching pulled me from my dreams. Little nails clawing. Followed by a very soft whining noise. How had I gotten back in my room? Were the vampires back? I looked at the window, but the curtains were still tightly closed. It was coming from my door.

No way they could get inside. Or so I hoped.

Maybe if I ignored it, it would go away.

More scratching and whining. That sounded dog-like. Or wolf-like.

I put a pillow on top of my head.

More scratching and whining.

I grabbed a tissue, ripped it in half, and shoved it in my ears. I sandwiched my head back in between the pillows.

More scratching and whining.

I threw off the covers and stomped over to the door.

On the other side was Dastien in wolf-form. He came up to my waist, and looked like he weighed a ton. Amber eyes stared at me.

I dropped to my knees and ran my fingers through his thick fur, searching for any signs of damage. "Are you okay? I was so worried—"

Shit. I probably shouldn't have said that.

I stepped away from him.

He lay down on the ground and covered his face with his front paws and let out a pitiful whine.

I gave it my best guess. "You're sorry?"

He sat up, and gave a soft woof.

Good thing Meredith slept like the dead.

I didn't know what to say. Now that I knew he was okay, some of my anger was back. The guy had been avoiding me after biting me.

But he did kind of save me.

He whined again.

"If you want to talk you should shift back to human. So you can actually talk."

He huffed.

"What? It's against the rules?"

He yipped.

"Guess I'm not going to find out about what happened with all the vampires then, huh?" He tilted his head to the side. "Well, thanks for saving me. But you're really giving me mixed signals. Ignoring me one second and ordering me around the next. I'm not sure why you're here."

He started sniffing at my belly, and I couldn't help but laugh as I tried to push him away. "I'm fine. Really. Just a scratch."

He tried to get between me and the door.

"You want me to let you in? It's like four AM. I have to get up in a few hours."

He sat, and looked up at me. I took a step back to close the door, but he darted past.

I growled. How was I going to get a huge wolf out of my room?

Maybe having Dastien there wasn't a horrible thought. If there were vampires around, then he would offer a measure of protection.

Shit. That's why he was here. To see if I was okay, and to keep watch.

I closed the door behind me. "If I let you stay, then there are rules. First, you will not—I repeat—will not be changing in the middle of the night. If I wake up with you naked in my bed, there will be hell to pay. Whatever it is that's going on with us, we're not at that part yet."

He tilted his head to the side and made a little coughing sound.

Was he laughing at me? "You should be thanking the Baby Jesus that I even let you in." Which wasn't entirely true. He'd gotten past me fair and square. "Second thing, I'm going to sleep. You keep me awake and you're out." I wasn't sure I could follow up on that threat, but it was the best I could do right then.

He jumped up on the bed, circled around once, and then plopped down—nearly taking up the whole thing.

I shoved at him. "Scoot over." I crawled under the sheets. It was dangerous, just giving in like that. If I had more energy to think about the implications, I would have kicked his hairy tush out of my bed. But I didn't.

Wolfy-Dastien moved so that he surrounded me. His warm wolf breath hit the back of my neck. He whimpered and touched his nose gently to the bandage.

"Cut it out." I shoved at him again, but he didn't move much.

Having him there should have weirded me out, but it didn't. His breath moved in and out, lulling me. I didn't have time to freak. One second I was thinking about how warm and relaxed I was, and the next I was in Dreamville.

Chapter Twenty-Seven

When I woke, it was to the sound of birds chirping outside my window. Bright light glowed at the edges of my curtains. I'd slept through the rest of night like a rock. I stretched as I reveled in my refreshed state of mind.

And then I remembered I wasn't alone.

I shot out of bed, but he wasn't there. I walked over to the bathroom.

Empty.

He was gone. I should've been glad. It shouldn't have ruined my good mood. But it did. It kind of hurt.

Why was I in a good mood in the first place? It's not like I really wanted him to stay with me. Did I?

That damned boy was bad for my brain.

I got ready as fast as I could, and peeked into Meredith's room. She wasn't there either. I checked the time. She'd be in the cafeteria still. I grabbed a pair of black lace gloves that stopped at my wrists and ran out the door.

When I got to the cafeteria, a boy was waiting at the door. He held out a tray for me.

"I don't need any help," I said. I cringed at my own words.

He looked at me like I'd just kicked his puppy. "You need extra protein after the attack. Just wanted to make sure you knew."

I was officially a terrible person. "Thank you," I said as I took the tray. "I didn't know. I really appreciate it."

He nodded, and walked off.

Hopefully some food would help with my mood. I piled my plate high with scrambled eggs, bacon, ham, and pancakes, and went toward our table.

Dastien's laugh carried over the voices in the room, warming me. He was sitting at my table. With my new friends. He pushed out the chair between him and Shannon without standing up. That was a slick move. I couldn't ever tell what was going on with him. He ignored me half the time, and the other half alternated between bossing me around and being so perfectly sweet.

It was beyond confusing.

Still, I couldn't just give him what he wanted all the time. That whole claiming me thing still bugged the crap out of me. I plunked my tray down next to Chris on the opposite side of the table. The conversation stopped.

"You smell...confused...annoyed...I don't know but I don't like it," Dastien said.

"That's really creepy. And makes me feel like I need to take another shower." I crumpled in my chair.

"Normal people say, 'You look upset.' Just FYI."

His smile faded. "I'll leave."

Shit. Now I'd kicked two puppies. "I'm sorry. I didn't mean that to sound...I just...I'm going to shut up now." I'd never had a boyfriend. Dastien was my first kiss. My first everything. Him sleeping in my bed meant something, even if he was a furball. It hurt that he'd left before I even woke up.

Was he embarrassed of me? Or ashamed? Or worse—was it only his wolf that wanted me?

I shoved my tray to the middle of the round table and rested my head on the cool Linoleum. A warm hand settled over my back.

"Don't touch her," Dastien growled.

I whipped my head up. Bossypants was back with a vengeance. "Seriously? Please don't tell me that after your days long disappearing act—which, by the way, you were painfully consistent with this morning—"

"Tessa—" Dastien started, but I held my hand up.

If we did this here and now I was totally going to cry. "Let's talk about it later."

No one said anything as I downed half my Diet Coke in one gulp. Maybe it would've been better to go for the regular Coke these days, but I'd grown accustomed to the taste. A girl needed a little something familiar when surrounded by the completely unfamiliar.

The sounds of the cafeteria as people moved around, grabbing their breakfast and chatting about last night's attack, filled the silence at our table as I took a bite of food.

Dastien looked across the room as Mr. Dawson walked through the door. They were having some sort of unspoken conversation that involved minute changes in body language. Dastien nodded and stood up.

"Catch you later," I said. It sounded pitiful, even to me. For once it'd be nice to be the one doing the leaving.

He walked around the table and squatted next to my chair. "I have to, *mon coeur*. I want to stay here with you, believe me. I need to win your trust. I'm sorry I left before you woke this morning. I'm an idiot and I didn't know it'd hurt your feelings or else I would have stayed. But I have to go now and I hope that later you'll give me yet another chance." He kissed my cheek and rubbed his nose from the corner where my neck met my shoulder up to my ear. He breathed in deeply, scenting me, and I felt it all the way to my core. "*Je t'aime, ma chérie.*"

My heart skipped a beat. Did he just say what I think he said?

No. I must've misunderstood.

I wanted to hang on to him, but stubbornness was in my nature. I wouldn't be forced into any relationships. But after last night, my resolve was weakening. Dastien was addicting, and I was hooked before I ever got to Texas.

I watched him until he was at the door. He glanced back and smiled, and then was gone.

Shannon scraped her chair against the floor as she got up.

Meredith broke the silence first. "Adrian, can you help me with my meta lab?"

"Hey, if you want help, babe, all you gotta do is ask. I love helpin' the ladies." He grinned.

"Don't be such a dork." She picked up a biscuit and chucked it at him.

He plucked it out of the air and took a bite. "Yum. Thanks." He winked at her. It was really nice to see them flirting. Meredith always counted herself out of the whole mating-game. Which reminded me… "So, why haven't you picked one?" I gestured to the tables of guys.

Everyone at the table stilled.

"I haven't shifted yet," Meredith said quietly. She looked down at her plate. "I had a run in with some witches a few years back. Mr. Dawson thinks they cursed me. I wouldn't want to stick anyone with that." Adrian reached across the table. "Hey. I told you I was working on it. *Brujo* blood, remember."

"*Brujo*?" I said.

"Witch. I've got some in my lineage a ways back. It's a pretty diluted but strong enough that I can cast minor spells."

"I know what *brujo* means, but isn't it just a bunch of hippie stuff. At least, that's what my dad always says about my cousins and they claim to be *brujos*."

Adrian studied me. "You looked a little Latin but your name threw me."

I nodded. "Half. Dad's one hundred percent white-boy. Mom's Mexican."

"So when you say cousin, you mean as in somewhere along the line we had a relative in common kind of a thing, or cousins as in mother's sibling's kids."

I laughed. Mexican families were typically really large. My mom joked that in her hometown on the

Texas-Mexico border everyone was cousins somewhere down the line. "As in my mother's nephews and my aunts and uncles and my grandmother...basically everyone on my mom's side."

He ran his fingers through his short black curls. "How are you just now telling me this?"

I shrugged. "I didn't realize it was a thing."

Chris nudged me. "It's a really big deal, and might explain a few things."

It explained nothing. "You guys are being extra weird, and that's saying something given the fact that you're already freaks of nature."

"You've got a bit of a pot and kettle scenario going on with that statement. You might be even more of a freak of nature than the rest of us." Chris leaned back to balance his chair on two legs.

I moved to knock Chris' balance off, but he laughed and slammed his chair down.

The bell rang. I hadn't even eaten my food. I was so screwed. The past few days had shown me that Meredith was right. Anytime I didn't eat enough, my temper was short. I had to eat to keep the wolf at bay, and with my moods running so hot and cold, I couldn't afford to skip a meal. "What do I do now?"

Chris grabbed my tray, and two slices of bread off his. He piled eggs, bacon, ham, and potatoes on one slice, and then topped it off with the other, making the biggest breakfast sandwich I'd ever seen.

"Adrian, toss me that biscuit," Chris said. He caught it without looking and cut the biscuit in half. He made a smaller sandwich with it. "Eat this now." He grabbed a napkin, wrapping the massive sandwich. "Eat this one in class. I'll bring you a snack later."

"That's sweet, but you don't have to," I said.

"It's no big deal. I have a study session first period. I have time to grab you something."

I looked into Chris' blue eyes as he got up. "Thanks. I seriously appreciate it." Everyone was already clearing out. It was nice to have a friend to look out for me.

"My pleasure, cutie."

Fire burned my cheeks, but guilt quickly washed the heat away. Why did I feel like I was betraying Dastien by flirting with Chris? It wasn't like we were married or anything.

"What is it with you? One guy not enough?"

I whirled to face Imogene. "Jealous?"

Chris stepped in between us. "Ladies. Ladies. Let's calm down. There's enough Chris to go around."

Imogene made circles on Chris' chest with her finger. "You wouldn't choose her over me? Would you?"

Even if she was a bitch, Imogene was gorgeous. Her brown eyes were large, just shy of being too big. With the make-up she wore, you couldn't look away from them. Her lips were full and red. I wondered if that was natural or lip-plumper.

"Yes. I would pick her over you."

She gripped Chris' shirt. Shaking him. "What?"

I was as shocked as Imogene was. He would pick me over her? It was one thing for Dastien to pick me. He was the one who bit me. He kind of had to pick me. But Chris had options, and he still wanted me?

Wow. I grinned. Maybe today wouldn't be so bad

after all.

Chris stared down at her. "I'd let go before you embarrass yourself any more than you already have."

She let go of his shirt and glared at me. "This isn't over between us. You'll regret—"

"That's enough. Go." Chris backed his words with so much power that the hair on my arms stood on end. Imogene growled as she stormed off.

"You're more dominant than her?"

"A lot of people are," Chris said. "She just likes to act tough and annoy the crap out of most everyone." His eyes were still glowing.

"What's with that?" I asked.

"Sorry." He closed them, and took a deep breath. When he opened them again, they were back to normal sky-blue.

"Why do they change?"

"Wolf. Power. Magic. Take your pick."

"Cool." I had no idea what that meant, but from the short answer, it didn't seem like he was up for chatting about it. I took a bite of my sandwich to keep myself from asking any more questions.

We started walking from the cafeteria to the class building. I noticed he was limping. "Hey, are you okay? Shouldn't you be in bed?"

"Nah. I'm fine." He tapped my bandage. "Quite a scare you gave us."

"You're telling me." I shuddered. "That thing was no Brad Pitt."

He reached toward me but hesitated. "Listen, you're going to have to face this whole thing before too much longer."

"You mean Imogene?"

He nodded. "She wants Dastien as her mate. They're family friends, and their parents have been trying to get them together ever since they were kids. Everyone's wondering what you're going to do."

"I honestly don't know." I took a giant bite to give myself time to think about what I was going to say. "I'm having enough of a time coming to terms with the possibility of going furry. Add in the whole choosing a guy for the rest of my life...that's a lot of pressure on a girl."

He grabbed my hand. "In the beginning it started with mated pairs. Meaning that the mates were two halves of one soul. It was easier then. You saw each other and you just knew. You were drawn together like magnets. If one died, so did the other. But that's legend now. People fall in love and if the wolves accept each other, then you're good to get married. But there's still no divorce for us. So be sure."

I knew exactly how that whole magnet thing felt, but that was crazy. I had my own full soul, thank you very much. "That sounds intense. How can I possibly figure out who I want to spend the next fifty years with?"

He laughed. "It's a lot longer than that. Try hundreds."

Chris had to be joking with this. The bell rang, and I was happy for it. "I gotta get to class."

"Dastien's my friend, but since you haven't decided yet..."

I didn't have time to move. He swooped down, and brushed his lips against mine.

I really want her to like me. She's so pretty and nice. And so much stronger than she thinks. I hope she doesn't pick Dastien. Please don't let her pick him. I know I could make her happy. She smells good.

My mind raced by the time he pulled away.

"Just something to think about. You have options."

He walked back down the stairs before I could remember to breathe.

I leaned against the lockers. My visions had changed for sure. Instead of seeing something that had happened to the person, I read their minds. And I heard things I didn't want to hear.

As much as I might have wanted it, I didn't feel for Chris what I felt for Dastien. And I couldn't read Dastien. Even if Chris was easy and fun and sweet, I craved Dastien. Chris' full-on kiss left me a little breathless, but Dastien's stupid barely-there kiss on my cheek shattered me.

Christ. This had just gotten way more complicated.

I banged my head against the lockers a couple of times. Why didn't I dodge the kiss? Or at the very least, why didn't I push him away? I'd never felt so guilty in my life. I wanted to upchuck the sandwich, but forced myself to finish eating it instead.

I wished Dastien hadn't left this morning. It'd be amazing if we could have an actual talk about what he wanted from me.

I needed a distraction.

Imogene walked past me with a devilish grin on her face.

I nodded at her. Distraction taken care of. I wasn't much for skipping class—I was already behind—but from what I'd put together from the little snippets of visions I'd had, that girl nearly got me eaten by vampires. I grabbed Meredith before she went into class. "I need to talk to you."

"Now? Because if it's about making out with Chris, then maybe it can wait." She waggled her eyebrows at me.

Perfect. My reputation didn't need anymore help in the negative direction. I'd bet money that's what put the grin on Imogene's face. "Not about a boy. Something bigger. I need to pick your brain and no, it can't wait. And no we can't talk here. Too many ears."

She tucked a chunk of her bright-blue hair behind her ear. "I know a place."

We went down the stairs to the first floor. We walked through the gym locker room to another set of stairs. The walls were thick concrete. Doors lined the narrow hallway, and flickering fluorescent lights made the space seem even smaller. Meredith opened the second door on the left. It was a tiny closet-like room, with a concrete bench built into one wall and that was it.

"Where the hell are we?"

"It's where we put feral wolves. Sometimes newbies flip out when they wolf-out the first time. So, they get thrown in here until they get their shit together."

Holy crap. I wondered if I'd spent any time in one of these during my missing week. If I did, I didn't want to remember it. "Whatever." I took a deep breath and laid out all of the visions I'd had from Imogene. At first, I thought I sounded a little crazy. It didn't take a genius to figure out that Imogene and I would never be friends. But when I got to the vision from when we were watching the news to getting pulled out of my window by the vamp, Meredith stood from the bench and started pacing.

I didn't have much but my suspicions and visions, but I knew something was off. "So what do I do?"

"We tell Mr. Dawson. You don't have any evidence. No proof but your vision of her thinking about vampires taking care of someone, and that's just…well it'll be your word against hers. You're more alpha than her, so you'd win. But it'd start a world of shit you don't need. Especially not after that kiss you had with Chris."

Why'd she have to remind me of it? This was supposed to be a valid distraction.

She walked to the door. "Come on. He'll be in his office."

Apparently, Mr. Dawson's office was on the first floor of the building where the infirmary was. A gray haired lady sat typing away at a desk. "Is he in, Mrs. Kilburn?"

"He is. Go on with you." She didn't look away from her monitor as she spoke.

Before Meredith could knock on his door, Mr. Dawson's voice came through the door. "Come on in girls."

Mr. Dawson's office was neat and orderly. Not a paper was out of place. A stack of manila folders was beside his keyboard. He finished typing something, and then nodded at us. "What can I do for you?"

"I have to talk to you, about my visions."

"I see," he said. "I take it you've already talked to Meredith about all of this."

Meredith nodded.

He motioned to the chairs in front of his desk. "Have a seat."

I pulled my hair into a sloppy bun as I gathered my thoughts. I laid everything out just like I had for Meredith. When I finished, I took a deep breath. This is where he could throw me out of his office for being crazy. "I think Imogene and Mr. Hoel brought the vampires to campus last night."

"That *is* something." Mr. Dawson leaned back in his chair.

"I know that Imogene and Tessa have a bit of a beef over a certain guy, but I really don't think this is about that," Meredith said.

He sighed. "I have to agree, but then this is something Rupert has been planning for a while. That Tessa got caught up in it is just lucky timing."

I snorted. "Awesome. I get all the luck."

"So what do we do?" Meredith said. "You can't let Imogene and her dad get away with this. They've exposed our school. Why would he—"

He stood from his chair. "Look, ladies. I appreciate you coming here and telling me this. You've confirmed a few of my suspicions. But this is really tricky stuff and I don't want you getting more involved. What's going on right now has been brewing for a while. Even if you don't know why Rupert would do it, I have a very good idea what his motives are and what he's planning. If you 'see' anything else, let me know, but don't go looking for visions." He came around the front of the desk and leaned against it. "Please don't make me pull pack on you. I don't want to have to order you to keep quiet about this."

Meredith lifted her chin, showing him her neck. Mr. Dawson nodded at her and then looked to me.

That was weird. "I guess I'll get back to class then," I said.

He sat there, saying nothing as we left.

We walked slowly back to class in silence, but I couldn't keep quiet for long. "So what do you think—"

"You heard what Mr. D said. We can't talk about it."

I rolled my eyes. "Come on. You'll really stop looking for answers."

"Yup. You have to obey your alpha. It's just the way it is."

Trusting that Mr. Dawson would look into it was one thing, but Imogene sicced vampires on me. There was no way I was letting that happen again. Plus, he hadn't actually ordered us. He'd made a strong request.

Chapter Twenty-Eight

Chris wasn't in the hallway when I got out of class. Which was a good thing. I hadn't figured out what to say to him. I'd never been in a place where I needed to let a guy down. Hell, I'd never even had a guy think about me in any kind of serious way. From the outside, it might seem nice, but the stress had my stomach in knots.

I opened my locker and found another sandwich and a bag of chips. I sighed. I was crazy for thinking that Dastien—the guy who kept bossing me around or running the other way—was a better choice. Chris was nice and funny and easy to be around and also hot. But the spark wasn't there. At all.

The spark was Fourth of July-sized with Dastien. We'd had a rocky start for sure, but I couldn't deny my intense attraction to him. But before I even thought about committing to him, he had to stop running away whenever things got hard and bossing me around. Otherwise, what was the point?

Two periods later, I sat in the cafeteria with Shannon and Meredith, but Adrian and Chris were missing.

I scanned the other tables, and realized that it wasn't just our guys that were gone. They were all gone. "Where is everyone?"

"You didn't hear?" Shannon asked.

I let her shitty tone roll off me. "Hear what?"

"The Cazadores showed up today. They're going to patrol campus at night. Everything might seem normal right now, but we're on full lockdown starting an hour before sunset."

Before I could ask what she meant, the doors flew open, banging against the wall. A group of twenty or so men strutted in. Each wore head to toe black. All the ladies froze in place and watched them as they piled food on their trays. When they turned to the room, the girls looked down, letting the guys take the dominant role. I sat up straight and met their gazes. The whole "women are the weaker sex" thing wasn't going to fly with me.

Donovan and Sebastian strolled through the doors.

"Oh my God. That's who those other two wolves were last night," Meredith said.

Donovan spotted me and winked. I waved back. Since I wasn't terrified of him anymore, I could actually notice that he was incredibly handsome. He wasn't as tall as Dastien, but he commanded attention in the same kind of way with his confident swagger. His black hair was tucked behind his ears. His smile showed off his dimples. He weaved through the tables toward us.

Meredith hit my shoulder. "Holy shit," she whispered. "Donovan Murry is coming over to us. He's gorge."

"Yeah. He kind of is, right?" He might have been a bit old for my taste, but he still looked a few years shy of thirty.

"Only totally."

He pulled a chair from the table next to us and sat in between Meredith and I. "How're you doing, lass?"

I grinned. That accent got to me in the best way. "I'm okay." The scratch had nearly gone away, and I only put a band-aid on today.

"We're checking out what you and Meredith here talked about with Michael. But we don't want you messing where you shouldn't be. Dangerous stuff, that. Okay?"

Wow. Mr. Dawson actually listened to me. Which meant that something was up. A million questions popped into my head. I opened my mouth, but didn't get a word out.

Donovan put a finger to my lips. "No. Remember what I just said?"

Meredith made a squeaking noise. Her cheeks were bright red. I'd never seen the girl blush before and had kind of assumed that she was un-embarrassable.

I couldn't stop the chuckle. "This is Meredith. She might be a little overwhelmed by you." Meredith punched my arm. Hard. "Ow."

"Tessa!" Meredith whisper shouted at me.

I laughed harder this time.

Their gaze met and I could swear I felt the heat of it burning. There were some major mutual

261

appreciation vibes going on.

"It's a pleasure to finally meet you, Meredith Savannah Molloney." He reached across me to grab her hand and pressed his nose to her pulse point. "I'll be seeing you again real soon."

What the hell. Donovan Murry was totally hitting on Meredith.

"Right. I best be off. You ladies enjoy your lunch." He gave us another of his smiles, crystal eyes twinkling.

Meredith punched my shoulder when he left. "Holy shit. Did that just happen?"

I fanned myself. "It totally did."

"He's so hot. And can't you just feel that power. God."

I laughed. "He is kind of potent. And while we're on the subject, I met Sebastian Braun too. Same deal with him."

Shannon pushed back from the table. "I'll leave you to your gossiping."

I couldn't win with her. It was much easier to not try.

"Don't worry about her. She's just jealous. Of both of us," Meredith said. The bell rang. "This isn't getting you out of spilling. Tonight. You will tell me everything. Especially about Donovan. Or face the consequences."

"I think I've had enough consequences for one lifetime." I giggled when she shoved me. "Tonight. I promise. When not so many people are around."

"Deal."

***

262

I should've known it was going to be a bad martial arts class when I walked into the gym and saw Dastien instead of Mr. Dawson. Everyone was already sparring. I guessed the attack made everyone a little on edge.

Chris waved me over. We started our normal stretching routine. I couldn't help but peek at Dastien. He stood reclined against the far wall watching as I stretched.

He mouthed, "Focus."

I quickly looked away, turning bright red for sure. I finally got into the fighting stance Chris had taught me, and tried to pretend Dastien wasn't there.

"Forgetting something?" Chris said.

I glanced at my feet, but they looked right to me. My shoulders seemed right too. "I don't think so."

"Gloves?"

My head so wasn't in gear. I tried not to act awkward, but was failing miserably. Every time I looked at Chris I felt guilty. Dastien watching me only made me feel extra guilty. I had to focus on the job at hand. After last night, I knew I was way behind on a key supernatural skill.

Plus, if I could get through this class, then maybe I could talk to Chris after and tell him he couldn't kiss me again.

I tucked my gloves in my waistband, and Chris nodded. "Let's work on flipping."

"I'm not a gymnast. Forget it. Let's work on something else. Something more practical, so I don't have another repeat of last night."

He laughed. "No. I mean you flip me. Over your

back. And this will help you. I promise."

I stepped away from him. "Now I know you've lost your mind. You're basically a foot taller than me and a ton heavier."

"If you do it right, that won't matter."

I listened to him explain the maneuver. It was a twist and squat with a little momentum behind it, not a feat of strength. Although he told me I could do it that way too. Which earned him an eye roll. I didn't care what they said about werewolf strength. Chris was bigger than me and there was no way I could lift him.

We went through each step, move by move. I had to grab his wrist and then spin around so that my back was to his front, which would wrench his arm. Then, I would squat a little bit to get my hip under his, and momentum, plus the fact that his arm wanted to stay connected to the rest of his body, would flip him over my shoulder.

Sounded reasonable. If only I could wear my gloves for it. I didn't need to hear about how he liked the way I fit against his body or how he thought I was sexy. My palms started to sweat. I didn't dare look in Dastien's direction. But I could feel him. Pacing. Barely holding his wolf at bay.

"You're moving too slowly," Chris said, drawing me back to the problem at hand. "Don't be afraid of hurting me. I promise I won't break. And even if I do, I heal quickly."

"But you're already hurt."

He slapped his leg. "This is nothing. Just a scratch."

"You're still limping. That's more than a scratch."

"Shut up. Just do it."

I stopped all the worrying and pulled the move. Chris went flying through the air, hit the mats and slid into the wall.

Crap. I needed to learn not to overdo it. I ran over to him. "Are you okay?" I nudged him with my foot. "Chris?" He wasn't moving. I leaned down to make sure he was still breathing.

"Boo!" he yelled.

I screamed and jumped up. "Damn it, Chris!" I took a deep breath, and kicked his side. "They should really pad these walls. One of these days I'm going to actually hurt you and I'm going to think you're faking and leave you for dead."

"I don't know why you never believe me. I really won't break." He stood up and pulled me against him. "I'm a werewolf," he whispered in my ear.

I didn't have time to laugh before an arm wrapped around my middle, ripping me away from Chris. Dastien set me on my feet, and turned—arms swinging. His fist met Chris' face. Chris flew through the air again, but this time the crack echoed through the gym when his head slammed into the wall.

Dastien lunged toward Chris. His hand wrapped around Chris' neck as he lifted him off the ground and rammed him into the wall. Chris hung limply.

"Shit!" I ran to them and yanked at Dastien's hand, trying to pry his fingers from Chris' neck. "Someone help!" The gym was quiet. Perfect. They'd just as soon let the boys kill each other as help me. "Let. Him. Go. Now!" I put all the force of my will into the words.

Dastien's eyes burned bright yellow. He took a

deep breath and let go. Chris slid to the ground. A little line of blood dribbled down his neck.

I knelt next to Chris and laid him flat. "Wake up. Please. Wake up, now. Chris! It's not funny this time." He wasn't waking up. "Someone get some help!" No one was doing anything., and I didn't know any first aid. Especially werewolf first aid.

Chris' eyelids fluttered.

"Chris? Can you hear me?"

"Werewolf. Remember?" he said. I could barely hear his scratchy voice. "We heal fast."

Now that I could breathe again, I got up and shoved Dastien. "You could have killed him!" All I got in response was a growl. Dastin's gaze stayed trained on Chris.

I reached a hand down to help Chris to his feet. Dastien's growl grew to a roar.

Chris dropped my hand like it was on fire. "Shit, dude. What's your problem?"

Dastien stalked toward him, and I blocked his way. A second later, water splashed all over Dastien.

Meredith peeked from behind him. "Did I hit you, Tess?" She held a large plastic bucket.

"No. Still dry." Mostly.

Dastien's shirt was soaked through. It clung to every muscle. He shook, spraying cold water over all of us, and my tongue stuck to the roof of my mouth.

Fuck. I finally got the whole wet T-shirt contest thing.

I didn't breathe as Dastien walked over to Chris, ready to step in between them if Dastien got violent again. He held his hand out. "Sorry."

Chris took the hand and got to his feet. "No big

deal."

Dastien walked to the door of the gym. "Class is over," he said before the door slammed behind him.

"I'm just going to check on him," Imogene said.

Meredith laughed. "Good luck with that one."

Imogene shot her a dirty look and quickly strode out of the gym after Dastien. I almost felt sorry for her. Almost. I caught Shannon's glare. Her arms were crossed, but she stayed rooted to her slice of mat. If she wasn't my friend before, this was so not going to win her over. Oh well. I was used to no friends. The fact that I had Meredith was awesome.

And I had a Dastien, whatever that meant.

Adrian was the only one to move as he took a few quick steps to close the distance. He inspected Chris' head. "Blood's just surface. It's already healed."

Chris grinned. "See. I'm just fine." The grin faded. "He snuck up on me. Damn it. No one's snuck up on me in forever."

"That's why he's the best," Meredith said. "Good thing I got the bucket. Looked like he was going for your throat."

"Thanks, Mer." They high-fived. "I totally owe you one."

"Speaking of buckets, where did you get it?" I asked.

Meredith pointed behind her. "There are always a few filled up in the room in case someone gets out of hand while we're sparring. But it's usually Dastien who dumps it over the student's head. Took a second for me to realize I needed to get it." She put her arm around Chris' waist. "Sorry."

"You did fine. No one expected Dastien to lose it.

He's usually so calm."

They stared at me. It was too much, especially with the rest of the class already staring. I took a step back. I had zero desire to know what they were thinking.

"Do you know what's up with him?" Chris asked.

I studied the mats. "Not a clue." My voice was a little too high pitched.

The door slammed and Dastien walked back to us with a mop. "Everyone out." Power rolled through the gym, giving me goose bumps. "You four can stay," he said to me, Chris, Adrian and Meredith.

Yikes. Shannon wasn't going to be happy about that, but I was kind of glad. If we were going to talk about what happened, I didn't need her negativity around.

Some of my classmates grumbled as they cleared out. Dastien finished mopping while we waited for the last of the eavesdroppers to go. I bit my lip as he cleaned. I wanted to ask Dastien what happened with Imogene, but he didn't look like he was in the mood to talk.

When everyone was gone, Meredith broke the silence. She sauntered up to him. "Glad you didn't forget cleanup duty, Daz." She rubbed her hand down his back.

Did she have to be so touchy-feely? My blood heated but I kept it under control, trying to remember that she was my friend. I concentrated on even breathing.

He cocked his head. "It's been a while, but I think I remember how it goes."

"Aren't you the cutest?" She leaned in and gave

him a kiss on the lips.

Red. All I saw was red.

I'm not quite sure how it happened. I don't remember even moving. One second I stood next to Chris. The next, Meredith was flat on her back, and I had her pinned to the ground. A bright red splotch spread across her left cheek.

I was growling when Dastien reached both arms around my stomach and lifted me off her.

"Shhh. I got you," he whispered in my ear.

My stomach bottomed out at the sound. The smell of him filled me—the scent of outdoors spread peace through my blood. He was like a drug.

And then came the shame. My face heated and I pushed Dastien's arms off of me. I hung my head and stepped toward her. "I'm so unbelievably sorry. I don't know what happened...I don't even remember hitting you, but that was totally inexcusable—"

Adrian laughed.

"It's not funny—" I started but Adrian cut me off.

"¡Joder! It can't be. That doesn't happen anymore." He helped Meredith up and ran his fingers over the mark on her face. "You've got *cajones* to try that. She hit you hard. It'll get worse before it gets better."

"It was worth it." Meredith straightened her clothes. "For the record, I called it."

She was ignoring my apology and I didn't blame her for it. I had to just keep going until she accepted. "I'm so sorry. I don't even remember moving. I swear I didn't—"

"Honey, please." She held up a hand to stop my babbling. "I made you do it."

What? I stepped away from her, my gaze darting between the four of them. "I don't understand."

"You'd only attack me like that if he was your mate. As in an actual mated pair. As in the other half of your soul."

It felt like I was floating.

Chris crossed his arms. "I never had a shot." He closed his eyes.

Crap. I'd hurt him.

Dastien stepped toward me but this was all too much. I dropped heavily to the ground and hugged my knees to my chest. I knew what they said was true, but the whole processing it thing was too much. I closed my eyes to think. Was he really my mate?

I'd been fighting my feelings for him. But why? I knew I wanted him. I knew it since I touched that paper in my father's office. But he kept pushing me away, and I kept pushing him away.

It had to end. I couldn't deny it. Especially not if I was going to slug Meredith over it.

A hand brushed my hair away from my face, but I kept my eyes shut. "*Mon cherie*, please. Open your eyes."

"Okay. I give up." I swallowed, and opened them. He was sitting cross-legged in front of me.

"We're not normal," he said finally.

I laughed. "You can say that again."

He smiled, and his dimples showed. "We're not normal. We never were. I spent a long time feeling not quite whole. And then I saw you and something clicked." He ran his hand down my cheek and I leaned into it. "Believe me, I would love to do this over. To start again and do it the right way. Take you on some dates. Get to know you better. Slower. I lost control for a second and I didn't even know what happened until it was done. I think the wolf knew that I wouldn't turn you. I would never take the risk of you not surviving the transformation. But what's done is done. Give me a chance."

"I'm not the only one who keeps running away."

He sighed. "I was trying to give you time to adjust. Everyone demanded that I give you time."

He was too far away. I wanted to be closer, so I just went with the feeling. I closed the space between us, sitting on his lap, and wrapped my arms and legs around him. I rested my head on his shoulder. "I think it's only making the whole thing harder for me," I whispered into his ear. "I feel lost and confused when you walk away. Angry. Hurt. I don't like it. I'm having enough of a hard time with the whole werewolf thing to also figure out a messed up relationship too."

It didn't take long for him to squeeze me tight. He scented my neck and placed a soft kiss on it.

"I'm sorry that you're stuck with me, but I'll spend the rest of my life making it up to you. I swear," he whispered. He let go, leaning back to see my face. "Okay?"

I nodded. "Okay." I startled at the sound of a throat clearing. "I forgot we weren't alone."

"Unfortunately not alone," Dastien said.

"Girl talk," Meredith mouthed when I met her gaze. "Do you want to go early to dinner?" Meredith asked aloud.

My stomach answered for me. "That would be amazing," I said.

"We'll stay here and help Dastien clean up," Chris said.

Dastien stood with me still attached. I dropped down to the ground and turned to go, but Dastien grabbed my hand. I pulled him down to me for a kiss. It was soft and quick, but still burned me all the way to my toes.

"Later," Meredith said as she pulled me away from Dastien.

We walked to the cafeteria. It was thankfully mostly empty, except for the workers who were busy setting out food for dinner. Most people were probably in the common rooms playing games or watching TV. We filled our plates and sat down.

"You're pretty quiet," Meredith said.

"It's a lot to take in. Did I just give into him?"

"Yup," she said. "But don't freak. You've got time. Even if Chris and I are right about what's going on. Doesn't mean anything has to change right now."

I let that sink in while I picked at my mountain of mashed potatoes. "It's not that. I feel like I've known him forever but he's still new. Like I've known that he was mine since I first saw him, even if I didn't really realize what that connection was or any idea of what it meant. It's a lot to get used to. Plus, all the rest of the stuff is throwing me off." I motioned down to the food. "Like this. I have to eat a shit-ton just to stay in control."

"It'll get better."

I snorted. "That's what everyone keeps saying."

"They're saying it because it's true."

I knew it would, but that didn't mean there wouldn't be more than a few bumps in the road.

Things were better with Dastien, but he'd mess up and I'd mess up as we figured it out. Once word got around, it'd be hell to pay with Shannon and Imogene. And that didn't even begin to count the whole vampire thing. And Mr. Hoel thing.

Oh and the whole turning furry thing. Christ. How had I forgotten that part?

Chapter Twenty-Nine

The boys joined us for dinner after they cleaned the gym. As soon as they sat, Imogene strutted into the cafeteria. She smirked at me and stopped behind Dastien.

My temper flared to life. I wanted her away from him. Now.

She ran her fingers through his hair and leaned down between Dastien and I. "I thought we were meeting outside?"

My trust in Dastien was still extremely fragile and she was trying to break that. I knew she was trying to get me to react, but I couldn't stop the growl that escaped from me. For some reason, I didn't care when my hands started changing.

Dastien pushed her away, and leaned into me until our noses were touching. He gently placed a hand on each of my cheeks as his eyes started to glow. "Shhhh," he said.

Waves of power ran through me. My muscles

turned to mush and whatever was rising up inside of me laid down.

"Okay?" His face still close to mine, close enough to kiss.

A silly grin spread across my face. Like he was reading my mind, he leaned in and gave me a soft kiss on the lips. I waited to see what his mind would show me, craved to know what was going on beneath the surface, but got nothing. My whole body tingled as he pulled away from me. He didn't get very far, since I was clutching his shirt in my hand.

He laughed, and pulled me to sit across his lap. "Better?"

"I'm not going furry." My words slurred together. "It's totally better."

Imogene snarled. She grabbed the table and flipped it into the air. Dastien stood quickly and blocked me from the flying debris. Chairs screeched across the floor as people dodged the table.

Luckily no one was sitting where it crashed. The force broke our table in two and chairs scattered across the linoleum.

When the din faded from my ears, Dastien stood between me and Imogene. "I'm sorry that I've hurt you, however unintentionally, but this is getting silly, Imogene."

"I'm sorry. You're my oldest friend. My best friend." She looked at the ground. "I apologize."

"It's not me you need to apologize to."

Her gaze met his again, but she shook her head. She kicked chairs from her path as she stormed out of the cafeteria.

I slumped into Dastien. He wrapped an arm

around my waist and looked down at me. His smile made me giggle. It was the same one from the night of the party—the one I hadn't seen since I woke at St. Ailbe's. It made him deadly gorgeous. I reached up to touch his face.

Meredith grabbed my arm and pulled me away from him. "Maybe a little less intense on the shushing next time. You've turned the poor girl to pudding."

I whined as she tugged me away from Dastien.

"Come on, Tess," she said. "Everyone's going to be coming in here soon for a pre-sundown dinner. We should get out of here before people see the mess and start hounding you. Plus, I think you could use a cold shower."

I stared back at Dastien as she dragged me out the cafeteria doors. He bent over, picking up pieces of the table. The only thing I knew about him was that we had the same odd taste in music and that his butt looked really awesome in those jeans. There was so much I didn't know about him. And I really wanted to know everything.

As if he could feel me staring, he looked at me and winked.

"Get me out of here before I do something really embarrassing," I said.

When we got back to the dorm, Meredith did as she promised and shoved me fully dressed into an ice cold shower. I screeched as the water came down and jumped out of the way.

"What the hell was that for?"

"You actually let me put you in the shower. That should tell you something about how you were acting."

I turned the hot water on full blast and closed the shower curtain. "It was like my brain capacity went from smartish to total dimwit in five seconds flat."

"You can thank Dastien for that. He over did it on calming your wolf. I hear it's like being drunk."

"Remind me to never get drunk." I shed my soaked clothes and stepped into the now steaming spray. My mind and body were out of my control. That was enough to chill me to the core.

***

Friday I woke up completely groggy. The sirens had gone off nearly every hour. I desperately wanted to look out the window, but we were under strict orders not to look. Plus, I wasn't going for a repeat, but worry for Dastien kept me up most of the night.

I probably should've known something was up when I saw Mr. Hoel at breakfast in the morning, but ignorance was bliss. He was the President of the Board and, as such, had decided that all us youngins needed a three-hour lecture about the situation on campus as it were.

There were more than a few nasty looks shot my way when news hit in my first period class. It seemed like he was using my example of getting snatched from the dorm for his talk. It was going to eat up everyone's—except for the Freshmens'—martial arts class. With vampires close by, that was the last class that anyone wanted to skip. Even for a day.

I was with them on that, but I didn't mind skipping Were history, which was kind of interesting-ish, or metaphysics, which seemed like a load of hogwash. This week's metaphysics lessons comprised trying to make magic have a scientific edge. I wasn't sure that any amount of rhetoric would convince me chemistry and spells were synonymous.

After lunch, we all piled into the gym. Folding chairs had been lined up and a podium sat in the front of them. I hadn't been in a room—other than the cafeteria—with the whole school before. Spread out across the cafeteria I didn't get much of a sense at how many people actually went to the school, but all in this room it felt both bigger and smaller. Smaller because of the number of people—there couldn't be much more than a couple hundred of us. And bigger because all the energy of the pack together made it feel like there were well over a thousand in the room.

Mr. Dawson, Sebastian, Donovan, and Dastien stood in the back of the room. Dastien and Donovan laughed at something Mr. Dawson said. There was really way too much hotness going on back there. The laughing only made them that much more attractive. Those two really didn't need the bonus points.

I found a chair between Meredith and Adrian. Chris was still keeping his distance from me after Dastien's freakout. I didn't blame him, but it chafed.

Once we were all settled, Mr. Dawson walked up and introduced Mr. Hoel. "Rupert Hoel is the head of the school board here at St. Ailbe's. He wanted to speak to you all about the vampire attacks on the school and the repercussions they could have on student life. I hope you'll all give him the attention he deserves."

I almost laughed. What if I didn't think he deserved any attention? Did Mr. D just give me leave to ignore the lecture? Nice.

"Thank you so much, Michael, for that introduction. I hope that in the next three hours you will come to learn a bit about vampires and the vampire threat. We'll also discuss relations with humans and the future of werewolves in this world. I do hope I have your undivided attention."

I snorted, and Mr. Dawson winked at me as he walked back to his spot against the wall.

The first hour of the lecture was spent talking about vampires and their abilities. Then the plans they had to keep us protected during the night when the vampires would be out.

But slowly what he was talking about changed. It was little comments here and there sprinkled in, but as I recalled each one, they added up to all the ways that werewolves were the best species on the planet. We had a merciful five-minute break and then it was back to the lecture.

The second hour turned my stomach. If there was any doubt that I disliked the man, it quickly disappeared. Mr. Hoel droned on about how humans were the weaker species and differences between the two. Throughout the course of that hour, I found myself grinding my teeth.

I'd heard this before—Caucasians versus African Americans, women versus men—same bullshit arguments. Anything but equality was just a load of crap. It made one half-white, half-Mexican, part-werewolf, part-*bruja* woman want to scream. I didn't fit into any nice little box in Los Angeles, and I sure didn't fit into any of Mr. Hoel's boxes now that I added a hefty dose of werewolf into the mix. I had a good feeling that I was a "lesser citizen" in his eyes. Mustering up the ability to give a shit about that was exceedingly hard. This was some Hilter youth bullshit that Mr. Hoel was trying to pull, and I sincerely hoped I wasn't the only one seeing through his line of crap.

The third hour was brutal. Halfway though I was jonesing to hit something. Or maybe just a specific someone. Too many of my classmates were nodding or clapping to his conclusions. Didn't they see how wrong this was?

When the time came for questions, I made sure mine was the first hand up.

I stood from my chair when he nodded at me. "I get that going to school here means that I have to listen to you wax poetically about how much better werewolves are than humans, but don't you think that you're being a little racist? Or maybe more appropriately species-ist? And what good would it do to really show up the humans? You want to start a species war in a world that is already ravaged by injustice. You talk about honor among wolves, but I don't see any honor in what you're implying."

I expected the open mouths and gasps from my classmates, but what I didn't expect was the clapping and cheering from the back of the room. I pulled out the sides of my invisible skirt and curtseyed before sitting down.

"I wouldn't expect you to understand," Mr. Hoel said. His words were clipped. "A former human would have little hope of grasping at the complexities of what we covered today and will cover in any future lectures."

I cleared my throat. "It's a good thing that being new isn't the same thing as being ignorant. I'm grasping your complexities quite well, I just happen to vehemently disagree with them. And I have to say your vitriol on the human condition really gets under my skin."

"I don't understand—"

"What? Were my words too big for you? Which ones, and I'll try to explain."

Meredith elbowed me. "Oh my God! Stop," she mumbled.

Mr. Hoel strode down the aisle toward me, but Mr. Dawson stepped between us. "Class dismissed. Everyone clear out." Mr. Dawson's order echoed in the silent gym. I wanted to stay and argue with the ignoramus but Adrian grabbed one arm and Meredith the other. They dragged me out of the gym.

"Do you have a death wish?" Meredith whispered. "You already know the Hoels have it out for you. Why'd you do that?"

I shrugged out of their grasp and continued walking to our dorm. "No one was contradicting him. I couldn't just sit there and let him think that we all agreed with that bullshit."

"Well, it was dumb," Adrian said. "He's a powerful enemy for anyone to have, but especially so for a recently bitten girl."

"Standing up against prejudice is never ever dumb."

He sighed. "That's not what I meant."

"Sure." I shrugged. "And look, it's not like he wasn't already my enemy. The only thing that changed is that everyone knows it. That could save my butt."

"I'm not sure if you're suicidal or a genius," Meredith said.

I grinned. "Go with genius. It's way more accurate." I held my fist out to Adrian and he bumped it.

"You're way more badass than me," he said.

"Thanks. I guess I'm gonna change and whatnot. Dinner in a bit?" They nodded.

I went up the stairs to my room. It wasn't until I got to my room that I let out the breath I'd been holding. Maybe going off on Mr. Hoel wasn't the best idea I'd ever had, but unless I figured out time travel, there was no changing it. And even if there was, I didn't think I wanted to.

One girl against three ass-Hoels. Those odds weren't so bad, were they?

Chapter Thirty

I woke up on Saturday totally ready for the weekend. The sirens had gone off all night again, and I couldn't be the only one a little on edge. My only hope was that I'd have a day blissfully free of people gawking at me or blowing my mind with crazy werewolf history or the "physics" behind magic.

A little R and R would go a long way to soothe my mental state.

I listened for people moving about the dorm, but the sweet sound of silence greeted me. The clock said it was eleven. Thank God for sleeping in. The only thing I needed to know was what to do with my day.

I peeked into Meredith's room, but she wasn't there. I hoped she hadn't gone somewhere too fun without me. What did people do on the weekend here anyway?

I threw on some clothes and grabbed a pair of cotton jersey gloves before heading down to the cafeteria. Adrian and Chris sat at the pristine replacement of our usual table. A few guys in all black were scattered around the room, but other than that it was nearly empty, my lucky day.

Chris reclined with his feet on the table. "How's it going?"

"Okay." I ate a bite of my omelet. At least the food was good. It would seriously suck if I had to eat the typical nasty school food by the truckload. "What are you guys up to?"

"Just hanging out," Adrian said. "Thinking about catching a movie."

I waited for a "want to come" but got an uncomfortable silence instead. Adrian squirmed as I stared him down. Why were they being distant all of a sudden?

Chris grabbed my hand. "We'd take you if we could. But we can't."

"Oh, that's okay. I'm sure you guys want time to do guy stuff or something. I'm sure Meredith is around somewhere."

The guys shared a look.

"You guys are totally acting weird. What's going on?"

"Don't be upset," Adrian said. "Meredith and Shannon went shopping."

That totally blew. I'd been dying to get off campus. The fence had been majorly creeping in on me the past few days. Maybe I'd just take my car and go for a drive. Grab some pizza and read a book.

Chris cleared his throat. "Look. You can't leave."

"What!" Now I was pissed.

Adrian raised an eyebrow. "You can't leave campus."

That irked me. Why was I just now hearing about this? "So what, I'm a prisoner?" These boys were driving me nuts. "I really wish everyone would stop beating around the bush and just tell me what the hell I need to know."

A scuffle came from under the table. Chris groaned as Adrian's foot made contact.

"You're not in control yet," Adrian said. "Until you get a handle on your wolf, you can't leave campus."

That was bullshit. "I'd never hurt anyone."

"Think about the past few days," Chris said. "You've been all over the place. We don't know what could happen, and if you were honest with yourself, you'd know it's true."

His words stung more than they should have. Even if they were a little right. I had a bit of an adjustment problem. It should be completely understandable, but I shouldn't be punished for it.

I pushed back from the table. "Got it. Thank you for telling me." They called to me, but I didn't stop. I had to find Mr. Dawson.

As I got closer to his cabin, I heard people yelling. I moved up the porch steps as quietly as I could. I leaned my ear close to the door.

"—completely out of control," Mr. Dawson said. "If he's—"

"We need proof," Sebastian said, his German accent thick with frustration. "Real proof! We cannot go to the rest of the Seven with your word."

"We're being attacked every night. The guys can't keep this up indefinitely. We have to find out what Rupert's planned before he destroys us," Michael said, his voice a low growl. "I'll read him—"

"Not going to happen. If we don't have proof, bringing him in will rip us apart. We're already divided, nearly evenly." Donovan's Irish lilt came through the door. "We cannot afford to be wrong. If ya—"

I took a step closer to the door. The board squeaked.

"Wait. We have a visitor." The door swung open to reveal Mr. Dawson's angry glare. "Is there something I can help you with?"

Yes. I want you to continue talking so I can finish eavesdropping. But I couldn't say that. "Uuuh… I want to go to the movies with Chris and Adrian."

"You've got superb timing, my dear. Talk to her, Michael." Sebastian clapped Mr. Dawson on the back as he walked out the door with Donovan. "I think you need to calm down a bit before we continue this."

Well that didn't go as planned. "I'll be with the guys. I won't hurt anyone."

Mr. Dawson stepped into his tiny kitchen. "Would you like a cup of tea?" he asked, but he didn't wait for my answer. His movements were jerky as he opened a cupboard and filled a dented metal kettle.

I took a seat in his breakfast nook. I didn't think of Mr. Dawson as a tea type. More like coffee or beer. He slammed the kettle onto the stove and switched the gas on.

No wonder the damned thing was dented.

He set a mug and tea bag in front of me. When the kettle whistled, he joined me at the table and poured the water.

I cleared my throat. "So I was right about Mr. Hoel? He's planning something big, right?"

"You're more trouble than I thought." I opened my mouth to ask another question but he shook his head. "You've got more than enough on your plate with everything else going on. I'm handling this." He took a sip of his tea. "Or trying to," he said under his breath.

I crossed my arms. "I can handle it."

"I'm sure you could, pup."

I'd have to figure out more about Mr. Hoel when Meredith got back from her shopping exposition. Which brought me back to why I was there to see Mr. Dawson in the first place. "Why can't I leave campus?"

"Because you won't be ready to be around humans until you've embraced your wolf."

"I'd never—"

He held up a hand. "Don't make promises that you might not be able to keep. It's going to be a hard transition—"

"It *is* hard. Nothing 'going to be' about it."

His mouth curved into a smile. "It *is* hard. I know you don't want to hear it, but this will—"

"Take time," I finished for him. I was exhausted from how many times I'd heard that lately. "I could just take my car and hit the road."

He lifted an eyebrow.

Right. Probably a bad idea. Especially now that I'd brought it up. "How long till I can do normal stuff?"

"That's entirely up to you. It could be tomorrow. It could be a year from now. I'd love to give you a firm date, but I can't."

Fan-freaking-tastic. "Is there anything I can do to change your mind? I'm only asking for a couple of hours off campus. And I'd be with Adrian and Chris. They wouldn't let—"

"No."

"This is totally unfair." I rolled my eyes at my own

cliché. I should be ashamed of myself. I sounded like a petulant teen.

His smile deepened, showing his teeth. "Every werewolf has gone through the same restrictions. That's why they come to this school."

That made me feel mildly better. "How long does it usually take? Give me a ballpark here."

He shrugged. "You're at one with your wolf when you're at one with your wolf."

Great. That wasn't vague at all. "A girl could get mighty bored on campus 24-7. I can't be held responsible for what I might do."

He chuckled. "There's plenty of studying for you to catch up on."

I gave him an even stare. I finally had friends to go out and do stuff with, and I wasn't about to waste my time twiddling my thumbs around campus.

"Here's the deal. You do some learning and try to adjust to the wolf today, and if you've improved at all, we'll see what we can do about tomorrow."

"A surprise?"

He nodded.

"An off-campus surprise?"

"Not sure. We'll have to see." Mr. Dawson went to the small wooden bookcase and pulled a thin hardback from the middle shelf. "Read this. I'll be back in a bit and we'll talk about whatever you have questions about. Okay?"

I glanced down at the cover. *The Werewolf's Bible* stared back at me. "I've got one of these."

"Oh, so you've read it?" He said it in a higher pitch than his normal voice. The guy knew perfectly well I hadn't read it.

"No, but—"

"Read." He strode to the door. "I'll be back in an hour."

I was stubborn only for a little bit. I sipped my tea slowly. Mr. Dawson was insane for drinking hot tea when it was a million degrees outside.

I braced myself for the visions that would come. When the first wave of them was over, I began to read. I hadn't finished the first chapter before the door slammed open.

"What are you doing here?" Dastien stomped over to me, his eyes a bright shade of amber. He was pissed and looking like a crazy-man.

"Reading." What was his problem? I lifted my mug and took a sip while he stared.

He gave a desperate laugh and sank into the seat across from me. "I haven't felt this out of control in years." He leaned forward, putting his head in his hands. "No. I don't think I was ever this inept."

I should've felt bad for him, but I didn't. It reassured me. If everyone thought Dastien was this awesome guy and he'd lost control, then me making an ass out of myself all the time maybe wasn't such a big deal.

"Glad I'm not the only one feeling crazy." I tugged on my ponytail. "Why'd you storm in here like that?"

He sat back. "It's too embarrassing to admit."

"That's a stupid thing to say. Now you have to tell me."

"I thought…" He scrunched his eyes closed. "I thought you and Michael…"

My mouth dropped open. "He's like the principal!" A smile spread across my face. The guy was jealous and I loved it.

"Yeah well, he's Alpha. He could handle you. If anyone here could take you from me…" Dastien let out a desperate sounding laugh. "I don't know what my deal is. I just keep thinking that you're going to change your mind about me. About us."

"You're saying that like it makes sense. Have you seen yourself?" I grinned when he started laughing. I picked up my book. "Everything has been out of my control lately. And now I found out I can't leave campus." I sighed dramatically. "I'm tired of not understanding. Ignorance isn't bliss. It's completely frustrating. I'm going to read this thing, and then I won't feel so freaking lost all the time. So no distracting me."

Before I could read one sentence, Dastien yanked the book from my hands. "You don't need this."

I narrowed my gaze at him. "Just because you're handsome doesn't mean you get to boss me around. I'm trying to learn some control. I can't be stuck at this school forever. I'll go crazy."

"Don't be so stubborn. When you feel lost or don't get something, just come to me. I'll always be there to help."

That was sweet. "I can't always lean on you. I have to figure this out for myself."

He nodded slowly. "I admire that, but sometimes it's smarter to ask for help when you need it." He walked around the nook and pulled me up. "Let's go for a walk."

My heart sped at the thought of being alone with him. It hadn't been just us since the party.

I separated our hands to pull off my gloves and

tuck them in my pocket. It was Dastien, and I never got much of anything from him. And if I got something from him today, I didn't think I'd mind it. Extra intel on the boy would be more than welcome. "Okay," I said. "Let's go."

He held out his hand. As soon as we touched, an electric spark stung my fingertips. I pulled away, shaking my hand. "What was that?"

Dastien looked at his hand as if it were a stranger. "I don't know."

"I'd say static electricity, but that doesn't quite cover it." I'd felt it in my soul.

"No. That was something else. Something more." He reached out again.

I hesitated this time.

"Let's just see if it happens again," he said.

I closed my eyes as I put my hand in his. It was different the second time. Something clicked into place and I could almost sense a line of energy connecting us. I gasped as it tightened around my heart.

When I dared to open my eyes, he was staring again at our linked hands. "What was that?" I said.

"I don't know for sure."

My heart raced. "Guess."

"Your heart's racing. Let's drop it for now. It can wait." He finally looked up at me. A slow grin spread across his face. "Trust me. It can wait."

"Okaaaay." Weirdo. But I had enough to worry about without this thing, whatever it was. "Are we still going on the walk?"

"I wouldn't let you out of my sight if I could manage it."

I tugged on his hand. "Not cool. That's more than a little stalker-ish, dude."

He laughed. "Okay. So that didn't come out right." He thought for a second. "How about I'd like to spend as much time with you as you'll let me."

I nodded. "Better. Just this side of Stalkerville."

He gazed down at me. "I thought girls liked that kind of thing."

"Yeah. It's kind of nice." I grinned.

Chapter Thirty-One

We walked in silence. I didn't know where he was leading me, and I didn't care. The ground crunched beneath my shoes. The smell of trees, grass, dirt and clean air was intoxicating. It wasn't the same air as LA. You had to breathe through the layer of smog there. Some days it was so thick, you couldn't even see the mountains. Totally gross. But in Texas, the fresh air made me long to spend time outside even in spite of the heat.

We reached a sharp drop. I glimpsed the rocky bed below us. "The creek?"

"Yep. We'll get heavy rains in the winter and spring and it'll fill up for a while, but by summer it's always dry," he said. "Want to go back or climb down?"

Caves pocked the wall on the other side of the creek bed. One of them looked large enough for someone to live in. Shadows filled its depths. But the thing that made me pause was the ladder that hung between it and the cave below. It was weather-beaten and missing a few rungs, which made it look ancient. "What's in those caves?"

Dastien looked where I pointed. "Some Native American drawings. It was a popular place for spirit quests."

"Seriously?"

"Yep."

Cool. I shaded the sun to try to get a better look, but it didn't do any good. "Can we go look?"

The side of Dastien's mouth lifted. "Sure. There's a small path down here. Be careful. It's steep."

I watched Dastien take the first couple of steps. His lithe movements mesmerized me. His muscles tensed and released under his tight grey T-shirt, and his jeans made his butt look so cute. I titled my head as I stared.

He chose that moment to look back at me.

"You coming?" A grin spread across his face. "What are you looking at?"

"Just enjoying the view." No guy ever caught my attention the way Dastien did. I studied his face, with its strong angles. His amber eyes seemed to be laughing at me, and his grin sure said I was amusing.

It took some effort to reign in my hormones.

I turned my gaze to the ground and started down the path. He wasn't kidding. It was steep. Dastien made it look easy as he climbed down, but dirt and rocks skidded out from under my shoes, dropping the forty feet or so to the bottom. I kept one hand against the cliff wall as we walked.

I gasped as I slipped, pebbles scattering.

Dastien grabbed my waist. "Careful."

"You didn't tell me I might die on this trail."

He didn't laugh like I expected. "I would never let you fall."

I rolled my eyes. "I was kidding."

"But I'm not."

The moment was too intense for words. He kept eye contact a second longer than was comfortable, and then turned back to the trail.

By the time we reached the bottom, I'd worked up a good sweat. I scanned up and down the creek. "It's so quiet." With the creek walls and trees cutting off even the normal outdoor noise, it felt like we were the only people for miles.

Dastien sat down on a large rock. "Yeah."

"It's peaceful here. I'm peaceful." I sat down next to him and took a deep breath. It was the most settled I'd felt in days. Years. I'd always been frazzled from the torrent of visions. Sure, I'd gotten used to them, managed them, but it was never easy. "Something's changed."

Dastien stared at me. He knew what was going on and the jerk wasn't sharing.

"What?" I said.

He shrugged.

"Why do I feel so calm?"

"I'm an alpha. One of the perks of being a strong alpha means that you can hold a pack." He laughed at the confusion on my face. "I've used it on you a couple of times. Made you feel calm. Settled down your wolf to stop the shift."

I crossed my arms. He had done something to me before, but I'd been too grateful for it to ask about what it was. "Are you doing it now?"

"Not exactly, but your wolf is content with mine."

His gaze was too intense to hold. I stared at the caves. "God. I've been acting like a crazy person." I sighed. "My temper's gone totally nutso."

"You'll be okay. Everyone goes through a phase where they feel like that."

I guessed that was true, especially after Imogene's display in the cafeteria. That girl was out of control for sure. Or maybe she was just psycho in general. Which brought the question up again. "Why?"

"Why what?"

"Why me? Am I really what you wanted? From what I hear, you had your pick of the girls. Why would you risk it? With me."

He ran a finger along my bottom lip. "You want to know what was going through my mind when I bit you?"

God. I wished he wouldn't do that. It took everything in me not to lick his finger. "Yeah. It might help."

"It's hard to..." He sighed. "Okay. So I guess I should start at the beginning. My whole life I've felt as if part of myself was missing. It was a nagging feeling, and it made me anxious. Irritable."

"You mean it made you a dick."

He chuckled. "You could say that. I wasn't mean to anyone, but closed off. And then a few days before you came...there was this sense one day when I was in Michael's cabin. I felt this presence and it was like something clicked. But just as it did, it was gone. I knew I was missing my other half, but had no idea how to find you. I kind of went a little crazy."

"It's not like I planned to do that—"

"So it was you?"

I nodded. "Nothing like that has ever happened to me before. I left that vision and punched this jerk from my class in his face. Broke his nose. In the middle of my dad's going-away party. It was kind of a disaster." And one I wasn't proud of.

His grin made me laugh. "When I first saw you at your house, for a second the wolf took over. He was drawn to you. Had to have you. I'd let you get away once already and he wasn't going to allow it to happen again." He started pacing. "I didn't get control back for days. I was restless, so I went to the mall. But after I talked to you—it only got worse. I convinced some of the guys to go hiking, hoping to burn off steam. And then I found you."

But why me? He wasn't giving me the answer that I wanted—needed—and a heaviness settled in my chest.

"What I did—it's unforgivable. And yet, I want you to do the impossible."

His amber gaze was so intense, I couldn't look away. My heart sped. "What do you want me to do?"

"I want you to forgive me. I want you to be mine."

I was short of breath. "You're not answering my question. Why me? You don't even know me. I don't know you."

"Don't lie."

He was frustrating the crap out of me. "I'm not lying! You're the one that's avoiding the question."

"Okay. So I don't have a perfect answer. When you meet your match you just know. The more we get to know each other, the more we'll know how right we are."

That warmed me. "Good answer."

His gaze turned from amber to gold. "I want to announce it to the pack at the next full moon."

That sounded serious. "Wouldn't Imogene oppose that?"

He grinned. "Jealous?"

"Hey! I'm not the one going around beating my chest. From what I've heard, she was the one you were supposed to be with, and isn't she your girlfriend?"

"She's not my girlfriend. She's my friend that's a girl. We grew up together. Our families went on vacation together. I think both she and her father wanted us to end up mated. And to be honest, I did give it a shot. But it didn't feel right and I ended it before summer."

I hugged my knees into my chest. The need for him filled me up, threatening to take any will power I had left. Whatever happened, I couldn't let him take over my life. I wouldn't let myself be that girl.

He knelt in front of me. "Give me a chance."

Crap. He was going to get his way. "This is way insane. I'm a normal, ordinary girl. Okay maybe not normal exactly, but normal-ish."

"You don't honestly believe that, do you?"

I narrowed my gaze at him. "If you wanted me so badly, then why'd you ignore me?"

"I was trying to let you adjust. To give you space. Like Mr. Dawson asked. Not to mention your family. It wasn't easy to stay away from you."

I opened my mouth with a retort, but he held up a hand.

"No. Not as hard as adjusting has been for you. But seeing the guys following you around..." His eyes flashed even brighter. He paced all the way to the other side of the creek and when he came back they were amber again. "I did something awful to you. Everyone thought it would be best if I stayed away, gave you time to get used to everything before I staked my claim as your mate."

It killed me to say it, but I had to ask. "And if I didn't want to be with you?"

"I'd let you go. Or try to." He ran his fingers through his hair, making it stand on end. "No. I don't know that I could do that. I'd wait. I'd do my best to win you over."

"Okay." I swallowed my nerves. "The whole mate word freaks me out. So let's just leave that out for now."

The smile that spread across his face made me melt.

Yep. He was dangerous.

"Deal." He held out a hand and pulled me off the bedrock.

His hand brushed against my arm and a tingle ran up it. "What's that?"

"Best guess?"

Something was better than nothing. "I'll take it."

"It's our mate bond settling in."

My heart kicked into over-drive. "Hey! Ix-nay on the ate-may word."

"Don't freak out on me. A deal is a deal. Our wolves are on a different level than us right now. But we'll catch up. We've got time."

"Time." My gut was screaming at me that I didn't need any time to know he was the one, but my brain knew better. "But don't I have to choose before my birthday?"

"I don't think they'll hold you to those rules." He brushed his fingertips along my face, and tucked a strand of hair behind my ear. "Just try to relax."

Heat spread through my body at his touch. "Right. Relax." The guy was turning me into a mumbling moron with the touch of his fingertips. This was bad news. Or maybe good news, depending on how I looked at it. I shook my head, trying to clear it. "Can I ask you a question?"

"You can ask me anything."

"How come I don't see anything from you?"

He raised his eyebrows, proving that I'd managed to catch him by surprise. "I'm not just an alpha. I'm Alpha. You'll only see what I want you to see. Or what you ask to see."

"How come I get stuff from Chris? Isn't he an alpha?"

He ran his hand over his stubble. "I guess you really do need to read the book."

I pushed him away from me, but he didn't budge. "Jerk. That's what I was supposed to be doing."

"What I meant was that there is alpha and then there is Alpha. The level of power a person has is unique to that person. I have more than Chris—much more than him—and since I found out about your abilities, I've been trying to guard my thoughts."

That made sense. Mom did that too. She wasn't as good as Dastien was, but she was decent at letting me only see some things. "One more. Why do you call Mr. Dawson, Michael?"

"That's his name."

I gave him a soft punch in the shoulder.

He grabbed my fist and opened it to link our fingers together. "My parents died when I was eight. Michael was their best friend, as were the Hoels. But Michael was the one who took me in, raised me."

I felt terrible for asking. "I'm sorry. That must've been awful."

"Thanks."

I stared at his larger hand enveloping mine. "Why did you leave? At the party after…" He'd run away that night. It bugged me that he'd done that.

"I didn't leave you at the party, but my wolf had control. I shifted and couldn't let myself get close to any of the other people there."

I remembered the wolf outside my window that night. "You waited outside my window?"

"Until your light went out." He pressed his lips together for a second. "And I was outside your room in the infirmary as you transitioned back and forth for days on end. You didn't stop changing forms until I finally broke into the room—"

I so didn't want to hear about that. I slapped my hand over his mouth. He bit it softly, and I felt it all the way to my core. I rubbed my hand off on my jeans.

"I can't undo what I did, but I can help you gain some control."

"You can?"

They'd told me that werewolves were stronger, but I couldn't stifle a gasp when Dastien picked me up as if I weighed nothing. He jumped onto a giant boulder.

He put me on my feet and sat. "Close your eyes."

I plopped in front of him and closed them.

"Take three deep inhales and exhales. Feel your body move. Feel the air come in, flowing down deep into your lungs, filling up your chest. Then follow it as it flows back out."

I recognized this from the yoga class.

"Focus on your hands...your feet...your arms...your legs...your chest. Feel the wolf deep inside of you. In the center of you, of who you are."

I opened my eyes after a few minutes. He was sitting there with his eyes closed. I felt bad about disturbing him, but then he opened one eye.

"Close them."

"Nothing's happening."

"That's because you're not relaxing."

I grumbled about having a hard time relaxing on a hard rock, but he ignored me. I don't know how long I sat there, before something clicked. I felt the rippling underneath the surface of my skin and gasped. "What is that?"

"You've nearly found her."

"Her?"

"The wolf."

"Shut up." I slapped his leg. "That sounds completely mental."

His golden gaze met mine. "She's a part of you. Once you start acknowledging her, she'll settle down and your moods won't be so erratic. She needs to trust you as much as you need to trust her." He laughed. I must've looked as confused as I felt. "Close your eyes again. Go back. See her. Feel her. She's there to protect you. To make you stronger."

I had thought of her as separate from me, but maybe she wasn't. The only thing I knew for sure was that it was complicated. I didn't really know what I felt, but when I opened my eyes again, I was steadier.

"Better?" Dastien said.

"Yeah. I think so?" I really hoped so. "Thank you."

"Anytime." He pointed up to the cave. "Still want to go take a look or head back?"

My stomach answered for me. I threw my hand over it. "Sorry. I think I might be hungry. I've got to get food fast or…" God. I just had a breakthrough and now I was going to ruin it. But I didn't want to shift.

"Don't worry. You won't change. Unless you want to?"

I waved my hands wildly in the air. "Definitely not. I mean what if I get stuck as a wolf?"

He touched his forehead to mine as he laughed. "You won't get stuck," he said when he caught his breath.

I shoved him. "I'm never telling you anything ever again."

He rubbed his thumb along my bottom lip. "That's not true."

"Yes, it is. I won't tell you anything when you do stuff like laugh at me."

His lips met mine. I wrapped my arms around his neck and pulled myself into his lap. When I felt his tongue, I opened my mouth and let him in.

When my stomach growled again, he pulled away. "Let's get you some food." He gave me one last soft kiss. "I'd do anything for you, Tessa. I know you don't realize that now, but you will."

That thought made me grin, even if I wasn't sure that it was true. He led us to a shorter part of the creek wall and started to climb. I'd never gone hiking without a clear-cut path before. It was fun, but hard. When we reached the top, rivers of sweat ran down the sides of my face. I lifted my shirt to wipe them away.

"Have a nice hike?" Mr. Dawson was standing there waiting for us.

I cleared my throat. I was supposed to be reading in his cabin. "Yeah. But I didn't read—"

"It's okay," Mr. Dawson cut me off. "Seems like it did you some good."

"I think so," I said.

Dastien stepped between Mr. Dawson and me. "I'd like to ask permission to leave campus tomorrow with Tessa. I'll vouch for her."

Mr. Dawson crossed his arms. "Where? When? For how long?"

"To the bookstore. In the morning. Just a couple of hours."

Mr. Dawson nodded. "Sounds like a good idea for both of you. Permission granted."

Shock filled me. "Really? Dastien can take me alone, but Chris and Adrian couldn't take me to the movies?"

Mr. Dawson smiled. I'd forgotten that he was handsome. "Yes. Dastien's already proven that he can keep you under control."

Shit. He probably knew about what happened in the gym. I don't think my face ever burned so much.

When Mr. Dawson left, I jumped up and down, tugging on Dastien's shirt. He laughed and put his arm around my shoulder.

"How did you know that I'd want to go to a bookstore?" I said.

"Who do you think set up your room?" He kissed my nose. My heart sped, wanting more. "Your mother gave me quite the lecture about keeping them in order."

I laughed at the image of her lecturing Dastien. She could be a bad ass when she wanted to be.

As we started back to school, one dark cloud hung over my otherwise sunny day. What was I going to do about Shannon? Not to mention Chris and all the other guys. At least maybe they would leave me alone now.

And then there was the problem of Imogene and her dad and the vampires.

I said a little prayer that everyone was still out having fun when I got back. But my luck had never been that good.

Chapter Thirty-Two

Gabriel and a few of the guys strode up to me as we walked down one of the paths to the courtyard. Dastien's hand came to rest on the small of my back and the guys stopped. I didn't need to look up at him to know he was giving them a serious stare down.

One by one, the boys looked at the ground and stepped back to let us pass. Being with Dastien definitely had its perks. Maybe the rest of the guys would quit telling me what and how much to eat.

A few heads popped up to stare at us as we entered the cafeteria. But after we'd gotten our food, he led us to a table alone.

"Chris said you're one of the best fighters."

He shrugged one shoulder. "I had the best teaching me. My father and Michael. The two of them sparring was one of my favorite things to watch." He leaned forward. "Do the rumors about you and our relationship bother you?"

"I'm used to being pointed at." I ran my fingers

through the ends of my hair. "I try not to let them get to me."

"But they do?"

I squirmed under his stare. He saw too much of me already. "I'm only human." He stayed quiet. "Whatever. You know what I mean."

"So you really like all the groups you wear shirts for?" he asked.

"Seeing as how I made most of those shirts—yes. I really do."

"Favorite show you've seen live?"

I chewed on my lip as I thought. "There was this Above & Beyond show that I went to a few months ago. It was epic. They played for two and half hours and the tracks were sick. They kept turning down the volume to let us sing along with vocals. You know what it's like when the whole crowd was in sync—dancing. It was just perfection."

"When was the show?"

I was never fantastic with remembering dates. "Mid-April-ish. At Avaland in LA."

He grinned. "I was there."

"Shut up." There was no way he was there. I would've noticed him.

"It was epic. The track they ended on—"

"Amazing, right? Gave me chills." I shook my head. This was crazy. "What's your favorite show ever?"

"I saw Apparat play in Munich. It was amazing."

"You've been to Munich?" It seemed weird picturing him anywhere but St. Ailbe's.

"I've traveled quite a bit. My father was from France, so I spent summers growing up there. As I got older, I roamed around Europe a bit." He shrugged. "I try to go to a new place every year. It's a thing."

"Sounds fun." I always wanted to travel more. "So who is Apparat?"

"You don't know Apparat?"

No way. He just out weird-music-ed me. "Should I?"

"Yes. For sure. I'll send you the tracks."

As we talked, he became more like a real person than an obsession—which should have eased my attraction to him, but it didn't. Every time he said something, I wanted to know more. He was sweet and laughed easily. Yet I knew from watching him fight vampires that he was dangerous.

When we finished eating, Dastien and I sat among the trees and did more control exercises. I got lost in the sounds of inhales and exhales, the wind softly breezing through the leaves, the chirps of the birds. I could've sat with him forever. My hands rested on my knees. It took me a while to realize they were getting hot. Then fingers slowly linked with mine. A lazy smile spread across my face.

"I have to go patrol, *ma chérie*. And you have to go inside before the sun sets."

I tightened my fingers around his. "No," I said, squeezing my eyes shut.

His lips pressed against my forehead.

I flopped onto the grass, tugging him down too.

He hovered over me, his weight on his forearms as he lightly brushed his lips against mine. I growled. That was not the kiss I was going for.

"Come on. I'll walk you to the dorm." He pulled me to my feet. "We're not going to have a repeat of the other night."

A shiver ran down my spine. Being inside was suddenly very appealing.

When we got to the entrance to the dorm, he spun me in his arms. His lips weren't soft this time. They demanded more. I closed my eyes and wrapped my arms around him, pulling him closer to me. His tongue brushed against mine, and I lost it. I gripped the back of his shirt in my hands, pulling my body flush with his.

By the time he inched back, we were both out of breath. His forehead rested against mine. "I'll pick you up in the morning for our trip off campus. Go inside. Be safe." I kept my eyes closed for a second as I leaned back against the door. His heat was gone, leaving me chilled. "Holy shit," I said to myself. He was beyond intense.

When I opened my eyes, he was already in wolf-form running across campus. A group of wolves waited for him next to one of the buildings. I watched until he disappeared from view, and then slid shakily to the ground.

It took me a few minutes to trust that my legs would work.

Meredith's room was empty while I got ready for bed. I guessed they were still out, but I wasn't upset about it anymore. Nothing they were doing could compare to what I'd experienced that day.

I went to bed smiling for the first time since I got to St. Ailbe's.

***

The next morning, I was already dressed and ready to go on my date-ish thing with Dastien when Meredith stumbled sleepily into my room.

I clicked off my music. "Sorry. Didn't meant to wake you?"

She waved me off and mumbled something incoherently.

I wore a flowy, short purple skirt and a grey tank top with flying little black birds printed across the front. "What do you think?" I said as I ran my hands down the skirt.

"About?"

"My outfit?"

"Are you going somewhere?"

I lifted my chin up. "Yes."

"Really?" She yawned and curled up on my unmade bed. "Mr. Dawson lifted the jail-time?"

"Kind of. Dastien is taking me to the bookstore. Mr. Dawson said Dastien would be held responsible for me."

Meredith laughed. "Wow. So. You and Dastien."

"Kind of." I couldn't stop the blush from spreading. "I guess. We're taking it slow. Very slow."

She jumped and swung me into a hug. "This is so exciting. Were we right? About the mate thing?"

"It's weird that you can just pick me up like that." I tapped her shoulder and she put me down. "And ix-nay on the ate-may. That word is now verboten. Freaks me out."

"Ha! Every girl here would kill for the connection that you guys have. Including me. So mate. Mate. MATE."

I stuck my fingers in my ears and sang loudly as

she talked.

She waved her hand in my face. "Okay. I'm over it." She looked me up and down. "And yes. Cute and casual."

A knock came from my door. "Come in," I said.

Dastien opened the door and leaned against the doorjamb. "You ready?"

My mouth went dry as I took him in. Well-worn jeans hung low on his hips. His white T-shirt had a bright colored map on it that looked almost like the London Underground but wasn't. I wanted to get a closer look but he distracted me with his smile.

Shit. He could lean against things so well. I cleared my throat. "What's on your shirt?"

He started to blush a little. "It's a bus map. For Westeros."

"You read George RR Martin?"

He grinned.

Why did we have so much in common? It was weird. "Let's go," I said as I tugged on a pair of gloves.

"You two crazy kids have fun," Meredith called after us.

"Goodbye, Meredith," Dastien said as he closed the door.

"God he's hot," Meredith said from behind the door.

I grabbed Dastien's hand, linking our fingers together. "We heard that!" I said.

He winked at me and my heart stuttered.

Before we got to the parking lot, Mr. Dawson stopped us. Faint shadows under his eyes showed his exhaustion. "You're needed."

Imogene stood next to Mr. Dawson looking pretty

satisfied with herself. All the hairs on the back of my arms stood at attention.

"Can any of the others handle it?" Dastien asked.

Mr. Dawson's lips thinned. "Afraid not."

Dastien squeezed my hand before letting go. "I'll be back as soon as I can."

He didn't spare me a second glance as the three of them took off. Every time I thought I was getting a handle on us, he disappeared. I swear I saw his back receding in the distance more than I saw his face. All the little doubts in my head telling me he was too good to be true reared their ugly heads.

It didn't help that he was leaning down close to Imogene as she talked to him quietly. Or that she looked back at me and grinned like she'd won this one.

I wanted to stomp my foot, to scream and kick something, just anything, but I didn't. Sinking to her level would be a mistake. If Dastien was really my m-word, then I'd have to trust him at some point, but the fact was that I didn't. Not fully. Not yet.

When I got back to my room, I plopped down on my bed. Something was going on. And where were Sebastian and Donovan? I hadn't seen them since yesterday afternoon. I had a funny feeling about it, but didn't know what to do.

I yanked on the ends of my gloves as I thought. I couldn't take them off and try to get visions. Could I?

"Back so soon?" Meredith said from the doorway.

"Something's up. Mr. Dawson said that he needed Dastien. So he left…with Imogene."

"Yikes." She sat next to me. "Well, I'm sure it's nothing big. I mean when your Alpha says shift, you say woof-woof. I'm sure he'll make it up to you."

"I know it's completely stupid, but I'm just having problems figuring out what to do." I sighed. "I guess I don't trust him. He bit me and ran. He ignored me. And when he finally gives me the time of day I swoon?" I punched my pillow. "Am I really that pathetic?"

She squeezed my leg. "You're not pathetic. Imogene is trying to mess with your head. You can't let that evil bitch win."

We sat there in silence for a minute while I stewed. The dorms were eerily quiet, but it was still early. And the weekend. And with Imogene gone...

"I have a crazy idea," I said. "But we could totally get caught and it might be a really, really, seriously bad idea."

Meredith rubbed her hands together. "This sounds like it starts with 't' and ends with 'rouble' and that is just my speed."

"Let's search Imogene's room."

Meredith laughed for a second before she realized I wasn't kidding. "You're for serious?"

"Come on. Everyone is asleep. Imogene is gone with Dastien. They're going to be at least a little while. I just want to look."

"That is a terrible idea. She'll totally know you were in there." She tapped her nose. "No way can you fool this."

She had a point. "Thing is, I really don't care if she knows I was in there. I just want to know what's going on. The girl tried to get me killed. And she's trying to take my ate-may."

"You know that 'ate-may' is just another way of

saying 'ma—"

I slapped my hand over her mouth. "Don't say it."

She pulled my hand away. "Fine. But it's the same thing."

"Whatever. You going to watch my back or what?"

"Not doing anything else right now." She shrugged. "Why not?"

I threw my gloves on the bed. "Let's do this."

Imogene's room was on the third floor. The door wasn't locked. "You wolves sure are trusting," I whispered to Meredith.

"We don't usually mess with each other's stuff. Your scent is like fingerprints, only way more obvious. It keeps you honest."

Imogene's room was messy. With how perfect she dressed—not even a hair out of place—I thought her room would be tidy. The sty was a surprise. Piles of dirty clothes covered the walking space.

"Dude," Meredith whisper-shouted. She held up a pair of jeans. "This pair costs like hundred dollars and she's just thrown them on the ground like they're trash. What the hell?"

I shrugged. Now that I was here, I didn't really want to touch anything. It was just so dirty. I stood in one place as I scanned the room, trying to decide where to begin.

"Here." Meredith handed me a journal. "Try this."

As soon as my fingers brushed the worn brown leather, I saw absolutely nothing. I closed my eyes, trying to concentrate. I shook my head. "It's not working."

I tried her pillow. Then ran my fingers along her

laptop's keyboard. Nerves made it hard to breathe.

Why wasn't I seeing anything?

"Try this one."

Meredith handed me a necklace. Its thin gold chain held a single tiny heart charm. It was simple and elegant—something I'd pick out for myself. That annoyed me.

I reached out and closed my hand around the necklace.

The vision knocked me on my ass.

Imogene was kissing Dastien.

I can't believe this is finally happening, she thought.

His tongue brushed hers and I could feel how happy kissing him made her.

I opened my hand and dropped the necklace on the pile of clothes at my feet. "This was a terrible idea." A hot tear ran down my cheek. "I think I'm going to be sick."

"Come on. Let's get the fuck out of here."

I hugged my arms around my stomach. It was in the past. He hadn't been cheating. But it sure felt like cheating.

That was something I never needed to see. *The curse of visions strikes again.*

Meredith moved to hug me, but I dodged it. "Sorry. Don't think I can handle any more visions at the moment."

We went back to my room. She sat at my desk. "What was it?"

I shook my head. "Something icky." But there was no unseeing it. "Dastien and her together."

"Shiiiiit."

I grinned in spite of my mood. "You're telling

me."

"Well, they broke up a while ago. Clearly she's not over it, but Dastien is. For sure. I know this stuff is not normal for you, but Weres don't cheat. It's not possible. So yeah, sucks that you saw it. But everyone has a past right?"

"Not me."

"Right. Visions." She balled up a piece of paper and threw it at me. "Enough with the pity party. Let's figure out our plan for today."

A plan? "You're not going anywhere?"

"Nah. About the mall...sorry for going without you, but, in my defense, Shannon had been pestering me. And then with everything with you and Dastien, she's been in a mood. I couldn't put it off."

She didn't have to apologize, but it was nice that she did anyway. "It's okay."

"No. It's not. Chris and Adrian found us at the mall after they saw how upset you were and gave us quite a lecture, and they were right. I should've left a note at least. When we came back, we saw you and Dastien were hanging. Shannon might be cranky but she'll get over it. She takes time to warm up to people."

We wandered down to the cafeteria. When we got there, the gang announced that they wanted to have a movie marathon. All werewolves. All day. Chris said I needed to learn more about being one of them. And this was the most fun way, even if the movies were horribly inaccurate. Then the debate really began— start with *An American Werewolf in London* or *Ginger Snaps*?

I found their love of werewolf movies fascinating.

Nothing was better than seeing their species depicted as monsters. Until recently I'd seen them as the bad guys too. There weren't that many movies where werewolves were the heroes. They were always a step away from zombies with their hunger for human flesh. A totally unfair assessment.

Halfway through *Ginger Snaps* there was a knock on Meredith's door. Mrs. Ramirez peeked in. "Did you order pizzas?"

Meredith popped up from her perch. "Yes. That's us." The door opened farther, showing three guys carrying pizzas stacked higher than their head.

"Holy shit," I said. "Meredith. There are only five of us."

Chris leaned over. "Five werewolves. And two of them are boys."

The pizza guys handed over the pizzas to Adrian and Shannon while Meredith signed the bill. When Meredith handed back the bill, the pale-faced pizza guys flinched. Why did they let human delivery guys on campus if they were so afraid of us?

"Thank you. You can go now," Meredith said to them.

"I'll be down the hall. Boys, you need to be in your own dorm before nightfall," Mrs. Ramirez said. "We're still on lockdown."

"Yes, ma'am," Adrian said. "We understand."

We ended up watching both *Ginger Snaps* and *An American Werewolf in London* before switching to *Buffy* episodes. Apparently season two was when it got good, because that's when Oz—the werewolf—joined the cast. It was quite possibly the most normal day I'd ever had. I never thought I'd be able to have friends, and spend the day relaxing with them.

But when I went to sleep that night, Dastien was the only thing I could think of. He hadn't stopped by. No calls or texts. Hell, I wasn't sure if he even had my cell number, but it still annoyed me.

The next morning I was getting worried about not hearing from him. There hadn't been any sirens, but that didn't mean he wasn't fighting vampires somewhere else. What if he was hurt?

I tried to push away my worry as the gang and I finished breakfast and then headed over to the school building. Starting my second week, the knots in my stomach had untangled somewhat, but it was still an adjustment.

Chris had been helping me with metaphysics during breakfast. We'd just left the cafeteria when I realized I'd forgotten my notebooks.

"I'll catch up with you," I said to Chris as I ran back through the doors.

I slid between tables and the mass of people heading out. Frustration filled me as I realized I'd be late for class. In my old schools, this wouldn't have been a big deal. But Mrs. Ramirez didn't look kindly on tardiness. She'd majorly reamed out Shannon when she was five minutes late on Thursday.

I snatched up my notebook. And then stopped.

Dastien was at a table in the corner talking to Imogene.

Why hadn't he come over to my table? He hadn't even said hello.

I stood there, frozen in time as they got up together. His arms wrapped around her in a hug. His smile was bright when he pulled away.

I let out a breath. A hug was just a hug. He'd said they were old friends. I couldn't let myself be the jealous girlfriend.

And then she kissed him. On. The. Lips.

Rage boiled my blood. I spun around, not wanting to see what happened next. I had to get out of there before I lost control and ripped her face off. Shit. Who was I kidding? I was totally losing control.

I wouldn't let him see me like this. I wouldn't let her see me.

Tears blurred my vision as I raced across the courtyard to class. I stopped just outside the room and took a deep breath. Everyone was already seated. I looked down, letting my hair hang in front of my face, and entered the room.

Meredith waved me over. "You okay?"

"No." But that was all I could get out before Mrs. Ramirez walked through the door.

She started lecturing, but I couldn't pay attention. Meredith tried to pass me a note, but I shook my head. I could feel the wolf pacing inside me, aching to get out. To squash whatever hurt me. But there was no way I would let that happen. Not in the middle of class. I just needed to concentrate.

Hair sprouted along my arms as I tried to focus on taking notes. I inhaled slowly and exhaled but it didn't help. My knuckles cracked and popped, forcing me to drop my pencil.

"Tessa?" Meredith whispered.

I caught Mrs. Ramirez's gaze. "May I go to the restroom?"

She watched me for a second before nodding.

The chair screeched as I pushed back from my

desk. I couldn't get out of there fast enough.

Chapter Thirty-Three

In the hall I found my favorite person, Imogene, looking through my locker. Half its contents littered the hallway.

I lunged over to her. "What the hell is your problem?"

"You go through my stuff. I go through yours." Imogene flicked one of my textbooks down the hall.

Okay. She had a point, but the girl was making a mess. "Can I help you find something?"

"Sure, *bruja*." The metal clanged as she slammed it closed. "Where's the *gris-gris*?"

"The what?" I didn't need this. Not from her. Not when my wolf was so close to the surface.

"You know—the voodoo charm. The spell. Whatever the fuck it is that you did to him." Imogene took a step toward me and crossed her arms. "I want it. Like yesterday."

Was she serious? "I don't have whatever it is that you're talking about. I didn't do anything to anyone."

I managed to get out the words through teeth that suddenly felt too sharp.

"There is no way he'd lose control like that without you doing something to make him lose it." She moved closer. "No way he'd leave me. Especially not for some half-human half-witch loser."

"It seemed to me that you two are still pretty damned cozy. So fine. You win. I'm not about to fight for some cheating asshole. He's all yours. But you need to stay away from me."

She took another step. I didn't move back. I let her come.

"If only it were that easy."

A frustrated laugh broke free. "You're crazier than I thought."

She shoved my shoulder until my back knocked into the lockers. "Give it to me."

I didn't like her touching me. And I sure as shit didn't like the way she had me cornered. "I don't have anything to give you. So get your hand. Off. Me."

She snarled and pushed me again.

My tenuous control shattered. Heat burned my skin and my teeth lengthened, nipping my lip. "Get your hand off me."

She moved her hand. Faster than I could track, her fist slammed into my face. My head whipped back, cracking against the lockers. I was too angry to feel any pain.

A door squeaked open.

"Tessa. Imogene. Stop fighting right now!"

I growled at Mrs. Ramirez. She looked at the ground and stepped back. Mrs. Ramirez whispered to someone to find Dastien or Mr. Dawson, but all my focus was on Imogene.

The next punch hit my stomach, and the air whooshed out of me. She hit my face again, and I tasted blood.

My wolf growled. A red haze narrowed my vision until all I saw was Imogene. My arms rippled as fur covered them. I launched myself across the hallway, throwing Imogene against the lockers. The part of me awakening was scary, but I was done being polite.

I punched and her nose crunched in response. I wrapped my arms and legs around her and twisted. We landed on the ground with me sitting on top of her hips.

"Stop. Moving. Now." I put a little power behind the words and she quit struggling. I didn't let go. I wouldn't be tricked twice. I sat up on top of her torso so she couldn't move, and put my hand on her chest to keep her still.

My anger blossomed as I stared down at her. My gloves ripped along the tips as my fingers lengthened and nails grew until it looked like something in between hand and claw. I was torn between what the wolf wanted—to end a rival for good, and what I wanted—to maintain some semblance of my sanity.

Imogene struggled under me. If she started to fight me again, I didn't know what my wolf would do, and that scared me. My nails drew blood as they touched the soft part of her neck. If I relaxed my hand at all, they would tear right through her flesh.

"Once I tell Dastien what a freak you are, he won't want anything to do with you. Look at your arm, caught between forms. It's disgusting."

Her comment pushed me over the edge. I growled

and let my nails penetrate her neck.

"Tessa!" Dastien sprinted down the hall. "*Merde.*" He dropped down on the floor next to us. "Tessa. Let her go." He pulled off his shirt and balled it up. "We've got to stop the bleeding."

He picked her over me. That thought had the wolf whimpering.

He put the wadded up shirt next to my hand and looked me in the eyes. "Let her go. Now."

Shock pulled me free of the last twinges of anger. All that was left was normal Tessa. Blood stained the front of Imogene's shirt. Her eyes rolled back in her head.

Bile rose in my throat.

Oh my God. I'd never gotten in a fight. Until martial arts class, I'd never hit anyone. Never even pushed anyone. I could have killed her. I crawled backwards until I hit the opposite wall of lockers and pulled off my stained and shredded gloves. Each classroom door was open with the teachers guarding it.

Why hadn't they stopped me?

"I need some help," Dastien said. His hand was wet with blood as he put pressure on the wound.

The teachers finally moved into action. Mrs. Ramirez reached them first. "Adrian, go grab Mr. Dawson and Dr. Gonzales. Hurry."

People poured out of the rooms, crowding the hallway. I couldn't stand them staring at me. I did the only thing I could think of, I ran.

It was cowardly, but I'd hit my limit. Dastien called for me to stop. To wait for him. But I didn't look back. He'd shown me time and again with his actions what he really wanted. Who he wanted. If he cared about me, he wouldn't have run away all those times. He wouldn't have been able to.

I flew out the front entryway of the school and followed the road to the main highway. I moved faster than I ever had before, my lungs barely registering the strain.

A sign led to town. I moved on autopilot, not caring where I went.

I slowly started to see familiar markers. And then I just ran faster.

I didn't stop until I got to the yellow house with the big tree in front. "Mom!" I raced up the porch steps and banged on the door. "Mom!"

Her feet clattered on the stairs as she ran to the door. "Oh my God, Tessa. What happened? Are you okay? Are you hurt?"

I looked down to see my shirt and my arm splattered with blood. "I don't know."

She pulled me inside. "Where's your other flip-flop?"

My left foot was cut up and bloody from running. Somewhere along the way, I'd lost one. "I don't know."

"Okay. Wait right here. I'll get the first aid kit."

I dropped the flip-flop by the door and went into the kitchen. I grabbed milk out of the fridge and the Oreos from on top of the freezer. I'd just burned some major calories and couldn't let my wolf get antsy from hunger while I was with Mom. I shoved two Oreos in my mouth and chewed quickly.

God. How had the day gone so wrong? I wasn't a violent person. I didn't attack people.

I hoped they weren't kidding when they said we healed fast, but since I was kind of a werewolf—I wasn't sure if she'd be okay. I didn't like Imogene, but I hadn't meant to hurt her.

Mom dug through drawers upstairs, and then water turned on, drowning out all the other sounds. She was a clean freak, probably washing her hands. I hopped up onto the kitchen counter to wait.

She came back carrying the first aid bin and a clean shirt of mine. We sat quietly as she cleaned my foot. I winced as she pulled out some gravel and poured peroxide over it. It bubbled white as it killed germs. I pulled on the fresh shirt as she worked.

She ripped open a bandage and then put it down. "Umm. The cuts have all healed."

I grabbed my foot. She was right. Once the bits of gravel were gone, my feet healed completely. Not even a scar marred them. "Thanks, Mom."

She moved away from me to throw away the dirty cotton balls. "You want to talk about what happened?"

"I hurt someone." Tears streaked down my face. "I'm completely lost, Mom. I don't know what to do."

"Tessa—"

"Dastien...he...I can't...And I can't control my feelings. One minute, I'm fine. The next I'm nearly ripping some girl's head off." I covered my face with my hands.

"Tessa!"

"I'm not joking. I could have killed Imogene. I'm a monster."

"Teresa Elizabeth McCaide." She squeezed my knee. "I don't care what happened. You're no monster."

I wanted to believe her. I wiped my hands down my face. "You don't know that. Not anymore."

"I do too. I'm the one who carried you for nine months. Who has taken care of you for the past seventeen—almost eighteen—years. I know my daughter. I don't care what happened—you're no monster. It makes me so mad that you'd think that. After all you've been through. You're still the same girl."

She was muttering under her breath about having a chat with Mr. Dawson when the doorbell rang.

I jolted down off the counter. "Who's that?"

She held up her hands. "I'm sorry, baby. I had to call them."

"You didn't." My own mother turned me in? That was so messed up.

I peeked around the corner to the front door. Through the window I could see Mr. Dawson and Dastien.

I flew out the back door, slamming it shut behind me.

Chapter Thirty-Four

I jumped off the back porch. Before I made it to the first tree, a hand grabbed my arm. I almost fell as I skidded to a stop. Dastien's scent enveloped me.

Why wouldn't he let me go?

I yanked my arm, trying to break free.

"Stop it," he said.

I stayed very still and slowed my breathing. He let go of my arm, and I took off. I didn't know why I was running, but if I stayed still, I would have to face him. Face what I had done. And what I was. Face our relationship or lack of it.

Screw that. Even if it made me a coward.

I hadn't taken more than a couple of steps before his hand gripped my arm again. He spun me around until my back slammed against a tree.

"Stop running from me. Please," he said.

"Let me go." My voice rumbled with the demand.

"No."

"I'm not going back."

His eyes turned the color of melted gold. "Why not?"

"Is Imogene okay?"

He took a deep breath and his eyes faded back to their normal amber. "She'll be fine. Because you're a Were, the wound will heal slowly. Not as slow as if she were human. But slow enough that she'll hate you."

"Not like we were destined to be bosom buddies anyway."

"I guess not." He set his knuckle under my chin, guiding my gaze. "What happened back there?"

"I could ask you the same thing."

His eyes flashed bright again and he released me. "What did I do?"

"I saw you. With her. After everything you said, you kissed her." I couldn't keep the hurt from my voice, which was mortifying. I looked away.

"Who?"

I gave him a second to figure it out.

"Imogene?" He let out a long breath. "Christ. If you think that, then you didn't stay long enough."

"I stayed plenty long. You left with her yesterday. You kissed her today. You've dated her before. Look, I know I'm not the most experienced person when it comes to guys—let alone werewolf guys—but seriously it doesn't take a ton of brainpower to know when your...whatever it is you are to me is cheating."

He sputtered and I held up a hand.

"So look at it from my perspective and tell me if you saw my ex kissing me what you would do. I walked away. Go me. But then I come back and she's throwing the contents of my locker all over the hallway. Shouting crazy shit about me putting a spell on you and wanting me to give her the *gris-gris*. I've had enough. The past week and a half has been extraordinarily shitty. This is my breaking point. I'm done. With everything."

His shoulders hunched as his gaze met the ground. "I have so royally fucked up everything and I really don't know how to fix it. From the second I met you, I've messed it up." His yellow eyes met mine. "I know you have no reason to believe this, but yesterday I was with the Cazadores. I didn't ditch you to hang out with her. I think she's covering up what her dad's up to by saying she was leading us to some vampires' den that turned out to be bullshit." He blew out a hard breath. "For the record, I don't want her. At all."

Good. I stared unblinking at him.

"It probably doesn't matter to you—the hurt is still the same—but I didn't kiss her back. I pushed her away, and told her what I've been telling her for months—that it's not going to work out. And now I can say the reason is because I'm mated to you. You're it for me. And now I've hurt you again because I was trying to spare an old friend's feelings."

Tears welled, and I focused on not letting them fall.

"I am yours," he said. "If you'll have me."

"You can't do this anymore."

"Do what?"

"Say the right thing and then act like the opposite is true. One second everything is fine, and the next you disappear. What was that yesterday? You just run off. You disappear. You don't call. You don't text. I don't see you or know if you're okay until I see you kissing some other girl. I can't do that. I can't turn my emotions off and on like that. I'm either all in or all out. And if you can't do that—if I don't come first, then for God's sake, leave me alone."

He pulled me to him. "I will get this right. I swear. I wasn't thinking."

"Like I said on Saturday, I'm on shaky ground enough with this whole werewolf thing without adding a guy into the mix. Maybe we just need a break."

He squeezed me tighter. "No. No break. We don't need a break. I'm not perfect, but I get it. I can't see you run away from me again. So we stop this. We're all in, because there is no other option for me. You're my mate. You're it for me. You have to trust me."

"Trust is earned."

"Then I'll earn it."

I finally relaxed against his chest. "Promise."

"I promise. You're my mate. My other half." He ran his fingers through my hair before tipping my chin up. "What happened in the hallway?"

God. He was going to say those nice things and then ask me that. Not cool at all. "It's not important."

He cupped my cheek. "Yes, it is. Please."

"No."

"Pretty please."

I laughed. "Forget it."

"You don't have to be embarrassed. It's just me."

"Exactly. It's you."

He gave me the saddest puppy dog eyes, and my will to stay silent wavered.

This was going to be embarrassing. "I was so

angry after I saw...I couldn't get control. I left class before I could humiliate myself—"

"Humiliate yourself?"

I rolled my eyes. "You know. Go furry."

He ran his thumb down my face. "That's not humiliating. That's what werewolves do."

"Yeah. But not in the middle of class."

"Sometimes in the middle of class."

I tried to shove him away. "Do you want me to tell you or what?"

He nodded.

"So I went into the hall and she was going through my locker. She started accusing me of some whacked out stuff. Demanded I give her my gris-gris, break whatever spell that I put on you." I couldn't stop the snort. "She pushed me into the lockers and something inside me snapped." I shook my head, trying to rid my mind of Imogene bleeding beneath me. "Why did she say my arm was so gross? I mean I think it's seriously weird. But I thought all of you shifted."

"Not everyone can do that. Only shift part of their body. Do you remember how you did it?"

"No."

"Are you sure?"

The little bit of trust I'd built up for him just moments ago started to crack. Was he going to call me a freak too? I tried to take comfort in what he'd already said, but a lifetime of rejection had me holding my breath.

I couldn't stand it anymore. I broke away from his hold and sat on the ground, resting against the tree. "You're making me nervous. Just say whatever it is and get it over with."

He squatted down in front of me and cupped my face with his hands. His lips softly brushed mine. I wrapped my arms around his neck and pulled him closer. The fear melted and my body burned. When he pulled away, I was breathing hard.

"Stop thinking the worst." He spoke as if I should understand words. My mind was utter mush with one kiss. He stood up and stepped toward my house. "Michael," he shouted.

Mr. Dawson stepped onto the back porch. "How's it going out here?"

Things were incredibly confusing.

"She doesn't know how she did it," Dastien said as Mr. Dawson walked toward us.

"Not surprising." Mr. Dawson sat down in front of me. "What you did back there took a lot of power."

Was he nuts? "Almost killing someone took a lot of power?"

"No. Half shifting your arm," Mr. Dawson said.

"I doubt Imogene would agree with you." I held his gaze. "Am I in trouble?"

He raised one eyebrow over his hazel eyes. "No. Imogene shouldn't have taunted you, but she's been trying to gain Dastien's power since they were pups. She was dead set on becoming his mate, regardless of how he felt."

A little growl slipped through me.

"Mate," Dastien said softly to me.

I tried to breathe through the jealousy. Dastien placed his warm hand in mine and calm poured into me.

"She's furious that you're more powerful than her," Mr. Dawson said.

I cleared my throat and tried to focus on what Mr. Dawson said. If I really was more powerful than her, why would she attack me?

"She was counting on you not realizing it," Mr. Dawson said. "You're dominant to Imogene."

Right. Meredith had said that too.

I leaned away from Dastien. "See, this is where I'm having problems. Who the hell talks about people being dominant?" I waved my hand to stop Mr. Dawson. "I know. I know. I probably should've read that stupid book instead of going for a hike."

The side of Mr. Dawson's mouth tipped up.

Great. At least my frustration was amusing to someone.

"In other words, when you give her an order, she has to obey." He let that sink in. "That and the possibility of you being mated to Dastien is more than she can stand."

Frustration burned into anger. "It's not like I deliberately stole Dastien from her." Dastien stayed silent. "Right?"

"I'm not something to get stolen from anyone. Neither are you. We're equal partners in this."

I put my head on his shoulder. Partners sounded much nicer than mates.

Mr. Dawson stood up and brushed the leaves off his jeans. "It's time to go back to campus."

Dastien nudged my shoulder with his. I felt connected to him in a way I couldn't describe. Like he was a part of me. I was losing myself to him and the wolf. Would there be anything left for me?

Dastien stood and reached down to help me up. He sighed when I hesitated. "This is hard on me, too."

Was I really that self-centered? I hadn't thought about his feelings. "I guess you seem so in control, I didn't think you had a hard time. Ever."

"Both of us have to learn to adjust. I'm taking it better than you because I've been a were my whole life." He let out a little growl. "But my wolf is out of control. I've been restless for the past year. And then I see you and everything else disappears. And you keep fighting it." He ran his hands through his hair. He was even hotter with it mussed. "My wolf wants to claim you. To make you mine. To protect you. But I'm trying to give you time, give you a choice even if it's killing me. It's why I keep messing up. I should've just staked my claim and let you deal with having me attached at your hip."

Knowing that he was shaken up made me feel better. I didn't feel quite so crazy. Or alone. I reached my hand up.

He yanked me to standing. "I admit I'm having a hard time and she's finally smiling?" Dastien said.

I chortled and it felt really good.

The back door slammed. Dad walked down the back steps in his work clothes. Even in this heat he wore a suit.

"Just what in the hell are you doing to my daughter that she runs—runs—the whole way home from school?" His tie hung loose around his neck. "You're supposed to be taking care of her because apparently we can't and it seems to me you're doing a shit job of it!"

Mr. Dawson tried to step in front of us, but I skirted around him.

"Dad!" I swallowed him in a hug. He smelled

good, even if it was an overwhelming mess of things—anger, dryer sheets, shampoo, relief.

He pulled away and looked at my face. "You okay?"

"I'm okay."

He kissed my forehead.

"Your mother called me. She's worried about you." He handed me a pair of white gloves.

I put them on. "Didn't seem like she was too worried. She called Mr. Dawson to come get me."

"Tessa. Your mother loves you very much, but we have to do what's best for you. We're both struggling to figure out what that is. How to handle this..." Dad looked beyond me and tried to push past. "I thought we agreed he would stay the hell away from my daughter."

Michael shoved his hands in his pockets. "I said he would, unless he was her mate. And he is."

"What is this bullshit! You can't marry off my daughter. She's only seventeen."

I stepped in front of him, but he moved me to the side. I was scared to push him back. I didn't want to accidentally hurt him.

"Calm down, Dad. You know I'm going to be eighteen really soon." He had a right to be upset. Hell, I was still a little upset. But I didn't want him to yell at Dastien.

"No one is going to make her marry me tomorrow. I would never force her to do anything she didn't want," Dastien said. "I know that's a lot coming from me. I can't ever take back what I did, but I hope eventually you'll be able to forg—"

Dad's face turned a bright shade of red. "You can

get the hell off my property. Now."

"Oh my God, Dad! Seriously. Calm down." I grabbed the back of his jacket as he strode toward Dastien. The cloth's rip stopped all motion in the back yard. Dad tried to get a look at his now ruined suit coat. "Oops." I hadn't meant to tear it.

"Teresa. Did you just rip my coat?"

I gave him a sheepish smile. "I'm sorry, Daddy. I honestly didn't mean to."

Dad pulled off the two pieces that used to be a jacket. "It's okay. I guess one less suit won't kill me."

The back door slammed again. "Tessa. What happened to your father's coat?"

"It was an accident. I'm sorry, okay?"

Dastien's chuckle was too soft for my parents to hear. My cheeks burned.

"Would everyone like to come in and have some lemonade?" Mom said.

"No, thank you. We should head back to campus," Mr. Dawson said.

Dad pulled me into his arms. "I don't care what he says, if something isn't right there, you come home. There are other options." His lips were set in a firm line when he pulled away from me.

"I'm going to be fine, Dad." I hoped I wasn't lying.

"Forgive me?" Mom said.

"Totally."

She came down and wrapped her arms around me. "Call if you need me." She pulled away. "And call your brother. He's freaking out."

"I bet he's having an awesome time in Austin and isn't thinking about me at all."

Mom grinned. "You'd be mistaken, kiddo."

We walked around the side of the house to the black Escalade parked in the drive. Dastien pulled a pair of flip-flops from his back pocket. "Missing something?"

"Apparently."

"They were like a trail to you. One not far from here, one at your front door."

I yanked them from his grasp. "Thanks." I slid them on and got in the car.

Dastien held my hand in the backseat as Mr. Dawson drove us to St. Ailbe's. I watched the trees fly past.

All too soon, we pulled through the gates, and into the small parking lot next to the main building. Dr. Gonzales ran up to the car.

"We have a problem," she said as we got out.

I barely heard the rumble Mr. Dawson gave before it stopped. "What now?"

"It's Imogene," Dr. Gonzales said.

Oh shit. "Is she okay?" I asked. "I mean, is she still—"

Dr. Gonzales held up a hand. "She's fine, although she might not be for long. Rupert Hoel is here—"

Mr. Dawson's door slammed so hard that for a second I thought the SUV might flip over.

"Why is he here this time?" His voice was too calm and soft.

"He believes you've lost control of the student body. That our prize student has gone Feral and turned a local. That the mutt is uncontrollable and almost killed his daughter. He believes this situation is very serious, and needs to be tended to. He demands that the two of them be held before a full tribunal."

What the hell did a "full tribunal" mean?

Mr. Dawson's fists were in tight balls as he looked off into the woods, at seemingly nothing in particular. At least I thought it was nothing until four people stepped out from beyond the thick. Four men wearing all black with no shoes. They flowed as one.

Cazadores. And I sure as hell didn't like the way they were watching me. Their eyes pinned me in place as they navigated around the last of the forest.

The tallest one stepped forward. "You'll have to come with us."

He couldn't mean me?

Chapter Thirty-Five

Mr. Dawson stepped in front of me, blocking the leader's path. "She won't be going anywhere."

"What would you have me do, Michael?" he said. He looked familiar, but I couldn't place where I'd seen him before.

"She's done nothing wrong, Trent." As soon as Dastien said his name, it clicked. He was the one from the bookstore.

"Dude. You're in trouble too," Trent said.

Dastien stood shoulder to shoulder with Mr. Dawson. I had to peek between them to see what was going on. "Fine. This is my fault. I'll go on trial. Alone."

"Everyone needs to calm down," Mr. Dawson said. "No one is going anywhere."

Trent reached for something in his back pocket. "I've got orders from—"

"I'm sure Rupert is forgetting that Sebastian and Donovan have already met and evaluated the situation here."

Trent's mouth dropped open before he recovered. He shook his head. "It's too late. Once a tribunal has been called for it can't be undone. Can it?"

Mr. Dawson's growl echoed among the buildings.

Dr. Gonzales put a hand on his arm. "We know full well that it cannot be avoided. But they're fine here. Dastien is a trusted Cazadore. He'll not run."

"And the girl? She nearly killed Imogene."

He was totally right. The image of my hand dripping with her blood flashed in my mind. I was going to be sick.

"She can wait in her room for Sebastian and Donovan to return," she said.

"Fine. James will stand guard at her door," Trent said.

"Where is Rupert now?" Mr. Dawson said. The power in his voice raised goose bumps all over my body.

"He's using your office," Dr. Gonzales said.

Mr. Dawson's fists clenched and released. Clenched and released. "Trent, you can come with me and Dastien. The rest of you can go to hell for all I care."

What was going on?

Dastien watched me over his shoulder as they walked toward Mr. Dawson's cabin. I couldn't help but feel a little lost without him.

Dr. Gonzales closed the distance between us, putting her arm around my shoulders. "It's going to be okay."

Jason gave a snort. "I'm not sure I'd promise her anything."

Finally someone was being honest. I hadn't seen Dr. Gonzales since I got to St. Ailbe's. Pretty much nothing had gone right since then. It took effort for me not to shake her arm off.

Dr. Gonzales' grey eyes flashed to silver as she growled at Jason. I hadn't thought of her as a fighter, but there was no mistaking the challenge she'd issued.

He stared at the ground. "Just my opinion. No offense meant."

"While you're here, you *will* show some kindness to Teresa. You wouldn't believe the pain and the struggle she went through just to survive transformation." Dr. Gonzales blew out her breath hard. "And now this."

I purposefully hadn't thought about what had happened in the week I'd been "asleep." For the first time, I kind of wanted to ask questions. I looked over at Jason and bit my tongue. Something about the way his accusing, flat brown eyes rubbed me the wrong way.

A hush fell over the girls eating popcorn and chatting in the common room when we entered. Just what I needed—a walk of shame.

"We're going to sort this out," Dr. Gonzales said as we climbed the stairs.

I didn't have much faith in that, so I kept my silence.

Jason cleared his throat when we got to my door. "I'll be here."

I stepped inside alone, and slammed the door in his face. The threat under his words totally wasn't appreciated. I kicked off my flip-flops and collapsed on my bed. As messed up as it was, being in trouble made me feel better about what I'd done to Imogene. Because in the real world, anyone who rips out someone's throat should seriously be put in jail. Or a mental hospital. Or something.

Meredith tapped on the bathroom door connecting our rooms before peeking in. "People are in a frenzy, and some wolf is guarding your door. What the hell is going on?"

"You're asking me?" She knew I didn't understand anything at this place.

She walked over to my desk and clicked a track. A crowd screaming over a live recording of an Eric Morillo mix boomed over the speakers. Meredith settled down next to me. "Tell me exactly what happened," she said softly.

"Imogene's dad is here. He called for some sort of a tribunal?"

Meredith jumped up so fast I almost fell off the bed. "No freaking way!" she whisper shouted.

"He's of the opinion that Mr. Dawson has lost control of the entire school, especially of me and Dastien."

All of the color drained from Meredith's face and she sat down hard on the bed. "That's not good. What you did was no big deal. I mean people get into fights all the time here. Even the Seven know that—it's normal for new weres." She was quiet for a second and then got up to pace. "It's gotta be more than just that. Mr. Dawson and Mr. Hoel have been fighting for years. They hate each other."

"Why?"

"Dastien didn't tell you about his parents?"

"He said they died."

Meredith nodded. "Mr. Hoel has always been kind of against hiding ourselves from humans."

I snorted. "Kind of obvious from his lecture."

"I know, right? The guy is a total dick."

I grinned. "Totally."

"Back in the day—Mr. Hoel, Mr. Dawson, and Mr. Laurent, Dastien's dad, were total BFFs. But one day Mr. Hoel got into it with a bunch of humans. He managed to get drunk—which is way hard with our metabolism—at some biker bar and called Mr. Laurent to go pick him up. By the time Mr. Laurent got there, the fight was in full swing. The only saving grace was that Mr. Hoel didn't shift. Mr. Laurent had brought his wife. They tried to pull him out of the fight, but then one of the humans grabbed the shotgun that the bar owner stored just behind the bar. Close-range headshot will kill anything. Mr. Hoel ran. Dastien was an orphan. Mr. Dawson never forgave Mr. Hoel for being a moron. They fought over Dastien's custody a bit, and animosity just skyrocketed from there." She scrunched her nose. "Mr. Hoel has been trying to undermine Mr. Dawson's place in the pack for a while now. He's such an asshole."

I stifled a groan. "And I played right into his hand."

"Not your fault." She paused. "I can't believe he's actually going for it. I mean he's been trying to get a foothold with the Seven for years. But this…"

I was starting to feel nauseated. "It might not be all that complicated. I did kind of attack his daughter."

She shook her head. "No. This is way fucked up.

Especially after the whole vampire thing. He might be using you as an excuse, but this isn't about you. This is bigger." She headed for the door.

"Wait. Where are you going?"

"Recon. We need more info."

"Good thinking. Keep me in the loop?"

"What am I? New?" She winked. "I'll be back in a few."

As I sat alone in my room, panic built inside of me, making the wolf rise closer to the surface. I closed my eyes and tried to do the breathing Dastien had showed me. I listened to the sound of the air flowing as it entered and left my body. My mind began to wander. I thought about the first time I'd seen Dastien. The intense pull that I felt between us. The day I first saw him. His sexy smile. The day I first heard his voice. I had way too many feelings about him. Mad. Attracted. Angry. Obsessed.

I pictured him pacing in Mr. Dawson's tiny cabin. Back and forth. Back and forth. His scent—woods, grass, dirt, and something spicy, something just Dastien—filled me. The vision of him grew sharper as my mind focused. His muscles rippled under his shirt as he paced. Heat warmed my body at the sight. Trent and Mr. Dawson were talking at the dining table. Dastien reached the end of the room and paced back toward me.

It took me a second to register the tingle that started in the bottom of my stomach and rippled through my body.

"Tessa?" he said.

Chapter Thirty-Six

I opened my eyes and jumped off the bed.

What the hell was that?

We'd linked. I'd done it again.

I decided that I had to try and lay back down. Rachmaninoff's Second Piano Concerto started playing. It took a second for it to click that it was coming from my cellphone. I grabbed it from the desk, but didn't recognize the number. "Hello?"

"Was that you? Were you here?" Dastien said.

"I think so. Hey, how did you get my number?"

"From Michael. Tess. Stay on topic. I could smell you. How did you do it?"

This was embarrassing. "I uuhh...I was thinking of you."

"You were?" I could almost hear his grin.

"Don't get a big head about it."

"I'm going to hang up now, and you're going to do it again. Okay? This time try talking to me."

"Can't we just—" My phone beeped. "—talk on

the phone?" I rolled my eyes. Seemed we were doing fine talking before he hung up.

I closed my eyes, and thought about Dastien. The way he looked after he chased me through my backyard. The tingles came, threatening to overtake me. This was way too intense.

I reached for my cell phone and dialed. He picked up on the first ring. "I need time to—"

"Just do it, Tessa." The phone beeped in my ear.

Did he just hang up on me? Again. What a jerk! Why couldn't we just talk on the phone like normal people?

My stomach rumbled. It'd been forever since breakfast. I caught the scent of bread. In the corner of the room, tucked beside my desk, was a silver mini-fridge. It was fully stocked with all the essentials.

I'd totally forgotten Meredith was going to set me up with it. A smile spread across my face. I actually had a real friend, and now I totally owed her one. Going downstairs to get food would've been a pain if the girls were still in the common room. And then there was Jason...

I grabbed a carton of whole milk, and made myself a peanut butter and jelly sandwich. And then made three more. I wasn't quite sure where all the food was going. Rationally speaking, I was pretty sure I physically couldn't fit three sandwiches and a half-gallon of whole milk in my stomach. But I ate until the cavernous pit was full, and then settled back down on my bed.

I breathed in and out slowly as I thought of Dastien and the way he smelled. The way he made me feel.

Then it happened again. My stomach dropped like I was falling two hundred feet. My body turned into one giant tingling mess and I couldn't get enough air. The next thing I knew I was in Mr. Dawson's cabin.

I stood just inside the front door hovering like a ghost. Being in two places at once was interesting. Talk about a vision overload.

The three guys were sitting at the table now—Trent, Mr. Dawson, and Dastien. Mr. Dawson was on the phone. He turned to me first, lifting one eyebrow, and then continued the conversation with whoever was on the other end of the call.

How did he know I was there?

"Dastien?"

He spun toward me.

"Is she back?" Trent said. "What is she saying?"

Dastien ignored him. "I've been reading up on mate-bonds. The thing is, the kind of bond we have, it's different than the usual kind. What we have is more than what they describe, and nothing I read said anything about this." He stopped in front of me. "I can smell and hear you, but I can't see you." He waved an arm where I was standing, and it went straight through me.

Every muscle ached with pins and needles. "How about you not do that again." I rubbed my hands over my arms, trying to make it go away. "Can they hear me?"

He settled down on the arm of the couch next to me. "I can't even. Not really. I hear you in my thoughts, not with my ears."

Weird. "Can you talk to me through thoughts?"

He sat quietly for a second and made a constipated-like face. I couldn't help but laugh at him. "Guess not," he said.

I wanted to reach out to him, but thought against it. "So is this really better than the cell?"

"It's definitely cheaper and more reliable. If we're separated, this could really come in handy." He paused. "Something's going on. We just have to figure out what."

"You're weirding me out, *mec*," Trent said.

"*Tais-toi*," Dastien said.

Mr. Dawson hung up the phone and cleared his throat. "It's official. No one has seen Sebastian or Donovan since they went to investigate how the vampires found us."

"*Merde*," Trent said. That was one French word I knew.

"How could this happen?" Dastien walked to Mr. Dawson.

"I'm not sure. Had to be an ambush of some sort. They can't be taken easily." He sighed. "I can't think that it's a coincidence that they go missing and Rupert shows up." He looked straight at me, even though he couldn't actually see me. "You may have been onto something bigger than even I thought."

Dastien started pacing. "The vampires have been acting up more the past couple of years. Especially recently. Do you think they could've found a leader?"

"No. You don't just change your behavior after centuries. There's got to be something more. I'm just missing it."

The door to Mr. Dawson's cabin swung open. Five guys in all black with guns ran in. There were three quick shots.

I screamed.

"Drugged," Dastien said. "Run."

Ice ran through my veins. I didn't know how to break the link. I checked on Mr. Dawson.

Mr. Dawson glanced at me like he knew where I was. "Out." The command rolled through me, pushing me out of the cabin. I tried to stop it, but the power behind it was too much. I sped through trees and buildings to get back to my body. It wasn't comfortable. By the time I found myself lying on my bed, I wondered if I'd ever feel right again.

I didn't have much time to think about it before Meredith strolled through the bathroom with Shannon in tow.

The music was still blasting.

"We've got news. And it's not good." Meredith said. Shannon hovered behind her.

I shot up from the bed. "Run. Now." I grabbed my cell phone and keys from my bedside table.

"Wait. What!" Meredith said.

The knob on my door twisted. "Window. Now. Fucking now!"

I leapt onto the windowsill and jumped down. The landing was easy this time, and I sprinted across campus like the hounds of hell were on my heels. I didn't look back to see if Meredith and Shannon were there. Maybe that meant I was a bad person, but Dastien was in trouble. I needed off this campus. I needed help from someone I could actually trust.

The parking lot was packed with big black SUVs. I clicked my car key, and set off in the direction of my car. Thankfully, I owned a black SUV too.

I was going to have to thank Axel for that one

again.

I spotted my car and unlocked the doors. For the first time I spared a glance behind me, and I was surprised to see not only Meredith and Shannon, but Adrian and Chris were there too. I wasn't sure when they'd shown up.

"Get in." I closed my door, and started the car. I didn't wait for them to buckle their seat belts. The gates were half-open as another SUV made its way into the parking lot. I swerved around it, and down the road.

"What in the fuck is going on!" Meredith said.

"Sebastian and Donovan are missing. And while I was linked to Dastien—long story—five cazadors broke down the door to Mr. Dawson's cabin and shot Dastien, Mr. Dawson and Trent with tranqs. Dastien said to run. When I broke the link, Jason was coming into my room. So I got the hell out."

A stream of curses came from my backseat.

"Tranqs. That's so damned cowardly," Chris said.

"¡*Conchesumá!*" Adrian hit the back of my chair.

"Whoa. Let's not break my car." What he said registered. "You kiss your mother with that mouth?"

"The word fits the man," Adrian said.

"Where did you guys come from anyways?" I said.

"We were in the quad walking back to the dorm from the cafeteria when we saw you jump from the window. When Meredith and Shannon followed we figured there's too much drama on campus today to not see what was going on with you." Chris squeezed my shoulder. "You're getting much better at the jumping from the window thing. That leap was a thing of beauty."

I snorted. "Fourth time's the charm?"

"Where are we going exactly?" Shannon said.

"To my house. Kind of obvious, so we can't stay long, but we need to regroup and find out what the hell is going on and what they're planning to do with Dastien and Mr. D. I have a really bad feeling. Sunset isn't far away and something tells me if we don't find them before then…" I took a calming breath. "We have to find him."

Chapter Thirty-Seven

I pulled up the driveway. Axel stepped out onto the porch. "You're home!" I said as I ran toward him.

"What's goin' on?" He hugged me tightly and my feet lifted off the ground for a second. "I heard something went down today and wanted to check on you. Why haven't you called me?"

"It's been a little intense." I paused. "You shouldn't be here. It's not safe."

He glanced past me as everyone got out of the car. "Then maybe you shouldn't have brought home so many wolves with you."

"Not them, you moron. Something just went down at school. Everything is beyond messed up."

A girl and a boy about my age stepped onto the porch. They looked enough alike—straight black hair, dark eyes, long straight noses, and full lips—to know they were related.

"Dude. This is not the time for a party," I said. "You and Mom and Dad need to get the hell out of town. Like yesterday."

"We know what's going on, Teresa," the guy said. His black hair just brushed the tops of his shoulders. He wore relaxed jeans that were ripped at the knee and his light blue *guayabera* made his skin look a richer brown. "We're here to help."

Chris nudged me. "Dude. Your name's Teresa?"

Typical. My full name is what he pays attention to. I shoved him back. "Shut it."

Axel put his arm around my shoulders, guiding me to the front door. "Come on. We need to talk."

I shrugged his arm off. "We don't really have time for that. I came by to get you guys out of here, and so that we," I motioned to my group, "could regroup."

"You have until sunset," the girl said. She smoothed down the skirt of her hot pink sundress. Her long hair was pulled back into a high pony tail. "Wasting time arguing now won't save your mate."

Adrian stepped up next to me and sniffed the air. "¿*Brujos*?"

"*Claro*," the guy said. "*Venga. Tenemos un poco de información que puede ayudarte.*"

Adrian stepped to follow the siblings into my house, but I stopped him. "Can we trust whatever information they have?"

"We don't have any reason not to trust them," Adrian said.

Meredith cleared her throat.

"Unless you're fighting one." Adrian had the grace to blush a little. "And then all bets are off. But normally, witches and Weres get along fine."

I thought it over for a second. If they had any information that could help me save Dastien, I couldn't ignore it.

When I stepped through the door, Mom hugged me tightly. "You can't call this time, Mom. No one can know where we are. Even if it might be the first place someone would look."

"Sure." She kissed my forehead and I saw her worries. Namely me biting my brother. "Can I get anyone anything to eat?" She didn't wait for a response as she dug through cupboards, piling snacks on the dining room table.

We so didn't have time for any kind of snacks. God only knew what was happening to Dastien. My skin rippled and I took ten long, deep breaths. Wolfing out in front of my family was not an option.

Food was probably a good call. I grabbed a couple of Oreos. "Thanks, Mom."

"Why doesn't everyone have a seat?" Dad said. "And then we can get back to what your cousins came here for."

I spun to look at them closer. If they really were related to me, I didn't remember them at all.

We settled in around the large table. Dad stood behind me, and Mom stayed near the door. I sat across from my "cousins," with Meredith and Chris on either side of me. Shannon and Adrian took the heads of the table, and Axel sat next to the guy "cousin."

Dad squeezed my shoulders. "Claudia, please." The name was familiar, but the last time I'd seen any of my mother's family was over a decade ago.

Claudia nodded. "It's really good to meet you. Again. Your parents told us that you didn't know about us or what your place was supposed to be here."

What the what? I glanced at Mom.

"I only did it to protect you. Living with *La Alquelarre* can be a bit much, and with what you could do and so young...it was better to give you choices. But when that wasn't working out for you, I thought maybe they could help."

The guy leaned closer. "I'm Raphael, Claudia's twin. Our mothers are sisters."

"We're *brujos*. Witches," Claudia said. "You were supposed join *La Alquelarre*—our coven—this year."

"Holy shit. This is out of control." Adrian clapped his hands, and then blushed.

Wow. I'd never seen him blush, and now he'd done it twice.

Adrian cleared his throat and sat taller in his chair. "It's really nice to meet you guys," he said in a much more controlled voice.

Raphael nodded. "*Igualmente*. Wish it could be under better circumstances." His gaze met mine again. His female counterpart might have been friendly, but this guy was all business. "Vampires are hanging out in the caves just north of your school. It seems your pack is having some problems with them?"

I moved uncomfortably in my seat. "It's not *my* pack."

Claudia and Raphael shared a look. "Nevertheless," Raphael continued, "you need to stabilize the pack. If you can't, there *will* be war. It seems one of your wolves thought it'd make him look good to humans if he brought a bunch of vampires here, have them tear apart this little town and the wolves would come to the rescue."

That sounded completely crazy. And totally like the Hoels. "How do you know?"

"Because we had a visitor at our house today. We were told, not so nicely, to stay out of the way tonight," Raphael said. "So we came here to talk to your parents, hoping that they knew some way to contact you."

Meredith slapped her hand on the table. "Fuck a duck."

"Language!" Mom said.

I grinned. Even when the world was going to crap, she was watching everyone's language. Maybe one day she'd realize it was a lost cause. "She's sorry, Mom."

Meredith scoffed, her jaw dropping open. I grabbed a handful of Doritos and shoved them in her mouth.

"If you don't take care of this problem, then *La Alquelarre* will," Raphael said. "I don't think any of your pack would like that."

This wasn't good. At all.

Chris growled, and I placed my hand on his arm. "Calm down." I focused back on the twins. "We want this taken care of as much as you do. And—"

"We're missing some of our alphas." Shannon cut me off, and I tried not to punch her for it. "Can you scry for them?" Shannon asked the twins.

"Scry?" I asked.

"It's a form of divination and can sometimes be used to locate someone in the present," Raphael said.

"I'm sorry. Our powers don't work like that." Claudia looked at me. "But hers do."

Everyone but Meredith expressed surprise. Chris must've noticed. "You knew about her and you didn't

357

tell us?" he said to Meredith.

"It was her secret to tell, ass—"

Mom cleared her throat.

"—dude," Meredith finished.

"¡Joder! I should've known when you said you were like half-*bruja* blood."

"Don't take it too hard. I've apparently gotten pretty good about hiding it." I sat quietly for a second as I gathered my thoughts. "If I understand everything right—which might be a stretch because I'm kind of a newbie—Mr. Hoel can't do this whole vampire attack thing with wolves more alpha than he is. They'd order him to stop. So he took out the four wolves in the area that are more than him the fastest way he could, tranquilizers, and then shoved them somewhere. But no wolf could be ordered to kill their alpha, they're not doing that. At least not yet. But even if Mr. Hoel pulls off today, he's going to have to deal with the alphas. So, my best guess is that he's going to ditch them someplace close to the vamps. Have them take care of them. Then celebrate with a lovely supernatural coming out party."

"Shit," Chris said. "It makes so much sense when she lays it out like that. How come she can see it and I couldn't?"

Shannon rubbed her forehead. "Because she's new to this life. She's seeing things we wouldn't dream of. Taking out your alpha other than at a full moon challenge is bloody disgraceful."

Knowing what might be going on and doing something about it were two completely different things. "We need to find them. They'll know what to do."

"The question is," Adrian said, "did they drop them in the caves with the vamps? Or did they stash them somewhere to be dealt with later?"

My face burned. "I have maybe a dumb question."

"There are no dumb questions," Claudia said with a smile.

"No. Only dumb people." When she started to retort, I started talking again. "Do vampires stay awake during the day or are they like dead-ish? I mean some movies have them where they just can't go out in sunlight, but others where they can't function when the sun is up."

"The second. When the sun is up, they're dead," Chris said.

"Caves." I glanced at my watch. "Mr. H would leave them in the den to be food when the vamps wake. That doesn't give us much time to get there, drag their asses out, and stop any attack on the town."

"I should mention that this isn't a small den. There are a lot of them," Raphael said.

"Think hundreds," Claudia said.

"Perfect. It's not like we'll be outnumbered at all," Meredith said.

"Shit." I slapped a hand over my mouth as soon as I let it slip.

"Tess!" Mom said.

"Sorry, Mom, but really—this is a completely shit scenario."

"Tess," Axel said. He'd been so quiet, I almost forgot he was there. "This seems really dangerous. I think you should leave with us. Let's just go."

"Sorry, broham. No can do." I smiled sadly. Things had changed so much in the past couple of weeks.

"She's right, Axel," Dad said. "Even if I want to lock your sister up to keep her safe, she's got a different path now."

That made me feel nearly like a grown up. Maybe I wasn't such a mess after all.

"You need to be sure before you go into a vampire den that the wolves are actually there," Meredith said, breaking the silence. "Can you connect with him? Like you did before?"

"Maybe. But what if he's all drugged-out still?"

Claudia reached across the table. "If you can connect with one of your pack, then I'll give you the power to strengthen the connection. Should be enough to see him even if they're unconscious and get an idea about their surroundings."

That seemed like a bad idea.

"You won't get anything off of me." She winked.

I didn't really know what she meant about power.

"You can trust her," Mom said. "She's family. She'll help."

My hand shook a little as I placed my hand in hers, but Claudia didn't comment on it.

I gasped as our skin touched. It was like sticking my hand in an electric socket. Or like drinking ten gallons of coffee. I was hyperaware of my senses, and since I was already part-wolf—it was majorly intense. The colors in the room were brighter. The scents stronger. I could hear every breath being taken, every heart beating.

"Now close your eyes," Claudia said, "and picture your mate."

I did. My consciousness raced out of my house,

through the wilderness, to a cave. Through tunnels. To four men huddled on the floor. They were chained. Their skin smoked where metal met flesh. Dastien and Mr. Dawson were still unconscious, but Donovan and Sebastian were awake.

"And who might you be?" Donovan said, looking my way. He sniffed. "Is that you, Teresa Elizabeth McCaide?"

"Can you hear me?" I asked.

Donovan and Sebastian looked at each other and then down at Dastien. "Wake," Donovan said. Power rippled over my skin, and Dastien gasped.

"*Merde.*" He groaned. "What is it? What happened?" he said as he took in his surroundings. "*Putain de merde.*"

"Dastien," I said.

His gaze met mine. "Please tell me you're not actually here."

If he could actually see me, then Claudia's extra juice was worth it. "I'm not there. But I'm coming. Just hang on."

I didn't give him a chance to say anything else. They were fine for now, but they wouldn't stay that way. I broke the link, and was back in my parents' dining room. "I know where they are. Let's go."

My chair toppled to the floor as I jumped up.

"One more thing," Raphael said. He went to the living room and brought back two small backpacks. "You'll need these."

"No way!" Adrian said.

The others fell in line, ooohing over them. "Am I missing something?"

"Weapons." Claudia grinned, revealing two deep

dimples.

"Not just any weapons," Adrian said. "*Bruja* weapons. They're the best."

"*Sí*," Raphael said. "For the one who doesn't wish to change and the one who cannot."

Meredith took the pack but held it away from her like it was going to bite her.

"I packed these special for each of you. You'll know what to do with what's inside," Claudia said.

That was kind of creepy. I grabbed the other backpack. "Great. Thanks. Now can we go?"

"Wait." Dad's hand clamped down on my shoulder.

I tried to contain my frustration. Did anyone else understand that we had extreme time constraints?

"You need to think this through more. What are you going to do when you get there? What's your plan?"

"There's no time. I'll figure it out when I get there." I hugged him quickly and stepped back. "Plus, from what I understand, if my mate dies, so do I. Can't live with half a soul, right?" I laughed, but it wasn't because it was funny. I left him sputtering. "Bye, Mom. Love you guys."

"I'm coming with you," Axel said.

I gave him a hug. "No, you're not. You're human. Love you. And don't stay here. Get your butts on the road ASAP."

We raced out the door and jumped in the car. Meredith's door was still open when I took off down the drive.

Chapter Thirty-Eight

I floored it down the road, trying to go in vaguely the same direction I remembered traveling in my vision.

"Do some navigating," I said to Meredith, who was sitting in the front passenger seat. "We need to go that way." I pointed straight and slightly to the left of where we were headed. "There has to be a better road. A turn off. Hell, a trail would do."

Beeps rang through the car as she tapped on the map looking for roads. "There's nothing!" Meredith frantically pushed more buttons. "Absolutely nothing. Do you have like a coordinate or something that I could punch in?"

I snorted. "Unfortunately, my visions don't come loaded with GPS." This wasn't going well. I swerved onto the shoulder. "We don't have long before sunset. We need to run from here."

Everyone in the backseat started taking off their clothes.

"What the fuck are you doing! This isn't orgy time. It's fucking kick ass time."

"We're going to shift, you idjit," Shannon said.

Harsh but she was right. I was being dense. They were probably faster on four legs. "Fine." I got out of the car with my witchy backpack and slammed the door. "Catch up with me when you're done."

I took off running. Wind whipped through my long hair as I sprinted. Meredith kept pace with me. She moved soundlessly but the heat her body gave off meant she wasn't more than a step behind me.

I gave out a girly cry when the wolves crashed through the bushes next to me before I realized it was just Chris, Adrian and Shannon.

I pushed harder. Raced around trees. Branches scraped my arms hard enough to draw blood, but I had to keep moving. I couldn't lose the feeling, the connection to Dastien. And if I didn't get there fast enough, he was going to be seriously hurt. Or worse.

I stumbled to a stop.

"What is it?" Meredith said.

"I don't know. I think we're here, but I don't see anything."

I scanned the forest. Oak trees towered above me, but there was a strange silence. I closed my eyes and focused in on Dastien—that bond that we had. It had gotten stronger since that first vision I'd had in Los Angeles, but it still took focus for me to find it.

We were close. Really close. I climbed up a massive fallen tree. The cave's entrance gaped behind the dead branches.

The three wolves were sniffing next to the entrance. The red wolf—Shannon—let out a quiet growl. I wondered what their wolf-y noses could smell that I couldn't.

Meredith moved closer to the wolves and inhaled deeply. "Do you smell that?"

I closed the distance to the wolves and a foul stench hit me. I pulled my T-shirt over my nose.

"Vampires," Meredith said.

"Why do they have to smell so bad?"
Meredith stared at me for a second. "They're undead. Piles of rotting flesh that live by drinking blood."

"When you put it that way, yuck. I guess when I think of vampire, I picture Brad Pitt or Robert Pattinson. More sexy, less stinky."

The black wolf—Adrian let out a quiet howl, and nudged the fallen tree with his nose. Shannon went under the tree and Adrian quickly followed.

I started to move the trunk over, but Meredith stopped me.

"Don't touch anything. It might be a booby trap."

I wondered how she knew, but didn't ask. We'd already wasted enough time. She slid herself under the branches. I followed her into the mouth of the cave. It stunk something fierce—worse than rotting fish on the beach—inside. I gagged and tried to focus on breathing through my mouth, but then I could taste the smell. My pulse hammered and I wondered if vampires could hear it like they did in the movies.

It was pitch black in the cave. "I can't see anything. Can you?"

The blond wolf—Chris huffed, and started walking into the darkness.

I pulled my backpack off and started digging around. If my cousins stuck a flashlight in there, I was going to owe them big time.

My hand touched a familiar shape, and I flipped the button. "Nice."

There were three tunnels ahead of us. Christ. We didn't have time to get lost.

"I'll go down this one," Meredith said. "Adrian, you go down that way—"

Chris turned back to human. Fully naked human.

I spun around. "Jesus. Give me some warning next time."

He chuckled. "Didn't mean to offend. But I wanted to tell Meredith that splitting up was a terrible idea. Have you never watched a scary movie?"

They started arguing, but I ignored them and focused on Dastien again.

He was down the left tunnel. I was sure of it. "This way."

"Wait. What?" Meredith said.

"Chris, go wolf again. I don't need to see your junk."

"He's furry," Meredith said after a few seconds.

"Good." I flashed my light down the left tunnel. "Let's go."

Every time we reached another fork, I did the same thing.

The stench became stronger with each passing step, until finally it got so bad that I gagged.

"Don't," Meredith said. "If you throw up, then I'm going to throw up."

"No promises."

We turned a corner, and Chris—in wolf form— jumped in front of me.

"Sweet baby Jesus," Meredith said. "I hope your

cousins packed us some fucking good weapons."

I swallowed. The next cave room was huge—at least a city block wide and long. The ceiling was super far up, a good fifty-sixty feet. There was a hole in it revealing the dark oranges of sunset. Night was only minutes away, and I realized that getting here had taken much, much longer than I thought it would.

Under the hole was a giant rock formation surrounded by stalagmites. Four bound figures sat atop it.

"You might be wanting to hurry up. They'll be waking up soon." Donovan's voice echoed in the cave.

Between their rock island and our perch on the wall, a sea of vampires lay dead on the recessed cave floor. We would have to hop down from our ledge, not impossible for us supes, and then hopscotch over each body. They'd left no clear path.

My heart pounded at the thought of walking over hundreds of sleeping vampires. But the thought of walking over hundreds of almost awake vampires was infinitely worse. I was the last to jump down from the ledge. I missed my mark and crunched awkwardly on a vampire hand. I couldn't move. More noxious fumes rose from the corpse, but otherwise he didn't stir. I tried to breathe as little as possible and not step on them, but they were so densely packed in the room, it didn't last for long.

The cavern was getting darker by the second.

Meredith and my three wolfy friends weren't as easily spooked as me. They ran off, leaving me to trail behind.

A vampire near my leg reached out, brushing my ankle. "Holy shit. They're waking up." Suddenly, I didn't care so much about stepping on them. I ran forward, glancing up only to keep track of the direction I needed to go, and desperately trying to keep my balance as I stepped on the barely moving vampires.

I let out a breath as I finally caught up. The three wolves faced outward at the seethe. Meredith was in just her bra, the remains of her shirt falling apart in her hands as she tried to remove the silver from Donovan.

Meredith cried out. "It burned through my T-shirt. I can't get them off. I can't get them off."

"Calm yourself, love," Donovan said. He looked like he was perfectly fine relaxing on this rock, but his skin was smoking where the chains touched him. There was no way that didn't hurt like a bitch.

She turned to me frantically. "I can't get them off. What are we going to do now?"

"How the hell did they get them on in the first place?"

"Special gloves made of inorganic material," Sebastian said. "But they didn't leave those behind after the cowards tied us up and left us here."

Perfect.

I didn't need to see the sheen of sweat covering Dastien's skin to know he was in pain. I could feel it nagging at the end of our bond.

"You're going to get out of this cave. Now." Dastien put a bit of power behind his demand, and I let it fly by me.

"Shut up." I couldn't let myself panic like Meredith was. There was no other option but to get Dastien out. I'd burn off my own hands before I'd leave him chained here.

I crouched by him. "I didn't walk through a room full of half-asleep vampires for nothing." The chain holding him was long, thin, and silver. It wrapped around his hands until it was an inch thick, and then the chain ran down his back to snake around his ankles. The chain had burned through his jeans. I swear I could hear a little sizzle coming from the silver against his skin. "I guess the silver thing isn't just in the movies."

Dastien's face was white with pain but he wasn't crying out. "No."

"Great. Well, good thing I'm new."

"You can't—"

Before he could stop me, I ripped the chains that were holding his wrists and ankles together. It didn't burn me at all.

"You're lucky your mate has *bruja* blood," Donovan said. "Me next, if you will, lass."

"Sure." I started to unwind the chain from around Dastien's wrists. Chunks of his skin peeled off when I moved the last bit of chain. I hesitated, not wanting to hurt him more.

"Do it."

I swallowed, and did it. Dastien muffled his cry. I knew it wasn't me who had put the chains there, but causing him pain still sucked. "You okay?"

"I'll be fine now. Hurry. We have to go." Dastien glanced up at the hole in the ceiling and then out to the sleeping vampires. "They should be up already."

He didn't have to tell me twice. I quickly unchained Mr. Dawson, Donovan, and Sebastian.

Adrian started growling. Chris and Shannon

quickly followed.

"Well, it was a fine attempt, but we will fight our way out after all," Sebastian said. The three alphas shifted into their wolf form quickly.

The cavern was silent, except for the soft growls of the wolves who now stood in a circle around Meredith, Dastien, and I. Movement rippled through the cavern as the vampires slipped soundlessly from dead to undead.

"Aren't you going to shift?" I asked Dastien.

"Not yet. What's in your bags?"

I couldn't look away from the vampires. There were so many.

"Tessa," Dastien said.

Shit. I was panicking.

"Her *bruja* cousin made them for us. Weapons," Meredith said. "Holy water."

Dastien took my pack from me and un-zipped it.

I had a second to think before I was soaked. "What the hell!" I wiped the water from my eyes.

"And she's back," Meredith said. She held up a bottle with a black cross on it over her head and dumped the contents. "Makes it harder for them to grab onto you if you burn the shit out of them."

"Here." Dastien handed me a large water gun, and then stuck two small ones in my back pockets. He pulled out some little glass vials filled with red and yellow grains and some green flakes. "I love your family."

"You've never really met my family. Hell, I just met my family." I grabbed one of them. "What is that?"

"They're spells. But from the color, they may as

well be grenades."

Meredith pulled out some vials filled with blue liquid. "I didn't get any like yours, but I did get these!"

"I don't know what those are," Dastien said. "I've never seen anything like it. How many do you have?"

"Your cousin was right," Meredith said. "I know exactly what to do with them. I've got three and that's plenty. These fuckers pack a punch."

Dastien muttered something and threw one of the red and yellow ones into the cave. An explosion reverberated against the walls. I put away my flashlight as the burning vampires lit up the cavern.

"Enough with the pow-wow. We're out of time," Meredith said.

"Right before you throw the vial, say, 'In the name of Jesus Christ, I purify you.'"

"Seriously."

"Yes. It doesn't have to be exactly that, but the intention in your head and heart when you throw it needs to be that. And you need to really feel it and believe it for it to work. That's the thing with *brujos*. They've got a bit of Catholicism mixed in with everything they do." Dastien kissed me. His lips were firm for a second, and then softened. "Stay beside me."

His clothes ripped and fell to the floor as he shifted forms.

"The wolves brought us some of their own for breakfast," one vampire's voice rang through the cavern. "And a witchblood."

A vampire floated above the rest. I left my backpack unzipped and put it on backwards. I stood, palming one of the vials in one hand and my holy water gun in the other. As the vampire gained speed, moving toward me, I threw the vial and said the words.

The explosion was easily three times as big as the one Dastien's gave off. The vampire screamed as decayed flesh melted from its bones. Flames rained down on the vampires below, burning them to a crisp.

All movement in the cavern stopped for a moment.

And then hell broke loose as the vampires in front swept toward us. The wolves ripped into the closest vampires.

"Your blood makes them stronger. You throw the vials. I'll back you up with water," Meredith said.

I tossed at anything that moved. Once they learned what our plan was, they stopped their freaky floating tricks. Any that Meredith got with her gun burned down to dust. It only took a squirt per vampire, but we didn't have an endless supply. And we were still grossly outnumbered.

"We need to get out of here," I said. "We can't hold them off here until morning."

"So what now?"

"We burn a path."

Donovan barked twice.

"I'm taking that as confirmation that my plan is good." As soon as I said that, the vampires converged to block the way out. "You assholes are just making this easier." I hoped I was right.

I threw the vials in quick succession. "I'll grab left and center. You take care of right. Wolves, don't let anything get us from the back." I took a deep breath. How the hell did I end up in charge here?

Jesus.

I counted to ten and slid down the rock formation, throwing vials ahead of me. The heat from the fire burning the vampires licked along my skin, but didn't last long enough to burn. Not looking at what I was hitting, I shot my water gun as quickly as I could with my left hand, and kept pushing forward as I threw the vials. When they hit the vamps, they burst into flames. It spread to the surrounding vampires within two seconds and then burnt out.

Throw. One. Two. Step.

Throw. One. Two. Step.

Throw. One. Two. Step.

The sounds of the battle grew behind me, making my stomach knot. I wanted to look back and see if Dastien was okay, but there wasn't time. He'd do his job, and I'd do mine. Our only shot of surviving was to keep moving forward.

It seemed like forever before we reached the mouth of the cavern, but we did.

I didn't know how many vampires were in the tunnels. If there were hundreds more, we were going to be totally screwed. I could see a good thirty up ahead. I reached for another vial and felt only a handful left.

Sweat rolled down my hairline. I threw another vial into them and used the sudden vampire torches to peek behind us. The light didn't reach far back into the cavern. It looked more like a stormy sea threatening to swallow us whole than individual monsters.

Shannon backed into me before throwing herself at the horde that still gathered behind us. There was no way to separate them from the cave walls until they moved.

This was bad. Really bad.

I threw my last vial and grabbed the other water gun from my back pocket. "Run!" I charged into the vampires blocking our way through the tunnels, dousing them with holy water as I ran. The blessed water wasn't as effective as whatever was in the vials. They took longer to spark, but burned for longer.

Flames licked my skin as I pushed forward, but I would heal. Teeth sank into my arm and I screamed.

Dastien leapt. His teeth sunk into its neck, and the head severed—spurting black goo all over me.

Holy shit. That was gross.

Another clawed down my side, and then I couldn't think anymore.

I moved in a flurry of action.

Run. Fight. Get out. Those were my only thoughts.

I don't know how I made it, but finally we hit the outside. I was bleeding from vampire scratches and the bite on my forearm burned wickedly.

"Wait!" Meredith screamed.

I spun to her. Were we not all out? I thought we were all out!

She pulled out the three blue vials from her back pocket, and tossed them into the entrance. She said something in French that I didn't understand.

The fire roared, knocking me back.

"What the hell was that?"

Meredith squatted a little and rested her arms on her thighs. "Just a little spell. You needed it. To activate the blue ones," she said between gasps. "I was saving it. In case we got out."

"In case we got out? In case we got OUT! Why the hell didn't you use it in there? We could've fucking DIED!" She was nuts. I was going to kill her for that.

"Calm yourself," Donovan said from behind me.

I would not turn around. I would not turn around. I didn't need to see Donovan's manly bits.

"You shouldn't stare, Meredith. It isn't polite," Donovan said.

Meredith blushed, but only glanced away for a second before her eyes were drawn back to him.

Shit. Now I wanted to turn around.

"We need to keep moving, ladies. As much as I'd love to sit back and have a pint, there's something else we need to take care of."

Forgetting that Donovan was naked, I started to turn around. Dastien nipped my hand. "Hey. I do believe the biting portion of our relationship is over." When I finished turning, Donovan was a wolf again. "Great. Now I can't ask him what he's talking about."

My arm was throbbing, but I ignored it. Dr. Gonzales had said vampire bites were bad, but it would have to wait. Donovan was right. We had things to take care of.

I tried to remember where the car was. This was so not the way we came in, and now it was totally dark. Finding Dastien was easier. I couldn't exactly link with my Tiguan. "Anyone have an idea where we parked?"

Chapter Thirty-Nine

After some debating and growling from the furry members of the group, we finally found our way back to my car. I had a brief moment of panic when I remembered that I hadn't locked it, and then relaxed. It was on a random dirt road in nowhere Texas.

My hands were shaking as we piled in. I folded down the back seats so the wolves could stretch out. "Alrighty then. I have no idea where I'm supposed to go."

Donovan—a black and brown speckled wolf—stuck his nose over the center console.

"I don't speak wolf. Meredith?"

"Dude. It's not like *Twilight* up in here. We can't read minds."

We shared a "we're stupid" look, and then I placed my hand on Donovan's head.

I didn't get any words, just pictures. Images. And I knew exactly where to go.

"Hold on to your hats." I did a quick U-turn and

floored it down the dirt road.

Thirty minutes later we pulled into the mall. I rolled through the parking lot until I found the brigade of shiny black SUVs.

I pulled even with them and then went out to open the back hatch. Meredith went to the closest SUV and coded the lock. She opened up the car and grabbed out a pile of gray sweats, pulling on a sweatshirt for herself first, and then turned to the wolves.

"Come and get 'em boys. And girl."

They took turns jumping back in my car to shift. Meredith and I were covered in nasty. I needed a shower something fierce, but it'd have to wait. We both changed into gray sweats in the other car as the rest were shifting.

While we waited, she handed me a pack of baby wipes, and I cleaned up as best as I could. When it came time for Dastien to shift, I nearly peeked, but stopped myself. Barely.

Once everyone was back to being human, we went in search of the pack.

We found them chowing down on the third floor food court looking completely conspicuous in their all-black getups. It was so strange seeing them among the humans. Normal people going about their day, oblivious to the fact that they were surrounded by werewolves.

A large group of kids and parents were eating burgers and fries. They'd pushed together five tables. Red and blue balloons were tied to the chairs.

Christ. They couldn't have picked a worse day to have a party at the mall.

The wolves sat scattered among the food court tables. Some stood off to the side, pretending to look in the windows of the nearby stores. I recognized a few from my classes. Including Imogene. A bandage wrapped around her neck, proof that I'd lost control before and could do it again.

Tension stretched thick as the wolves scanned the mall, waiting for something that would never come. Thanks to us. And my cousins' well-made potions. I was totally going to have to thank them for their awesome packs o' badass. Maybe if I asked nicely, they'd show me how to make those vials.

I didn't spot Mr. Hoel until we turned the corner. In the back of the food court next to the bathrooms, a group of werewolves stood around a man. He was standing on a chair addressing the group.

It took me a second to realize that even through all the mall noise, the wolves could hear what he was saying. They might not have been looking at him, but they were listening. The way they moved and nodded with his points and pauses gave it away.

Dastien's hand warmed the small of my back. "You okay?" He whispered against my ear.

No. I was so not okay. The man was on his soapbox preaching about how even if the vampires didn't show up they still needed to take the place of superiority tonight.

"They are lesser. They are weak. We've been slaves to them for centuries as we kept them safe. Without payment. Without a thank you. Blood shed and lives lost, and they don't even notice. We cannot hide anymore. Not with cameras everywhere—in buildings, on the streets, in everyone's hands. We must choose when we reveal ourselves, and the time is now."

I shoved past Mr. Dawson, Sebastian, and Donovan. Maybe it was the wrong move, but I couldn't help it. If it made me weaker because I was part-human, then so be it.

I made my way to the center of the group gathered around Mr. Hoel. "Everyone out of my way. Now."

They scattered at the command.

Dastien moved to stop me, but I shook my head.

Mr. Hoel looked down at me. "Ah yes, the human half-breed here to—"

I didn't let him finish whatever insult he had. I kicked the chair out from under him, and before he could react, punched him in the face.

When he moved to attack me, Donovan stepped between us. "I wouldn't do that if I were you."

Dastien grasped my arm. "Come on. Let's let them handle this."

I nodded and stepped away. I would've apologized to them for going after Mr. Hoel, but I couldn't bring myself to. I wasn't sorry.

"Everyone go back to St. Ailbe's." The sound of Sebastian's voice echoed in the mall, and everyone turned to stare at us. "Except for Rupert," Sebastian said.

The humans looked confused, but then came to whatever conclusions they could as they witnessed the mass exodus of uniformly dressed people.

A few of the wolves had the grace to look embarrassed, but not Imogene. I tried to ignore her as she walked toward me.

Dastien turned us toward the exit and I kept pace beside him.

One second I was thinking about how quickly we could get back so that I could shower, and the next something plowed into me and I was falling two stories to the ground. This time I couldn't right myself before I hit.

The hard tile cracked against my back. Screams echoed through the mall, but the pain blocked them mostly out. It hurt to breathe, and I was pretty sure I'd broken something.

A foot collided with my side, and I rolled, coughing as I tried to desperately get air into my lungs.

Then everything froze. I wouldn't have noticed it, except for the sudden silence in the mall. It was mega-eerie.

Claudia's face appeared in front of me. "Sorry. I didn't see her move or else I would've frozen her before she hit you. We only just got here. Had a meeting about who is taking over in your place. It went on forever." She seemed to notice that I wasn't moving. "Are you alright?"

"Grand," I wheezed. "Thanks. I'm just going to hang out here for now."

"Glad I could help." She smiled. "Be right back. Going to reanimate the other wolves."

"Fantastic." If we were gone when the humans came out of it, they wouldn't panic so much.

I glanced around from the ground and noticed that everyone in the mall was frozen. It was like someone hit the pause button on life. Dastien was a few steps away. Imogene was above me, poised to slam her fist into my face. Donovan was hovering directly above me mid-jump between the third and second floors.

If I hadn't been in so much pain, I'd find it equal parts freaky and rad. I wondered if I hadn't ended up with the Weres, then maybe I would've learned how to do this freezing people trick.

Claudia stood in the middle of the floor. Raphael was by her side, holding her hand. She raised her arms above her head and he mimicked her move. Together they muttered something. And then the wolves could move.

"Shit," I said as I realized almost too late what was happening.

I slid away just before Imogene could land her punch. The tile under her fist cracked.

Dastien tackled her and pinned her to the ground. "Why?"

"Because I had nothing left to lose. You're gone. My father is in trouble. And she gets everything. It's not fair."

I laughed, albeit a little hysterically as I was also in pain, but still the laughter bubbled free nonetheless. "What a load. I've gotten nothing but shat on my entire life. I finally get a little bit of good—if you ignore the whole biting thing, the going furry thing, the nearly getting offed by vampires that look suspiciously like zombies thing, the finding out I'm a witch thing, and the kind of losing my mind thing—but hey—at least I got a guy." I snorted. "Because that toooootally makes everything worth it. Right? Now I can just go enjoy being barefoot in the kitchen for the rest of my crazy long-lived life."

I sat up, and pain ricocheted through my body. It took my breath away for a second. "God that fucking hurts," I said when I could breathe again. "Anyone know what a broken rib feels like? Because I may have several. On top of the vampire bite—which by the way—is burning something fierce. It's gray around the edges, too. Should I be worried about flesh rot? Because getting a rocking case of necrotizing fasciitis would round out my day in really fantastic way."

Somewhere along my rant, everyone that wasn't already frozen turned to look at me.

"Anyone have a name of a good dermatologist? Anyone?" I paused. "Anyone?" Still got nothing. "Bueller?" I sighed. Wolves really had no sense of humor.

Dastien turned to look at me while still pinning Imogene to the ground. "Are you feeling okay?"

Meredith, Chris, Adrian and Shannon came down the stairs, taking the focus off of me.

"Holy shit," Chris said. "She totally nailed you."

"Shut it," I said. "Where's Mr. Hoel?"

"Mr. D and Sebastian have him," Adrian said. "They're escorting him back to campus in one of the SUVs."

"Perfect. So, cuz, how long does the freeze last?" I said.

Claudia leaned heavily against her twin. "Thirty seconds longer at best. I wish I could do more, but it'd be best if we left. Like now."

Raphael muttered something to his sister, and she shook her head. They took two steps, but she lost her footing. He swept her up.

"Is she okay?" I said.

"*Sí*. She'll be fine. Doing a spell this big takes a toll."

Interesting. They turned to go, but I shouted out to them. "Hey. Thanks for those packs. They saved our lives."

"*De nada*," Raphael said. "Once you're feeling better, come visit us. There are things you should know. Things you could learn."

"You know. I might take you up on that." I needed to learn to fight, and if I could get some of their awesome powers to help me, then maybe I'd stand a chance.

Claudia grinned. "We'll leave you to it." She glanced at Mr. Dawson. "If you need help from *La Alquelarre*, let us know."

"*Gracias. Vaya con Dios.*"

"Y tú también."

Once my cousins were out of sight, the wolves went into action.

The humans started slowly moving. It was past time to get out of here.

"Dastien," Mr. Dawson said. "Take Tessa back with the pups. We'll deal with Imogene and her father."

Dastien rose from where he had Imogene pinned, pulling her up with him.

"Imogene," Mr. Dawson said.

"Yes," she said. Her gaze was on the ground and her shoulders hunched over.

"You will stay here with me. We need to have a long chat about your future in this pack."

"Yes, sir."

I kind of hoped she got kicked out.

Okay, I totally hoped she got kicked out. The girl was a menace. I didn't want to know what else was going to happen. All I wanted was a shower.

And something for my arm. And my back. And my ribs. Just generally something for my entire body would be good.

"You guys," I said to my new friends as we exited the mall. My vision was starting to blur and my skin was clammy. "I wasn't joking about the whole vampire bite thing. It's really burning. Do you have, I dunno, some kind of balm or something for that?"

Dastien stiffened next to me. "I thought you were joking about the bite." He grabbed me. "Please tell me that vamp who had your arm didn't sink his teeth. Please tell me I killed him in time."

"Can't tell you that." I stuck out my left arm. It was swollen around two large punctures and a ring of smaller ones. "The red and puffy wouldn't bother me so much if it wasn't also turning a blackish-gray around the actual puncture marks. Is that a bad sign?"

Meredith said something but I couldn't make it out. I couldn't make anything out.

"You guys. I'm not feeling so hot." I managed the words before my body turned to Jell-o and the world went black.

Chapter Forty

I blinked my eyes open. I threw my hand over them as the sun threatened to make my head explode. My body didn't hurt, except for one spot.

I'd been in here for the past three days, in and out of consciousness. Today I'd been more in than out. I touched the gauze and tape that covered the bite. A shudder ran through me at the memory of that nasty vampire's teeth ripping through my flesh.

The chair beside my bed creaked. Dastien. A smile spread across my face that warmed my whole body and I peeked through my fingers.

We were in one of the medic rooms on campus. Dastien sat scrunched in a chair beside my bed. "How're you feeling?"

"Better." My voice sounded particularly scratchy.

"How's the bite?"

"Still burns."

He grunted. "Vampire bites are nasty."

I raised an eyebrow.

"Okay, maybe all bites are nasty."

Meredith came through the door. "You're up!" She threw herself on the bed next to me. She'd been by a few times but I always seemed to miss them. "Thank God. No one could take Dastien being all grumpy anymore."

"I'm nearly better. Right?" I glanced at Dastien.

"Right," Dastien said. "The vampire venom had time to work its way into your system before we neutralized it. Another half-hour and you'd have been dead. Although if you told me about it—"

I growled. We'd been over this a million times, but from what I could tell, he wasn't going to let up anytime soon.

He sighed. "You'll be out of the bed tomorrow."

I touched the bandage again. God. Who knew there were worse things than becoming a werewolf? "I'm so glad I'm not going to turn into a vampire. I don't think there's enough product in the world to fix what's wrong with their faces."

"Gross!" Meredith laughed. "Hey, now that you're out of the woods, let's move you to your room. I'm sure Dr. Gonzales would okay it."

"That would be awesome." I let out a shaky sigh. "If you give me a sec, I'll change out of this hospital gown."

They grumbled about it, but left.

I reached into the bottom cabinet where my clothes were last time. Jackpot. I pulled on a pair of jeans, white T-shirt, and some flip-flops.

By the time I was changed, I was sweating, but I did it. Dastien was going to have to carry me back to my room. There was no way I'd make it.

The idea wasn't completely terrible.

I yelled through the door to tell Dastien and Meredith to come back, but instead Imogene walked in and shut the door behind her.

She was wearing skinny jeans and a flirty tank. Her hair was pulled back and her face was make-up free. She didn't look bad, but she didn't look like herself either. "I'm not here to fight," she said as she leaned back against the door.

"What do you want?"

"Don't worry. I don't want to be friends."

"Good." I crossed my arms and ignored the bit of discomfort.

She smirked. "I just thought I'd say that I'm sorry for the way I acted. I know you probably don't give a shit, but I've spent my whole life trying to get my dad to notice me. I've always been a big disappointment. I wasn't a boy. I wasn't alpha enough to do him any good. As lame as it sounds, my one shot in life was tied to becoming Dastien's mate. When you came here, things got a little out of hand. I would love to blame what I did on my wolf, but I can't. I was pissed. My life was falling apart and it was your fault. I did what I thought—and what my father agreed—was best." She looked away and blew out a heavy breath. "I've talked a lot to Mr. D and Dastien the past few days. I'm probably going to get kicked out of here, and lose my sister if I can't convince her to go with me, but that's what I get because of the choices I made. I'm not asking for your forgiveness either." She scoffed. "I wouldn't forgive me."

I didn't know what to say. Or if I should say anything. Her talking to Dastien—even though I knew it had happened—made me want to hit her, so I stayed silent.

"Anyhow. I just wanted to apologize for being a bitch. Dastien's my best, oldest friend and I want him to be happy. So make him happy." She turned on her heel before I could say anything else.

Well, shit. If anyone had told me that I'd feel sorta bad for Imogene Hoel, I would've told them they'd lost their mind. But I kinda felt bad for her. It took major *cajones* for her to come here and apologize. I respected that.

***

That night, under the light of the moon, the senior class sat around a bonfire in the middle of the woods northwest of the school. Much to my annoyance, Dastien had carried me the whole way. Even if I couldn't walk for long on my own yet, it was a little humiliating. As soon as he put me down, he'd wrapped a blanket around me and tucked me close to his side.

Mr. Dawson, Sebastian, and Donovan stood in front of the fire with Imogene. She had a backpack on, and a large duffel at her feet.

I had to respect her as she stood there ramrod straight, gaze focused above us, ready to face her fate.

Once everyone was seated, Mr. Dawson stepped forward. "You all know what happened with Imogene and her father. But here today, we're going to ignore her relations. This is a decision her peer pack must make as she plotted against and harmed some of our own. I could make the decision, but all of you would have to live with it. And so you must decide."

He put his hand on Imogene's shoulder. "Imogene Hoel stands before you ready to be cast from the pack. Should you decide that as her fate, she will walk away from here with what she has and should she ever appear again—come as an enemy. Or you can decide that she stay on."

Mr. Dawson glanced around the circle. "The vote will be placed, and the majority will rule. May fair hearts and minds rule your decisions."

He paused. A few murmurs filled the night, but were soon quieted. "If anyone has anything to say to sway the decision, now is your time to speak."

I looked around the fire. No one glanced her way. "Are you going to say anything?" I asked Dastien. He sat on the log next to me. His fingers twined with my ungloved ones.

"No, ma cherie. I'm not in your class and I'm not in your peer pack. I'm only here to help you to and from the meeting."

Right.

As the seconds turned into minutes, my heart started to race. I couldn't sit here and let them do this to her. Not after she apologized to me. As much as I wanted her gone, she'd made a mistake. Lord knew no one in my old schools ever listened to me or gave me any second chances. I couldn't condemn her to the same fate.

"Help me up," I whispered.

"What are you going to say?"

"Fine. Don't help me up."

Dastien growled as I stood. He kept his hand wrapped around the back of my calf, making sure I stayed upright.

"Hey, everyone. Tessa here." I paused as everyone looked my way. "I know I'm new and I really have no idea how this is supposed to go or what I'm supposed to say or…I'll stop rambling. The thing is, I guess I'm the one here that should want her to go the most. I mean—she tried to take my guy. She nearly had me kidnapped by vampires. Twice. Because of her dad, my guy actually was kidnapped by them. She attacked me. Twice. One of which was a total sucker punch, which was way lame."

Dastien's hand tightened around my calf.

I reached down and ran my fingers through his hair as I looked out among my classmates—my peer pack. "What I'm trying to say is that yeah—she's done bad stuff, but maybe she's not a terrible person. People make dumb mistakes all the time. And yes, hers were really seriously stupid, but I think if we give her a second chance, maybe she'll be better. She knows what she will lose now and how quickly things can go wrong. She'll have to earn back our trust, and it won't be easy, but if she's willing to work for it— then I think we should give her a shot."

My strength waned, and Dastien stood, holding me against his side. "All I know is that everyone deserves a second chance. Maybe that's really human of me. Maybe that's not how things work here. But I really hope it is. I vote she stays."

I looked over at Mr. Dawson. "I'm tired. Is it okay if I don't stay for everyone else to vote?"

Donovan smiled. "Take her home, pup."

He smiled down at me. "Ready?"

I nodded, and he swung me up into his arms.

I met Imogene's gaze. "Good luck," I mouthed.

A tear rolled down her face and she wiped it away. "Thank you," she mouthed back.

Dastien lifted me into his arms, and I rested my head on his shoulder. I couldn't control what anyone else did, but I had to do what felt right for my own conscience. Speaking up for her when no one else would felt right.

Somewhere between the fire and my dorm, I fell fast asleep.

***

Three days later I was going stir crazy. My days were filled with trying to figure out the homework on my own and resting. The good thing—or maybe it was bad—was that my peer pack decided to let Imogene stay. I hoped speaking up for her didn't end up being a wrong move on my part, but I felt that I'd done what was right. Even if Meredith disagreed. The vote hadn't been unanimous in the end, but Imogene had gotten enough to stay.

The vampire venom was gone, but its effects lingered. Everyone was being really great about it. They came by to hang out in shifts—to bring me homework, give me a bit of gossip, or play cards. Dastien stayed almost all the time, and spent the night in his wolf form in my bed. Apparently we were stretching the rules a bit, but since he stayed furry after hours, no one said anything. Even with the distractions, I wasn't going to last much longer cooped up.

It might have been Saturday, but I'd be damned if

I stayed in my pajamas for another day. I grabbed some clothes from my closet and went into the bathroom to get ready for the day, leaving wolf-Dastien sleeping in my bed.

When I got out, he was gone. I peeked into Meredith's room. "Have you seen Dastien?"

"He's grabbing his stuff. Thought you'd like a day out."

A silly grin spread across my face. "A day out? Does that mean I've been cleared for my regularly scheduled life to resume?"

"You've been a good little patient." She patted my head, and I knocked her hand away. "But you're now free to leave the confines of your room. Dr. Gonzales checked on you last night and cleared you."

This was amazing news. "I'm seriously in for something normal."

Dastien came in with car keys in hand. "Ready?"

"Totally."

We walked to the parking lot and then I stopped. Adrian, Chris and Shannon were leaning against a Porsche. The SUV kind, but still. "Seriously?"

"You don't like my car?" Dastien said.

I pointed to it. "That's not a car. It's a Car."

"Graduation present."

Meredith elbowed me in the side. "Yeah right. Didn't you know he was loaded?"

"I guess it never came up," I said.

"You can call home on the way." Dastien held out a phone as he opened the door for me. "If you want, we can stop by."

I snatched it from him as I jumped in, and quickly dialed Mom. She answered on the first ring. Dad was home and she said she'd get Axel to drive down for dinner if we all wanted to come eat. I told her we'd be by in a couple hours and to think each wolf was like ten humans. She laughed and said she'd go buy burgers in bulk.

I was still processing everything. Somehow the witch thing was easier to deal with than the shifting. Hopefully. I still hadn't gone furry, but I knew that it'd happen soon. When it did, I'd deal with it. Just like I'd dealt with everything else.

Dastien held my hand as he drove. The spark that went between us was strong. I felt more connected to him than ever before. He glanced at me. He was happy, content. And thanks to our bond, I knew that he liked the feel of his hand in mine.

He gave it a squeeze and I knew he could feel what I was feeling. It was nice to be on the same page with someone. We still had some stuff to work out, but I didn't doubt that it would. When we had to face the tribunal, we'd do it together. As a team.

My friends were laughing and talking in the back seat. Shannon hadn't said anything to me, but I had hopes. She'd get over Dastien eventually. There wasn't another option for her. Or for me. Dastien was mine.

The laughing stopped as we walked toward the mall. "Norms. Ten o'clock," Adrian said.

Rosalyn, Carlos, and a few others whose names I couldn't remember were walking toward us. It felt like forever since the party, but it'd only been little more than three weeks. So much had happened.

I stopped walking. Dastien looked from me to them. He gave my arm a little tug and strode straight toward them. As soon as Rosalyn saw me, she stopped talking to Carlos.

I cleared my throat. "Hi."

"Hi," she dropped her gaze to the ground. That was weird. She wouldn't meet my gaze? I scanned the group. They were all staring at the pavement. One girl in the back started to stink. Like fear. It made my wolf want to play. I peeked up at Dastien.

He brought my hand to his lips, and gave a mischievous smirk. "Good to see you, Rosalyn. It's been a while."

"Yeah."

"I'm sorry I had to turn you down for that date, but I'm sure you understand."

What a total hypocrite. She'd tried to get Dastien? A growl slipped from me. Meredith and Adrian started laughing like a pair of hyenas.

"Come on you guys. I need ice cream." The Cedar Ridge High crowd parted as Shannon walked through them.

I waited a second until Rosalyn looked up. "See you around." Her face lost all color. She was totally afraid of me.

Maybe this werewolf thing wasn't so bad after all. I had a boyfriend—mate—whatever, that I was figuring things out with. A kickass girl friend, which was a first. Sure, there was the whole tribunal thing, the witch thing, the whole Imogene thing and Mr. Hoel still being on the run. It wasn't all sunshine and rainbows, but I'd be ready for whatever came my way.

I had a feeling that my life was going to start being a whole lot of fun, and I didn't need a vision to tell me that I was right.

Who needed normal anyway?

The story continues in the second book of the Alpha Girl Series. Pre-Orders available December 17, 2013. For more information, check out:

www.inkmonster.net/alphagirl

Acknowledgements

First off, thank you so much to my Seton Hill University Writing Popular Fiction family. It was among you that I found my voice and learned to write. Thank you to my mentors: Karen Williams, Lee McClain, and Maria Snyder. You ladies are amazing.

Thank you to my critique partners: Chris Von Halle, Lynn Salsi, and Jenny Gottsch.

Thank you to Lauren Stone. I'm so lucky I got you as a One. You slaved with me over this novel for years. I couldn't have done it without your help. I'm sorry to say that you're stuck with me forever.

Thank you to Kime Heller-Neal. I couldn't have done the final revision. Thank you for pushing me that last little bit. You rock.

Thank you to my mother-in-law, Kristi Latcham, who helped proof. Something that I'm absolutely terrible at doing. You're a lifesaver!

Thank you to everyone else who ever critiqued me. I love getting notes, and every time I got them, my writing improved.

Thank you also to Christina Bauer, my partner in publishing crime. You kick ass.

Thank you to my family. I'm blessed to have each and every one of you in my life. I don't have words for how much I love you all.

And finally, thank you to my husband. You're

amazing. Thank you for being my partner. For picking me up when I had a bad day of writing and cheering me on when it was going well. I can't do it without you.

To anyone who wants to write, my advice is this: Read a ton. Then, read some more. Write every day. Finish a draft. Allow yourself to let it be a shitty one. And then get yourself some good critique partners and listen to them. They're worth their weight in gold.

Aileen Erin is a lover of all things nerdy—from Star Wars (prequels don't count) to Star Trek (TNG FTW), she reads Quenya and some Sindarin, and has a severe fascination with the supernatural. Aileen has a BS in Radio-TV-Film from the University of Texas at Austin, and an MFA in Writing Popular Fiction from Seton Hill University. She lives with her husband in Los Angeles, and spends her days doing her favorite things: reading books, creating worlds, and kicking ass.

39971538R00231

Made in the USA
Lexington, KY
19 March 2015